Meredith Jaffé is the author of four novels for adults: *The Tricky Art of Forgiveness*, *The Dressmakers of Yarrandarrah Prison*, *The Making of Christina* and *The Fence*. Her bestselling novel *The Dressmakers of Yarrandarrah Prison* was voted in the 2021 Booktopia Favourite Australian Book Award Top 50 and the 2022 Better Reading Top 100. She also writes for children.

She regularly facilitates at writers' festivals and other author events. Previously, she wrote the weekly literary column for the online women's magazine *The Hoopla*. Her feature articles, reviews and opinion pieces have also appeared in the *Guardian Australia*, *The Huffington Post* and *Mamamia*.

Books by Meredith Jaffé

FICTION
The Fence
The Making of Christina
The Dressmakers of Yarrandarrah Prison
The Tricky Art of Forgiveness

CHILDREN'S FICTION
Horse Warrior

The Dressmakers of Yarrandarrah Prison

Meredith Jaffé

HarperCollinsPublishers

HarperCollins*Publishers*

Australia • Brazil • Canada • France • Germany • Holland • India
Italy • Japan • Mexico • New Zealand • Poland • Spain • Sweden
Switzerland • United Kingdom • United States of America

HarperCollins acknowledges the Traditional Custodians
of the land upon which we live and work, and pays respect
to Elders past and present.

First published in Australia in 2021
This edition published in 2022
by HarperCollins*Publishers* Australia Pty Limited
Gadigal Country
Level 19, 201 Elizabeth Street, Sydney NSW 2000
ABN 36 009 913 517
harpercollins.com.au

A catalogue record for this book is available from the National Library of Australia

ISBN 978 1 4607 6326 1 (paperback)
ISBN 978 1 4607 1363 1 (ebook)
ISBN 978 1 4607 8830 1 (audiobook)

Cover design and embroidery by Emily O'Neill
Cover images: Flowers and needle by shutterstock.com
Author photographs by Rachel Piggott Photography
Meredith Jaffé's newsletter header by Michelle Barraclough, Fresh Web Design
Teacups and teapot by Seb Cumberbirch/Unsplash
Typeset in Bembo Std by Kirby Jones
Printed and bound in Australia by McPherson's Printing Group

MIX
Paper from
responsible sources
FSC
www.fsc.org   FSC® C001695

To Beau —
never be afraid of what you don't know.

Chapter 1

When Sharon enters the room, Derek doesn't know where to look. It's been five years since his sentencing hearing, him standing in the dock, hands clasped to prevent the trembling. He expects she's changed since then – haven't they all – though, looking at her now, it's still easy to see that Sharon is his ex-wife's sister. They don't look the same exactly, but there's something about the general heft of her that declares a shared gene pool.

The clusters of chairs and tables populating the visitors' room slow Sharon's progress. She gives the families, sweethearts and men in prison green a wide berth, as if being poor or a criminal is contagious. Even so, Derek admires her bravery, for that's what the force of her walk says: 'I am here.'

Here is where Sharon has never been, until now. Five years he's served. Five years with only the rare visit from his lawyer. Last time was to advise Derek his final appeal had failed and he'll serve every day of his seven-year sentence. 'You'd get less for murder,' some bright spark had joked at the fancy do they'd splashed out on at the golf club for Lorraine and Derek's fifteenth wedding anniversary. How right they were. Plenty of men in here are serving less time for crimes more serious than his. Murder might be diabolical, rape a terrible violence, whereas stealing, or, in Derek's case, embezzlement, is a crime against another person's property. And people value their property highly. Still, he's more than halfway through now. Every day he wakes up with less time ahead than the day before. It's what gets him out of bed in the mornings.

'Derek,' Sharon says by way of greeting, plonking herself down on the plastic chair screwed to the floor.

No peck on the cheek then.

Still, he can't help but smile, he's so damned pleased to see a familiar face. 'You're looking well,' he says, kindness forcing the lie through his teeth. She wears an optimistic shade of foundation that has settled into the lines that map her face. Lipstick has bled through, feathering the gentle curve of her lips. Beneath her strong perfume, Derek detects the stale odour of cigarettes. She's still smoking then. He can't blame her. He would too if he could, but Corrective Services has banned smoking, killing off a popular pastime and creating a black market in one fell swoop.

'Can't say the same about you,' she says, reaching for her handbag, forgetting it is currently stuffed inside one of the lockers that line the corridor outside the visitors' room. At a loss what to do with her fluttering hands, she clamps them together on the laminate tabletop.

Derek lets that one go through to the keeper. He'd have thought it was fairly obvious that prison disagreed with most people. The food's no worse than the meals Dad dished up after Mum had gone, but the daily grind wears a man down. The constant surveillance. The constant vigilance. He can barely remember the last time he had a decent night's sleep.

Sharon fishes around inside the pockets of her coat. Finds a balled tissue, which she dabs at her face, then tucks into her sleeve. It pokes out, smeared with lipstick and foundation. 'I guess you're wondering why I'm here,' she says, her jowls settling in the folds of her neck.

'Too right,' he says. Ever since last Wednesday when Young Carl told him she was visiting, the question's been on Derek's mind. What possible reason could his ex-sister-in-law have to set foot inside a prison? He hopes it's good news, but he doesn't like his chances.

'I'm not here for me,' she rushes out, as if Derek has openly questioned her presence.

'To what do I owe the pleasure then?'

She leans forward, as if sharing a confidence. 'If Lorraine knew I was here, she'd kill me. Lolly's more than happy to let you stew in your own juices, but ...'

But Sharon's not like that. Physical similarities aside, Sharon couldn't be any more different from her sister. A bit like him and his brother, Steve.

Sharon shakes her head, gives him a sorrowful look. 'God knows you've made a complete fool of yourself, I can't pretend I think otherwise. I've been over and over it a thousand times and I really can't fathom how you could throw everything away like you did.' A ripple of discontent sends a shudder through her shoulders. 'I promised myself I wouldn't go down that path. Lorraine can say what she likes but as far as I'm concerned, it's punishment enough you're in here.'

It wasn't punishment enough for Lorraine, though. She filed for divorce right after the sentencing hearing, and, with that, their twenty-two-year marriage was over. Derek's wedding ring remains zipped inside his wallet, which is secured inside a bag with his clothes and keys for a house he no longer owns, waiting for his release.

Derek keeps his trap shut. He has no desire to rehash the ins and outs of how he became a resident of Yarrandarrah. And he's willing to bet Sharon isn't making the seven-hour round trip to examine his conscience.

'But that's not good enough for Lolly, is it?' Sharon goes on, oblivious to Derek's internal machinations. 'No, she has to rub your nose in it and turn Debbie against you too.' Physically, his daughter, Debbie, is cut from the same cloth as Sharon and Lorraine, but personality-wise, she's always reminded Derek of his long-lost mother. Not that it makes a squirt of difference. Lorraine succeeded a long time ago in making him feel that his input, from the sperm to the parenting, was incidental.

Sharon leans closer, her generous bosom pillowed by the tabletop. 'You know that's why she refused to register for the phone service. Didn't want Debbie talking to you. Said it was for her own good, that she needed to move on.' Sharon sits back with a huff. 'It makes me spitting mad, but you know as well as I do that Lorraine's always had a mean streak.'

Derek takes a deep breath, the hurt a clenched fist in his chest. 'That's why I write to her.'

Sharon looks surprised. 'What, letters?'

'I write to Debbie every week. And Dad.'

Sharon's surprise turns into indignation. She's a woman used to having her finger on the pulse and is none too happy to discover she's not as reliably informed as she thinks. 'Lorraine's never mentioned any letters.'

'I never miss a week,' Derek replies, pride seeping into his tone. He does the arithmetic in his head. 'That's two hundred and sixty letters rounded down to the nearest year. Plus a card each birthday.' Although Christ knows it's a miserable selection at the buy-up. He pins Sharon with a stern look reminiscent of his teaching days back at Turnley Vale High. 'You're not the only one who knows what Lorraine's like. Debbie's smart enough to keep her mother in the dark.' At least, he hopes that's the reason.

Sharon braces her forearms on the table. 'That's why I'm here.'

'Sorry, Shaz, but my interest in talking about Lorraine is zero. Can we change the subject?'

Sharon shakes her head furiously. 'Not Lorraine, you idiot. Deborah.'

This startles him, especially because Sharon used her full name instead of Debbie or Debs. Weighing out all three syllables can't be good news. He shifts in his chair, casting a sideways glance at Young Carl hovering in the corner. The officer always tries to look like he's not eavesdropping on the conversations playing out around him, but Derek's not fooled. Carl is a stickybeak of the first order. He can't help himself. Derek pitches his voice low. 'Is everything all right?'

Sharon retrieves the tissue from her sleeve and dabs at her nose again. 'Oh, she's more than all right, Derek. She's getting married.'

Well, the saying goes 'you could have knocked me over with a feather', and that's exactly how Derek feels. 'She's too young!' he splutters.

'Tell me about it.'

Derek leans closer then immediately pulls away, assaulted by the sharpness of Sharon's perfume. 'Well, did you tell her that? Did you tell her she's too young to be …' He's about to say 'wasting her life on some fella', but catches himself in time. After all, he's in no position to be casting aspersions on other people's marriages.

'Of course I did. Or more to the point, that Ian's too old for her.' Sharon glances around the visitors' room, as if the wives and girlfriends, mothers and sisters, have ears for anyone else's troubles but their own. 'He's thirty-bloody-two! What business does he have dating a 21-year-old? *And* he still lives at home with his mother.' She offers this last fact with a note of triumph, then adds, 'I mean, he's got a university degree and a good enough job, so why does he still need to live at home?'

It's clear she's not looking for a response, which is lucky, because Derek is too shocked by Sharon's revelations to give her one. His first reaction is that Debbie should be dating boys her own age, but then she never really did. In high school, she was the girl whose boyfriend had his own car while her friends made do with the pineapple-faced youths from the selective school up the road. Debbie preferred boys with real jobs who took her to the Ming Dynasty for dinner, not Macca's.

Derek had protested about this. That be they eighteen, nineteen or twenty, these young men were not taking Debbie to flash restaurants because they fancied a few dim sims and the lemon chicken. Why tolerate a giggling teenager for any other reason than the promise of something better for dessert than the fried ice cream? But Lorraine didn't share his concerns.

Derek shakes off the plague of memories. 'Are you sure she's serious?' he asks, hoping Debbie might be merely overtaken by the idea of getting married, as if this Ian was Ken to her Barbie, rather than actually planning to go ahead with it.

Sharon throws herself back in her chair, which squeaks in protest. 'You've got to be joking? You should see the size of the ring.'

Is it real? The words almost tumble out, but he stops himself. Five years in Yarrandarrah have made him cynical. He opts for a more diplomatic question. 'What else do you know about him?'

Sharon rolls her eyes again. Derek finds this gesture strangely comforting. She's been an eye-roller since way back when they met in the staffroom at Turnley Vale High. It's her favourite gesture of disgust. 'Mr Fancy Pants is a mortgage broker. He helps people get home loans.'

'Not himself then, if he still lives with Mum.'

Young Carl snorts back a laugh and Derek shifts in his chair. They've been getting too loud. Derek shoots him a look and Young Carl mouths an apology.

'Oh, don't you worry, Derek. He owns a portfolio of "investment properties".' She hooks her fingers around the words. 'That's how he can afford them.'

'And that's where they're planning to live, is it? In one of these investment properties?' he murmurs, because there's more harm than good if the other crims think Derek's hit pay dirt.

Sharon wrinkles her nose. 'You'd think so, wouldn't you? But Ian's decided they need a new place, a house in a nice neighbourhood with decent schools.'

Derek digests this nugget of information, wondering whether Debbie cares either way. Still, it's a small consolation to think that this Ian might be financially dependable.

'So when's the wedding?' he asks, hoping they're planning a long engagement so Debs has a bit of time to grow up and there's a chance he might be out in time.

'October. Debbie's keen on a spring wedding.'

Derek starts. 'That's only seven months away. Don't tell me, Shaz.'

Sharon flutters her hand, forgetting the clutched ball of tissue, which rolls across the floor and wedges against the table leg. 'Nothing like that, thank God. Though I have to admit, I had the same reaction. Fortunately, we've been spared the indignity of a shotgun wedding.'

That's a relief. At fifty-one, he's too young to be a grandfather. 'What's the rush then?'

Sharon nudges the ball of tissue with her foot, scoops it up, and returns it to the cavity of her sleeve. 'Apparently love cannot wait,' she says with a smile.

'But surely Lorraine's tried to talk her out of it?'

Sharon's smile vanishes. 'Truth be told, Lorraine can't wait to be an empty nester. Now she's got Garry, I mean,' she says, referring to Lorraine's replacement husband. She sighs, her shoulders sagging. 'Don't ever tell her I said this, but a part of me gets why you did what you did. Lorraine's always been a grasper. It's hard to feel sorry for a man like Garry Johns, but I don't think the poor bloke knows what's hit him.'

'Don't waste time feeling sorry for that prick.'

'Yes, well, you would say that, wouldn't you?' Sharon waggles her head. 'Be that as it may, I have no idea why Lorraine is the way she is. She always rode roughshod over you. *And* she's done her damnedest to mould Debbie into the same shape.' She shoots him a look of apology – whether for her words or her gene pool, Derek can't be sure.

'So what do you want me to do about it? I can have a chat with Debs and see if I can talk some sense into her, if you like?'

Sharon throws back her head and laughs, her fillings glinting under the fluorescent lights. 'Oh, Derek. Missing the point as usual.'

He stretches his palms flat on the table, feels the tension strain through his fingers and up through his wrists. What more is there to say? One of the most important milestones in his daughter's life and he won't be there to walk her down the aisle.

'Weddings are expensive,' Sharon throws at him.

Derek sniffs, resisting the urge to remind her that his and Lorraine's wasn't. A plain old registry affair, immediate family only, followed by the roast special at the pub. Lorraine's parents barely had two coins to rub together, and being fresh out of teacher's college himself, his salary didn't amount to much. They'd all agreed it was better to use their money to buy a home rather than splash out on a fancy party.

'As you can imagine, Lorraine doesn't want Debs to miss out,' Sharon continues. A serious furrow cleaves her brow, reminding Derek of the school secretary she once was. 'To quote my sister, she "deserves the full catastrophe".'

Derek winces. He can hear Lorraine saying those exact words.

'Of course, that's the problem, isn't it?' Sharon catches Derek's eye. 'Because you don't have a cent to your name.' 'Anymore' hangs between them, unspoken.

Derek tries his hardest to hold her gaze, but his eyes fall to the gouged laminate tabletop.

'And since Lorraine's got the pip you can't pay for the wedding, she's decided you don't deserve to know about it either. It's petty beyond all belief, but, then again, we are talking about Lorraine.' Sharon sits up straight and tall. 'Which is why I'm here. Whatever else you may be guilty of, no one could ever doubt your love for Debbie.'

Her kind words warm Derek's soul. He clears his throat. 'Who's paying for this shindig then?'

'Not Garry, if that's what you're worried about,' she rushes to add. 'Ian's footing the bill. He's booked the reception centre down by the river. Chosen the seven-course degustation menu. And Champagne. Not sparkling wine, proper Champagne from France.'

The maths teacher in him does a quick calculation, reels at the numbers. Depending on how many guests they invite, the cost could run into the thousands, the tens of thousands. His chest constricts, as if someone is wrapping a belt around it and is tightening it, notch by notch. He remembers this feeling, what it made him do. It's winching him in so tight, for a moment he worries he might be having a heart attack.

'There's no nice way to say this, Derek, but if you think you're going to stroll out of here after seven years and get a warm welcome from Debbie, you're a bigger fool than you look. A girl never forgets her wedding day. And she'll never forget that her dad wasn't there to give her away.'

'What do you expect me to do, stage an escape?'

By the look on Sharon's face, she almost says yes. Then she softens. 'No, of course not. But mark my words, once Debbie's married, she won't be your little girl anymore. The cord will be cut.'

Sharon pauses, distracted by a small boy who is picking at the edges of a large scab on his knee and eating the scrapings. A trickle of blood oozes into his greying sock. Disgusted, she turns back to Derek and eyes her sorry excuse for an ex-brother-in-law. Not for the first time, she remembers Derek as he was when Debs was a toddler. How happy he and Lorraine had seemed. But something went wrong between the pair of them. Derek grew quieter and shrunk in on himself. Lorraine grew brittle. Sitting there, she can see the man's misery radiating off him. Sharon sighs.

'Forget all this nonsense with Lorraine. She's got you set, but Debbie's different. You two used to be close, she has good memories to fall back on. You've got to make a big gesture, something to surprise her.'

'Time,' calls Young Carl, his rubber soles squeaking on the linoleum.

Feeling the moment slipping away, Derek grabs Sharon's hand and gives it a squeeze, surprised by its soft warmth. 'Don't you worry, Shaz, I'll think of something. That's an iron-clad promise.'

In her eyes he sees sadness, or maybe pity, he can't be sure. 'I truly hope so,' she says, patting his hand then gently shaking him off.

Sharon stands awkwardly, stiff from spending her allotted time in a cold plastic chair. She pats her hair into place, then sighs. 'You always used to tell Debbie that you loved her to the power of infinity. Remember that? "Finny", she used to say. Then the new neighbours moved in with that scruffy terrier. His name was Fynn, remember? She thought you loved her to next door and back.' Sharon chuckles at the memory. 'Funny how these things just pop into your head.' The smile disappears and Sharon catches Derek's eye. 'I think now's the time to prove it, don't you?'

With that she marches to the door, hips rolling with every stride. Derek doesn't shift from his spot until the flap of her coat disappears around the final corner.

'Shuffle on, Dezza,' says Young Carl.

And Derek does as he is told. Because even though Young Carl is as nice as officers come, there are still rules. He has to be searched, signed out, searched and signed back in again on the wing. Just enough time to be back for lunch, then off to the prison hospital for his afternoon shift cleaning the wards. Plenty of time to think of a way, any way, he might prove his love to Debbie before the opportunity is lost forever.

Chapter 2

Derek wakes the next morning with Sharon's visit still fresh in his mind. He lies there, listening to the sounds that mark the start of day. The jet of piss hitting the back of a stainless-steel bowl. A fart, rude and loud. The rhythmic swish of a toothbrush.

Yawning, he stretches his arms above his head and hits the wall. He's yet to find the edges of his space in here. A month ago, he went from sharing a two-out in the old block, to a one-out of his own in the new C Wing. No more rusty metal-framed bunk beds. Instead he has a sleek modern job secured to the wall on the long side. It reminds him of summer holidays, when his dad, Clive, would take him and his brother, Steve, on the sleeper up to Brissie to see their nan. The carriages had the same narrow bunks, with thin mattresses and pancake pillows. They'd eat dinner in a special dining car, where people served him food that was heaps better than what Dad dished up at home. And Derek didn't have to do the washing-up afterwards.

But the best bit about the trip was watching the world rush by his window. He'd sit there until stars blanketed the sky. Then he'd wake at dawn to see the sun rise over the lush cane fields racing past. It felt like they had landed in a tropical paradise. Even after all these years, the memory remains fresh.

At four by two metres, his cell is a lot bigger than those sleepers. With the bunk jammed in the corner and the tiny desk and chair bolted next to it, there's no room to swing a cat, but he doesn't care. He knows he's lucky; in some prisons the men sleep three to a cell. A cell of his own is a privilege beyond compare. He gets a bit of peace, a bit of solitude, a bit of privacy, and it makes it a lot easier to stay out of harm's way.

Derek shifts his feet to the floor and looks out the window while he waits for the blood to flow back into his legs. This view hardly changes from one day to the next. There's not much to see except a corner of the exercise yard and a patch of sky, but it faces east and Derek counts this as a blessing. The morning light, however feeble, is his to enjoy.

He hears the crunch of the lock, first one bolt then another being pulled back, and Young Carl's face swings into view. 'Morning, Dezza,' he says, his smile as broad as his hips.

It's not the young bloke's fault, but he's way too nice for this job. Always cheerful and upbeat. Derek wishes he could like him for that, but the truth is it grates on his nerves. He'd never say so out loud, though; he's not that mean.

Derek stands and tests his weight on each foot. 'Morning, boss.'

Young Carl sticks his thumbs through the belt loops of his trousers. 'Ready for breakfast?'

Derek once made the mistake of telling Young Carl that breakfast was his favourite meal of the day. Ever since he shared this intelligence, and every time Young Carl scored the early shift, he has made this running joke about what's on the menu.

But because Young Carl is a nice bloke, Derek plays the game. 'I'm bloody starving, mate. It'd better be good,' he says, his stomach releasing a timely rumble.

Young Carl's generous cheeks turn pink. 'Well, you're in for a real treat this morning. We've got bacon, poached eggs, baked beans and toast. I might even be able to swing you a bit of grilled tomato if you like,' he adds with a wink.

'Sounds terrific,' Derek says, rewarding the officer with a quick smile.

Satisfied, Young Carl tips two fingers to his temple in a small salute and moves off.

Derek sighs and fills the basin so he can have a quick top-and-tail before brekkie. He'd give his eye teeth for a decent fry-up. Even just a bit of bacon would do. But there are only two menus in this joint, summer and winter, and breakfast is the same whatever the season: doughy white bread, a carton of milk, a tiny packet of cereal like the ones his nan used to give them from the variety packs, minus the variety. There are sachets of instant coffee and artificial sweetener, single serves of jam and margarine. The only choice Derek needs to make each day is whether to eat the bread as it is with a bit of butter, or fight for access to the toaster.

He's towelling off when a man with a flat head pokes his nose through the doorway. 'You and Carl got a thing going on, have you?' he snarls, making a lewd gesture with his forefinger and thumb.

Bloody Ando. A nasty piece of work if ever there was one.

Derek sucks in air, pumping himself up to a bigger size. 'Rack off. I don't know what his problem is,' he says, ignoring his heart thumping around his chest like a trapped blowfly.

Ando crosses his skinny biceps, which are swirled with tattooed sleeves. 'Yeah, well, if you know what's good for you, you'll make sure I'm the first to know, won't you, Dezza?'

Derek picks up his t-shirt, but he's too frightened to slip it over his head. That's all it takes in here. A sliver of inattention, and a fist to the solar plexus will drop him like a sack of potatoes. Mustering his bravado, he says, 'Mate, be sure of it.'

Ando lingers a moment longer. Derek's terrified the vicious little squirt is weighing up whether to belt him anyway. But with a grunt and a final warning stare, Ando swaggers off down the corridor, no doubt looking out for his boss man, the even nastier Jacko.

Once he's disappeared, Derek deflates and slips on his t-shirt. He joins the line of prisoners making their way down to the rec room for breakfast. He spots Parker three in front and hurries to fall in step.

'Morning,' he says with genuine cheer. Parker's friendship is one of the few things Derek can bank on in here. He's always up for a half-decent chat or ready with some useful advice on surviving the stay.

'Morning, Dezza,' he rasps, phlegm gurgling in his throat.

It's slow going. Parker's nudging eighty. His knees aren't what they used to be and most days he's got a shocking case of the tremors. A strip of duct tape holds the bridge of his glasses together and there is a diagonal scratch across one of the lenses after an encounter with a crim who demanded Parker hand over the newspaper he was reading.

The old man pauses and punches his chest, releasing a hacking cough. When he's recovered his breath, he says, 'I read in the paper that this is the hottest March since 1939.'

'Is that so?' Derek replies, hiding a smile. Parker is a one-man Bureau of Meteorology, able to recall the exact date of the hottest day on record or the highest rainfall, a habit lingering from more innocent times growing up on a farm.

'But they're wrong, you know,' Parker continues, indicating he's ready to walk on. 'The temperature gauge hit forty back in '56.' He pauses. 'Mind you, we measured in Fahrenheit back then, so the gauge would've read 104.'

Derek's about to comment on Parker's powers of recall when a young crim barges past and snarls 'Paedo' at Parker, before shoving the old man into Derek. He catches Parker and steadies him, glaring at the perpetrator, who turns, sneers and mouths the word again.

Derek is fuming. Parker's no more a sex offender than he is, but these young hooligans assume anyone over seventy who's locked up has to be. Something about past crimes catching up with them. Parker's in for a heist that went wrong and saw him accidentally put a hole in a man's chest where his heart used to be. Any fool can see he's not a paedo.

The encounter is a stark reminder that while C Wing might be an upgrade, the reality of their situation hasn't changed much. As they walk along the corridor, Derek reads the cards next to the cell doors. The names and years tell a sorry tale. He knows his own card all too well. Brown 7. Parker is serving seventeen. Overnight they bussed in a newbie. Maloney 8. That's all Derek knows about him: a surname and the length of his sentence.

Derek's troubled by this; not by the number and certainly not the fella's surname. It's just that yesterday the card read 'Evans 18'. Where have they taken Evans? And why? Evans has disappeared into the dark of night. Ghosted.

Downstairs in the rec room, Derek sees Parker settled before fetching his own breakfast tray and finding a spot at the long table. He sinks a little when he notices the Doc sitting three down on the opposite side, unmistakeable with his slicked-back hair, the defiant set of his jaw, and an enviable level of confidence. Derek thinks back to the Doc's card: Lyall Life.

The Doc acknowledges him with a nod. Derek nods back.

'Heard you had a visitor,' the Doc says, stirring sweetener into his coffee. 'Turn up for the books, isn't it?'

Somehow, the Doc scored the prize gig of prisoner librarian. Not only does it mean he has a one-out, but it also gives him access to anyone who's doing education or wants to read, use the computers, or research their appeal. By default, he knows everybody's business and he files it all away in that enormous brain of his like one of his library cards, saving it up for when he might need it most. It says 'Life' on the Doc's door, but that card isn't big enough to write the full truth. Multiple life sentences for murdering little old ladies in their beds. Defenceless seniors who met their end at the hands of the very doctor who had taken the Hippocratic oath to do them no harm. In another time and place, Derek would cross the road rather than talk to the Doc, but in here he doesn't have that luxury.

Derek stabs at the margarine and smears it over his bread. 'My sister-in-law came to visit.'

'That a first?'

Derek nods and reaches for a packet of jam. An inmate comes over and deposits a plate of toast in front of the Doc. Derek savours the aroma, wishing he'd braved the queue for the toaster. The crim digs into his pockets and scatters handfuls of margarine and Vegemite on the table. Where the hell did he get Vegemite? Derek doesn't want to know.

'What did she want?' the Doc asks, slathering his toast with the contraband breakfast spread.

The men within listening range fall silent, hoping for a nugget of tradeable information.

'My daughter's getting married.' Saying the words out loud makes it seem so much more real. An image of Debbie flashes through Derek's mind: caramel curls, golden tan, a little dimple in her cheek to match her smile. Not old enough to commit for life.

'Pregnant, is she?'

Derek's head shoots up. It's not like he didn't ask the same question, but the Doc's got no right to judge.

A smirk dances across the smug crim's lips as he waits for Derek to take the bait, but Derek's not falling for that old trick. He chews and swallows. 'Apparently not.'

'When's she tying the knot then?' comes from two seats up.

Derek daren't look at the speaker. It's an unfortunate turn of phrase from a man who strangled his wife with her own pantyhose. 'October.'

'Long before you're out then,' quips another, and the men snigger.

The Doc shoots the joker a filthy look and the smile falters. To Derek, he says, 'So not pregnant but getting married in seven months. He must be quite a catch.'

How's Derek supposed to know? Sharon's description of Ian – which now he thinks about it, did she even tell him the man's surname? – was sketchy enough. Thirty-two, living at home with his mother. A mortgage broker, owner of an unstated number of investment properties and in love with Debbie. Hopefully. None of which he intends on sharing with this lot.

Derek sips his coffee. 'A spring wedding at a function centre is the sum total of my knowledge.'

The Doc sucks Vegemite off his thumb and indicates for the bloke next to him to swap seats so he can sit closer to Derek. He taps the table in the space between them, a frown troubling his brow. 'Tradition dictates that the father of the bride pays for the wedding.' He pauses for effect, glances around. 'Have you been squirrelling something away for a rainy day, Dezza?'

Derek refuses to answer; that'd be like flicking a lit match into a petrol tank.

'Saving up for just such an occasion?' prods the Doc.

Or poking an angry crocodile with a sharp stick.

The Doc stretches his arms and cradles the back of his head. All smiles. 'Oh no, *that's* right. You're skint.'

The men burst out laughing. Derek flinches and buries his gaze in the depths of his coffee. What he'd give to wipe the smile off the Doc's face. Thinks he's the smartest man in Yarrandarrah because he's a doctor and the prisoner librarian. Whereas everyone knows why Derek's a guest of the Australian taxpayer.

There's a hierarchy among the long-term residents in this joint, determined by a blend of time and crime. Men like Jacko and the Doc are kingpins. Even Parker earns more respect because he put a hole in another man's chest. If the new kids knew that, they wouldn't be so quick to call him names. But Derek? Stealing money to chuck it down a poker machine's gullet isn't a crime, it's pathetic.

Derek's silence prompts the Doc to have another dig. 'Poor girl. Not only is her father financially constrained, he won't even be there to give her away. She must be so proud.'

Derek jerks to his feet. Two of their breakfast companions also jump up, looking to the Doc for their cue. Derek ignores them and glares straight at the arrogant man.

The Doc breaks eye contact. 'Oh, let him go,' he says, waving the others down. 'It's time for muster anyway.' He looks at Derek, feigning concern. 'Sorry, Dezza, I didn't realise I'd hit a nerve.'

Though his temper boils, Derek puts a lid on it. He picks up his tray and chucks the rubbish in the bin. Refusing to look back, he heads straight for the stairs, desperate for the sanctuary of his cell, hating himself for being such a gutless wonder.

But the Doc can't leave well enough alone. 'I'll pop my thinking cap on and see if I can come up with a brilliant idea to help you out,' the Doc calls after him, earning a roar of laughter that rolls over Derek in a breaking wave.

Chapter 3

Derek sits up late into the night, working on his sewing. It soothes his nerves and, by the following day, he is calm again.

That afternoon, he finds a quiet spot in the rec room. He sits with a cup of coffee by his side, a few sheets of paper piled in front of him, his sole blue ballpoint balanced between his teeth. So far, he's written the date and the words 'Dear Debbie'. Normally, he writes his letters on the weekend to break up the long days during lockdown, but the circumstances warrant him making an exception.

'Why don't you just call her?' Parker asks, turning the pages of the *Yarrandarrah Chronicle* to the Opinion section.

Derek lays down the pen and rolls his shoulders. 'Nah. Waste of time.'

'Yeah, I know what you mean,' Parker replies. 'Access to the phone service is a pain in the arse.'

It's a fair point. When he first arrives, a bloke has to give the powers-that-be a written application with a list of people he wants to call. They check the numbers are real and that the nominated person will accept the call; a bit like the old days when you rang overseas. Derek went through the process, dutifully writing down Lorraine's and Dad's home phone numbers. Then, as an afterthought, he added his brother Steve's, just in case there was a family emergency.

'Nah, it's not that. I don't want to put her on the spot, know what I mean?' Which is completely untrue. Derek would like nothing more than to hear his daughter's voice. But despite his friendship with Parker, he's never told him that when the authorities checked if the parties were happy to receive Derek's calls, his dad was the only one who said yes. Lorraine refused. Steve too, although that was less of a surprise. He was always a shit.

Parker looks at Derek with his pink-tinged eyes, waiting for more. Discomforted by the old man's silence, Derek elaborates. 'What's bothering me is why Sharon came all this way to tell me Debbie's getting married when Debs could have dropped me a note?'

The pink-tinged eyes remain as blank as Derek's notepaper. 'Then I realised that Debbie was probably worried about how I'd react – her being so young and all. So she's not going to tell me in a letter, is she? Far easier to send Shazza as her missionary.'

'You mean emissary?'

Derek frowns, weighs up the two words. 'No, I think you'll find it's missionary.'

'Orright.'

Derek nods, convinced this must be how things panned out. 'My job now is to put her mind at ease.' He gestures to the notepaper. 'I'm going to tell her how surprised and delighted I am to hear her news.'

'Orright.'

Derek had hoped for a slightly more enthusiastic response from Parker, but undeterred, he ploughs on. 'It's all very well this Ian's paying for the wedding but as father of the bride, I insist on making a contribution to the day.'

Parker sparks up at this. 'Yeah? How are you going to manage that?'

Derek considers his response. Thanks to his sewing and his shifts at the hospital, he has two hundred bucks plus change in his prison trust account. 'It depends what she wants. I'm thinking something nice, you know, something you can keep forever.'

'Like a vase or something?'

Derek's thoughts immediately fly to the blue cloisonné vase his mother had kept filled with flowers in the centre of the kitchen table. Cornflowers, hydrangeas, agapanthus, delphiniums or even morning glory at a pinch. But her favourites were always the tiny forget-me-nots that grew near the garage. Except for the lemon tree and the veggie patch, everything in their garden had blue flowers; blue was his mother's favourite colour. Derek recalls how she always referred to the vase as a family heirloom, which sent young Derek's eyes wide with wonder. Imagine people like them owning heirlooms. It disappeared after she left – who knows where Dad put it? – and the garden was left to grow wild until his dad poisoned the lot with Round Up then turned it back into lawn. The only remaining feature being the Hills hoist.

'I was thinking along the lines of something practical, like a clothes dryer.'

Parker sniggers. 'It's a rare bloke who says "I love you" with a clothes dryer. Maybe chuck in an ironing board as well.'

Derek bristles, but realises Parker has a point. 'Yeah well, maybe I'll ask her for a couple of ideas.' And hope whatever she suggests comes in under two hundred bucks.

'Or you could ask Jane,' says Parker.

'Jane?'

'Why not?'

'I hadn't thought of that,' but Derek considers it now. Apart from Sharon, Jane is the only woman with whom Derek has had contact since he's been in. Seeing her every week has been the only thing keeping him sane.

'Women tend to have a better feel for these things,' Parker adds.

'I've got Backtackers tomorrow. I'll ask her then.'

'Sounds like a plan.'

Derek stands and stretches. 'Want another coffee?'

Parker peers at the clock high on the wall. 'Normally I'd say no, but since it's Wednesday, I might take me chances.'

Wednesday night is film night on the wing. Most of the blokes who can't afford a TV, which is pretty much everyone, hang out in the rec room after dinner. Doesn't matter how awful the movie is, they all squint at the small flat screen bolted in the far corner and pretend they're enjoying it.

'Are you gunna come back for the fillum, mate?'

Derek reviews his options. 'No thanks. I've never been a fan of *ET.*'

'C'mon, live a little. Keep an old man company. We can even pretend we've got choc tops.' Parker wheezes with laughter.

'No offence, but there's something about the little alien and his constant requests to phone home that does my head in.'

'Is that right,' Parker says with a sharp look.

Derek shifts uncomfortably on the spot. 'Yeah, well, who does he think is going to answer? He's lost in space. He's MIA. They've probably already written him off.'

Parker breaks into a smile. 'You're probably right.'

Relieved to be off the hook, Derek collects his stationery. 'I might finish this letter in my cell instead.' His thoughts drift back to his chat with Sharon. The look on her face when he told her he wrote to Debbie every week. Lorraine would go off like a Roman candle if she found out Derek was corresponding with Debbie. Derek smiles at the thought. He fetches Parker a coffee and says his farewells.

As he leaves, he scans the rec room and finds the Doc deep in discussion with one of his book-club mates. Looks like Derek's struck lucky, and can sneak out unnoticed. His mood brightens and he whistles to himself all the way back to his cell. He'll write this letter, do a bit of sewing, then tomorrow is his favourite day of the week. All in all, things are looking up.

Chapter 4

Jane drives her little green hatchback, affectionately named Fern, along the flat miles that link the town to the gaol. She's bored of listening to ads for water tanks, cattle drench and Mick's Slashing, and the reception is pretty crummy this far out anyway, so she turns off the radio and makes the most of the time alone to let her thoughts drift. It's one of the pleasures of being an only child – she enjoys her own company. Forty-five minutes of uninterrupted bliss.

At the security gate, Jane shows her ID to the duty officer through the car window. She searches for an empty space in a shady corner of the car park. Once parked, she turns off her phone and slings it and her wallet in the glove box before locking it. She never brings a handbag on Thursdays; it makes one less thing to worry about and not all the crims are on the inside. She grabs the bag of tapestry kits and her sewing tote from the boot and, laden like a packhorse, aims for the reception block.

Jane signs in and swaps her ID for a personal duress alarm, which she hangs off her waistband. Wearing one always makes Jane feel more like a target, not less so, but she'd never be allowed inside the gaol without one so there's no use complaining. The duty officer runs a scanner over her and her bags, checks the approval, and only then is she free to continue.

Officer Petty is waiting to escort her through to the admin block. She offers a small smile in greeting and he beams back. In silence, they walk the corridor that links the education block and the reception building. She looks out the windows framing the exercise yard. A few men are running laps, others are shooting hoops, but most stand in clusters, heads bowed, sharing secrets out of ear's reach of the patrolling guards.

The next set of windows frame the chapel garden. The roses are in full bloom, spilling over the sandstone path that circles a statue of the Madonna and Child. The tranquillity of the scene is somewhat destroyed, though, when the Riot Squad stomp through in full regalia. On their way to who knows where, but their presence always spells trouble with a capital T.

At the air lock, Officer Petty punches in the security code and the door clicks open. They pass through another set of doors into the room where a bank of screens displays images from all over the wing. Only once they're through to the other side does Carl speak.

'It's as hot as Hades today, isn't it?'

Not the most inspired conversation starter, but Jane appreciates the effort. 'Terribly. It's supposed to be autumn!'

'An Indian summer,' he agrees.

They both fall silent again. Fortunately, it's not much further to the sewing room. They pass the prison library where men sit at ancient computers stabbing at the keys, or grouped around small tables reading the newspapers. A prisoner with slicked-back hair scowls as he sorts through books and stacks them into piles. Then they pass the education room, where there is a literacy class in progress, and arrive at the sewing room.

Officer Petty unlocks the door and stands aside so Jane can enter. He unlocks the box of scissors and the sewing machine, then returns to the corridor, ready to tick the men's names off the list attached to his clipboard.

Jane begins laying out the ziplock bags containing the new needlework kits on the table – simple cross-stitch for the beginners, like pin cushions, Christmas decorations and lavender bags, on one side; the more difficult kits for the advanced sewers, like crewel work and free embroidery, on the other. It's not long before she senses a presence and looks up. As usual, Derek Brown is the first man here. She smiles in welcome. 'Good afternoon.'

He murmurs hello and deposits his embroidery on the nearest available chair so he can lend her a hand.

Their Backtackers is part of a national network run by the charity Connecting Threads. There are women like Jane all over the country teaching male prisoners meaning and purpose via quilting and embroidery. Derek has been with Backtackers a lot longer than most; he's one of her shining lights.

Derek picks up a tapestry kit featuring a peacock design. It's an absolute beauty, one of Jane's favourites. The fanned tail is stitched with golden thread and silken emeralds and blues. The effect is quite dazzling. 'My mother used to have a set of throw cushions just like this,' he says.

'It's gorgeous, isn't it?' she replies as he passes it to her. 'I can put your name on it if you like?' She glances at the work laying on the chair. 'Looks like you've almost finished that cushion.'

But to Jane's surprise, Derek drops the kit back on the table. 'No, no, let the others have first pick. I don't care what I work on, as long as my hands are busy.' As if to emphasise the point, he fetches another kit and passes it on without even a glance.

From the way he keeps averting his gaze, it's fairly obvious Derek has something on his mind. Well, that makes two of them. Jane also has a dilemma and Derek is the perfect person to ask. He doesn't gossip, which is more than can be said for some of the other Backtackers.

She's about to ask Derek his opinion when three men enter carrying canvases in various stages of completion. Officer Petty ticks them off the list, then tucks his clipboard under one arm in order to open the door a little wider for a prisoner burdened by a large quilt, for which he receives a grunt in thanks.

'Afternoon, Mick, Brian, Sean,' Jane chirps and receives a chorus of cheerful hellos in reply. 'Les,' she adds as he scuttles past her to his favourite spot in the corner.

Not all women would feel comfortable spending their afternoons teaching sewing to a bunch of crims. She's under no illusions these are good men, but equally the years teaching at Yarrandarrah have made her realise that no one is all angel or all devil. At any given time, she has a baker's dozen, each with their own particular issues. Jane's policy is to take each man as he comes. It's simpler that way.

'Let's see what I've brought in today, shall we?' Jane begins. From experience she knows there's no point asking to see their works in progress until they've had a sticky at the new kits. They're like kids in a candy shop, jostling each other out of the way to get the packet they want.

Big Mick with his swollen knuckles is drawn to the intricate patterns. More than once, he's told her how it eases his arthritis. Les prefers plain stitching, so it's no surprise when he reaches for a simple geometric pattern and slides it to one side. Brian picks up a tapestry with a snarling leopard and purses his lips.

'Don't be put off by the spots,' Jane says, tapping the pattern. 'It's a 4.5 mesh canvas and you're using wool. It's not as hard as it looks.'

'Jane's right, Brian. You're more than ready for a bigger challenge,' Derek chimes in.

Half of Brian's face is covered by a burn that runs down his neck and disappears under his collar. It's the result of a heist that went horribly wrong and saw Brian trapped in the burning getaway vehicle. Whenever he smiles at Jane, it's like his face splits open. It's taken her a little while to become accustomed to Brian's smile, but she reminds herself that at least she can bring one to his face.

Sean flings his quilt over two tables shoved together to make a workbench. The men stop to admire it, for it is a work of art.

Jane spreads the quilt over her hands. Within the black border swirl rich reds, greens, purples and golds. One of the many rewards of this job is seeing hard men like Sean learn to express themselves through their stitching. In his work, Jane senses his inner turmoil. This is a man whose emotions run deep. 'It's truly beautiful. You must be so proud.'

'Jeez, Sean, that's fuckin' great,' Mick adds, rubbing a corner between his thumb and finger.

'Your hands better be bloody clean, mate, or I'll …' Sean glares menacingly at Mick.

'Now, now, Sean,' Derek intervenes. 'We all know the rules.' He turns to Mick. 'All right?'

Mick frowns and wipes his hands down his pants. 'I washed them twice. And scrubbed under me nails. It's the grease, you know, it's a bugger to get out.'

Sean eyeballs him a moment longer, then turns away with a nod. Mick, like the rest of the blokes who work in the kitchens, reeks of rancid fat. The smell alone is enough to clog a man's arteries, but it's not Mick's fault. He didn't ask to work in the kitchens, but someone has to otherwise they'd all starve.

'He could put that in the Charity Ball, couldn't he?' Brian says to Jane as he settles in his chair.

Each year, the Connecting Threads Charity Ball showcases the best of the Backtackers' work. The well-heeled splash money around buying up quilts, wall hangings and cushions in a frenzied auction. Some of the items end up in museums, or hung in parliament houses and corporate foyers. And this year will be even more special as it marks twenty-five years since Connecting Threads first ventured into the prison system and created Backtackers.

Jane busies herself pinning labels identifying the stitcher to the completed tapestries. 'Yes, we definitely need to think about that. The Charity Ball seems like ages away now, but the time will fly.'

'Maybe for you, love, but not for us,' Mick says.

Blushing at her faux pas, Jane concentrates on writing details on the labels and stacking each completed kit in the plastic bag to take away.

'Sean's the best quilter there is,' Brian continues.

'Sean's the *only* quilter there is,' Les throws from the corner.

Jane often wonders why Les comes to Backtackers. It can't be for the company. He says nothing most of the time and when he does open his mouth, nothing pleasant comes out.

'There are many quilters across the Backtackers network,' Jane corrects. 'Although few do work as fine as yours, Sean,' she quickly adds lest he takes offence.

It's true, the quilt is exceptional, and definitely should be included in the Charity Ball. It's just that it only showcases *one* man's work. To her way of thinking, the most beautiful quilts at the Charity Ball are the collaborations where a whole Backtacker group spends the year working on a single quilt. They usually pick a theme that resonates with the men, something that speaks to their lives in prison, so that it offers them the opportunity to reflect on who they were on the outside versus how they feel about that version of themselves now. Jane would love to do a similar group project but she has a significant hurdle. Apart from Sean, none of her Backtackers have shown the slightest bit of interest or, in some cases, the necessary skills to make a quilt. Anyone would think the sewing machine was armed and dangerous.

Officer Petty steps into the room and adds his admiring comments to the mix, earning a smile from Jane and gruff embarrassment from Sean. Jane notices Derek giving Officer Petty a look of annoyance, before he ducks his head over his work once more.

Derek can't help but notice Young Carl fawning over Jane. It seems he's not immune from wanting Jane's approval either. Almost to a man they are lonely and bored in here. Without the support of family or a regular life, Jane is a beacon shining a light into their dark corners and chasing away the shadows. But what's Carl's excuse? He gets to go home at night, shrug off his uniform, and twist the top off a beer. Derek concentrates on pushing the needle through the canvas, feeling his way back up to the front of the work, ploughing it down again, soothed by the repetition, feeling time slip away.

'How are you going, Derek?' Jane asks, appearing at his shoulder. Startled, he drops his needle and it dangles by its thread. Pinching it between his fingers, he weaves it through the mesh then shows her his work. 'Almost done.'

'Are you going to stitch the border for the flange or have you decided against it?'

Derek holds the canvas at arm's length. 'It'll look better with.'

'I agree.' Jane hovers by Derek's side.

Words tumble through his head. 'Jane, I'm wondering if I can seek your opinion on a personal matter.' Hmm, is that the right way to lead in? Maybe he's better off saying, 'Jane, I have news. My daughter is getting married!' But then she might think all he is looking for is a 'Congratulations!' That's the thing, though, isn't it – what exactly is the question?

Derek does a quick recce of the room. The other blokes are busy sewing and chatting. It's now or never. He takes a deep breath and dives in. 'Jane …'

'Derek,' she says over the top of him, her expression serious, 'as you know, this year is Connecting Threads' twenty-fifth anniversary.' He swallows his question.

'I think I may have mentioned that they've planned a series of commemorative cushions. We were supposed to have the kits months ago, but it looks like they won't arrive until next month.' Jane fiddles with the pendant watch that hangs at her neck, a familiar gesture indicating anxiety.

Derek restrains himself from placing a comforting hand on her arm.

'Apparently there were issues with one of the dye lots, not that it matters now. The point is, while the work itself is not difficult, it means we're behind schedule. If we're going to have any chance of finishing them on time, we'll need a fourth stitcher.'

The look on Jane's face tells Derek that this news is on the same scale as a national disaster. Why, he can't say. It's hardly her fault and time is one thing the stitchers have ample of.

But she's right. A fourth stitcher would make all the difference. Derek surveys the heads bent over their needlework. Mick is showing the new recruit, Jarrod, how good stitching looks almost the same on the wrong side as it does on the right. The young bloke's face collapses in dismay when he compares the higgledy-piggledy mess of his own needlework with the exactness of Mick's. But Mick has a way of showing the newbies how anger makes for poor stitching. The irony is not lost on Derek. Mick is serving fifteen years for a brawl he started and had a good stab at finishing. While he was working as a bouncer.

He returns to the problem at hand. 'Well, there's Mick, for sure. And Sean of course,' he adds, nodding at the sandy-haired crim engrossed in his quilt. 'That goes without saying.' Derek takes stock of the men in the room. Frank and Vince, Ahmed, Pete, Riley, Suresh. They were down to eleven, but now Jarrod's joined them they are back up to twelve. They could squeeze one more in but it'd be a tight fit. Derek beckons Jane closer. 'The trouble is, there are a lot of beginners in Backtackers at the moment.'

'I know. Losing men is a constant headache.'

She's dead right. The system ships men in and out like a Coles warehouse. Rarely does a man leave Backtackers because he's done his time. Some just can't hack stitching. Some have their privileges revoked, and taking away a man's stitching is punishment all right. Though it causes more problems than it solves. Fourteen hours in your cell each night are long hours to fill. Best to have something to occupy yourself, take the mind off your troubles. 'At a pinch, Brian might make a fourth,' he offers.

A look of understanding passes between them. The truth is, a snail would stitch faster than Brian.

He purses his lips, weighing up the options. 'Let me sound out Mick and Sean and see what they say.' He means later, when they're not all sitting around gossiping like a bunch of nannas.

Jane doesn't look too reassured by this. He gets where she's coming from. Outside of these four walls, no one but them will care if Yarrandarrah Backtackers fails to deliver their allocated

number of commemorative cushions. Except that's not how
they roll. It goes against the grain for any of them to start a
project and not finish it. That's one of Jane's gifts to the men –
finish what you start. But Derek has problems of his own and
a glance at the clock high on the wall tells him their time is
almost up. He can't face another week stewing over Debbie's
wedding present. He has to make his move. 'Jane,' he says.

Jane starts and blinks at Derek. 'Yes?'

'While I've got you, I wonder if I could ask your opinion
on a personal matter.'

A flush creeps up Jane's neck. Personal exchanges are off-
limits because it fosters intimacy. Men can try to cultivate a
relationship with the volunteers then lean on them for favours
that are not altogether legal, let alone palatable.

Sensing Jane's discomfort, Derek realises he'll have to just
blurt it out, otherwise she'll think he wants her to run drugs
for him, or worse. 'It's my daughter, Debbie, she's getting
married.'

Jane releases her breath in a long exhale.

Derek's grateful Jane didn't go straight for the 'How
wonderful! When's the big day?' kind of line. Encouraged by
her silence, he plunges ahead. 'See, she's my only child. Her
getting married is a once-in-a-lifetime event – well, hopefully –
and since I can't be there, I want to buy her something special,
you know, that has meaning, but I just can't figure out what
might be best.'

Jane offers a sympathetic grimace. 'And no one wants to end
up with three fondue sets,' she says, with a look that clearly
shows she's talking from personal experience. 'Does she not
have a gift registry?'

The words send shivers down Derek's spine. He can see
Lorraine and Debbie as clear as day. Dressed up to the nines,

slipping into the comfy chairs and guzzling a glass of bubbles while the sales consultant prints out long lists of items from manchester, glassware and kitchenware. All but giving them the keys to those glass cabinets with their expensive displays of silver and crystal.

'I'm not sure,' he mumbles.

'I'm a little out of touch with weddings myself. I seem to be in the phase where I am either going to christenings or divorce parties.' Jane smiles at Derek, before glancing at the little pendant watch hanging around her neck. 'Look, we're almost out of time today. Let me sleep on it. I'm sure I'll be brimming with ideas by next week's meeting.'

But she doesn't sound confident and, to be frank, Derek feels a bit let down. After his convo with Parker, he'd pinned his hopes on Jane coming up with the perfect solution. The truth is, he hasn't seen Debbie in five years and girls change. He's no longer sure he knows Debbie like he used to. The wrong gift could be the nail in the coffin of an already fragile relationship. She's his one and only daughter. If he lost her, it would be a disaster.

Chapter 5

After finishing his shift at the hospital the next morning, Derek heads to the rec room for lunch. Parker's already there, tray to one side, reading his newspaper. Being old, he doesn't have a job to fill the hours, and he's shown no inclination to further his education. Parker's life revolves around meal times and impromptu chats.

'How'd you go with Jane?' Parker asks, as Derek bites into a limp salad roll leaking soggy tomato.

Derek removes the lone slice of beetroot, which has stained the bread purple, and discards it on the plate. 'Disappointing, mate. Disappointing.'

'Yeah?'

'She said she'd try and come up with some ideas by next week's meeting, but I'm not getting my hopes up.'

'So what's your plan B?'

Derek picks up his lamington and pockets it for later. 'I might ask Dad for his two cents. He's been known to pull the occasional rabbit out of a hat.'

Parker responds by burying his head in the sports section, which Derek reckons is his way of saying he doesn't like Derek's chances. At least Parker's kind enough not to say so out loud.

Derek makes short work of his salad roll and heads back to his cell. He checks no one is lurking about, then slides his stash of notepaper out from under the mattress. Nothing in here is sacred, and while it wouldn't take a genius to flip over Derek's mattress, a cell that looks empty is less inviting to flitting fingers.

He pops the lamington to one side and uncaps his pen. In his last letter, he told Clive about Debbie's forthcoming marriage. He hasn't had a reply yet so he's not sure where to start. Maybe he could ask Clive what gift *he's* thinking of getting and see what the old man throws back. That way it won't look so obvious that Derek is on a fishing expedition. He smiles to himself. Yep, that's the way to go about it.

'What are you looking so happy about, Dezza?' comes a voice from the doorway.

It's the Doc, a Scrabble set held together by an elastic band under one arm, a transistor radio and a magazine in his other hand. Derek's heart sinks.

'Feel like a bit of entertainment?' the Doc asks, entering Derek's cell and plonking the Scrabble set on the desk.

Derek scrambles onto the bunk so the Doc can have the stool and glances at the magazine. *Interior Style*? That doesn't sound much like the Doc's taste. The corner of his letter pokes out from under the set but he decides to leave it there rather than risk drawing the Doc's attention to it. This surprise visit rankles him. The whole point of a one-out is the absolute joy and pleasure of being alone. As the Doc well knows, since he's in one too. If Derek had wanted the Doc's company, he'd have gone looking for it. And he wasn't about to do so after their last conversation. But by Yarrandarrah standards, Derek is an educated man and there's not too many men in here who can give the Doc a decent game.

'You can have first pick,' the Doc says, generously passing over the cloth bag of tiles.

Derek mutters thanks and is relieved when he draws an S, the Doc an L.

'Looks like I've got first go,' the Doc says with a grin, then counts out seven tiles.

Derek perches on his bunk, his chin near level with the desk, while the Doc straddles the round stool, their knees almost touching. Still, it's better than playing in the Doc's cell, where men are constantly popping in, asking if the Doc wouldn't mind returning a book for them or keeping the newspaper aside or helping them write a letter home. Let alone the fact that the Doc's personal collection of books teeters on every available surface. Even with the best will in the world, there is nowhere to play.

The Doc opens with KYLIX, earning him a handy fifty-four points.

Derek's rack is a shocker. He's got the Q, but, with no U in play, he responds with KART for eight.

The Doc switches on his transistor radio and classical music gently swirls in the background. He hunches over his tiles, his fingers flying over the rack, then slaps down PRETZELS across two triple-letter squares.

'Forty-five,' he announces. 'Plus a bonus fifty for using all seven letters.' He double-checks Derek adds his score correctly, seemingly oblivious to the insult. The Doc knows Derek was a maths teacher in a former life, but then again he also knows Derek's crime.

Satisfied Derek has lifted his score to 149, the Doc checks the time and turns up the volume to listen to the news. Despite the fact not much happens in Yarrandarrah, the Doc likes to stay connected to the outside world, even if it is only through the ether. Derek delays taking his turn and they sit in respectful silence so the Doc can engage with the universe.

'With the local government elections looming, mayoral candidate Nicholas Fischer has again come under fire from the opposition,' intones the newsreader. 'Councillor Susannah Cockburn has called on Mr Fischer to quash rumours that if he is elected mayor, he will cut funding to services such as Meals on Wheels and the local youth outreach service.'

'Looks like that Cockburn woman's got Fischer's number,' the Doc says, reaching into the green bag for seven new tiles.

Taking this as his cue, Derek adds a B and an O to the X. 'BOX for twelve,' he says, writing down his score. He's miles away from beating the Doc unless he can find a clever spot for the Q.

Once normal programming resumes, the Doc turns down the volume and they play the rest of the game in silence. As the Doc contemplates his closing move, Derek plays with his Q and waits. The Doc lays out CATCHY and grins.

'Looks like I've won again, Dezza.'

Derek reveals his remaining tiles and the Doc frowns. 'What'd you hang on to the Q for? You've had ample opportunity to play it.'

'Not everyone is a walking dictionary, you know,' Derek replies, struggling to keep his petulance at bay.

The Doc snorts and, to Derek's annoyance, picks up the uneaten lamington. 'I've been thinking about this wedding of yours,' he says, breaking it in half and taking a bite. Wiping his fingers clean on his trousers, the Doc flicks through the pages of *Interior Style*. 'The women on E Block love these home-decorating mags. They're full of craft patterns and recipes, stuff like that. They come in handy, especially in the self-contained units where they have their own kitchens.'

He finds the page he wants and shunts the magazine over to Derek. It's open at a double-page spread of gifts. The caption reads, 'Kitchen Tea Inspirations'. In between the flowers and ribbons and cupcakes cluttering the page are pastel-coloured gadgets, glassware and fancy-looking candles.

'Fifty dollars for a candle!' Derek exclaims.

The Doc looks over and taps at a cooking pot enamelled in an attractive shade of pale blue. 'I was thinking more along the lines of something like this.'

Derek peers at the price. 'Four hundred and seventy-five dollars,' he splutters. 'I could buy nine and a half of those squiffy candles for that amount.'

The Doc gives him a cool stare. 'I don't think you can buy half a candle.'

But the blue's got Derek thinking. The idea just hasn't solidified into anything useful yet.

'It doesn't matter, you know.' The Doc regards the other half of the lamington, then pops it in his mouth. 'The truth is, the only gift your daughter would really want is for you to be at the wedding. And that's not going to happen, is it?' He brushes desiccated coconut from his tracksuit pants. 'Didn't you say you write to your daughter every week?'

'That I do,' Derek replies.

'Does she ever write back?'

There's that belt again, tightening around his chest. 'None of your business.'

The Doc shrugs and begins pouring the tiles back into the cloth bag. 'I didn't mean anything by it, Dezza. I just thought it might be easier to ask her what she wants and be done with it.' He packs up the racks and board and wraps the elastic band around the box. 'As per usual, you're overthinking this. Make a simple statement and move on. That's my advice.' He points at the magazine. 'Drop that back round when you're done, would you?' With that, he picks up his radio and Scrabble set and strides out of the cell.

Derek reflects on the bizarre conversation. He doesn't care what the Doc says – in no way, shape or form does a casserole dish, even a four hundred and seventy-five–dollar one, say, 'I love you.' It says, 'I'm obliged to acknowledge your special day.' It says, 'I've got deep enough pockets to buy a decent gift.' At a pinch, he concedes, it might even say, 'I wanted to buy you something that will last forever.' A sort of vote of confidence that the marriage will last at least as long as the warranty. But what it will never, ever say is, 'I love you.'

He leaves the magazine on top of his letter and retrieves his tapestry kit from under the bunk. He lays the threads in a row on the desk and shuffles back on the mattress until he finds the wall. Derek unfolds the pattern, reminds himself where he was up to, then picks up his needle and pushes it through the canvas. Up and down his needle goes, Derek absorbed in the task, the winched-in feeling loosening, his mind gently drifting and bobbing on a tide of thoughts.

He thinks back to the casserole dish. His mother would probably have liked it. Apart from the blue cloisonné vase she filled with flowers from the garden, his mother also had a collection of willow-patterned knick-knacks in the special display cabinet in the lounge room. And she had those throw cushions with the peacocks on them, just like the kit Jane had brought in, arranged on the gold bedspread in her bedroom. Combined with the white shag pile carpet, the total effect was all class. He used to sneak in there just to admire how beautiful it was. She had the magic touch when it came to decorating, did his mum.

Derek gasps as the thought he was searching for smacks him on the forehead. God, he's an idiot. Debbie doesn't want a four hundred and seventy-five–dollar casserole pot or a collection of fifty-dollar candles stinking of lemongrass and lychee. She wants something that comes from the heart. Something personal and unique. It's been staring at him the whole time. He's going to *make* Debbie's wedding present. Yep, a set of peacock throw cushions, just like his mum's. The idea is pure genius. He can't wait to see the look on Jane's face when he tells her.

Chapter 6

A sunbeam alights on Derek's tapestry where it rests on his chest. The colours are dazzling in the early morning light. He's fallen asleep sewing again.

'Wakey, wakey, hands off snaky,' an officer bellows down the corridor. Laughter follows the clanking of keys as men are released into the relative freedom of the deck after fourteen hours of isolation.

As he rises from his bunk, his door clicks open and Young Carl stands there, all smiles. 'Rise and shine, it's another sunny day in paradise.'

Derek turns his back and relieves his bladder.

'You're going to love what's on this morning's menu,' Carl continues.

Derek pulls his tracksuit pants up over his Y fronts. God he hates Y fronts. He's a boxer-shorts man himself, but the authorities don't allow them. In case some idiot transforms the elastic into a garrotte or some such nonsense.

'C'mon, guess what's for breakfast.'

'I'm thinking baked beans on toast,' Derek says wearily, throwing his jumper on over his t-shirt.

Carl shakes his head and smiles. 'No, we had that last week. How about this? Belgian waffles with whipped butter and maple syrup, a pot of plunger coffee and freshly squeezed grapefruit juice.'

Derek gives him a thumbs-up, then hurries off to find Parker and head down for his real breakfast. The last time he'd seen waffles was when they went to the golf club to celebrate Debbie's twelfth birthday. Lorraine liked the club, said it was genteel, but Derek hated forking out hard-earnt cash for a fancy breakfast when they could have just as easily whipped up something special at home.

They'd barely sat down when Lorraine ordered the eggs Benedict and a glass of bubbles.

'I'll just have the toast,' Derek told the waitress.

'For goodness sake,' Lorraine snapped. 'You can have toast any old day of the week,' and she'd looked at him the way she always did by then, disappointment scouring her features. 'He'll have the country breakfast,' she said to the waitress and smiled in that condescending way reserved for anyone she deemed beneath her.

Derek knew he'd never get through all that food. And he also knew that Lorraine would pick at his plate, then take the leftovers home for the dog. As if she wasn't fat enough already, poor thing.

'Have the waffles, Debs. They're Belgian,' Lorraine had instructed and, with a sigh, Debbie did as she was told.

But the surprise showed on her face when she had her first mouthful. 'They're really yummy.'

And, with a triumphant smile, Lorraine had skewered a morsel, her fork greasy with hollandaise, all but saying, 'I told you so.'

Derek picks up his tray and joins the queue straggling past the serving bay. It's stacked with pre-packaged items that might constitute a nutritionally balanced breakfast but have all the appeal of eating the very cardboard containing them. A million miles away from Belgian waffles and a view of the eighteenth fairway.

Derek yelps as pain shoots through the back of his leg. He whips around and sees a boy with a horrified look on his face.

'Shit! Sorry, mate, I'm really sorry,' the kid says, trying to dab at the back of Derek's thigh with a scrunched-up paper napkin.

He knocks the hand away. 'What the hell did you do that for?'

The young man cowers as crims circle around them, saying things like, 'Yeah, bro, what'd you do that for?', 'He did that on purpose you know,' and 'You should teach him a lesson, Dezza.'

Panic flashes in the young man's eyes. He too recognises how fast this could turn nasty. It's lucky for him he's spilt coffee on Derek and not someone like Jacko. That man has a mean streak as wide as the Hume Highway.

'Did you do that on purpose?'

The kid's gaze flickers sideways. 'I tripped.'

A loud guffaw meets this explanation, earning comments along the lines of, 'Yeah, mate, and bullshit builds houses.'

Derek ignores them. The kid deserves some credit. For one thing, he's smart enough to keep his eyes down. He knows the drill.

'Be more careful next time,' Derek says in a stern tone, hoping it's enough to satisfy the others. He leaves the warning hanging between them and goes in search of a vacant seat. His thigh stings, but it could be worse. He's never been on the receiving end of a violent temper but he's seen plenty of examples in the prison hospital; stitches, broken bones, you name it. Derek eases himself into a spare chair in the corner.

'Can I sit with you?'

The boy slides into the opposite seat, a pleading look on his face. Derek studies his lean brown frame, his liquid eyes and generous mouth. Sitting with Derek might single a man out as a soft cock, but better to be a wimp than the darling of some of the thugs in here. Looks like his can attract the wrong kind of attention.

'Sure,' Derek says. He pours milk over his rice bubbles, leaving enough for his coffee later. He glances over at the table on the far side. 'But wouldn't you rather sit with the other Kooris?'

The boy turns and signals hello to a group sat around a nearby table, receiving nods in reply. 'Nah, I'll catch 'em later.' He picks up a packet of jam and flips it between his fingers. 'I didn't really trip, eh.'

Derek ponders this over the snap, crackle and pop of his cereal. There are only two ways this can go and he's too old to be targeted by some pipsqueak looking to make a man of himself. It reminds him of standing in front of a classroom of bored teenagers, sweltering in the hot summer afternoons, watching the clock until bell time. Making trouble rather than wrestling with algebra.

'What's your name?'

'Maloney. Joey Maloney.'

Aah, the newbie. Maloney 8. No gossip yet on what the '8' is for. Judging by the size of him, probably something stupid like stealing cars. He notices Parker tottering towards them, concentrating on balancing his tray in his shaking hands. Derek turns back to Maloney. 'How are you settling in?'

The boy shrugs, a fluid movement that reminds Derek of a dancer. 'It's different. I was in the Bay before this. I dunno why they moved me, eh?'

Parker plonks his tray down next to Derek's, supports his weight on the table, and lowers himself into the chair. 'The powers-that-be move prisoners all the time,' he says, hands shaking as he struggles to open his cereal. 'Truckloads of 'em shunted across the state like cattle.'

Derek takes the packet from Parker, opens it, and pours the contents into his bowl. The old man grunts his thanks and unfolds his newspaper, tapping his glasses back onto the bridge of his nose.

'What's the deal here then?' Maloney ventures, folding his jammy bread in half and shoving it in his mouth. 'I mean, which jobs pay the most?' Maloney continues as he chews.

Derek shoots him a sharp look. 'That's a bit forward. You've only been here five minutes.'

'I made hospital scrubs before this, but do you reckon I'd get a look-in here?' Maloney taps his spoon against the back of his hand.

Christ, does the kid ever stop fidgeting? Derek knows Maloney's sort. Junkies whose lives run on feeding their habit. Doing whatever it takes to get the next fix: stealing, setting up their friends, wheedling with the dealers or trying to outrun them. It made for a life of high drama and beat the heck out of flipping burgers, just ask them. Inside, the drug addicts were instantly recognisable, their bodies constantly in motion in a way that reminded Derek of a demonic marionette. The junkies share a strange camaraderie and there're plenty of drugs in gaol if you know the right people. But the price the dealers extract is extortionate, and Derek isn't just thinking about the cash. Even smoking cigarettes can get a man in with the wrong crowd and not many can afford twenty bucks for a single fag.

'You've got Buckley's, mate,' Parker says, turning to the weather page. 'Unless you've got special skills, everyone starts on cleaning duties.'

Derek looks to Maloney's rolled-up sleeves, searching for track marks. 'Why are you so desperate for cash?'

Out of jam, Maloney butters a slice of bread and sprinkles it with artificial sweetener. He looks to his elbow and shakes his head. 'I don't do drugs. Drugs are for idiots.'

Derek and Parker share a knowing look. Petrol or glue sniffing then – it's always something.

'It's me Aunty,' Maloney continues. 'She's gotta bung hip. She can barely walk, eh.'

Derek plays with his cardboard cup. There'll be bruises on the boy; there always is. On his belly, in his groin, between his toes.

'What do you do then?' Maloney asks, pouring sweetener on another slice of bread. 'You've been in a while; haven't ya? You must know which are the good gigs.'

Derek scowls at him.

'On your door,' Maloney adds. 'Seven years.'

'And you're serving eight.'

Maloney balls up his half-eaten bread and shoves it in his gob. 'Yeah, well, I'm not guilty of nothin', eh.'

Parker chuckles. 'Mate, I'd love a dollar for every crim who's said that.'

Maloney squares his thin shoulders and glares at the old man. 'I'm up for parole at the end of the year. I'll be gone before you know it.'

Derek eyeballs Maloney. 'So you can sew?'

The kid swings back on his chair, his wide smile revealing even white teeth. 'My Aunty taught me, the one with the gammy hip. I can sew anything.'

Derek doubts that. Not a single man joined Backtackers with more than a passable nod at a decent stitch, himself included. 'Yeah, well, making hospital scrubs is one thing, but hand-stitching is another thing entirely.'

Maloney's hand flutters to his chest. 'Tell me about it. Most of the men I worked with couldn't even sew a straight seam.'

'And you can, can you?'

Maloney grins. 'Aunty is the best sewer in town. She does repair work at the drycleaners but at night she sews costumes for the local theatre group. Gets commissions too. You know, formal dresses, stuff like that, eh.' Maloney expands with the telling, his hands sketching the words in the air.

Derek squints at him, wondering what this has to do with a skinny kid in prison greens.

'I been sewing since I was this high.' Maloney indicates a height that suggests he was about six years old. 'I'm a dab hand with a Bedazzler,' he adds with a wink.

Derek doesn't get the joke, but before he can ask, he sees the Doc zeroing in. He knows exactly what the Doc thinks of Backtackers, so he decides he'd better say his piece before the mercurial crim joins them. 'There's a sewing group on Thursday afternoons,' he says quietly. 'But I warn you, this is serious work. We're on commission and Jane won't put up with any nonsense.' Which isn't quite true. Jane's a big softie.

'And who's this sitting in my chair?' the Doc asks, banging his tray on the table. Parker jumps and spills his coffee all over his newspaper, reducing it to a soggy mess. Maloney jumps too, almost falling off his seat. Parker glowers at the Doc, but says nothing as he tries to rescue his paper.

To the boy's credit, he quickly composes himself and sticks out his hand. 'Joey Maloney.'

The Doc ignores the offered hand and nods instead. 'I hope you've washed those. The best way to spread germs is via hand contact, and you don't want to get sick in this joint. Might be the death of you.'

Maloney laughs, but Derek doesn't. How many little old ladies met their end? Two? Ten? Twenty? And it certainly wasn't through lack of personal hygiene.

Chapter 7

The following Thursday, Derek arrives at Backtackers filled with anticipation. He can't wait to tell Jane about the peacock cushions; he's sure she'll agree that it's a genius idea. But when he gets there, Jane's stuck in a corner with Les and Derek is forced to wait his turn.

Sitting next to Les, Jane wonders how much more she can add to a conversation about the intricacies of half-stitch. Part of her wishes Les would evolve beyond his current skill level but as the man himself says, 'Best to stick to what you know,' even, it would seem, if what one knew wasn't very much at all.

She looks up and notices a young man hovering in the doorway. He has the most gorgeous crop of thick black hair and such expressive eyes. He stands there, his fingers tying themselves in knots, those eyes searching for a friendly face. Jane makes her excuses to Les and goes to rescue him.

But Derek beats her to it.

'You made it then?' he says by way of welcome, which to Jane's ears sounds a lot more like, 'What the hell are you doing here?'

A hurt look shadows the boy's face. Concern furrows Jane's brow. Derek hastens to make the introductions. 'Joey, this is Jane.'

At the boy's obvious surprise, Derek explains, 'First names only in here, mate. No jail talk and no' – here Derek gives Maloney a stern look – 'inappropriate comments.'

'It's always lovely to see new faces, Joey,' Jane says, glancing at Officer Petty.

Keeping a firm grip on his clipboard, the officer waves a slip of paper. 'Permission slip came through this morning.'

Relieved that everything's in order, Jane ushers Maloney over to her chair and finds a spare to sit beside him. 'Have you sewn before?' she asks, reaching in her basket for an offcut of linen, thread and a needle.

Maloney launches into his story about his Aunty and her costumes for the local theatre group. When he repeats the joke about him being a dab hand with a Bedazzler, Jane snorts with laughter. Derek makes a mental note to find out what on earth is so funny.

She instructs Maloney to give her some sample stitches then turns her attention to Derek. Jane smiles at him, the laughter still in her eyes. 'Have you given any more thought to the commemorative cushions? Have we a fourth stitcher?' Her perfume, light and floral, invades Derek's senses. Another note assails him, something tropical in her hair. Coconut? He swallows. 'Mick and Sean are good. Mick reckons it's a toss-up between Frank and Brian?' He says it as a question and Jane knows why. Brian might be slow, but he's easy to get along with, which is more than can be said for Frank, who likes to think he's one of the better stitchers. Unfortunately for him, no one else shares that opinion.

Derek glances around the room. He'd rather keep this conversation between him and Jane, and while the Backtackers aren't jammed in like a packet of Arnott's Assorted Creams, they are close enough to hear every word. Then again, Jane's only here three hours a week, so he lets the excitement win and spits it out. 'I've thought of a gift for Debbie's wedding.'

'Ooh, a wedding! I love weddings,' Maloney exclaims, abandoning his sewing in order to float his hands about his face. 'The silk, the lace, the whole confetti and Champagne thing. When my sister got married, Aunty made her this dress that was so heavy it took two of us to lift it.'

Jane raises her eyebrows at Derek before acknowledging Maloney. 'That's lovely work, Joey. Can you show me some chain stitch?'

Realising he has overstepped the mark, Maloney buries his head in his sewing.

She gives Derek a nod of encouragement. 'I'm all ears.'

Derek lowers his voice, making sure Jane is the only one who is all ears. 'You know that peacock tapestry kit you brought in last week?'

'Ye-es …'

'I've changed my mind. I've decided I will make that cushion, if it's all right with you.'

Two lines form between Jane's eyebrows, little furrows of confusion. 'I'm not sure I understand what that has to do with your daughter's wedding present.'

Now it's Derek who's confused. 'Remember I said that my mum used to have a set of cushions on her bed? With peacocks on them. And, bang, just like that, it came to me the other night. I should make Debbie a set.' He grins at Jane, waiting for her to make the connection.

Jane hesitates. As much as she loves sewing and knitting and pretty much all things crafty, she can't imagine her twenty-something-old self would have been thrilled to receive a set of handmade throw cushions, with or without the peacock embroidery. She searches for the diplomatic middle ground.

'It's a lovely thought. Something handmade is worth a thousand times more than a purchased gift.'

Derek deflates. It sounds like Jane thinks he's a cheapskate and he didn't mean it like that.

'You could make her wedding dress,' pipes up Maloney, handing Jane his sample work.

'That might be a bridge too far ...' Jane says tentatively.

Which Derek reckons is her way of saying that's the dumbest idea she's ever heard. And she'd be right. Cushions are one thing, but a wedding dress is a whole other ball game.

Jane turns her attention to Maloney's work, marvelling over the neat stitches scrolling across the cloth. 'This is excellent,' she says, surprised and delighted to have someone join Backtackers who can actually sew. 'I think you did a bit more for your Aunty than Bedazzling.'

Mick and Sean drop their work and come to see what the fuss is all about, cutting between Derek and Jane. 'You could be a brain surgeon,' Sean says, turning over the linen to admire the neat offside.

Maloney dips his head to hide his pleasure.

'Looks like we've found our fourth,' Mick adds, shooting Maloney a grudging look of praise.

With a glum heart, Derek watches Jane and Maloney sort through the new kits. So he hadn't lied. The kid can stitch, all right. They finally decide upon an intricate pattern of wreathed roses. It's one of the tricky ones; a free embroidery with no pattern printed on the fabric, meaning Maloney will have to copy the design by eye. Jane pulls out the instruction sheet and starts running through it. With some satisfaction, Derek notes the kid's smile shifts to a worried frown. Not such a clever clogs after all.

Out of the blue, Sean suggests, 'What about a wedding quilt?'

Jane spins around. 'That is a brilliant idea! Why didn't I think of it?'

'What the hell's a wedding quilt?' Mick chips in.

Sean searches the shelves behind the sewing machine for a book and thumbs through it until he finds the section he's looking for. 'See here?' he says, holding up a double-page spread filled with photographs of different quilts.

Jane points to a picture of a quilt with a wedding ring pattern. 'My nanna has one of these, they're quite traditional but there're so many to choose from.'

She's not wrong, either. There's a chequerboard patterned one with a panel in the middle for the couple's name and date of marriage. There's one with a heart in the centre and the words 'Please sign our quilt' sewn above. Another with 'Mr and Mrs Right'. Yet another with 'Bride and Groom' sewn onto plain panels in the midst of an exquisite appliqué pattern.

'There's no way in hell I could make something this complicated in six months. I'm not bloody Sean,' Derek says. 'Anyway, what's wrong with my idea?'

Sean snaps the book shut and shoots daggers at Derek. As far as he's concerned, Derek's lucky Les is in Backtackers because Les makes Derek look like a ray of sunshine.

'Nothing,' Jane says, taking the book from Sean and returning it to the shelf before he's tempted to use the sharp corners to show Derek how he really feels. 'I'm sure your daughter will love a set of cushions.'

Mick and Brian share a look. As fathers of daughters themselves, they can almost guarantee what the reaction would be. Mick whispers to his mate, 'He hasn't got an effing clue,' and Brian sniggers.

Longing to rescue the situation, Jane offers her own suggestion. 'Or what about a trousseau?'

'Underwear?' Lumbering Sean with his overdeveloped biceps and gym junkie's rolling gait turns a deep red. Suresh and Riley start giggling like schoolgirls, but Ahmed looks like he's about to have heart failure at the mere suggestion.

'A trousseau is not just underwear,' Jane replies, sounding sharper than she means to. 'They originated in the days when a young woman lived at home until she wed. Her relatives and friends made items for her to take into her marriage. Underwear, yes, but also nightgowns, embroidered pillowslips, monogrammed napery. Items a young bride might need to start her own home.'

The men fall silent as they contemplate the items on Jane's list. Unfortunately for Derek, his brain has frozen on the image of his little girl dressed in suspenders and garters and a push-up bra.

'Wouldn't it be cheaper just to go to the shops and buy a set of towels?' asks Pete, completely missing Jane's point.

'I refuse to make girl's pyjamas,' Frank says, disgust written all over his face.

'Noted,' Jane says coolly, knowing full well that Frank thinks making a nightgown is beneath him.

'I could do some nice scalloped edges on a set of napkins for you,' Mick pipes up. 'Personally, I like damask, but it's a bit much with lace. I reckon plain linen's the way to go.' Mick thrusts his hand in Derek's direction where a sample of dainty lacework lays in the meat of his palm.

Derek makes a show of admiring it, wondering what on earth Debbie would do with such a thing.

Jane smiles at Mick, glad to have found at least one ally. 'Exactly. A set of embroidered hand towels never goes astray either, perhaps monogrammed with her initials.' She turns to Derek. 'Is she changing her name?'

Now it's Brian's turn to muscle in. 'Yeah, what's this bloke's name then, Dezza?'

Embarrassed that he doesn't know the bridegroom's last name, Derek makes one up. 'Carter. Ian Carter.'

'So will your daughter be Carter then?' asks Jane.

Derek doesn't answer. He's trying to imagine what Deb's mortgage broker looks like. Maybe tall and thin with glasses. Because the marriage of opposites is supposed to work out best. That's what they'd said about him and Lorraine.

A voice shouts in his head. 'You and Lolly are the perfect couple, Derek. You know how to make the money and she knows how to spend it!'

Derek starts as if Garry Johns is right there beside him, clapping his shoulder so hard the froth from his beer slides over the rim of the glass. Garry's face looming in too close, making sure Derek's got the joke. Interpreting Derek's weak smile as a yes before swivelling around to Lorraine, who titters and flaps her hand at Garry as if he is the life and soul of the party when all he is, is the president of the golf club. How Derek hates Garry Johns. He feels no remorse for the pain he inflicted on that buffoon. He deserved everything he got, including Lorraine.

'Are you all right, Derek? You look a bit pale. Do you want to sit down?' Not Garry Johns' hand weighing on his arm, but Jane's. She leads him over to the chair next to Maloney, the gentle waft of her perfume calming him.

'Sorry to rain on everyone's parade, but trousseaux are so old fashioned,' Maloney says, head bent over his frame. Derek can't believe how fast he sews, how quick and even his stitching is. He'd dismissed Maloney as all puff and no powder, but he was wrong. The sick Aunty may be a furphy, but Maloney is well and truly a stitcher. 'Next you'll be suggesting a glory box as well. I mean, hello? What century are we living in?'

Jane flushes. She's allowed herself to be carried away by the thought that she might at last have found a group project for the

Backtackers. Joey is right. To a twenty-something, a trousseau is equally as bad as a set of homemade throw cushions.

Maloney crosses his legs, dangling the frame over one knee. 'My Aunty says a woman never forgets what she wore on her wedding day. All that money and razzle dazzle is about creating a lifetime of memories.'

'He's right about the money, you know,' Brian chips in. 'I couldn't fuckin' believe it when me daughter Crystal got married. Weddings are a rip-off. You order a fruitcake from the cake shop and it'll cost you so much, but say it's for a wedding and, bang, straight away they hit you up for three times that amount.'

'When Kaz told me our Samantha was getting her dress made, stupid me thought it was because she was trying to save money,' Mick chimes in. 'I'd read some of those wedding magazines on the toot. I'm not even talking hundreds, I'm talking *thousands* of dollars on an effing dress! So I thought, great, go for it, get a homemade jobbie. Almost had a heart attack when Karen slips me the invoice. I said to her, "What's it made of? Fucking spun gold?"'

Not to be outdone, Maloney adds another story. 'My cousin was marrying some bloke out Erindoroo way.' He rubs his thumb against his fingers. 'Loaded. Four thousand head of cattle, canola. You get the picture.' Maloney flaps his hands. 'Anyhoo, they went all out. Watered silk and Aunty embroidered the entire skirt in some special design that was supposed to bring my cousin luck and prosperity. The whole bodice was hand-stitched in seed pearls. That dress was something else, eh.'

'And did it?' Sean asks.

Maloney frowns. 'Did it what?'

'Bring her luck and prosperity.'

'I s'pose. She's got five kids now,' Maloney says with a broad grin.

The men cackle with laughter. Brian gets a bit carried away. 'Yeah, right. So what did Samantha have on hers then, Mick? The Rabbitohs?'

Mick's smile disappears in a flash. Brian's eyes go wide with alarm. He's gone too far. Mick's lost his jovial punter look and suddenly seems to fill twice as much space. Brian, who's not the sharpest tool in the box, is desperately trying to think of a way out of this. Taking the piss out of South Sydney's rugby league team is already sailing a bit close to the wind, but having a go at Samantha is a recipe for disaster.

'Settle down you two,' Sean tosses at them from behind the sewing machine. It's a warning that he's watching them. Given he's the only Backtacker who's bigger than Mick, it's all that's needed for Mick to shed his anger and resume his friendly barman persona. Brian shoots Sean a look of thanks.

Jane's been listening to the men, wary but not alarmed by their behaviour. The blokes rarely step out of line at Backtackers and she'd rather they sort their differences out with words. She knows they'll calm down as soon as they pick up their stitching. No one wants to lose their place in the sewing program.

She picks up Maloney's embroidery and studies his handiwork. An idea is taking shape in her brain but she wants to see if the men can get there by themselves. It would be better that way. 'Well, we certainly have no shortage of excellent stitchers, whatever you decide on, Derek.'

'Making a wedding dress is a stupid idea,' Les throws from his corner.

Maloney's smile evaporates. 'What d'you mean?'

Les's eyes dart from Mick, to Brian, to Sean, as if daring them to disagree, then he lands on Derek. 'For starters, what size is she?'

Derek thinks back to the last time he saw Debbie. No, he doesn't want to think about seeing Debbie in court. He delves further into his memories, to a time when they were still a family. He can easily picture her soft curls, blue eyes that flashed between bemusement and disdain. Quizzical eyebrows like some Hollywood starlet. He remembers her spending hours in front of the mirror, practising how to raise just one. But after a certain age, a father is careful how he looks at his daughter. Average height, taller than her mother, shorter than him. Strong legs. Busty.

He gives a helpless shrug. 'Haven't got a clue. What size are most women?'

'A fourteen, but she's young so maybe she'd be a ten or a twelve. Does that sound about right?' Jane replies.

Derek nods, but Jane gets the sense he really has no idea.

'It won't matter if it's a bit out,' Maloney says. 'We can make it with a generous seam allowance and adjust it after a fitting.'

Mick guffaws. 'A fitting? How the hell are we going to do fittings exactly? The gov's not going to let her in here and we're a bit short on privacy in the visitors' room.'

'After we make the mock-up, we can get her to try it on. Or I could get her measurements, then we'd be certain,' Jane suggests.

Maloney shoots Mick a smug glance. 'Once we know the style of dress she wants and we have her measurements, we're as good as gold.'

Derek's not so sure. He can't imagine Debbie, or Lorraine for that matter, being thrilled about Jane turning up on their doorstep. No, far simpler to stick with throw cushions and keep the Backtackers out of it.

'Did it occur to you ning-nongs that Derek's daughter has probably already picked a dress? It's one of the first things girls do, after booking the reception centre and the chapel,' Vince lobs in.

The excitement fizzles out like a damp firecracker. Jane straightens the edges of the tapestry kits on the table. Mick picks up a skein of thread. Derek retrieves his needlepoint, but makes no attempt to work on it.

'Jane can tell her not to bother. That we'll make the dress. It's Derek's way of being a part of the wedding, to be there on the day ...' Maloney's enthusiasm dies on his lips when he notices the look on Derek's face.

'Well, I think it's romantic,' Jane says. She turns to the men, her cheeks warming to pink. 'I think Derek's daughter is lucky to have a father who can make her wedding dress. We could easily hand-stitch a design onto the skirt, just like Joey's Aunty. Then it wouldn't be any old wedding dress, it would be a work of art.'

The men regard her and Derek regards his shoes. This is his gift, his daughter – what's it got to do with anyone else?

'A quilt means we won't waste our time,' Sean says with a degree of petulance.

'Unless she hates it and sends it off to Vinnies,' Maloney retaliates.

Sean flinches as the words find their mark.

Jane glances at the clock high on the wall. 'Look, we don't have to make a decision today. Let's mull it over and discuss it again next week.'

She looks at each of the men in turn, willing them to see the obvious possibilities. Between them, they have all the skills they need to make a dress, if only they believed in themselves, and for once in their lives, worked together. She looks at

Maloney, at Derek, and her gaze lingers on Les, the negative Nellie who goes out of his way to put a dampener on just about anything, and she feels her resolve strengthen. She addresses the Backtackers.

'Making a dress is a statement. A declaration of Derek's love. How could she possibly say no?'

Chapter 8

'Ouch!' Debbie jerks away from the invading fingers of the pencil-thin girl and scowls at her reflection, all seven of them. The array of mirrors show her from angles she's never dreamt existed.

'It'll be much easier if you stand still,' the girl replies, smiling, though her tone is acidic.

Debbie imagines snapping the stick figure in half.

'For heaven's sake, Deborah, stop fidgeting,' Lorraine instructs from the embrace of a deep lounge.

Debbie pulls away as the girl's manicured talons fiddle with a zipper that refuses to budge past her hips. 'There's no point, Mum; the dress is too small.'

Lorraine wriggles to the edge of the couch, nostrils flaring. 'It's not the dress, Deborah.'

'Yes it is. It's designed for someone who's' – Debbie pauses and points at the shop assistant – 'built like her.'

They both regard the petite blonde standing before them, with her perfectly tinted roots, buff spray-tanned forearms and pouty lips that must cost her a fortune to maintain. Polished toes peek out of expensive sandals. She is a sleek advertisement for the dreams promised by the volumes of organza and satin, lace and taffeta displayed in the windows of La Chic Bridal Boutique.

When Debbie said yes to Ian, she'd imagined a simple affair, immediate family only, and a seamless transition into matrimonial bliss. Not this. The moment she told Lorraine that she and Ian were engaged, her mum became a woman possessed. The wedding preparations feel like that movie where they are on a runaway train and no one knows how to stop it and there's a ticking time bomb that they have to disarm or they're all going to die. Except in this case, the ticking bomb is her mother. And this assistant, whatever her name is, is like the sidekick character who keeps chucking obstacles in the heroine's path, making it impossible to save everyone.

'Are you all right?' the stick insect asks, pinching Debbie's arm.

Flinching, Debbie realises she's practically hyperventilating and forces herself to calm down. No one warned her that the word 'wedding' would turn her mother into a monster or that choosing a wedding dress would become her worst nightmare. She stares at the assistant, trying to remember her name. After so many bridal shop visits, these assistants have started to blend into one. Was it Tash? Tory?

'Let's have another try,' Tash Tory says, and, with her will to resist flagging, Deborah scrunches in her abs and hopes for the best.

The girl carefully unzips the dress a little to release the small fold of flesh gripped in its teeth, then with a motion like ripping off a Band-Aid, runs the zipper up its full length.

Sighs of relief swirl around the room. Tash Tory fiddles with the fit, prodding and poking Debbie into the dress. 'There,' she announces and steps back to admire her handiwork.

No one says a word.

This particular dress, strapless with a boned corset, is her mother's choice. Debbie's stomach strains against the lace with all the appeal of a jelly mould. Her breasts, defying gravity in the tight bodice, press high as if searching for her chin. Debbie fears if she sneezes, the pair will topple out and bounce up and down like when she and Ian went bungee jumping in New Zealand. The only redeemable feature about this mountain of fabric is that it falls over the edge of the pedestal, concealing her worst feature: her thick ankles. She can't even move in the thing, which is a shame, as she'd like nothing more than to run away from this train wreck.

After the third attempt, Lorraine manages to escape the lounge and moves into position, front and centre. Her eyes are moist. She clasps her hands to her bosom. 'Oh Deborah, don't you look beautiful.'

Tash Tory snorts, then rushes to disguise it with a cough.

Debbie narrows her gaze. She goes to draw a deep breath, preparing for a sharp retort, but the constraints of the dress prevent her from doing so. 'It's too tight,' she squeaks.

'Well, you know what they say,' Tash Tory says. 'Hashtag shedding for the wedding.'

'She's right you know, Debs,' says Lorraine. 'Six months is plenty of time to lose a few kilos.'

'Six months!' exclaims Tash Tory, her eyes round with horror. 'Haven't you left it a bit late?' She doesn't wait for an answer, as she's concentrating on lifting the flesh off the top of the bodice so she can undo the hook and eye.

As Tash Tory pulls down the zipper, Debbie gulps in air like a drowning woman hitting the surface of the water. 'I'd prefer a dress that fits,' she says.

Tash Tory doesn't seem to hear her. 'Preparation is absolutely essential,' she continues, untangling Debbie's feet from the gown. 'Chase and I got married last spring.' Her eyes take on a dreamy look. 'We had the wedding on the beach at Maradhoofeydhoo.'

Debbie and her mother share a look. Marahoo what?

'Fortunately, I had twelve months to get myself in shape, otherwise I don't know how I would have done it.' She carefully arranges the dress on its hanger, as if it were a religious artefact rather than an extravagant waste of fabric, and returns it to the rack. 'Beach weddings can be so unforgiving,' she says with a knowing look. 'Although at least I didn't have to worry about shoes.' Tash Tory giggles and tosses her hair.

Debbie glares at her, shivering as she stands there in her underwear in the arctic air conditioning. Lorraine sinks back into the womb-like embrace of the lounge.

Tash Tory tilts her chin at Debbie. 'You need a battle plan to get yourself in shape. Guest lists and seating arrangements are easy. How you look is the only thing that matters.'

Tash Tory turns to Lorraine, and ticks items off her immaculate nails. 'Number one is diet, obviously. For the first three months I did the 5:2 with a twelve-hour fast, then ramped it up to 3:4 in the last nine. The trick is to restrict your calorie intake to between eleven am and four pm. On the in-between days, it's no dairy, no wheat, no alcohol, no red meat and *no sugar*.' She gives a delicate shudder. 'What really makes the difference is a hydro-colonic cleanse every month. You know, to remove waste and impurities from the large intestine. It's not as expensive as it sounds. If you buy a package of ten sessions, it's only $1599.' Tash Tory opens the drawer of a cabinet tucked discreetly in one corner. 'I think I have an Eternal Wellness brochure here somewhere. Oh, here it is,' she says, pulling a brochure from the pile and handing it to Debbie.

'Weekly facials are also a must, plus exfoliate, exfoliate, exfoliate,' Tash Tory goes on. 'I can't emphasise it enough. And drink at least three litres of water a day.' She grimaces attractively in Lorraine's direction. 'I know water tastes blah but it's calorie free and removes all those nasty toxins. And it does wonders for your skin. It doesn't matter which dress you choose, skin is everything.'

Debbie casts an anxious glance at her own. She's always considered her skin to be one of her best features. No freckles or moles and she's never really suffered from pimples. Although right now, under the pink-tinged glow of the overhead lights, she looks like a cooked lobster.

'And the other critical thing is exercise.' Tash Tory frowns at Debbie's torso.

'I do exercise,' Debbie responds, struggling not to sound defensive.

'She does too,' pipes up Lorraine from somewhere in the depths of the couch. 'Zumba three times a week.'

Tash Tory gives a sad shake of her head. 'You need an intensive program of HIIT and weights every other day. Especially hand weights to tone the upper arms and shoulders. Everyone is going to see you from all angles and you don't want them to be revolted.'

Debbie clenches her stomach muscles.

'The trick,' Tash Tory continues, waving a finger in front of her lips as if sharing state secrets, 'is slimming shakes only for the last week so you're guaranteed a flat tummy without compromising your health.'

'Is that what you did?' Lorraine asks, fighting her way to the edge of the couch.

Tash Tory runs a hand over the bones of her hips. 'Absolutely. And I've kept up my routine since the wedding because it feels so great! Here, let me show you.'

She retrieves her iPhone from the cabinet and pulls up her wedding photo album. 'See what I mean?' Tash Tory says, scrolling through thousands of images. 'Photos can be so brutal.

Especially on your wedding day. I mean, imagine if I hadn't looked after myself before a shot like this.' Tash Tory pauses at a photo and enlarges it before shoving it under Lorraine's and Debbie's noses. 'Hashtag no filter,' she adds with a satisfied smile.

Debbie eyeballs the photo of Tash Tory in a slip of a dress that hugs her pert bottom and showcases her flat abs. She must have had hair extensions because the tips of her balayaged hair brush the top of her butt. No filter? Probably because there was no need. There isn't one centimetre of Tash Tory that hasn't been physically enhanced or minimised.

Tash Tory sighs as she flicks through her memories, 'The natural look is totally in, but it's so unforgiving.'

'Can I get down now?' Debbie cuts across the self-congratulatory praying mantis.

Tash Tory's smile evaporates and she swipes her phone shut. 'But you've only tried on six dresses.'

'I've had enough for one day,' Debbie says, desperate to escape Tash Tory and her fashion magazine ethos. The only way she'd ever be as skinny as this emaciated creature was if she lived on air. Even the thought makes her hungry. 'I really need a steak.'

Tash Tory winces.

'And a jacket potato with sour cream and cheese,' she adds with a touch of malice.

With an 'oh', Tash Tory's hand flies to her lips. She looks like she's about to throw up.

Debbie feels a sliver of satisfaction. 'And for dessert' – she pauses, pretending to think about it – 'probably the double caramel chocolate mud cake with whipped cream *and* ice cream.' A victorious smile plays at the edges of her lips. She might be standing on a pedestal in her knickers, but she has Tash Tory on the ropes now.

But Tash Tory is an old hand at breaking brides. She raises one perfectly threaded eyebrow and says, 'In that case, I'll see what we have on the super-size rack.' With that, she disappears behind one of the concealed doors, leaving Debbie cold and deflated, with seven versions of herself staring back, each one reflecting the tears brimming in her eyes.

Chapter 9

'It's the lead item on every channel,' declares the Doc, rubbing his hands with glee. 'They're twisting themselves in knots trying to find someone other than themselves to blame.' Around him, the crims cheer.

The Doc is in the centre of the rec room with his radio turned to full volume. Men crowd around him, shoulder to shoulder, wanting to hear how Yarrandarrah has hit the big time.

'Shut up, you moron, I can't hear!'

'Did he say three got out or four?'

'I bet you it was Fitzy's idea.'

Through the forest of drab prison green, Derek sees Young Carl hovering with the other guards. This incident isn't funny to them. It will require mountains of paperwork, hours of dissection and examination.

Parker and Derek stand on the sidelines, watching the melee. 'What I want to know is,' Parker mutters, 'how the hell did four men make it over a six-metre-high perimeter fence topped with razor wire using nothing but wheelie bins?'

Derek shrugs. 'No idea,' he says, dipping his head in the direction of the guards, 'but when they catch the buggers, there'll be hell to pay.'

Since the breakout happened, headcounts have been upped to five a day. Prisoners stand outside their cells waiting to be checked off like recalcitrant schoolchildren. The dogs have been in every single day.

Derek studies Young Carl, thinking how lucky the bloke was to be rostered off that day. It's the kind of mistake he can just imagine Carl making. Though, in all fairness, no connection has been found between any officers and the two mattresses and the bung security camera in the car park.

'Somebody's been using visiting time to talk about a lot more than how the kids are doing at school,' Parker says with a phlegmy chuckle that catches in his throat and doubles him over.

Derek thumps his back until Parker waves him away.

Maloney saunters over and nudges Derek in the ribs. 'Thought it might have been you, Dezza. Thought you might have decided to go and measure up the wedding dress yourself.'

Parker wheezes with laughter and Derek scowls. Maloney's a bit mouthy for his liking. 'Don't be so bloody stupid. It might have escaped your notice, Maloney, but some of us prefer not to draw attention to ourselves.' Derek steps away, emphasising the distance he wishes Maloney would keep.

'Yeah, Maloney,' snarls Jacko from where he sits. 'If I were you, I'd shut that big mouth of yours if you want to see five more minutes on God's earth.' At six foot four, Jacko has a strong forearm and a long reach, as evidenced by the state of some of his victims in the prison hospital. Anyone stupid enough to ask will be left in no uncertainty that Jacko hates poofters. And, judging by the look on Maloney's face, he knows it.

'You're not entertaining the idea of making a wedding dress, are you, Dezza?' the Doc asks, switching off his radio.

Derek shoots the kid a filthy look. What goes on in Backtackers is supposed to stay in Backtackers. 'We talked about it, but I don't think the idea's got legs.'

He tenses, waiting for a generous slug of the Doc's ridicule. Mind you, it might put Maloney in his place if the Doc agrees with Derek and throws a wet blanket over the whole suggestion. But the Doc simply says, 'Anything worth doing has its challenges, Dezza. I can't think of a good reason not to try.'

'I can think of plenty,' Derek snaps.

'Name one.'

'Well, for starters, I've never made a wedding dress in my life.'

A smile twists the Doc's lips. 'Is that the best excuse you can come up with? I'm sure your sewing circle mates will be happy to pitch in, isn't that right, Joey?'

Maloney grins at the Doc, clearly thrilled to have found an ally. 'I told 'em I've made heaps of dresses. For me Aunty, you know, the one I told you about.'

The Doc nods at the kid. 'Precisely. Problem solved.'

Derek shakes his head. 'She's *my* daughter and it's *my* gift. I've already decided on what I'm making her and I don't need to involve every Tom, Dick and Harry to do it.'

The Doc says nothing. Just crosses his arms and contemplates Derek. The scrutiny gives Derek the jitters, but he does his best to maintain eye contact. Then the Doc asks, 'What are you scared of, Dezza?'

This fells Derek's gaze in one swoop. 'Nothing.'

'I'm getting the sense that you're reluctant to go out on a limb here.'

Derek snorts. If only it were that simple. He can't get the Backtackers involved. How many favours can one man owe? No thank you. He's been in debt before and look where that landed him. 'There is a lot more at stake in making a wedding dress than making a set of cushions, isn't there?'

The Doc shrugs, conceding the point. Encouraged, Derek goes on. 'Once I tell Debbie I'm making her wedding dress, then I have to deliver on the promise, don't I? I can't leave her high and dry.'

He glances from Parker to Maloney to the Doc. No one is disagreeing with him. With a surge in confidence, Derek expands the argument. 'Imagine this. Debbie's wedding day is just around the corner, and she's expecting a custom-made wedding dress, handcrafted in this fine facility.' He waves his arm round the room. 'Any one of us can be here today, gone tomorrow, which means we have no real control over the production process. And what if we can't get our hands on all the materials we need? A half-finished dress is no good to anyone.' There are so many reasons *not* to make a wedding dress, Derek is beginning to wonder why he ever entertained the idea.

'But Jane …' Maloney begins.

'Is not a miracle worker. She's subject to the same rules we are when it comes to what is and isn't allowed in here.'

'He's got a point, you know,' says Parker.

'Thank you. I cannot have Debbie depending on me to deliver a wedding dress and then failing to meet that expectation because of variables beyond my control.' Derek tilts his chin at the Doc, glad to be able to put the old crim back in his box.

The Doc scratches his nose, sniffs, then clears his throat. 'Bulldust.'

All three men turn to him.

'You can go blah, blah, blah all you like, Dezza, but what I'm seeing, what I'm hearing, is a man too frightened to take a risk. I find that quite incredible coming from you.'

'What do you mean?'

'C'mon, Dezza. You're a mathematician, a gambler, you know all about risk. How does that saying go – nothing ventured, nothing gained. Sure, don't make the dress, nothing lost. But what happens if you *do* make the dress? What does that tell your daughter, hey?'

Thank goodness the Doc doesn't spell it out, but Derek blushes just the same. 'And what if I tell Debbie I'm making the dress and then stuff it up? Get her hopes up only to dash them? That doesn't say "I love you", that says "I'm a dickhead".'

'To my way of thinking, Dezza owes no one nothin' and if he says he doesn't want to make the frock, then that's the end of it,' says Parker, folding his newspaper in half.

The Doc fails to disguise his disappointment. He pockets his radio then moves the Scrabble set to the centre of the table, indicating the subject is closed.

It's a rare day that the Doc can be reduced to silence. Derek should be elated, but he feels something else that he just can't put his finger on. Smaller maybe?

The Doc sets up the board and motions to Derek to take the place opposite. Derek curses internally. He needs to get back to his cell and get stuck into his sewing. He wants to finish this current cushion so he can make a start on the first of the peacock tapestries for Debbie. He'll have to complete them on the side, as personal projects don't earn him a cent and he needs the pay. The last thing he has time for is another one of the Doc's blasted Scrabble games.

But he sits down all the same and reaches in the bag. He pulls out a P.

The Doc pulls out a W and, with a snort of disgust, throws it back in the bag. It's bad luck, but Derek knows better than to offer him first go. The Doc's a stickler for the rules.

Maloney grabs the chair next to Derek and starts leafing through a discarded motorcycle magazine. 'What's that you're playing?'

'Scrabble. Surely you've heard of it?' Derek replies, turning his rack away from Maloney's curious eyes. Shuffling his tiles, he wishes for vowels, any vowel, besides the single I in his possession.

'Nah, never played it.'

Derek lays down BIND. 'Seven, doubled for going first, makes fourteen.'

The Doc forms the word URBANITE around Derek's B. 'That's ten times two for the double-word square, plus fifty for using all my tiles makes seventy all up.'

The Doc writes down his score and the tone is set for the rest of the game.

'What's an urbanite?' Maloney asks.

The Doc ignores him while he counts out seven fresh tiles and slots them on his rack. Derek can almost see words cascading through the Doc's head as his fingers flick back and forth over the tiles. He'd answer Maloney, but he's not a hundred per cent sure himself.

The Doc frowns at Derek. 'It's your go.'

He knows that. Derek just wishes they were playing in Polish; hardly any vowels in that language. He puts down DUMB using the Doc's U.

'Guys? Urbanite?' Maloney tries again.

'An urbanite is a person who lives in an urban centre,' says the Doc. 'It comes from the Latin *urbanus* meaning pertaining to a city or city life, specifically Rome, but it only came into common usage in the nineteenth century.'

Parker pulls his newspaper up in front of his face, so the Doc can't see him roll his eyes.

As the game continues, Maloney sounds out each word played in the manner of a third grader. The Doc corrects any mispronunciations along the way and offers definitions, often without being asked. Derek's mood grows darker – the constant chatter is ruining his concentration. The Doc ends up winning by over a hundred points, leaving Derek holding an F, a Y and a V. The demerit points widen the margin further but victory buoys the Doc's mood.

'Feel like joining us in a game?' he asks Maloney. 'I'll thrash you, but you're in with a good chance of beating Derek here.'

'Nah, I'm tired. I might hit the sack.' Maloney gives a theatrical yawn, leaving his motorcycle magazine exposed on the table.

The Doc swoops. He flattens the pages and makes a show of flicking through the articles. Derek can't be certain, but he's willing to bet the Doc has little to no interest in motorbikes. He looks more like a Jaguar man.

And, as mouthy as he usually is, Maloney stays silent. Not gaining the rise he hoped for, the Doc shunts the magazine across the table. Maloney leaves it there, unclaimed.

The Doc checks the time and turns on his transistor radio. The theme tune for the news plays and the newsreader leads with the prison breakout. Distracted by the pollies and their opinions, the Doc doesn't notice Maloney steal the magazine back, shove it in the waistband of his trackpants, and pull his jumper over the top.

'In local news, mayoral candidate Councillor Nicholas Fischer today visited the Yarrandarrah Community Centre to meet voters benefiting from the council-funded Senior Citizens Animal Therapy program, SCAT. Councillor Fischer said that pets are important companions for the elderly who can often feel isolated in their communities. If elected, he says he will increase funding to this important service to the people of Yarrandarrah.'

The Doc snorts. 'Bloody political point-scoring.'

'I don't know why you bother about what goes on outside. It's not like anyone listens to us,' Derek says. He slurps the last of his coffee and crushes his cup, keen to get away and get stuck into his stitching.

Fischer's challenger, Susannah Cockburn, is in the middle of offering her opinion when the Doc snaps the radio off.

'I'll tell you why. Because that clown cares more about pensioners' dogs than showing us a skerrick of humanity. This from a man who is on the record for calling this joint "a holiday camp". He wants to talk about reaching out into the community? How about improving the literacy program here so the likes of Maloney can learn how to read?'

'I can read!' shoots back Maloney.

The Doc snarls and snakes around the skinny boy. Derek tenses. The Doc looms towards and over Maloney's wiry frame. His hand darts out. The kid swings away, but he's too late. The Doc holds the furled motorcycle magazine.

He opens it at an article comparing the merits of a number of bikes. He stabs the page. 'What's this say then?'

Maloney doesn't move. He's coiled tight. His eyes flick to Parker, but the old man sticks to his crossword.

'What does it say?' the Doc thunders.

'Give it a rest, Doc,' Derek snaps. Maybe it's a hangover from his teaching days, but assuming you're better than someone just because you know more than them is one thing guaranteed to get up his nose.

The Doc wheels around. 'Keep out of it, Dezza.'

Maloney can't leave without going past the Doc, and despite Derek's firm words, Maloney knows Derek's no use to him. The kid takes a tentative step towards the open magazine. He peers at the page. His mouth works around words he cannot voice. He adjusts his position back and forth, as if he's having trouble reading without his glasses. But Maloney doesn't wear glasses.

'I can't.' He hangs his head, close to tears, his rich black hair wisping at his neck.

The Doc says nothing.

'I was never much good at school,' says Maloney. 'I liked playing footie with me friends, and art. But reading and maths and stuff was too hard, eh. I kind of stopped going after primary. Aunty let me hang out with her and she'd tell me stories as she worked. I like stories.' Maloney looks up at them, the memory firing in his eyes.

The Doc smiles and hands Maloney his magazine. 'You're in luck. So do I.'

Chapter 10

An outbreak of food poisoning has filled the hospital. Some idiot's been making home-brew again and, instead of helping his mates get merry, they're all chucking their guts up. Two of them are on respirators. It makes Derek late for Backtackers and, by the time he arrives, he's fizzing with anxiety.

Tensed in the doorway, he takes in the scene. Jane examines a set of tapestry kits on the table and checks them off on one of her lists. Beside her, the sewing machine whirrs as Sean works on his quilt. Mick is teaching Brian how to make a running border of fly stitch. Derek's tension unwinds. He gravitates to Jane's side. The graphic 25 is a dead giveaway. At last, the kits for the commemorative cushions have arrived.

'I cannot tell you how relieved I am,' Jane says, pressing a hand to her chest as if to still her beating heart. 'We can finally get started, and now we have Joey,' she ducks her head in Maloney's direction, 'we'll easily meet the deadline.'

Derek glances at the kid, busy sewing his roses and humming a vaguely familiar tune. A thread of annoyance tightens his jaw. Maloney might have won Jane's approval with his fancy stitches and funny stories, but the kid is sorely mistaken if he thinks good stitching makes him a good man.

Jane touches Derek's elbow and beams at him. 'I took the

liberty of speaking to my mother, you know, about the dress. She thinks it's a fantastic idea.'

Derek is speechless, but his mind whirrs faster than the needle on Sean's sewing machine. What has got into everyone? Everywhere he turns, people are trying to talk him into making the wedding dress. If he didn't know better, he'd swear the Doc, Maloney and Jane were in cahoots.

Jane's smile falters. She's been so looking forward to sharing the news with Derek but from the look on his face, he seems far from delighted. She says gently, 'You are still planning to make the dress, aren't you? I thought we'd agreed.'

Derek's neck prickles, aware of the growing silence in the room. To a man, the Backtackers are straining to catch their conversation. The belt tightens one notch, then another.

Jane too realises the room has grown awfully quiet. She rushes to include the other stitchers. 'Some of you might recall that my mother, Marion, runs the haberdashery store in town. She thinks the wedding dress is a brilliant idea.'

'I told you before, the girl will already have bought a dress,' Les mumbles around the needle clamped between his lips.

Brian lays down his hoop, glad to have an excuse to escape the difficulties of fly stitch. 'I reckon we'd make a dress ten times better than one from a shop. Plus then she'd know, wouldn't she?'

Sean takes his foot off the treadle and stares at Brian. 'Know what?'

Colour diffuses over Brian's one good cheek. 'You know what I mean,' he says, his voice gruff with embarrassment.

'Nah, mate, I'm not sure we do,' Mick adds, feigning innocent confusion. 'Why don't you spell it out for us?'

Brian shoots daggers at him. Mick doesn't even flinch. Maloney keeps his head bent over his stitching, but his shoulders shudder with ill-contained laughter.

'To prove he loves her,' Brian blurts out, his cheek now a violent shade of crimson.

Mick grins and Sean releases a series of small snorts. Les's needle slips to his lap.

'Exactly,' Jane beams, ignoring the schoolboy humour. 'All the skills we need to make this dress are right here in this room. Imagine what we could achieve if we worked together.'

I'll tell you what we'd achieve, Derek longs to shout, *a bloody fiasco*.

Jane senses Derek's lack of enthusiasm. Perhaps it was a mistake to mention working together. He's a funny creature. Not unfriendly exactly, more like awkward, as if he's in prison due to some administrative error rather than because he is guilty of a crime.

She returns her attention to the men. 'There is one issue, though.' A faint blush creeps up her neck. 'Mum's offered us a generous discount if we buy the materials at her store, but, even so, we will still need to pay the wholesale cost for the fabric and bits and bobs.'

And just like that, the mood deflates. Every man in this room has a job, it's the rules. Cleaning, gardening or working in the kitchens keeps the prison running and occupies time. But they're not paid the same rates as they would be on the outside. All in all, money is a scarce commodity.

Frank picks up his needlework. 'I'd help out if I could, but I send what I can to the missus.'

Maloney smiles in apology. 'My Aunty.'

'Yeah, well, my son Jason needs braces. Christ, don't start me on that,' Brian says with a shudder.

Sean fiddles with the tension control on his machine as he says, 'I need every penny.'

Sean has no family. With no one to send him parcels of underwear or toiletries, let alone little luxuries like a book or a set of playing cards, every cent he earns has to pay for the basic necessities of life.

Derek, on the other hand, feels like Jane's just dealt him the winning card. He tries to infuse his voice with regret. 'Ah well, it was a nice idea while it lasted.'

Hearing Derek's disappointment makes Jane wish she'd kept her trap shut. She could easily afford to subsidise the project and now all she's achieved is getting the Backtackers' hopes up for nothing.

'What about a payment plan?' Mick suggests. Derek's hands curl into fists.

'That's a great idea,' says Suresh.

'And you don't need to buy everything at once,' chips in Maloney.

Derek only has two hundred odd bucks in his account and he's got the sneaking suspicion that's nowhere near enough for a dress. As opposed to the cost of cushions.

Jane claps her hands together. 'First things first. Next week I'll bring in some wedding magazines and we can pick a dress we like. Fortunately, patterns are pretty cheap; it's the fabric where things start to get expensive.'

The belt around Derek's chest tightens another notch.

'Fabric doesn't have to cost squillions,' Maloney says, placing his needlework on a vacant chair. 'Sometimes my Aunty makes a dress for a couple of hundred bucks. Lots of girls come to her with big ideas and no budget.'

Sean shifts the heavy quilt across his lap. 'Like how?'

Maloney moves a couple of chairs out of the way to clear some space. With a flourish, he twirls around and strikes a pose. 'Here I am, it's my wedding day.'

'What a beautiful bride,' sniggers the new kid, Jarrod.

'Jeez, the groom must be old, blind or stupid,' mumbles Les.

Maloney simpers and dismisses the comments with a wave. 'I'm walking down the aisle,' he says, sashaying across the room, head lowered, casting demure looks through the veil of his long lashes. 'The guests watch me pass but mostly they're gunna see me from behind, eh? I've got a long train so you can't see much of what's underneath.'

'That's a relief,' jokes Mick.

Jane approaches Maloney and indicates for him to turn around so the others can see his back. 'Even with a short train, what draws the eye is the shape. A keyhole or a low V for instance,' she says, drawing each image across Maloney's back.

'You can't have bare flesh on your wedding day. You're s'posed to be a virgin,' Brian says, shaking his head in disgust.

Raucous laughter fills the room.

'What? I'm not saying whether or not she is a virgin, but the whole bloody point is she's supposed to *look* like one. Otherwise, why bother?'

A waggle of heads concedes the point and Maloney explains, 'Think about what you see in the wedding photos. Once she lifts the veil,' and he mimes this, eyelashes aflutter, 'the dress is just a front panel, eh.'

'He's right. The fabric doesn't need to be expensive; it just needs to *look* expensive.' Jane's excitement draws the men in. 'You can make a dress out of pretty much anything, but if you cut the pattern incorrectly, or the stitching is poor, or the finishing is second-rate, it doesn't matter how much you spend on the fabric, it will still be a bad dress.'

Derek's heart plummets into his socks. He really, *really* does not want to make a wedding dress. How is it even possible in three hours a week?

'We can finish it off with all sorts of details – embroider the hem and the neckline, maybe scallop the edges of the veil,' Jane adds.

Derek can see how careful she is to include each and every one of their strengths, which just makes him feel worse.

'This is what I would do,' Maloney says, holding up his tapestry hoop for all to see. Mick takes it from him, tilts it towards the light and studies the stitching before passing it wordlessly to Brian. Brian squints at the work, holding it close to his face. Les takes it from Brian, holds the hoop at arm's length, then shakes his head and passes it to Sean. After some moments, Sean gives a low whistle and hands it to Jane.

She finds the words none of them have voiced. 'Oh Joey.' Her fingers hover over the wreath of roses; the muted reds, apricots and delicate pinks. 'This is exquisite.'

Derek peers over her shoulder. Every stitch is perfect. Rather than wait until he has completed the basic cross-stitch, Maloney has begun the fancy overlay work, rose by rose. Derek picks up the illustrated instruction sheet that came with the kit, and compares the picture with Maloney's handiwork. It's as he thought. Maloney has used the basic design as a foundation and added many more layers. He's created veins within each petal and tiny French knots rise out of the centre of some flowers, as if the stamens are upright. Every leaf has a scalloped edge. When he holds the hoop at a distance, it is as if a real wreath of roses lies on the cloth.

'Not bad for a kid who can't read the instructions,' Derek murmurs, returning the hoop to Maloney.

Maloney slips him a sly smile. 'I've had lots of practice.'

'You see?' Jane appeals to the men. 'We can do this. If we keep the design simple, are modest in our choice of fabrics, with our stitching skills we can create a truly wonderful dress.'

The room is silent as the Backtackers contemplate the prospect. Derek doesn't know what to think. Despite himself, Jane's obvious passion for the project is reeling him in. There are little images dancing before his eyes. Of Jane's surprise and delight when he unveils the completed dress, him bursting at the seams with pride. Of Debbie walking down the aisle wearing a dress of his creation.

He shakes off the images. The idea is completely impractical. For starters, he can't make this dress on his own. Even he can appreciate that the stitching is only one part of an elaborate process. And how is he supposed to ask Debbie what she wants? He opens his mouth to speak, but Sean gets in first.

'Well, don't count on me. I have to have this finished by the Charity Ball,' he says, returning to the sewing machine and hunching over his quilt.

Jane's hopes splutter and die. She's pushed too hard. It's one thing for her to believe the men can make this dress, it's another thing entirely for them to believe it themselves. Without Sean, she has no machinist. She may as well kiss the whole idea goodbye.

'I'll help,' Maloney says, his gaze fixed on Sean's mop of strawberry blond hair.

Jane turns to the slip of a boy. She senses that beneath the mouthiness and the flippant attitude lies a vulnerable soul.

'As long as you put in a good word for me,' he says, grinning at Jane.

Tempered with a huge dose of street smarts. Because Jane doesn't need him to spell it out. Maloney's referring to his annual review. 'Of course, I'll do what I can,' Jane replies, although she doubts a good word from her will have much sway with the case review committee.

Derek watches this exchange with mounting annoyance. First Maloney is hogging the limelight, flouncing about in his pretend dress then showing off his stitching, and now he has the gall to ask Jane to put in a good word with the gov. The manipulative little sod.

It's only later, when he finds Parker, that Derek can finally say out loud what he would never say to Jane's face. 'The problem is, Jane's a soft touch.'

'Yeah?'

'Maloney spent the entire three hours big-noting himself in front of Jane, sucking up to her. The poor woman thinks Maloney's being helpful, but all he wants is a clean report card to show the parole board.'

Parker just blinks at Derek in reply and Derek takes that to mean he should go on.

'I mean, I'm a big boy, I can look after myself. But Jane …' Derek pauses and shakes his head. 'Jane's the type of woman who needs a nice fella who can make sure no one takes advantage of her good nature. And she's certainly not going to find that among this bunch of self-serving crims, is she?'

Parker stays silent.

'As much as I hate to say it, I don't think I've got any choice but to go along with this wedding dress idea. With any luck, the Backtackers will soon lose interest and then I can send Debbie the peacock throw cushions.'

Parker finally decides to share his thoughts. 'Lady Luck's not really ever been with you though, has she, Dezza?'

'What do you mean?'

'I think you're looking at this arse about tit. Maloney's not the only one who could earn some brownie points by making this dress.'

'Don't be bloody stupid.'

'For chrissakes, Dezza, for a smart bloke you're as dumb as batshit sometimes.'

'What?'

'Just think about it, mate.'

Chapter 11

Jane watches the men leave, escorted by the officers who will see them returned to their wing. People are usually horrified when she tells them she volunteers at the prison, imagining she is brave in the face of an ever-present danger. Many can't understand that week in week out, she listens to exchanges dominated by a different kind of brutality, men yearning for family, community and a normal life outside the boundaries of these walls. She knows that if they could, they'd be propping up a bar curing their loneliness with a schooner of ale and a bit of banter. Instead, they are stuck with her sewing tapestries, as she tries to provide some respite from the tedium and troubles.

Officer Petty sticks his head around the door jamb. 'Ready to go?'

Jane nods and double-checks she's locked away the scissors, then puts the lid on the sewing machine and locks that too. It's the same ritual every week, although why anyone would be stupid enough to steal the very tools that help them with their sewing is beyond her. She steps into the corridor and waits for Officer Petty to lock the door behind them.

They walk the length of the corridor towards the air lock. Past the Indigenous inmates' art class and the library, where she sees the prisoner with slick-backed hair handing around copies of a book to a group of prisoners seated in a semi-circle. A book club? The idea makes her smile.

'So d'you think this wedding dress has legs?' Officer Petty says at her side.

Jane turns her smile on him. 'I know some of them are making their excuses, but I'm sure once we've chosen a pattern and start actually making the dress, they'll soon warm to the idea. Don't you think?'

Almost every week, she walks the length of this corridor with Officer Petty. He's not like a lot of the guards. He's gentler, seems keen to believe that most of the men in Yarrandarrah deserve the opportunity to put past mistakes behind them. It's an admirable quality.

Officer Petty's walkie-talkie erupts and screeches instructions from somewhere inside C Wing. He turns down the volume. 'Don't worry about Sean, he'll come round.'

Surprised, Jane pauses. 'Actually, I was thinking about Derek.'

At the air lock, Officer Petty enters the security code and the door clicks open. The men on duty barely glance at them as they pass through and they walk in silence back to the reception building. Once there, Jane unbuckles her personal duress alarm and swaps it for her ID in the cabinet. The weight lifts from her, in more ways than one.

Sunlight slants across the grey linoleum. Carl lingers while the other officers scan her person, then her sewing tote and the bag of tapestries.

'Anything exciting planned for the weekend?' he asks, passing her back her belongings.

'Not really. My flatmate's running for mayor so I'll probably be handing out leaflets or working the sausage sizzle.'

Officer Petty's face lights up as if struck by a bright idea. 'Would you like to catch a movie on Saturday maybe? The new *Star Trek* is on in Corondale.'

Jane hides her surprise at the invitation and amusement at his choice of movie.

'Or I think that one with the famous Pommy actress is showing too.' He squints, trying to recall her name.

'Judi Dench?' Jane suggests, though his description could apply to any number of British actors.

'That's the one.'

Jane wonders how old Officer Petty is. Or rather, if he knows how old *she* is. Judi Dench is more her mother's vintage than hers.

Mind you, Jane's a bit over the election. Boxes and boxes of leaflets, campaign t-shirts and bags of balloons have turned their house into a veritable obstacle course, and just about every weekend for the past several weeks has been taken up with campaigning. She could do with a night off. Besides, he *is* quite cute.

'All right,' she says.

'Excellent. I'll swing by and pick you up. What's your address?'

'Let's just meet outside the cinema,' Jane says. She finds her notebook and pencil. 'Do you have a first name?'

'It's Carl.'

Jane smiles at him. 'Nice to meet you.' She writes down her number, tears off the page and passes it over.

Carl slips it into his pocket. 'I'll message you after I finish work so you have mine too.'

Jane nods. Mobile phones are banned in prison. The officers have to keep them in their lockers until the end of their shift.

'Well, I better go,' she says, grabbing the door handle. 'Um, I guess I'll see you Saturday.' She shoots him an awkward grin, then escapes into the sunshine.

Jane draws a deep breath, filling her lungs with fresh air after the hours in a tiny room thick with the scent of grown men. Almost immediately, she begins to perspire. It's unseasonably warm for April and poor Fern's not parked in the shade this week. When she opens the driver's side door, a wall of heat rushes out. Jane leaves it open while she puts the tapestries in the boot and takes her phone and wallet from the glove box. She checks her messages. There's a reminder that her library books are overdue. Another from Susannah asking her to pick up some milk.

The drive home follows the harsh line of metal fencing back towards town. Past the local swimming pool, bereft of water now summer is officially over. Her thoughts drift back to Carl. His kind eyes, his gentle smile. She wonders what he looks like when he's not in uniform and laughs at the unintended implication.

Jane swings right at the new footie stadium and follows the long straight road. She switches on the radio to hear Susannah ranting about the amount of money the current council has wasted on infrastructure projects like the stadium and the sculpture drive designed to attract tourists. 'All this,' Susannah says, 'at the expense of improving the opportunities for the youth of Yarrandarrah. If we invested in our young people, perhaps more of them would choose to stay and build their lives here, rather than move to the city.'

Jane turns down the volume. She's rather fond of the sculpture drive. It started at the tip, then sort of grew from there. Now there are all sorts of strange beasts cobbled together out of broken and discarded objects: a dinosaur riding a bicycle, a horse made out of horse shoes. Although Susannah has a point. The three main sources of employment in the town are the prison, the council and the primary school. Without them, the population of Yarrandarrah would consist mostly of land agents desperately trying to flog drought-stricken properties, and farmers wishing to sell up.

She turns into her street, where a smiling Susannah warmly greets her from every telegraph pole. Jane parks Fern behind Susannah's silver sedan.

'Hello,' she sings out as she plonks her handbag on her bed. Susannah doesn't answer her; Jane can hear she's on the phone. Jane strips off her sensible skirt and blouse, unhooks her bra and slings it in the laundry basket, then slips into a loose sundress and lets down her hair. She follows Susannah's voice into the kitchen. Her flatmate lounges at the table, bare feet resting on a chair, her high heels next to her briefcase on the floor, laptop open in front of her. Susannah gives a little wave as she finishes up her call.

'How was your day?' Susannah asks, tossing her mobile onto a pile of paperwork.

'Pretty good. Head office finally delivered those kits for the Charity Ball. I'm supposed to return them at the end of July, so hopefully there'll be enough time.'

'Your mother called,' Susannah says, her attention already diverted by the glowing screen of her laptop. 'She wanted to know what happened with the wedding dress.' Susannah glances up at Jane. 'You never told me you were getting married.'

Jane laughs. 'God no. Once bitten, twice shy.' Her thoughts drift back to her date with Carl, but she decides not to tell Susannah in case it's a one-off. After all, she barely knows the man. She flops in a vacant chair. 'One of the inmate's daughters,

Debbie, is getting married. We're thinking about making the dress as a sort of project.'

'Group therapy?'

'Not quite.' Jane pauses, considering Susannah's words. 'Well, yes, maybe.'

Susannah's fingers fly over the keyboard. When she pauses to add yet another item to her to-do list, Jane voices the question that's been bugging her all the way home. 'What do you think my chances are of getting the bride-to-be's measurements?'

Susannah rests her chin on her hand and studies Jane, disbelief mingling with curiosity.

'Having those would make our lives so much easier,' Jane continues. 'Guesswork is fine, to a point, but what if she's not a standard size? Her father hasn't a clue.'

Susannah snorts. 'Name me a man who does.'

Jane shakes her head. 'That's not what I meant. I don't think he's seen her for a while. I don't think he has much money either. What if we go to all this effort, at his expense, and end up with a dress that doesn't fit?'

'But surely she's already got a dress. No offence, but money aside, the whole project sounds like a recipe for disaster.'

Jane stares at the ceiling while she gathers her thoughts. 'I wish you could see these guys. People watch those gritty television dramas and think prisons are hotbeds of violence but the gaol is more like some perverse boarding school. These men aren't pure evil, they're just trying to get through the day, like everyone else. Joy is in short supply.'

'C'mon, four of them escaped the other week!'

'I know, but the men I teach aren't like that. You can't hold them responsible for a few rotten apples.'

'More like a barrelful.' Susannah trails a finger over the keyboard to collect the dust. 'I know how important

Connecting Threads is to you, but these men are in prison for a reason. It's one thing to teach them how to sew and, sure, making the dress might help alleviate the boredom, but you're only one person, Jane. You can't save them all.'

Jane studies her hands. Susannah didn't see the fire in some of the Backtackers' eyes when they talked about the dress. The idea inspired them. She can't fight the feeling that making this dress could be a golden opportunity.

Susannah closes her laptop and rests on her elbows. 'Okay, knowing how stubborn you are, let me ask you this. How on earth are you going to turn up on this girl's doorstep and say, "Hello, you don't know me from a bar of soap, but would you mind stripping down to your undies so I can measure your bust?"' Her kind expression takes the edge off her words.

Jane can't imagine it, that's the problem. She goes to the fridge and finds a quarter of a watermelon. 'Here's the thing,' she says, removing the cling wrap and setting the quarter flat side down on the chopping board, 'it's not just the making of the dress that's important.' She cuts off two generous slices and removes the rind, flicking the pips into the sink. 'It's about forgiveness, Susannah. This is the perfect way for Derek to apologise to Debbie for his past mistakes. When she wears the dress, Debbie will know how much he cares about her.'

Jane returns to the table with the plate of fruit. Susannah takes a slice, cupping it in her hand so the juice doesn't drip on her blouse. 'And if she doesn't?'

Jane licks her sticky fingers. 'I refuse to go down that path.' Out the window, a lone magpie perches on the fence, its wings arched away from its body in an attempt to cool down. 'We will make a truly wonderful dress. She will see all the love poured into it. Only a total cow could fail to be moved by such a significant gesture.'

'Jane, I …'

'And I won't be the one to deny him the opportunity.' Jane tilts her chin, daring Susannah to disagree.

Susannah studies her flatmate. Jane might be stubborn but she's also thoughtful, kind, and desires to think well of others. The complete opposite of Susannah who has spent far too many years hanging out with people sniffing around political power to share such a rose-coloured view of the world. 'I'm just worried that you're setting yourself up to be hurt.'

Jane droops a little. 'I know. And look, honestly? It's all theoretical anyway. I'm not sure all the men are convinced.' She thinks particularly of Sean and the way he looked at Maloney showing off in front of the Backtackers. 'It might end up being just a bit too much like hard work.'

But her words ring hollow and they both know it. Susannah and Jane have known each other since day one at Yarrandarrah Primary. Some might say Jane's a little flaky, but the pair have one thing in common, apart from a pathological hatred of white bread, devon and tomato sauce sandwiches. They are both passionate about anything they set their minds to. If she has her sights set on mending broken hearts with a dress, nothing Susannah, or anyone else for that matter, could do or say will stop her.

Susannah's mobile sings out the opening bars of the Bee Gee's 'Stayin' Alive', jerking her back to reality. As she listens, her eyes narrow. 'Is he now? Mmm. Why does that not surprise me?' She sighs. 'Yeah, thanks for the heads-up.'

Susannah tosses her phone on the table.

'Bad news?' asks Jane.

'Bloody Fischer. Wait till I tell you what he's planning now.'

Chapter 12

For some inexplicable reason, Derek feels the urge for company, and, unusually, not his own. He blames Jane and Parker and that blasted wedding dress. The conversations spool through his brain in a continuous loop, and, in the end, he abandons his letter to Clive and makes his way downstairs to the rec room. There he finds Parker leafing through the local paper, or what's left of it after numerous grubby fingers have rubbed it thin searching for an update on the escapees.

Derek slides into the opposite chair. 'What's tonight's movie then?'

'*Cheaper by the Dozen.*' Parker snorts. 'That muck they serve up is almost as bad as the food.'

Derek chuckles, although it's true. The rules technically allow them to watch movies classified up to M15+, but not with their gov in charge.

'That gov treats us like bloody children. Worried a decent fillum might overstimulate us. Christ, a John Wayne would do. Even a Doris Day. Mongrels.' Parker shakes out the paper, although Derek can't tell if it's out of anger or because of his tremors.

'I used to love going to the cinema,' Derek says. 'Sitting in the dark with a bag of popcorn and a choc top.'

Parker's rheumy eyes turn misty. 'Yeah, it's nice being in the dark. Even if tonight's movie was half decent, it's not as good as sitting in a picture theatre.'

The old man's right. There's always someone making wisecracks or talking at top volume throughout the interminable ninety minutes. Tonight, a ghetto blaster, or whatever they call the damn things these days, thumps out the jaw-rattling beat of some rapper with an attitude problem. All in all, what passes for entertainment serves as a miserable reminder of the life they have forsaken.

The Doc sits at the other end of the table, immersed in a book. One of Jacko's thugs slides in beside him and palms him something, saying, 'Right, mate?', then sidles away.

Without missing a beat, the Doc slips the contraband into his pocket and turns the page.

Drugs is the first thought that springs to mind, but Derek's pretty sure drugs aren't the Doc's scene, either taking or slinging them. Not that it stops crims approaching him. After all, he *is* a doctor. And desperate men will do pretty much anything to escape reality.

The Doc lays the book aside, cover down so Derek can't read the title. It's thin, no more than a couple of hundred well-thumbed pages, its cover creased, a corner bent.

The Doc withdraws the Scrabble set from beneath his chair and places it between them. 'Ready for a thrashing?' he asks with a grin.

Curiosity gets the better of him, so Derek excuses himself to Parker and moves to a closer chair. 'Why are you in such a good mood?'

'It's Wednesday, Dezza. My busiest day of the week. Yarrandarrah Library delivered fresh stock including two new book-club sets. Can you believe it? You should have seen the looks on the blokes' faces when I handed them around. The timing was perfect. We'd pretty much exhausted everything we had to say about *To Kill a Mockingbird*.'

Since the Doc's been prisoner librarian, he's managed to increase the book-club membership to such an extent he's had to split the group in two. It's a strange crew though, Jacko being a prime example, as well as that other bloke who's always hanging around with him. Carruthers.

'The thing you need to understand, Dezza,' the Doc goes on, warming to his theme, 'is that, unlike the newspapers and the magazines, book-club sets are hard to come by. You see, we have to rely on the regional library network to update their sets first.'

The Doc shakes the bag of tiles and passes it to Derek. Derek pulls an S. The Doc a V.

'When the books get a bit tatty, instead of binning them, Yarrandarrah Library sends them to us. There's no hope of securing any recent releases.' The Doc lays down ZENITH off Derek's JUMPING, not even pausing to comment on Derek's use of all seven tiles, although he does note the bonus fifty points.

'Beggars can't be choosers,' throws in Parker.

The Doc shoots him a sour look. 'I disagree. Just because we're residents of this fine establishment doesn't mean we don't deserve a decent read. In fact, I'd argue that we are *more* entitled to one than a member of the general public. They have a lot more options on how to pass their time than we do.'

Derek places down CHIEF using the Doc's H. The Doc's swift rebuke is QUIZ off the Z for a double-word score. 'Shouldn't have left that one open, Dezza.'

Too late, Derek realises he could have laid down FIZ or FEZ. It wouldn't have made a squirt of difference to his score, but it would have blocked the Doc's forty-four pointer. 'What books did you end up with?' he asks.

'*The Kite Runner* by Khaled Hosseini, which should prove popular, and *Big Little Lies* by Liane Moriarty.'

Parker chortles. 'That's gunna go down well, isn't it?'

'What do you mean? *Big Little Lies* consolidated Moriarty as an international bestseller and the television series was a huge hit.'

'Be that as it may, I know those blokes in your book clubs, Doc, and I can't imagine them being thrilled having to read a book by and about sheilas.'

'*To Kill a Mockingbird* was written by a woman and it's about a little girl,' Derek tosses in.

'That's right,' says the Doc.

'Yeah, but it's about justice and courts and that. Something *relatable*,' Parker says.

The Doc sits up straighter and rolls his shoulders. Derek can see he's building up for one of his lectures. Bloody Parker. He can be a real shit-stirrer when it suits him, but why does he have to do it when Derek's around?

'How's it hanging?' Maloney appears from nowhere and grabs the chair next to the Doc.

Derek's surprised Maloney has the guts to make an appearance after the other week's tirade. He checks the kid's back pocket for a furled magazine, but there's nothing. No sign of his stitching either.

The Doc suddenly hunches over his rack, furiously clacking his tiles, the sound amplified by the unusual silence of the transistor radio.

Oblivious to the Doc's mood, Maloney starts cleaning his nails and nattering quietly to Parker. Derek waits for the Doc's next move. JALOPY off the J for thirty-six. Derek manages

PANTO, but the Doc hits back with EXODUS off the U, quickly followed by WEAKLY off the E when Derek fails to take advantage of the open triple-word square. Since Derek has a run of vowels, he's stuck watching the Doc destroy his lead and take the game.

'You were off to a strong start, Dezza, but you ended up playing like an old woman. What's up?' the Doc asks, after laying down his final move and tallying the scores.

The irony of the Doc's statement is not lost on Derek. Is this how the Doc lured his victims into his good graces? A friendly game of Scrabble with a cup of tea and a couple of Monte Carlos to sweeten the lovely old ladies? It is obvious the Doc was once handsome before prison sucked the life out of him. Derek imagines he could have been a real charmer.

'Yeah, I don't know, got a bit on my mind,' Derek replies.

'Thinking about the wedding?'

'Nah,' he says, even though that's a straight-out lie.

The Doc packs up the game and secures the box with the rubber band. Then he reaches into the pocket where he secreted whatever it was the inmate gave him earlier. His brazenness alarms Derek until the Doc unfurls his palm to reveal two AA batteries. Unclipping the back of his transistor radio, he replaces the dead ones and the radio springs to life.

The Doc closes his eyes as the sound of an orchestra swells and swirls around them. Maloney takes this as a sign that it's safe to approach and edges closer. He's got his eye on the Doc's book and Derek's pretty sure the old crocodile is watching the kid through his half-closed lids, waiting for the moment to pounce. Maloney stretches out a tentative hand, turns the book around and studies the cover.

Stern capitals fill the top of the page. Beneath is a man's face drawn in harsh black lines. He has a thick moustache and his sorrowful eyes stare into the distance. Maloney frowns, whispering broken syllables. He is not alone. Even Derek is unsure how to pronounce the author's foreign name, rich in consonants.

'*One Day in the Life of Ivan Denisovich*,' the Doc announces, startling them all. 'A Russian classic.' He grasps the book with both hands as if greeting an old friend. 'The author won the Nobel Prize for Literature.'

Maloney says nothing. His eyes dart from the Doc to the book, suspecting, quite rightly to Derek's way of thinking, that the Doc is having a joke at his expense.

'Solzhenitsyn. Aleksandr Solzhenitsyn.' The name rolls off the Doc's tongue as if Russian is his native language.

Maloney looks perplexed.

'I've never heard of him,' Derek says in Maloney's defence.

'You should have. He was a mathematician like you.'

Derek winces. Sure, he studied maths at university, but he had no higher ambition in life than teaching. Calling him a mathematician is a bit of a stretch.

The Doc pushes the book towards Maloney. Maloney picks it up by one corner, and opens it to a random page. His lips tremble with the effort of sounding out the words. The Doc's cruel prank angers Derek. When Debbie learnt to read, it was *Green Eggs and Ham*, not Russian literature written by a man with an unpronounceable surname.

'I can't,' Maloney says, flinging the book down and folding his arms across his chest.

Derek tenses, waiting for the Doc to ridicule Maloney further, but the Doc surprises him. 'I know,' he says. 'I'm sorry to say the easy-reading section of the library has diminished somewhat over the years.' The Doc removes his reading glasses and puffs warm air onto the lenses. 'But if you stick with it, I think you will enjoy it. It's about prisoners trapped in a gulag in northern Kazakhstan, where the winters are bitter and men died as a matter of daily occurrence.' His voice quivers with emotion as he polishes the glasses. 'It's about suffering the worst kinds of deprivations a man can imagine. Fighting nature and the system that incarcerates them.'

'It doesn't sound funny.' Maloney's words wobble with doubt and Derek could quite cheerfully give the Doc a piece of his mind. He has no right to go meddling in other people's business. He should learn to leave well enough alone.

The Doc shakes his head slowly back and forth. 'You're quite right. It plays to a deeper human emotion than that. It speaks to our souls. This is what you must learn to read, not trash like motorcycle magazines.'

Maloney sits straighter, turns side on like the street fighter he probably is. 'I like motorcycle magazines.'

'The pictures you mean.' The Doc's words carry the whiff of contempt. 'If I am going to teach you to read, you will read books that enhance your knowledge of the human experience.' He reaches across the table to recover the discarded novel. 'Few works will teach you more than this. You'll see.'

Derek doubts Maloney will be able to get through a single page. Before he avoided spending time at home, he used to love reading Bryce Courtenay, James Patterson, or a bit of Michael Robotham. Lorraine preferred thin romances or a thick Di Morrissey. Debs never read much, not once she discovered boys. The point is, not everyone's a reader, and it's certainly not the badge of honour the Doc seems to think it is.

'Let me start reading it to you and you can decide if you want to read more,' the Doc offers and turns down the radio. Derek glances at Parker, wondering if this is their cue to leave, but the old bloke's eyes are darting back and forth between the

Doc and Maloney like he's at the tennis. He is clearly enjoying this far more than the movie.

The Doc opens the book and smooths the pages in a gentle caress. Against the background of canned laughter, doof-doof music, and the call and banter of the men, he begins to read.

It's a performance. He takes his time, weighing each word and relishing the pauses. By doing so, the Doc brings the story to life, engrossing Maloney, them all, in its telling.

When the Doc finishes the chapter, Maloney says, 'Does this Ivan Den— Deniso …'

'Denisovich,' completes the Doc, laying down the book. 'Does he what?'

'Yeah, him, does he die there?'

The Doc clasps his hands behind his head and stretches out his long legs. 'Well, given that the author drew upon personal experience to create Denisovich, no, he does not die in a camp.'

The obviousness of this statement passes over Maloney. Derek expects a smirk from the Doc, but instead he expands on his answer. 'Solzhenitsyn wrote the book about his experience in the Stalinist camps. Given the horrendous conditions, it is more surprising that he didn't die there, as over a million men did, but lived to the ripe old age of eighty-nine.'

'But how'd he survive? There woulda been freezing snow and ice and not enough clothes, eh.' Maloney shivers, as if even the thought of it is enough to chill his bones. Not surprising, given the kid comes from up north where the rainforest meets the sea. He's probably never even seen snow.

'I think the Doc is talking about how suffering forms us. That life is intrinsically unfair,' Derek suggests to take the pressure off poor Maloney.

The Doc appraises Derek over the top of his glasses. 'Indeed. Every day we're incarcerated is a challenge to stay sane, to stay out of trouble. We, at least, will not be taken out and shot. In this country, there is no death penalty. We are clothed, fed, and watered; given the most basic of human necessities. By contrast, our gulag is comfortable.'

And despite himself, Derek can't help but admire the Doc's ingenuity. To pick a novel so unintimidating in size yet so pertinent to their personal dilemma. The canny bastard.

'Did you hear the news then?' the Doc asks, switching his attention to Derek.

'What news?'

The Doc bestows a superior smile. 'Clearly you don't read the papers.'

'Why bother when I have you?'

The Doc leans on his elbows and closes the space between them. 'As you well know, our dear friend Nicholas Fischer is running his election campaign on the basis of fiscal responsibility. You know, all that nonsense about budgets and surpluses and how he's a safe pair of hands. He's been rattling the council's chain about the amount of ratepayers' money used to fund the town library.'

'I think you're mistaking me for someone who gives a stuff about the elections, Doc. As Dad always said, don't vote, it only encourages them.' Derek chuckles and Parker joins in, but the Doc doesn't even raise a smile. Nothing from Maloney either. He's too busy staring off into the distance with those big brown eyes.

'Well, you should care,' says the Doc. 'The weekly supply of books from Yarrandarrah Library has a direct flow-on effect to services like the literacy scheme and the education programs.'

Derek glances at Maloney, wondering what's caught the kid's attention. 'Half the guys in here are functionally illiterate and most of them only do the literacy program to stay off basic.'

'I think you're confusing illiteracy with stupidity. They're completely different things.' The Doc taps the empty table. 'You know, Dezza, not all of us are content to spend our days in our cells hoping the world will pass us by. You might actually learn something if you got off your bum and came to book club or joined one of my journal-writing workshops, or God forbid, offered your own skills to help those less privileged write the odd letter home.'

'I don't sit in my cell all day. I've got my shift at the hospital and Backtackers,' Derek retaliates.

The Doc huffs. 'And tell me, Dezza, how does you being part of the sewing circle help anyone, apart from yourself?'

Derek's speechless. Not because the Doc called Backtackers the 'sewing circle' – he always calls it that – but the insinuation that Derek never does anything to help anyone but himself, well, that hurts. As if the Doc teaching Maloney to read is for any reason other than to put the kid in his debt.

'My point is that our future mayor is on the record as saying that the public expects criminals to be sent to prison to *be* punished for their crimes rather than *as* the punishment for their crimes. I bet you Councillor Fischer hasn't read a book since he left high school. He has a hide telling us what we can and can't read, to take away our right to better ourselves and find a way to connect with each other or the rest of the world. Reading is not a privilege. It is our basic human right.'

Derek refuses to look at the Doc. Instead he lets his gaze travel the room. It comes to rest on Sean, sitting in a corner, alone, staring at something on this side of the room. As soon as he realises Derek is looking at him, Sean shifts off his seat and leaves the rec room. Derek looks around him, wondering what had caught Sean's attention. There's no one here but the four of them, and they've all got their backs to Sean except for Maloney.

He turns back to the Doc. 'You seem to be working on the assumption that men like Jacko are worth saving. I've got news for you, Doc. Book club isn't going to make Jacko a better person. He'll still be a thug, just with a better vocabulary.'

'Yeah, Dezza's right,' Parker interjects. 'Anyway, apart from whingeing to us, what are you going to do about it? Write a letter to the editor?' He winks at Derek.

The Doc opens his mouth, on the verge of issuing a sharp retort, then pulls up short. 'Do you know what, I think you've hit the nail on the head.'

Derek snorts. 'What? You reckon a letter to the *Yarrandarrah Chronicle* is going to make a squirt of difference? C'mon, Doc. I know you think you're a big swinging dick in here, but outside you're nothing but a crim.'

The Doc shrugs. 'So? At least I'll go to my grave knowing I tried to make a difference.'

He doesn't say it out loud, but Derek can sense the unspoken 'unlike you', and he does not like the way it makes him feel. He does not like the feeling at all.

Chapter 13

Derek lies on his bunk, waiting for the night sky to recede. What day is it today? He compiles a list of things he did yesterday and deduces that today must be Thursday. His favourite day of the week. Well, normally. He shuffles over to the hand basin and splashes water on his face, then lathers it with soap. Derek takes his time shaving, careful as always, to avoid meeting his own eye. When he's finished, he drinks from the tap then sits on his bunk to wait.

Right on cue, his cell door springs open and Derek turns to face Officer Carl Petty.

'Morning, Dezza. Glorious day for it,' Young Carl chirps, rubbing his hands together. It might be glee, but the truth is the mornings are becoming colder now Easter's been and gone.

'Yeah?' Derek replies, folding the pages of his latest letter into three and carefully easing the letter into an envelope.

'It's Thursday, your sewing day,' Carl persists. 'When Jane comes,' he adds and Derek's guts go cold. Since when did Young Carl care so much about Backtackers? He thinks about the way the officer loiters around at sewing group. Always smiling at Jane and dropping small compliments on their work. Derek leaps to the inevitable conclusion. Young Carl's taken a shine to Jane. Jesus wept. It's one thing after another in this joint.

He tucks the letter under the mattress, flattens the sheets.

'And to celebrate, we've got a real treat for brekkie.'

Judging from Jane's enthusiasm about this wedding dress, Derek suspects she has an over-romanticised view of marriage. Clearly, she's never tied the knot herself. But Jane's always struck him as a practical kind of person. Surely she won't return any romantic notions Young Carl might be cultivating. Jane will have her sights set on someone with a little more wherewithal than a prison guard.

'Blue cheese and mushroom quiche, served with a salad of baby rocket leaves lightly dressed in caramelised balsamic,' Carl announces.

Derek nods and pretends he's busy with the zip of his tracksuit top so he doesn't have to look at the would-be suitor. He'll have to watch Carl at Backtackers now. Run interference so he can't cosy up to Jane. The thought of someone as nice as her tangled up with a no-hoper like Carl makes him feel sick to the stomach.

'Hurry up, Brown, we haven't got all day,' barks Officer Cheryl Blackburn from behind Young Carl. She transferred from the women's wing a couple of months ago. Derek hasn't had much to do with her, but the word is she likes to throw her weight around and, judging by the size of her, there's a fair bit of it to throw.

But on this occasion, Derek's pleased to see her. The distraction gives him a chance to escape. He slips past Carl and hurries down to breakfast, eager to put as much distance between them as possible.

As he picks at his tray, he remembers the original reason he woke up feeling less than overjoyed about today's Backtackers meeting. Jane said she'd bring in wedding magazines so they could choose a style. He's had a whole week to make up his mind about whether he's prepared to commit to this project. He's still on the fence and it's not a particularly comfortable place for a bloke to perch. After today, there'll be no going back. And it seems everyone has a bloody opinion. He's got Parker telling him it's a good way to earn brownie points with the governor, and Maloney seems to be having similar thoughts. The gov won't know what to do with himself, there'll be so many glowing reports about the Backtackers by the time they've finished the dress. He's got the Doc telling him 'nothing ventured, nothing gained'. Not to mention the Doc mounting a one-man campaign to help Maloney with his reading, which really has nothing to do with the wedding dress, except it irritates Derek like an itch that won't go away. And Jane, of course, is desperate to make it. Which leaves him where?

Jane sets up the sewing room as if it is any other Thursday. She has brought in another set of the commemorative cushions for the Backtackers working on the Charity Ball project, as well as the new peacock tapestry Derek requested. The rest she leaves hidden in her sewing tote.

She's had all week to build up her courage. By her standards, what she's planning today is a bold move and, like all bold moves, it has the potential to backfire. Jane has carefully constructed an argument for each of the men, her weapons hidden in her sewing tote. There is so much at stake. Jane sorely hopes she can pull this off, and when the first of the Backtackers ambles through the door, she knows there is no turning back.

Maloney enters the sewing room and greets Jane with a smile. He grabs a chair from the semi-circle she'd carefully arranged and moves it to his favourite corner near the edge of the workbench, where he can lay out his thread and have a direct line of sight to the sewing machine. He casts his eye over the table where Jane has placed the peacock tapestry.

Maloney tuts. Derek's no more a peacock than he is a rooster, that's for sure. He's more like one of Aunty's chooks. They're all different, those girls, and they don't call it the pecking order for nothing. Derek's the sort who never goes anywhere without his little mate to keep him company. Puts himself to bed when it's dark, pops on his roost then down again at first light to spend the day scratching about until it's time for bed again. Whereas the Doc is the boss chook, telling everyone else where to go, stealing their worms. And the chooks like Derek squawk a bit, but they're secretly glad they're not the chook in charge who has to stop the magpies nicking their feed or warn the others when there's trouble about. The problem is, the Doc doesn't come to Backtackers, so Maloney guesses he'll have to step in as boss chook and help Derek make up his mind.

Mick and Brian come in, engrossed in a discussion about the merits of silverbeet, Mick from a cook's perspective, Brian from a gardener's. Jane gestures for them to take the two chairs to her left, hoping they don't realise that today she has set up the room to suit her purposes. Les heads straight to his corner, acknowledging no one. She nods to Sean who needs no stage directions. He takes the seat he always takes at the sewing machine and nods hello at Maloney. Maloney beams back.

By the time Derek arrives, each of the chairs, bar one, is taken. He casts a wary eye over the table. No wedding magazines. But he sees Jane has brought in a new peacock tapestry and he feels instantly lighter.

Now she has her full complement of stitchers, Jane puts her plan into action.

'I decided against bringing in the magazines. There's simply too many choices and we really must make a decision this week.'

She reaches into her sewing tote and retrieves a bundle tied up with a simple ribbon. Jane undoes the bow and fans the patterns across the workbench. Picking one at random, she holds it out to Derek.

He hesitates a moment, then takes it. The brand is Simple Sew. On the front is a picture of a young girl who models an attractive lace dress. It is high at the neck and has long sleeves. She wears a matching headband in her hair.

'It's a bit short, isn't it?' comments Mick, pointing to her long, tanned legs. 'I don't think girls should wear dresses like that on their wedding day. It lacks class.'

'Unlike you, eh, Mick?' quips Sean, laying aside his quilt. 'This is nice,' he says, selecting one with a slip of a girl in the arms of a swarthy-looking Lothario. The man wears black-tie and she leans into his arms as if they are dancing. The dress is floor-length and gathered at the waist, displaying only a modest amount of cleavage.

Vince takes the pattern from Sean and scrutinises the cover. 'It depends what time of day she's getting married. It says here, "Dance the night away in this relaxed fit blah blah blah". Is it a day or evening wedding, Dezza?'

'How should I know?'

'This is pretty,' says Brian, choosing another.

'You mean *she's* pretty,' laughs Frank, elbowing him in the ribs.

Curious, Derek peeks over Brian's shoulder. He's right. The girl is lovely. She sits on a step eating a slice of cake smothered in pink frosting. But this design has a plunging neckline and the girl has a much smaller bust than the one Debbie inherited from her mother. Mick's got a point. You can't have your daughter looking cheap on her wedding day.

'This is a bit like the one my Crystal wore,' Brian says, showing them an old-fashioned ball gown with masses of skirt.

'I like the gauzy bit across the chest,' Derek says, searching for one redeeming feature.

'It ticks the modesty box,' agrees Ahmed.

'Her waist can't really be that tiny, can it?' Mick adds.

'Although, it will use a lot of fabric,' Jane feels compelled to point out.

'She looks like a meringue,' Maloney says, taking the pattern from Brian. 'To get away with a dress like this, she'll need to be tall, otherwise she'll end up looking like one of them toilet roll dollies. How tall is she, Dezza?'

Derek holds his hand level with his nose. 'About this high. She has a …' He hesitates. He'd prefer not to be thinking about any of Debbie's 'departments'. 'She has a large …' and he cups his hands away from his chest.

The men nod and give aahs of understanding

Jane briskly gathers the rejected patterns into a pile and delves into her sewing tote for the pattern she held in reserve. 'Well, in that case, this might be ideal.' She holds it up. 'It has a simple neckline, and being floor-length and high-waisted, makes it slimming and elegant.'

'Now that's classy,' says Mick with a nod of approval.

Sean takes the pattern from Jane and examines the notes. 'Long straight seams will make it easy to sew.'

'Quick too. It won't take long to make,' says Maloney, giving Jane a sly wink.

'I like the scalloping on the veil,' Brian pitches in.

Jane blushes and smiles at Derek. Hope bubbles to the surface, buoyed by the men's enthusiasm. Her plan may very well be working. Trying to sound casual, she says, 'And what about you, Derek? Can you imagine your daughter wearing this?'

He takes the pattern from Sean. Jane's right, the dress is elegant in its simplicity, but what would Debbie make of it? Last time he saw her, she was sixteen, an age when girls try on new identities. For a while, she played with all black, smearing her eyes thick with kohl and mascara. Thank goodness that gave way to pastel jeans and ballet flats. But now that she's a young woman, her tastes have probably matured.

As a father of daughters himself, Mick senses Derek's consternation. 'Well, for starters, do *you* like it?'

'I agree with everything that's been said, but I don't know.' Derek shrugs. 'Maybe she'd prefer something fancier?'

'Too easy,' Maloney chimes in. 'We can add a crumb catcher around the neckline. Scatter some crystal pearls and chatons over the skirt. She will sparkle.' His hands dance, capturing his enthusiasm.

Derek studies Maloney. He's in his element. If Derek says yes, then the dress won't be the only thing that shines.

Jane crosses her fingers. Maloney is right. With their combined skills, the Backtackers can easily transform this simple design. All they need is Derek's permission, but she cannot read the look on his face. He's thinking of something – the question is, what?

Derek reflects on his conversation with Sharon. She'd said Derek had to prove to Debbie how much he still loves her. That Debbie will never forgive him for not being there on her wedding day. If he makes the dress instead of the peacock throw cushions, will Debbie then know how deeply he cares about her? He's not sure. Although in a way, the dress has the distinct advantage of allowing Derek to be there on the day. In that sense, making Debbie's wedding dress would kill two birds with one stone.

The stitchers all stop what they're doing and wait for his verdict. Jane feels like she's about to burst. Maloney silently pleads with him. Sean hunches over his sewing machine, head bowed as if in prayer. Mick bounces lightly on the balls of his feet and Brian's making this strange clicking sound with his false teeth. From his spot in the corner, Les watches and waits.

Derek has the strangest sensation, like he's holding the whole world in the palms of his hands. As if one word from him will change their lives forever. The thought leaves him feeling a little light-headed. He's not sure he's ready to be responsible for other people's happiness. Based on his past performances, he's bound to make a botch job of it.

Saying yes means he's effectively giving Jane permission to deal the deck. Who knows what cards he'll end up with? But one thing's for certain – he'll never know unless he plays. He looks them each in turn. The band around his chest is so tight, he can barely breathe. It takes all his effort to deliver the one word they want to hear. 'Okay.'

Brian smacks Mick on the shoulder, Maloney and Sean exchange fist bumps, all acting like they've won the jackpot.

Jane claps her hands in delight. She can smell victory, but Jane has one more ace up her sleeve. Affecting nonchalance, she reaches into her sewing tote. 'I know I'm being a bit presumptuous, but I thought we may as well look at some swatches while we're at it.'

With that, she spills the contents of a supermarket shopping bag over the table. As she hoped, the men cluster around her, jostling for positions. Satins, silks, taffeta, laces, organza and tulle are separated into 'no' piles and 'maybe' piles. Everyone has an opinion. An underskirt in satin with an organza overlay goes up against shot silk. They dismiss antique white lace as being too fiddly to work with. Colour is a whole other topic.

'Ice, ivory, champagne, mushroom,' Brian reads from the labels.

'Is there no such thing as plain white?' Mick complains.

'Another thing to consider is that photography can change the way a colour shows up, so we might need to choose a white with a bit of blue in it, so it comes up properly white in the photos,' Jane points out, only to be met by groans of disbelief.

After a contest of ideas, the Backtackers go full circle and decide to stick to plain white duchess satin.

'It'll make the details shine, eh,' Maloney says. His imagination has already moved on to finishing the dress, always his favourite part. Ever since Aunty's fingers started getting stiff in cold weather, Maloney's taken over all the embroidery and beading. These boys don't know what a treat they're in for.

The men smile, imagining what they can do with this blank canvas. All except Derek. Now he's said yes, he wishes he could take it back. He's allowed himself to get carried away. There's no way he can afford a flash wedding dress. And he really should ask Debbie what she thinks before spending his hard-earnt readies on a dress she might not even want. He doesn't want to dampen the mood, but he has to ask. 'How much will this set me back?'

Jane's been expecting this question. 'Mum and I have had this exact conversation. We've agreed to donate the pattern for the cause.'

'That's real good of your mum,' says Brian.

'There you go, Dezza, one less thing to worry about,' adds Mick

'Good old Jane, eh?' says Frank.

'It's not the most expensive item by any stretch,' she says, hiding her fluster by packing away the patterns and swatches. Her face brightens. 'The great thing about duchess satin is that it only costs around ten dollars a metre wholesale.' She runs her finger over the instructions on the pattern. 'We're looking at around eight metres, plus zippers, buttons, thread and trims, of course. Oh, and the lining.'

Derek studies the floor. For years, financial embarrassment has been his cringing companion and here it is again. The sour truth is that he can't afford even a simple wedding dress. The band winches tighter. He should tell the Backtackers to forget it. He can't ask the fellas to go out on a limb for him. The whole idea is crazy.

'It's not about the money,' Sean says and Derek blinks at the unexpected source.

'He's right. It's a gift, you're telling her how you feel,' Brian says, carefully avoiding the L word.

The only contact Derek has had with Debbie in the past five years is via the post. He'd give anything to hear the sound of her voice, to have a good long chat like they used to. He loves Debbie with all his heart and he'd like nothing better than the chance to prove it. He glances at the peacock tapestry kits on the table and tries to see them through the eyes of a young woman. He can't.

'We really must make a decision today,' Jane says, sensing Derek's self-doubt and fearing she's losing him. 'It's not like we have all the time in the world.'

Maloney goes to say something and Jane shoots him a warning glance. He shuts his mouth again.

Derek looks at the faces of his fellow stitchers and wonders why they care so much about this dress. Sewing is a distraction from the everyday grind of life in prison and all the crap that goes with it. And there is no end of pleasure in making beautiful things. But stitching is more than that. It's an act of defiance; a way to make sense of a world gone mad. Stitching sets them free.

'All right,' he says. 'Let's go with the duchess satin.' He'll just have to save his pennies; no more extravagances like chocolate from the buy-up.

Excited comments fly back and forth about how amazing this dress will be. The chatter brightens the room, their everyday projects momentarily forgotten. Maloney prances about, drawing spectacular variations of the dress with his hands. Laughing, Sean shares a comment with Mick and Brian. Les sulks in his corner, his lips stitched tight, glaring at Maloney. Sean's smile falters.

Maloney feels like he's a kid again, and been cheeky and got away with it. Thanks to him, Jane has her project. And thanks to Jane, he will now have a good review to put before the parole board at the end of the year. Plus the Doc's teaching him to read. That's gotta count as self-improvement, eh? At this rate he'll be home in time for Christmas. Aunty will be beside herself.

He glances at Sean, the sandy-haired crim's attention like bathing in winter sun, but something's distracted him and now his eyes are downcast. Maloney spins away. A tiny part of him feels bad for using Jane and Derek to get what he wants, but then, as they say, every man for himself.

He taps Derek on the shoulder. 'You should ask Jane to go and get Debbie's measurements.'

Derek's fragile joy pops like a child's balloon. Astonished, it takes him a moment to find the words. 'I can't guarantee she'd get a warm reception, if you know what I mean.'

'Don't ask, you don't get,' comes the tart reply.

Derek shoots Maloney a withering look. The kid sounds exactly like the Doc. 'Yeah well, be that as it may, my ex lives in the city. It's a three-and-a-half-hour drive each way. I can't ask Jane to do that.'

'C'mon, what's the worst she's gunna say?'

'Ask who what?' Brian butts in.

Maloney shrugs and twirls away. Before he can answer, Derek catches sight of Jane. Jarrod's asking her a question. As they chat, she tucks a loose strand of hair behind her ear and looks up. At Carl. Hovering in the doorway with a big grin plastered all over his face. Blushing, Jane ducks her head to hide her smile. Embarrassed, Derek looks away.

'Well?' prompts Brian, scratching his name and date on the form for borrowing scissors. 'No secrets in here, Dezza, you know that.'

Derek has no choice but to spit it out. 'Maloney reckons I should ask Jane to go and measure up Debbie. You know, so we don't waste our time, or fabric.'

Brian pulls a face. 'That's it?'

Derek shrugs.

'Well, what are you waiting for?'

The belt winches tighter.

'Ah, for Pete's sake, you big wuss. I'll ask her.' And before Derek can beg him not to, Brian is standing next to Jane.

He gestures at Derek, stranded in the middle of the floor, and starts talking. Jane gives a careful nod then walks over to Derek.

'I'd have to go this weekend because it's the elections the weekend after and I'm running the polling booth at the primary school.'

'Oh, it was only an idea, it doesn't really matter.'

'It's no trouble. I can take the completed commemorative cushions into Connecting Threads' head office while I'm there.'

Derek's not sure this is a good idea. Lorraine can be all sorts of trouble. But Brian's eyes are boring into him and Maloney's defiant look dares him to say no.

Jane passes him her notebook and Derek swallows. He scrawls down Lorraine's name and address and hands back the notebook. 'I should warn you, my ex can be a bit prickly.'

'It will be fine, Derek,' she reassures him. 'I'm sure there's nothing to worry about.'

But Derek's not convinced. From where he's standing, there's plenty to worry about. Worse still, there's bugger all he can do about it.

Chapter 14

'Not only have we chosen a pattern but the men have even agreed on the fabric,' Jane says, flopping on Susannah's bed and kicking off her shoes. 'And to top it all off, I have Debbie's address so I can go and get her measurements.'

For a good minute, Susannah says nothing. Then she raises her gaze to meet Jane's in the mirror. 'You know that will never work, don't you? She won't want a bar of you.'

'Of course it will work. It has to. Making the dress by guesswork leaves far too big a margin for error. And it's not like poor Derek has the means to start over if we stuff it up.'

Susannah breaks eye contact and turns side on, first one way, then the other, concentrating on her reflection. 'Do you think this says "approachable capable leader" or "uptight corporate cow"?'

Jane studies her friend's outfit. Black pencil skirt, crisp white business shirt, black patent leather heels. The matching jacket is draped over the chair in the corner. Susannah dresses for the council chambers as if it were a corporate boardroom. 'It is a little severe,' she says tactfully. 'Maybe wear your hair out? Or change the blouse to something more feminine?'

Susannah snorts. 'Do I look like a woman who has a collection of Liberty prints?'

Jane smiles. 'No. But lucky for you, I am.'

In her bedroom, she searches the neat rows of brightly patterned fabrics hanging in the wardrobe. The collection started with a gift from her grandmother for her sixteenth birthday. When she was a student, she used to scour the inner-city op shops near the art college and later found more in the funny little boutiques hidden in the back lanes surrounding Connecting Threads. She rubs the soft cotton of her favourite blouse, with its cheerful trail of cherry blossoms, and thinks of Maloney and his exquisite roses. Life is strange how it can deny a person so much, but then endow them with a gift so special it casts a shadow over all their shortcomings.

Jane drops the sleeve. Susannah won't go for full-on flowers. She selects another with a simple geometric floral repeat. If you look closely enough, the violets are obvious, but at a distance the flowers disappear. It's feminine without being too girlie.

Susannah views the blouse with a raised eyebrow. 'I'm not sure that says "future mayor".'

Jane slips the blouse off its hanger. 'Trust me, it will look brilliant under the jacket.'

Susannah exchanges her white business shirt for the blouse. Jane holds up the jacket and she shrugs it on. 'Done up?' Susannah asks.

'I don't think so. It's important to remind people of the difference between you and Nick Fischer. You're a true local who's on their side, not some plant from Macquarie Street. And to that end ...' Jane releases Susannah's ponytail and her long blonde hair cascades over her shoulders. Jane smiles. 'Better.'

Susannah frowns at her reflection. 'Are you sure I don't look like a high-class hooker?'

'Don't be an idiot. But if that's what's bothering you, wear sensible heels.'

Susannah's eyes widen. 'I can't! Nick towers over me. Anything lower than these and I'll be talking to his navel.'

'Could be worse.'

Susannah grabs her briefcase, handbag and car keys. 'I better skedaddle, I'm late for the Chamber of Commerce lunch. We've invited the members from Corondale branch in an effort to cement the numbers prior to the election. A week doesn't leave us much time, you know.' She pauses in the doorway. 'Are you sure you're allowed to visit a prisoner's family? I mean, I sort of assumed it would be against the rules.'

'For heaven's sake, Suze! We're making a wedding dress. Debbie's measurements might be important to us, but it's hardly passing on state secrets, is it?'

Susannah looks thoughtful. 'Even so, maybe you should double-check. Even if it's not a breach of the code of conduct, you don't know what any of these men are in for, what their families might be like. You could be walking into trouble.'

A twinge of annoyance pinches Jane. Susannah is making assumptions about her Backtackers. Judging them for what they did, not who they are. It's precisely the reason she wants to make this dress, to challenge those assumptions. 'No offence, Suze, but I think you have enough on your plate without worrying about me. I'll be fine.'

Susannah glances at her phone, checking the time. 'I really have to go. Look, it's usually me who says "if you don't ask, you don't get", but, in this case, I think you need to tread carefully. Maybe ring this girl first?'

Jane stands, brushes down her skirt, and collects her shoes. 'Derek said he doesn't have her number. Anyway, as Joey pointed out, it's better if I see her in person so I can get a sense of her shape.'

Susannah doesn't buy this Derek's argument. As if he wouldn't know his own daughter's phone number. The more Jane tells her, the louder those alarm bells start ringing. 'Do me a favour and ask your new boyfriend what he thinks. The last thing you want is to get in hot water over a stupid dress.'

Jane simply nods and glances away. Once she hears Susannah's car back out of the driveway, she picks up her phone and brings up Carl's number. His current profile picture is the Malaysian chicken curry he served up on Monday night. Her finger hovers over the phone icon. She checks the time. Carl will be on shift. Jane lies back on Susannah's bed. She stares at the ceiling with its curls of flaking paint. She doesn't need to involve Carl. It's her project, her responsibility. What possible harm can come from meeting Derek's daughter?

The next day, Jane leaves Yarrandarrah straight after she and her mum close the shop at lunchtime. She buys a coffee to sustain her on the long trip and double-checks she has a tape measure and her notebook with its precious address in her handbag. She hadn't been totally honest with the Backtackers when she said could drop off the completed commemorative cushions while she was there. As if the Connecting Threads head office would be open on weekends. But she is pleased to have an excuse to get out of election duties, and the long drive gives her plenty of time to think.

As the miles peel away, she lets her thoughts drift, occasionally changing the radio dial whenever static interrupts the program. Her mind goes to Carl. Already they are falling into an easy routine. First the movies on Saturday night, then he cooked her that amazing curry on Monday night. A quick drink at the pub on Wednesday. He looks nice out of uniform, dressed in jeans and a shirt, untucked to hide his slight paunch.

There's something safe about his softness. His goodnight kiss is gentle, respectful, if a little chaste. But each time she closes the door on him, she feels grateful he hasn't pushed for more. It's easy to fall into bed with someone; much harder to get out of a relationship that's no good for you.

On the outskirts of the city, Jane switches off the radio so she can listen to the sat nav directions. She drives through a leafy suburb populated with mansions squatting side by side, and soon the computer tells her she has reached her destination.

Jane listens to the engine tick and cool. She glances at the house on the corner. It is large, angular, grey and glassy. A high hedge marks the boundary. In the driveway are two cars: a white Mercedes and a silver Suzuki hatch with pink personalised plates. DEBS 101.

It's the right house then. Yet Jane remains inside her battered old Toyota, pinned there by doubt. She grabs the tape measure and her notebook and hides her handbag under the passenger seat. She adjusts the rear-view mirror and slides on a layer of lippie. Then she pats the dashboard and says, 'Wish me luck, Fern.'

Debbie flops on the modular lounge. 'My feet are killing me,' she moans.

'Stop whingeing,' Lorraine shouts from the kitchen, slamming the kettle on the bench for emphasis.

Debbie closes her eyes, shifting her focus from her aching feet to her throbbing temples. She has grown to hate shopping, more so because now she has to endure it in the company of her mother. That woman is unstoppable, undaunted in the face of four floors of boutiques at Oaklands Mall. Over a lifetime, Debbie has collected many unpleasant memories within the glistening confines of shiny-floored, shiny-staffed shops. Even entering a shopping centre car park can make her break out in a sweat.

Her mother deposits a cup of Earl Grey on the occasional table beside Debbie. 'Your problem, young lady, is that you're too fussy,' she says, placing a plate with a rainbow array of Italian cream wafers next to the tea, then plonking herself down in the wing chair. 'We have been to every single bridal boutique this side of the city. If you ask me, they all stock the exact same dresses. The only thing that changes is the price tag. But, oh no, none of them are good enough for you, are they?'

Debbie scrolls through the photos on her phone chronicling yet another day's shopping expedition, looking for ones suitable for social media. She tries out different filters on some, deletes others, anything to stop herself saying something she might later regret. Having decided on a photo to post, she types out a caption and adds their wedding hashtag, #DebsnIan4Evs, then sips her tea. What would be the appropriate hashtag to describe today's experience? She types #bridezilla then quickly deletes it.

'I was never lucky enough to have the choices you do, let me tell you that for free.' Lorraine crams two wafers in quick succession into her mouth before going on. 'I would have given my eye teeth to have had the full catastrophe you two are planning, but your father was too stingy. More concerned about squirrelling away money to buy that shoebox we called a home than celebrate our actual wedding day. I should have realised then that the writing was on the wall.'

Debbie cringes. Even before he went to prison, her mother never missed an opportunity to have a dig at Dad. It hurts to think of her father. She hasn't seen or heard from him since the day of his sentencing. Too ashamed, she supposes. But not even a card? A phone call?

Lorraine pats her helmet of platinum blonde hair. 'Fortunately for me, I met Garry.'

Debbie can't help but let a derisive snort escape, and she hunches over her phone to hide her expression.

'What?' Lorraine snaps. 'Don't go criticising your stepfather, young lady. If it weren't for Garry we'd be living on the streets.'

'Yeah, right, Mum.' Debbie refuses to make eye contact. She types in #thefullcatastrophe and hits enter. She was young when Dad was locked up, but even she thought Garry Johns appeared on the scene pretty quick. The guy thinks owning a house backing onto the fifth fairway of Oaklands Golf Course makes him someone special.

'I never asked for the "full catastrophe", Mum,' she says, picking up a wafer then abandoning it as a vision of Tash Tory's perfectly manicured finger waving no-no appears in front of her. Instead, she types 'shedding for the wedding' into the search engine and starts scrolling the results as she speaks. 'Ian and I wanted something low-key with just our closest friends and immediate family.' How she regrets saying no when Ian suggested they buy a Fijian wedding package and elope.

Lorraine harrumphs, struggling to cross her legs in the tight skirt binding her thighs. 'That was never an option. What you'll understand when you grow up is how easily people's noses get out of joint if you don't include them on the guest list.'

Debbie clicks on a link that reads, 'Wedding Day Diva – 12 weeks to divine!!!' 'But I don't even know half the people you want to invite. Who exactly are Nina and Terry?'

Lorraine purses her lips, looks down her nose. 'Nina was my chief bridesmaid. And Terry is her husband. Although he used to be my boyfriend, before I introduced them.' She dismisses the relationship with a wave. 'Anyway, that's water under the bridge.'

Debbie matches her mother's expression. 'I thought you and Dad were married in a registry office. You can't have had a chief bridesmaid. Anyway, aren't they called a maid of honour?'

Lorraine picks up another wafer and pops it in her mouth, refraining from speaking until she has swallowed. 'Don't split hairs, Debbie. I still had a bridesmaid and it's the done thing to invite Nina to my daughter's wedding.'

Debbie returns to her gallery of photos. Early on, she's smiling and posing for the camera. By the time she scrolls through the blur of wedding dresses to today, she's looking anywhere but the camera. Debbie hates to admit it, but Tash Tory has seared it into her brain. She's going to be photographed from every angle and, judging from these photos, it's not going to be pretty.

She remembers her mother's original point. 'The reason I haven't chosen a dress yet is because I look awful in every single one.'

'And I say, you're too fussy.'

'Mum! I'm not spending thousands of dollars on a dress that makes me look ...' She falters. She doesn't even want to think the words, let alone say them out loud, yet they echo around her head. Fat. Frumpy. Ugly. Tears prick her eyes. Ian says he loves her curves, but clearly whoever designs wedding dresses doesn't.

Lorraine deposits her tea cup with such force, it rattles the saucer. 'Now you listen to me, Deborah. You get one chance at this,' she hisses. 'The wedding photos will be sitting on your mantelpiece for the rest of your life. So you better make sure that you can look back on your wedding day, from your hair to your shoes and everything else in between, with pride. There'll be plenty of time later for regrets.'

Debbie looks at the mantelpiece. There is her mother, adorned in a silk shantung day suit in an eye-popping shade of vermilion, holding a matching bouquet. Garry wears a tie the same colour and a kerchief tucked into his pocket, along with a vermilion rose.

Her mother follows her gaze. 'And while we're on the subject, I fail to see why you refuse to let Garry give you away. He *is* your stepfather.'

The tears evaporate. 'I've already asked Uncle Steve.'

Lorraine's neck flushes to a hue closely resembling her silk shantung day suit. 'I don't want that man at my wedding.'

'It's not *your* wedding!'

Lorraine dismisses Debbie with a wave. 'You know what I mean.'

'Why don't you want him there? Because of Dad?'

Lorraine's lips shrink to a tight moue, her bosom heaves. 'One of my deepest abiding pleasures, apart from no longer being married to your father, is no longer having to put up with his drunk of a brother. He is *not* coming to the wedding.'

As Debbie opens her mouth to retaliate, the doorbell chimes the opening bars of 'Edelweiss'. They both turn and stare towards the front door. Who could it be at this hour on a Saturday?

'I'll get it,' Debbie says, glad to escape the escalating tensions. 'It's probably Ian.' Although she isn't expecting him until six. They are taking his mother to the Ming Dynasty for her birthday. Debbie was hoping they could go somewhere fancier like Roberto's Ristorante, but Ian's mum loves the Chinese, especially their famous prawn cutlets.

All smiles, Debbie swings open the front door to find a stranger standing in the portico. A woman with tousled curls, wearing a floral dress and draped in a shawl against the chill. She has what appears to be a tape measure clutched in one hand. Debbie's first thought is that she's a Jehovah's Witness; after all, it *is* Saturday. But don't they normally travel in pairs? And they hand out copies of *The Watchtower*, not tape measures. Debbie pulls the door close behind her. 'Can I help you?'

'Hello, my name is Jane.'

She doesn't look like a God-botherer. They're not usually this pretty and they certainly don't wear dresses with plunging necklines.

'Are you Derek Brown's daughter?' the woman goes on.

Debbie flinches. Her mother no longer refers to her father by name. Even Auntie Sharon rarely does.

'Who is it, Deborah?' her mother sings out from the lounge room.

Debbie pokes her head inside and calls, 'Just a door-knocker about the elections, Mum,' and closes the door properly. 'Why do you want to know?' she asks Jane. 'Has something happened?'

'Your father is fine,' Jane rushes out. She bites her bottom lip and stares into the strappy-leafed cordylines guarding the front door. She takes a deep breath and returns her attention to Debbie. 'I work for a charity called Connecting Threads, you may have heard of it?'

Debbie shakes her head. Slightly deflated, Jane ploughs on.

'We train prisoners in needlework as a way of building skills and earning money. Your father is one of my stitchers.'

Debbie laughs. 'Dad can't even thread a needle.'

A serious frown furrows Jane's brow. 'Your father is a very fine stitcher. He's one of my best.'

Curious, Debbie stares at her. This Jane woman seems mighty fond of her dad. 'Why are you here?'

Jane squeezes the tape measure, as if this will bring her luck. 'I believe you're getting married in October.'

Debbie starts. 'Who told you that?'

'Your father, of course.'

How does Dad know? Her mother's refused to speak to him for five years and never let Debbie anywhere near him. Mum always said it was because Debbie had already suffered enough thanks to her father and she owed him no favours. Except here is this stranger, happily standing on the door step, telling her what a fine stitcher he is. Part of her wants to attack this Jane for painting her father in a positive light. *She's* the one who's been hurt. Dad got what he deserves.

But part of her wonders who her dad has become. *Your father is a very fine stitcher.* Five years is a long time.

Jane sees anger and vulnerability play out across Debbie's face and wishes the ground would swallow her whole. Susannah was right. She should have called, not ambushed the poor girl on her front porch. Sure, she expected Derek's daughter to be surprised to see her here, but also thrilled to know she was in her father's thoughts. How did Derek know about Debbie's wedding if it wasn't Debbie who told him? The mother perhaps? Whoever it was, it's too late now. She can't leave empty-handed after promising the Backtackers she'd get the measurements.

As she opens her mouth to speak, the door swings wide revealing a stout woman with dyed blonde hair lacquered into a pert bob. 'We already know who we're voting for, thank you,' she says in a very bad posh accent, elbowing her daughter aside.

Debbie shoots Jane a warning glance.

The woman, presumably Debbie's mother and Derek's ex-wife, Lorraine, looks like the kind of woman who never takes no for an answer. Mustering her courage, Jane says, 'This is going to sound a bit odd, but I volunteer at Yarrandarrah Correctional Centre ...'

The words have barely left her lips when the woman's gaze narrows, her enormous bosom heaves, and her genteel accent vanishes. 'Go inside, Deborah. Whatever this woman wants has nothing to do with you.'

'But Mum …' Debbie protests.

'Actually, it's Debbie I need to see,' Jane rushes out, sensing her chance slipping away.

Lorraine steps closer. A smudge of electric blue mascara on her cheek catches Jane's attention.

'Now let me make myself clear. I've protected my daughter from that lowlife scum for five years. I will not, do you hear me, I will *not* have anyone associated with him anywhere near my family. Now, get out before I call the cops.'

Shocked, Jane almost falls as she backs down the stairs.

'Mum, don't be ridiculous,' says Debbie angrily. 'She's armed with a tape measure, not a knife.'

Lorraine turns on her daughter, using her enormous bust to press her point. 'I told you to go inside.'

'Get real, Mum. I'm not sixteen anymore,' Debbie says, seeming embarrassed by her mother's rudeness. Turning to Jane, she asks, 'What's the tape measure for, anyway?'

Jane blinks away tears, horrified at the mess she has made. She didn't mean any harm. But that woman! How could someone as nice as Derek ever be married to this witch? No wonder he was so reluctant to give her the address.

She takes a deep breath and stares at the women in front of her. Mother and daughter are so similar, especially the shape of them, although Debbie is a good head taller and a welterweight compared to her mother. But where the mother's features are set by disapproval, Debbie's features are a gentler echo of her gene pool. Even so, neither of them look at Jane with anything resembling warmth. With a sinking heart, she realises her mission has failed. Jane swallows her disappointment, and says, 'Forgive me, I think I've made a mistake.'

She turns on her heel, and tries to maintain a dignified pace back to the car. Thank goodness Fern starts first time. Jane wrenches the steering wheel full circle and does a U-turn. At the end of the street, she risks a glance in the rear-view mirror. Debbie has disappeared, but the mother is still standing there, making sure she leaves. It sends a shiver down Jane's spine.

Chapter 15

Parker shakes out the pages of Monday's newspaper. 'Listen to this, Dezza: "Newly elected mayor, Nicholas Fischer, says he is thrilled to accept the invitation to tour Yarrandarrah Correctional Centre, a major source of employment in the electorate. 'The destinies of this town and the gaol are inextricably linked and this economic partnership is crucial to all our futures,' he said on Sunday at a barbecue held at the Victor Simpson Memorial Park to celebrate his electoral win."'

'Who's he bloody kidding?' the Doc snarls. 'Pompous prat. He's the mayor, not the bloody premier.'

But the rest of C Wing buzzes with excitement about the visit. Wherever he is – in the hospital, in the lunch queue, even when he is having a shower – Derek endures a thousand theories as to when the mayor will come and what he will make of them.

It is only a few days later, that the rumours are confirmed. It's not a royal visit; it isn't planned months in advance. After muster on Wednesday, the guards inform them that the mayor will arrive the following morning.

'I, for one, am majorly unimpressed,' Derek shares with Parker over a cup of coffee in the rec room. 'Jane was a no-show last week and now they've cancelled Backtackers because it's considered a "security risk". We're supposed to be cutting out the pattern for the wedding dress. It'll never get made at this rate.'

'You've changed your tune,' observes Parker.

Derek shrugs him off. 'You know me, mate. Anything to keep the peace.'

'Yeah, well, don't think you're so special, Brown,' muscles in Cheryl Blackburn.

Derek starts, unaware she's been listening in.

'Everyone's in lockdown during the visit,' she says, and struts off to rain on someone else's parade.

Derek waits until she's out of earshot. 'Bloody ridiculous. What do they think we're going to do? Attack him with a bunch of embroidery needles?'

'Look out, trouble's about,' Parker says, nudging Derek in the ribs.

Derek turns to see the Doc marching towards them, grinning like a Cheshire cat.

'Have a bit of news for you fellows.'

Derek and Parker exchange glances, wondering what intel the Doc's gleaned from his many sources.

He perches on the edge of his seat and puffs out his chest. 'Mayor Fischer has specifically asked that his grand tour includes the library. Which means the gov has given me special dispensation to show him around, explain how it works. You know, make us look good.'

Make *you* look good, you mean, thinks Derek. Christ, the Doc will be dining out on this for months.

'It's the perfect opportunity to show Mayor Fischer how important the library is to morale. After I've worked my magic, he'll never dream of cutting funds to Yarrandarrah Library.' The Doc cracks his knuckles. 'Anyway, can't stay, I need to get the joint ship-shape.'

Derek watches him depart, self-importance inflating his already oversized ego, sharing the news with a favoured few on his passage to the admin block. 'You'd swear it was the Doc who's been elected mayor.'

Parker chuckles. 'You know what they say, Dezza. Pride cometh before the fall.'

During the mayoral tour, Derek completes his second commemorative cushion, then starts on a note to his dad. He wants to give Clive a before and after impression of the tour, since it's odds on there'll be some interesting titbits to share. If nothing else, it makes a change from his usual inquiries about lawn bowls and his father's health.

He's not wrong about there being news from the tour. Afterwards, Young Carl is full of it. Proud it was him unlocking and locking gates in the mayor's wake.

'And it wasn't only the mayor,' he says, hovering in Derek's doorway the following morning. 'The media unit sent a film crew and Fischer had more guards looking after him than you lot.'

Derek chucks him a smile then makes a beeline for the rec room. Crims crowd the place, sharing morsels of information, trying to piece together the whole story. In light of the special occasion, an officer tunes the telly to the morning news and they gather around to watch highlights of Mayor Fischer spinning his spiel.

'Today's visit was about familiarising myself with Yarrandarrah Correctional Centre and the people who work there. To meet the officers, the administrative staff, the volunteers, and the chaplains. To inspect the new wing, which provides inmates with more spacious accommodation and better facilities than any other institution in this state.'

'Sounds like we're staying at the bloody Hilton,' Parker whispers in Derek's ear.

'More like Hotel California.'

The mayor finishes with, 'It has been a valuable opportunity for me to observe firsthand the day-to-day lives of the men and women in Yarrandarrah Correctional.' As he speaks, the camera pans across the piggery and the vegetable gardens where men in prison greens are picking produce. It then cuts to a shot of prisoners delivering the produce to the kitchens. Derek spots Brian, a grin cracking open his damaged face, holding up a bunch of beetroot.

'Christ,' Parker murmurs, shaking his head in disgust.

'Hey look, there's Carl. Look, Carl, you're famous, you're on the telly,' a crim yells across the rec room. His comment meets with a chorus of crowing and laughter.

Young Carl stands next to the mayor in the sterile zone. In the background, through the wire mesh, four prisoners are visible playing tennis. The camera captures the moment when one is serving, his racquet arched, the ball launched skywards as the others hunker down at the net, ready for the return volley.

'Jesus,' Derek mutters.

Then things go from bad to worse. The shot switches to one of the Doc in the library. He wears a smile – actually, grimace might be a better word for it – as he shows the mayor around the stacks. The place is immaculate and, somehow, the collection seems to have doubled overnight. The shelves are heaving with books. The coverage finishes with a shot of the Doc showing the mayor a thick hardback with a shiny new cover.

'Where'd you get all them books?' asks Parker, voicing Derek's thoughts.

The Doc taps the side of his nose. 'The blokes leant me their personal copies and, as you know, I own tonnes. I lined the front shelves so it looked like we had all the latest releases. There's bugger all out the back,' he says with a cackle.

The coverage switches from the prison to the old Town Hall. Nicholas Fischer stands on the steps and looks straight down the lens of the camera, his expression one of resolute concern. 'When I toured Yarrandarrah Correctional Centre today, I was particularly impressed by the new C Wing, with its innovative design and contemporary fit-out. The new wing houses an education centre and centralised library that is stocked with more of the latest titles than my bookshelves at home.' Mayor Fischer chuckles at his own joke.

The Doc smirks.

'Unfortunately, the same cannot be said of Yarrandarrah Municipal Library.' The mayor pauses for effect. 'Since the opening of the state-of-the-art facility in nearby Corondale, patronage of the town library has steadily dwindled. To bring the library building up to the requisite standards will cost this council several million dollars. Money we simply do not have and a debt with which we cannot in all consciousness further burden ratepayers. Although this saddens me,' and he adopts an appropriately sombre expression, 'the only option is to close the town library at the end of the month. This will put an end to the duplication of services and free up resources for other critical projects.'

The Doc's smile falters. A vein throbs at his temple. 'That cunning bastard.'

'Not wasting any time, is he?' adds Parker, concealing his amusement behind the pages of the newspaper.

Derek, on the other hand, actually feels a bit sorry for the Doc. It's not often he misreads a situation and this time it's blown up in his face. 'Fischer's planned this. He tours the prison in the morning, looking like the big hero,' Derek says, opening one palm. 'Then in the afternoon he announces the closure of the town library.' Derek holds out his other hand. 'By putting the two images side by side, it makes him look fiscally responsible without actually having to blow his own trumpet. It's nothing but political opportunism.'

The Doc's face is as dark as thunder. 'But don't you see? Closing Yarrandarrah Library means no more books for us.'

'Well, I can't see how …'

'What's that on your face, Doc?' Parker asks, pointing to a spot on his own cheek. 'Is that a bit of egg?'

The old man's trembling, but it's not his usual tremors. Parker's fighting to hold back his laughter. It's a rare day Derek thinks poorly of Parker, but it's a low blow to hit a man when he's already down.

In an attempt to show a bit of support, he says, 'Don't worry, at least you've got your personal collection. The prison library will have to get by on the resources it already has.'

The Doc shoves his breakfast tray aside so hard that it almost shoots off the table. Derek rescues it just in time, and sets it to rights.

'You don't understand,' the Doc thunders. He looks from Derek to Parker and back again. 'How would you feel if they suddenly shut down your sewing circle?'

Maloney chooses that moment to join them. 'They're not closing Backtackers, are they?' he asks, taking the chair next to the Doc. 'I'm up for parole at the end of the year. I need a good annual review.'

'Don't worry, mate. It's only an example,' Derek soothes.

'Don't be so sure. I've seen it all before. First will be the library, then they'll cut funding for any of the rehab programs they reckon aren't delivering results. Who knows where the gov will draw the line?' Parker adds.

Alarmed, Derek looks to Maloney, who shrugs. They both turn to the Doc.

'Right now, the crux of the issue is this: no library means more than no books. It means no magazines, and no newspapers,' the Doc adds, curling his lip in Parker's direction.

Parker pales. 'What! That can't be right?'

The Doc nods slowly, pinning Parker to the spot. 'We're all going to suffer. Every single one of us.'

Derek quickly races through the probabilities and reaches the same conclusion as the Doc. Plenty of men will be spewing.

'You could always subscribe,' the Doc says, affecting nonchalance.

'You know I can't afford it,' Parker spits back.

'What if a few of the fellas pooled their resources and shared a subscription?' Derek suggests, trying to defuse the tension.

'Why should we have to use our hard-earnt cash to pay for something that by rights should be free?' splutters Parker, breaking into a paroxysm of coughing.

Calmer now, the Doc drains the dregs of his coffee, crushes the cup, and lobs it into the bin. 'See, cutting the weekly delivery of books has flow-on effects. From the literacy and education programs, to the book clubs, and to the blokes who need help with their appeals or letter-writing. If we let this happen, self-harming will skyrocket. And that's only for starters.'

'Men like Nicholas Fischer think crims like us don't deserve a single act of kindness,' Parker says.

'Well, in fairness, we don't deserve to be happy, do we? I mean, we're here for a reason,' Derek points out.

The Doc slaps his thighs. 'Bulldust. The deprivation of my liberty *is* my punishment. No one has the right to refuse me the opportunity to exercise intellectual freedom. That's what a library really does. It saves souls. Whether it's to learn something new or escape the boredom, who cares? Nobody gets hurt and, in a lot of cases,' he glances at Maloney, 'it does a lot of good.'

Derek also looks to Maloney. Against all odds, *One Day in the Life of Ivan Denisovich* has led to another classic, *The Catcher in the Rye*. He can't help but admire the Doc's strategy: slim volumes chosen for their underwhelming size and overwhelming themes. The Doc has a valid point, except for one thing. 'Stirring the pot will put you in no end of trouble.'

The Doc laughs, the harsh sound grating against Derek's ear. 'Who cares? I'm in for life anyway. And unlike you, Dezza, I'm not prepared to sit on my arse and accept my fate.'

Derek turns from the blow, as if the Doc had struck his cheek, not casually tossed out cruel words. For a brief moment, he had admired the Doc's passion and selflessness. But the truth is, without books, the Doc's life is meaningless. Strip him of the power and authority he gets from being the keeper of information, and the Doc's simply another crim trying to find a way to fill the endless hours. In the end, the Doc's the same as Derek, Maloney, and everybody else in this joint. All he cares about is looking after number one.

Chapter 16

Jane lies on the couch, her feet draped across Carl's lap, content after a meal of chilli sautéed scallops followed by quail in a lime marinade. Divine doesn't even begin to describe it. The CD player racks up another disc and Bryan Ferry croons in the background. Carl blames his dad's vinyl collection for rooting his tastes firmly in the eighties but from where Jane lies, this feels like a blatant attempt at seduction.

Carl starts massaging her instep and Jane lets a small sigh escape.

'A penny for your thoughts?' he asks.

Jane stretches and yawns. 'Actually, I was thinking about Backtackers. I don't think I've ever missed two weeks in a row.'

'Well, it wasn't your fault – it was because of the mayor's visit.'

Jane pats around until she finds her wine glass, sits up and takes a sip. 'That's not entirely true though, is it?'

Carl stops massaging her instep and finds the bottle of tempranillo. He tops up both their glasses. 'Stop beating yourself up. It was one week. No one cares whether you really had a cold.'

'*I* care. So should you. At the very least, you should despise me for lying. You thought you were going out with a nice person, and then I reveal that I was so embarrassed about failing to get Debbie's measurements that I'd rather fake a cold than face up to the Backtackers. I'm a coward.'

Carl's fingers run from her instep to her ankle, sending a tingle all the way up to her neck. 'Maybe I find cowardice a turn-on.'

Jane hoots with laughter. 'Trust you to find the silver lining.' She removes her foot from Carl's hands and tucks it beneath her other leg. 'I've been thinking.'

'Uh-oh.'

'Shush, hear me out. What if I tell Derek I *did* get Debbie's measurements?'

Carl frowns. He's clearly not following her logic.

'I had heaps of time to have a good look at her, enough to make an educated guess.' Jane reaches into her handbag and retrieves the little notebook. She flicks through to the page marked with a satin ribbon. 'I drew a sketch after I left and wrote down some numbers. See?'

Carl takes the notebook from her and studies the drawing.

'He'll never know,' Jane adds, warming to her idea. It would solve so many problems, at least until she can figure out a way to get the proper measurements.

Carl looks up from the notebook. 'Except one thing. Derek writes to his daughter every week. He'll find out. Then where will you be?'

Jane wriggles along the couch until Carl is so close, she can see each and every eyelash brushing his cheeks when he blinks. 'I'm not so sure he does write to her, you know. When I told her he was one of my finest stitchers, she looked surprised. Don't you think Derek would have told her about Backtackers? It's the highlight of his week.'

Carl's fingers brush her neck as he tucks an errant curl behind her ear and traces the line of her jaw. 'You don't know anything about Derek. For all you know, he could be a mass murderer.'

Jane pulls away. 'Is he? He doesn't seem the type.'

Carl smiles, but it doesn't reach his eyes. 'You know I can't answer that.'

Still, Jane entertains the fleeting fancy that she might be facilitating a dress for a murderer. It might explain why his daughter was so distant and why his ex-wife was downright rude. 'You're right. Whatever Derek's crime, it's none of my business. It's not my job to judge him, or any of them.'

She leans closer and places her lips against his. An invitation. He cups the soft nape of her neck and they kiss and kiss again. A ball of heat forms in her belly.

Then another thought occurs to Jane. She pulls away. 'What if Derek's ex is the one doing the misjudging?'

Carl threads his fingers through hers, tethering Jane to him. 'Don't get involved, Jane. Tell Derek the truth and go back to tapestries. No good comes from meddling.'

Jane lets herself fall forward and Carl is beneath her, running his fingers down her spine and over her hips. Leaning on her elbows, she looks into eyes the colour of an autumn sky. Carl stills and Jane can feel the rise and fall of his chest pressing against her. She smiles at him and he smiles back.

'I've come too far to turn back now,' she says.

Chapter 17

Derek hurries to Backtackers, grateful to escape Parker snarking about the newspapers, the Doc fuming over the books, and the whole bloody mess. Two weeks he's missed, thanks to Jane's absence and the mayor's visit, and quite frankly he's desperate to talk about something other than politics. But he slows on approach to the sewing room. Is it out of line to ask Jane how Debbie looks? Did Debbie indicate whether she missed him as much as he misses her? Or would asking anything be overstepping the mark?

'Afternoon,' Young Carl says, although he barely glances at Derek as he ticks him off the list. He's too busy making eyes at Jane, who's standing at the workbench surrounded by Backtackers. She looks up and smiles. At Carl.

Disgusted, Derek elbows past him and taps Mick on the shoulder. The crim moves aside to let Derek into the circle.

'Not like you to be late,' Mick says, unfolding a wisp of tissue paper.

A roll of fabric lays on the workbench. Wound up tight like that, it's hard to imagine it being transformed into a beautiful dress. Jane's expression is solemn. Derek's heart sinks.

She clears her throat and addresses the Backtackers. 'I went to see Derek's daughter.' Jane produces a notebook and shows the men her sketch. Only Maloney steps closer for a better look. 'Derek's right,' Jane continues, 'she has a big bosom but is quite slender through the waist.'

Maloney pulls up his t-shirt, revealing his stomach. 'About this big or smaller?'

She studies his torso then pulls the tape measure from around her neck and whips it around his waist. 'Smaller.'

'What if I suck in my stomach?' Maloney asks, clenching his abs.

Jane tightens the tape measure another inch. 'Perfect.'

Mick sniggers.

'What the hell's so funny?' Derek demands.

Mick wipes the tears from his eyes, chortling as he tries to get the words out. 'I'm just wondering how we're going to get around the fact Maloney's as flat as a pancake.'

Brian starts laughing. Then Les and Sean join in. Jane stifles a giggle. Even Carl chuckles.

Maloney rolls his eyes. 'Your problem, Mick, is that you have no imagination.' He saunters over to Sean's quilting basket and flutters his eyelashes at the big sandy-haired crim. 'May I?'

Sean turns an interesting shade of pink that makes his freckles stand out, and nods curtly.

Maloney holds a piece of wadding to his pouting chest. 'If the lovely Miss Jane here finds me a brassiere, all we have to do is stuff it with this and ta-da! Instant bust.'

Mick snorts. 'Are you telling me that part of this dressmaking caper is putting up with you in your scanties?'

'Jesus Christ. I didn't sign up for this,' says Brian.

'Regular pin-up girl,' comes from Les.

Maloney flings the wadding back in the basket. 'You got a better idea?'

The smile disappears from Mick's face. 'Don't be like that, Joey. We're only mucking about. Anyway, Jane's got us the measurements and the fabric. If you're happy to be our model, then we're as good as gold.'

Jane rummages around in her sewing tote and produces a sturdy white bra. 'And to Mick's original point, as it so happens, we are now the proud owners of one E-cup brassiere.'

She holds it aloft and the Backtackers grow silent. It's not exactly an attractive specimen. The straps are frayed and the lacy cups are covered in tiny pills of grey. There's a stain under one armpit that leaves Derek wondering.

Maloney takes it between two fingers and sniffs. 'Who gave us this ratty old thing?'

'We have CWA President June Makefield to thank for her generosity.' Jane gives Maloney a mock serious look. 'Would you mind slipping it on for us? I have washed it.'

Maloney goes over to the corner of the room for a modicum of privacy. Back turned, he whips off his jumper and t-shirt and fastens the bra. He moves the hooked side around and slips his arms through the straps. Jane goes over and helps him adjust the fit.

'Jeez mate, looks like you've done this before,' jokes Mick.

Maloney spins around and strikes a pose. 'Maybe once or twice,' he says with a wink and a toss of his head.

Brian sniggers. 'You look bloody ridiculous.'

Derek presses his lips together to contain the laughter. Brian's right. Maloney standing there in his Y fronts and a saggy-titted bra hardly qualifies as a sight for sore eyes.

Maloney huffs and shoots Brian a scathing look. 'You're hardly one to talk,' he says, giving him the once-over.

Derek's not alone in noticing Brian suck in his gut.

'Now, now, everyone, settle down,' Jane says, delving into Sean's basket and passing Maloney some scraps. She turns away as he stuffs the cups and pokes them into place. 'A couple of smaller bits would be good,' he says over his shoulder.

Jane complies and the rest of the Backtackers watch on, eager to see the end result.

This time when Maloney turns around, his chest is high and proud. If he was in the kid's shoes, Derek would have died of embarrassment, but Maloney models the bra like he's a regular superstar. 'Hello, boys,' he says and blows them a kiss.

To a man, they are rigid with shock. No one knows how to react.

Maloney cracks up. Hands on his knees, he's laughing so hard he can barely spit out the words. 'You should see your faces, eh.'

Mick grunts. 'Yeah, well, it's fair to say the officers in the security room are getting a bit of X-rated entertainment for the afternoon.'

This meets with chuckles all round.

'Christ,' says Brian, 'they'll be banning us next.'

The laughter dies.

'They can't do that, can they?' Mick asks, frowning at Jane.

'Of course not. Connecting Threads has nothing to do with the local council.'

'They'd better not bloody try,' adds Frank.

'Do you know,' says Sean, 'someone nicked my copy of *Power* magazine. Came back from breakfast and it was gone.'

The Backtackers share blank looks.

Sean adds, 'You know, me weightlifting magazine. It's not even mine. It belongs to the library. The Doc'll kill me.'

One look at Sean and his rippling body mass assures Derek there's not a hope in hell the Doc would take him on, but he sees the kid's point.

'What do you expect now we're not getting our weekly delivery,' grumbles Brian.

'Laws of supply and demand,' throws in Les from his corner.

And here was Derek thinking Backtackers would be an escape from the dramas of C Wing.

Maloney interrupts the grumbling. 'Can we hurry up please? I'm getting goose bumps on my goose bumps.' He illustrates this with a dramatic shiver.

Jane bustles over and whips the tape measure around his new and improved bust. She fetches more wadding. 'May I?' she asks before ever so gently stuffing the cups. She checks the measurements. 'Not bad.'

'So what did Dezza's daughter say when you told her about the dress?' Sean asks from behind the safety of the sewing machine.

Jane stiffens. She keeps her gaze firmly fixed on the wall behind Maloney's shoulder. If she catches Carl's eye, she won't be able to carry this off. 'She was surprised, obviously. She hadn't realised her dad was such a good sewer.' Jane hopes her tone conveys the right amount of lightness, after all, what she said is actually true.

Maloney's watching her though, she can feel it. She risks a glance and sees the fleeting pulse of realisation followed by the slightest of raised eyebrows. Jane exhales and turns to face the men. 'As it happens, she hasn't chosen a dress yet. Lucky for us.' A bead of perspiration trickles between her breasts.

A wave of heat passes over Derek, leaving him hot and clammy. He wishes he didn't have to ask this in front of the other Backtackers, but he won't get another chance. 'How is she? Debs I mean,' he adds, as if Jane would think he'd be asking about anyone else.

Jane hears her mother's voice whispering in her ear, 'Oh what a tangled web we weave when first we practise to deceive,' and she's twelve years old again. Caught red-handed at her mother's dressing table holding the almost-empty bottle of Chanel No 5 in one hand and a tiny jug of water in the other. She tamps down a rising sense of panic. What was she thinking? Well yes, she knows what she was thinking. It'd taken her so long to get the men on board. She can't let them down now.

'She's a lovely girl, Derek. I can see why you're so proud of her,' she replies. Should she mention the mother? Probably not.

A lovely girl. Jane's warm words unlock Derek's heart. He hadn't realised how much his reluctance to make the wedding dress had come down to nerves. But if Debbie approves, that changes everything. Jane's simple words have delivered a thousand Christmases all at once.

Maloney rattles the container of pins. 'Pardon me for interrupting, but at this rate we'll be making the dress for Dezza's granddaughter. If you want my services, we'd better hurry up. Otherwise, I'll be out on parole and you Neanderthals will be left high and dry.'

Jane turns to the men and smiles, despite the fact her pulse races at an amazing clip. Lying has never been her strong suit. She's glad the moment is over. 'Joey's right. Shall we make a start?'

While Maloney dresses, Jane unrolls the fabric across the workbench. Mick carefully unfolds the pattern and lays out the sheets of tissue paper on the adjacent table.

Derek looks at the fabric. The warm fuzzy feeling fades. Something is terribly wrong. He casts his mind back to their last meeting. They'd agreed on the duchess satin. It was shiny, expensive looking. Nothing like this fabric. He clears his throat. When nobody notices, he clears it again. Jane looks up, her mouth bristling with pins. 'Is this the fabric then?' asks Derek tentatively.

Jane laughs and spits the pins into her palm. 'Sorry,' she says, patting them dry with the hem of her skirt. 'What do you mean?'

Maloney lifts up the tail of the roll and runs it over his hand. 'Yeah, we decided the duchess satin was a bit old-fashioned, so we thought we'd go for something with a bit more oomph.' Maloney drapes the fabric over one shoulder and across his hips. 'Nice, eh?'

In this light, Derek can see straight through it. He fights off a vision of Debbie walking down the aisle like the emperor in that fairy tale. For all the world to see, like some common little …

Jane darts him a smile. 'This fabric is for the mock-up.'

Maloney bites his lip, trying not to laugh. Mick and the others are less successful and break out in guffaws. The new kid, Jarrod, looks confused but laughs along. Even Les, who rarely says boo to a ghost, is tittering like a schoolgirl.

'What?' Derek snaps. 'What's so bloody funny?'

Jane clasps a hand to her breast and tries to regain her self-control. 'I'm sorry. Remember? We talked about it. Before we make the actual dress, it's best to make a mock-up.'

Derek blushes. No, he does not remember. In fact, why is he the only one here who doesn't have a clue?

Maloney offers him a sympathetic smile. 'See, what you do is fit the pattern onto the muslin and cut out the shape. Then you baste it so you've got an idea of what the dress will look like. You can make changes to the design, length, sleeves or whatever before cutting into the real fabric. Makes sense, eh?'

'Baste it? Sounds like we're making Christmas dinner not a bloody wedding dress,' says Mick.

'It means to loosely sew it together,' Jane explains.

She steps away from the workbench and smiles at Derek. He looks over his shoulder at the Backtackers staring back at him. 'What?'

Mick grins. 'Well it's your dress, Dezza. Don't you think you should do the honours?'

Jane passes him the shears. 'He's right. You should cut the pattern.'

'Yeah, mate,' chips in Frank. 'It's not every day a man gets to make his wedding dress.'

That sets them all off again, but their laughter peters out once Derek stands poised over the workbench. He studies the pieces of pattern pinned to the fabric, then picks up the corner of the piece closest to him.

'Try to cut as close to the edge of the paper as possible,' Jane says, nudging him into action.

Derek flexes his hand and slides the fabric between the shears. 'Measure twice, cut once,' he hears Clive saying in his head, and he can smell the garage, pungent with fresh sawdust. This is it then. The point of no return. 'Here we go,' he says under his breath and makes the first snip.

Not one man picks up his stitching. Tentatively at first, then with growing confidence, Derek cuts out the pieces, pausing now and then to blot his forehead with his sleeve. When he is done, there are patches of pattern and fabric scattered across the workbench like one of those jigsaw puzzles with a thousand pieces of sky.

Jane starts gathering them into a pile. 'There's not really enough time left today to start the basting. We may as well save it until next week.'

'Will I have to use the machine?' Derek asks, casting a worried glance in its direction.

'If we machine-baste it, we'll have the mock-up done in no time. That's when things get really exciting.' Noticing Derek's worried frown, Jane adds, 'I'm sure Sean will be a wonderful teacher.'

One glance at the sandy-haired con is enough to tell Derek how Sean feels about this encroachment into his territory.

'I'd really appreciate it, Sean,' Jane says softly.

The young crim's shoulders relax. 'Yeah, all right.'

'Which reminds me,' Jane says, rummaging inside her sewing tote. She withdraws a slender volume and hands it to Derek. 'I thought this might help.'

He studies the cover. *Sewing for Beginners*. Judging by the furled corners and yellowed pages, it's very old. On the inside cover is a woman's name written in faded ink. Violet Dempsey.

'My grandmother's,' says Jane.

Derek doesn't know what to say. He's a mess of gratitude for this woman who has done so much for him, brought so much joy into his life, and somehow, brought him the most precious gift of all. He holds the book to his chest and smiles at Jane. 'Thank you.'

Chapter 18

On Saturday, Jane arrives home after her shift at the haberdashery store to find Susannah at the kitchen table immersed in the weekend papers. She's still in her pyjamas, even though it's past midday. She looks a mess. Her skin has broken out and pimples scour her cheeks. Goodness knows when she last showered. Too busy eating Tim Tams and licking her wounds.

'Fischer has a bloody hide,' Susannah announces, shaking the creases out of the paper and turning the page. 'Take a look at this,' she says, handing it over.

Jane dumps her handbag and puts the kettle on to boil, then turns her attention to the head shot of Nicholas Fischer filling the front page. It's the photo from a week and a half ago on the steps of the town library. She scans the article. It's a rehash of everything Fischer said in his original announcement about closing down the library. Jane puts down the paper and spoons tea leaves into a teapot, wondering what sort of response Susannah wants.

'It's complete bulldust,' Susannah says, taking the second-last Tim Tam from the packet.

'Which bit?'

'The bit about the library being too expensive to repair. Fischer wants everyone to believe the building is full of asbestos, termites, faulty wiring and whatever else he can dream up.

But the truth is, he wants the precinct rezoned so his property developer cronies can knock it down and build a retirement village.'

Jane brings the teapot over to the table. 'Seriously? Isn't that illegal or at least a conflict of interest?'

Susannah scoffs and piles her hair on top of her head, securing it with an elastic. It only serves to highlight how thin and pale she looks. Gone is the woman dolled up to the nines, always ready for a photo opportunity or a chance meeting with an influential voter.

A memory niggles at her. Something Sean had said at Backtackers this week. Jane stirs honey into her tea and follows the train of thought.

'The town library supplies the prison with new releases and requested titles,' Jane says slowly, thinking out loud as she stirs. 'And if you're doing one of those open university courses, you can order in the textbooks you need. Plus they provide free newspapers and magazines, which are so crucial, of course.'

Susannah glances at the spread of papers over the kitchen table. 'Why "of course"?'

Jane's phone pings. It's a text from Carl, asking her if she feels like going to the pub tonight. She texts back a smiley face. 'Well, most of the inmates can't afford to buy reading materials themselves. The weekly delivery from the town library is a lifeline.'

'How come you know this and I don't?'

'The Backtackers don't sew in silence, you know,' Jane says, nabbing the last Tim Tam, dunking it in her tea and popping it into her mouth. She licks the melted chocolate from her fingers. 'One of the inmates is the prisoner librarian. I believe he runs a book club and supports the literacy program as well.' Jane pauses and tries to remember the name of that grumpy older guy with the slicked-back hair she sees every time she passes the library.

'I know for a fact that Corondale Library won't be maintaining services to the gaol.' Susannah picks up a notepad and jots down some thoughts. 'When you think about it, this decision to close the local library affects a whole lot of vulnerable people. Prisoners aren't the only ones who can't afford to buy books or want a quiet corner to read the papers.'

Jane's phone pings again. 'Do you fancy dinner as well?' reads Carl's text. She posts back a thumbs-up.

Susannah opens the lid of her laptop. Her fingers perform a mad dance across the keyboard as she speaks. 'Fischer doesn't give a stuff about the library or the impact of closing it on the local community. And most of the councillors are in his pocket. We need public pressure. An action group so we can tackle him head on.'

Jane notices a spot of colour in Susannah's cheeks and smiles to herself. This is exactly what Susannah needs to get over her shock loss to Nick Fischer. A new cause to champion, with the added bonus of a bit of revenge politics on the mayor.

The neighbour's dog releases a volley of barks and the tin lid of the letterbox slams shut. That's odd. The postie doesn't usually deliver on Saturdays. Jane leaves Susannah tapping away to investigate. Outside, their neighbour waves over the fence and shouts, 'Wrong letterbox, love. I've just popped it back in yours.' The old dear's up for a chat, filling the bird bath from the hose as an excuse. Her horrible little terrier comes snuffling over for a chat too. It's one of those dogs that is supposed to be white and fluffy but always end up with those pinky-brown stains all over it. It tries to lick Jane's hand, but she pulls sharply away.

'Oh, he doesn't bite, love. Don't be frightened.'

Jane smiles and discreetly wipes her fingers on the back of her skirt. As penance, she listens to the lonely old dear for a while, but eventually Jane signals the chat has come to an end by retrieving the misdirected item from the letterbox.

As she walks up the front path, Jane flips over the stiff envelope and stops in her tracks. In the top left corner is the Connecting Threads logo. Opening the envelope, she finds a letter from the Secretary of the Organising Committee of the Connecting Threads Charity Ball. Jane scans the contents, then returns to the middle paragraph.

In recognition of your years of service to Connecting Threads and the Yarrandarrah Branch of Backtackers, the Board cordially invites you to be the keynote speaker at this year's Charity Ball.

Her? Keynote speaker? Jane reads the invitation again, then races inside to share the news.

'Suze, you'll never guess,' she calls down the hallway.

'What do you think of FOYL?' Susannah asks, without looking up from her keyboard.

Jane pauses, confused. 'Foil?'

Susannah swings the laptop around so Jane can see the screen. 'FOYL. Stands for Friends of Yarrandarrah Library. Incorporated. I've already registered the name.' She beams at Jane, looking extremely pleased with herself. 'Your mother's agreed to be president.'

'My mother?'

'Well, *I* can't be. I'm a councillor. I need to be seen to be at arm's length; supportive but not actually running the show. Marion's going to talk to the CWA and VIEW Club ladies and help rally the troops. Together, we're going to wipe that smug smile right off Nick Fischer's face.'

Susannah snaps shut her laptop and stretches. 'Which reminds me, can you find out the name of that prisoner librarian? I'd love to have a man on the inside.' She checks the time on her phone. 'Gosh, it's almost two. I'd better grab a shower. I'm meeting the head librarian for coffee in an hour.' She springs to her feet and heads for the bathroom, leaving Jane stranded in the middle of the kitchen clutching her letter.

Susannah pops her head around the door. 'Sorry, what did you have to tell me? Good news I hope?'

Jane passes her the invitation and waits as Susannah reads it.

'Wow! You really have hit the big time now, haven't you?' she says, returning the letter. 'Let me know if you want help writing your speech. I've had tonnes of practice.' With that, she disappears into the bathroom.

Jane goes to her bedroom, removes the pile of clothes from the chair at her desk and sits in front of her ancient laptop. As she waits for it to fire up, she thinks about her reply. She's been a volunteer sewing teacher with Connecting Threads for over six years. The speech will be a chance to tell everyone about her Backtackers' wonderful work and how the most important job Connecting Threads does is inspire hope. She opens a new document window and starts to type her acceptance letter, then abandons it to ring Carl instead.

She drums her fingers on the desk as she waits for him to answer.

'What's wrong?' he asks without preamble. 'Have you changed your mind about tonight?'

'No, no, of course not. You're not going to believe what I've been asked to do.' Jane can't sit still. She paces the room as she brings Carl up to speed, her free hand punctuating her points.

'You'll say yes?'

'Absolutely. This is a once-in-a-lifetime opportunity. How could I possibly refuse?' Jane smiles at her reflection in the cheval mirror parked in the corner near the window. 'And I've had the most brilliant idea.' She picks up the hem of her skirt and twirls in front of the mirror. 'The wedding dress is the perfect way to showcase the Backtackers' superb work.' Her mind flits to Joey. Thank goodness she has someone in the group with his skills and experience. Between them, this dress will be spectacular. 'Imagine the look on the audience's faces. People will be talking about our dress for ages.'

Jane pauses, waiting for Carl to agree that her idea is pure genius. Instead, all she hears is silence. 'Carl?'

'I'm here.'

'What's wrong?'

Jane can hear him fidgeting down the line. 'At the risk of pointing out the obvious, as of this moment, Debbie doesn't know about the dress and Derek doesn't know that you've lied about getting her measurements. How on earth are you going to ask him if you can borrow the darn thing?'

Jane flushes with guilt. 'No, no, that's not what I meant. I'm talking about a slideshow presentation showing the stages of making the dress. Photos of the Backtackers making the mock-up, Joey modelling it, you know, each step. That way people will see that this is about creating something beautiful, building friendships, bonding over common goals. The dress is a symbol of all that and more. It's brought people together – you and me, Sean and Joey ...'

'Sean and Joey?'

'Yes, isn't it obvious? If they're not already an item, they soon will be. And I know it was wrong to tell Derek that Debbie let me take her measurements, but you saw the look on his face. He clearly loves his daughter very much. What's one little white lie stacked up against all these happy people?'

'I don't know, Jane. There's an awful lot of ifs in this scenario. You'll have to get permission to take photos and convince the gov that it will be good publicity.'

'Oh, I hadn't thought of that.'

'And even if you get permission from the gov, you can't just turn up at Backtackers and start snapping photos. Some of the blokes might not want their photos shown in front of hundreds of people.'

'That's a good point.'

'And you are going to have to come clean with Derek before your good intentions blow up in your face. After all, technically it's his dress.'

'I will, I will, when the time is right. But the whole argument becomes academic if we don't actually *finish* the dress. Don't worry. This is Derek's big opportunity to shine and I'm not going to fail him.'

By the time Jane hangs up, she's convinced herself that the wedding dress and the Charity Ball are a match made in heaven. If she closes her eyes, she can see how it will unfold. The gasps of admiration from the audience. Tears – the good kind. The wedding dress will prove the redemptive powers of the gentle art of sewing. That no matter what mistakes we've made in life, there's always a chance to turn over a new leaf. All it takes is a little bit of nurturing and good things can blossom.

She quickly finishes her acceptance letter, then opens a new blank document to write a letter to the governor.

Chapter 19

Reading *Sewing for Beginners* makes Derek feel closer to Jane. He can see a younger Jane, hair tamed into pigtails, sitting at her grandmother's sewing machine, tongue poked between her teeth as she concentrates on following her grandmother's instructions. Violet seated beside her, helping Jane guide some pretty fabric through the machine as they make the library bag on page sixteen. And young Jane would be trying so hard to please her grandmother, not just because that is her nature, but also because Violet has promised her a slice of madeira cake and a glass of milk for morning tea if she does a good job.

'Never mind,' Violet would say when Jane grew tired, the project still incomplete. 'We can finish it next week.' And little Jane would smile up at her grandmother, a gap where her two front teeth should be.

Derek sighs and taps his own front teeth. There's no way in hell things will ever be that peachy between him and Sean. Even if there were cake.

Mick casts aside his commemorative cushion. 'Where have you been, mate? You're holding up the show.'

Derek apologises and hurries over to the sewing machine. Sean nods to the spare chair, making no effort to vacate his position. Derek's heart sinks a little. A glance at Jane proves

Brian has consumed her attention with the mess he's made of his commemorative cushion. He's not really supposed to be working on them, but how could Jane say no when he asked? With a sigh, Derek takes the spare seat and pops his tapestry under the chair.

'Right, let me show you how it's done, mate,' Sean says and so the lesson begins.

Maloney stands at the workbench, facing Derek and Sean. His hands work independently of his eyes, as he pins together pieces of sample fabric while watching Sean teach Derek. He passes over a section, is disappointed when Sean takes it without looking. Sean demonstrates to Derek how to feed the pinned pieces under the foot, the right tension on the needle, just enough pressure on the footplate.

'How are you coming along?' Jane asks, joining them.

Maloney shrieks, his hand flies to his chest. 'You scared the bejesus out of me!' earning an amused apology from Jane, but at least Sean looked at him for a moment.

'I thought I'd show him how it's done then get him started on an easy bit.' Sean tilts his head at Derek.

Jane can see where this is heading. Forcing poor Derek to play sidekick while Sean takes over the actual sewing and preserves his territory over the machine. She glances at Maloney, who's making eyes at Sean unbeknownst to the sandy-haired con. 'Lovely, well, let's see if Derek's been paying attention.'

There is not enough room for Sean to hover in the corner, which forces him to step closer to the workbench where he accidentally brushes against Maloney. 'Sorry, mate.'

Maloney looks up and holds Sean's gaze for a moment. 'All sweet.'

Derek moves into the warm spot left by Sean. He positions the fabric beneath the foot and lines it up with the pattern. He can't quite bring himself to apply pressure to the plate. In his mind's eye, the fabric races every which way like an out-of-control dodgem car.

'Breathe, Derek,' Jane soothes.

'Careful you don't sew your thumb while you're at it,' warns Sean.

Derek's world shrinks to the square inches surrounding the sewing machine foot and the scraps of white muslin trapped beneath. He gently eases the machine into action, beads of sweat on his top lip, the taste of salt on his tongue as he rams the tip between his teeth.

When he's done, he passes his handiwork to Jane. She holds it up and checks the seams. 'Some of my students at TAFE can't sew as well as this,' she says, and Derek blushes with pride.

'Do you teach sewing?' asks Maloney. 'Away from here, I mean.'

'I do.'

'What? You give people a piece of paper that says they can make a dress?'

Sean grunts at Maloney, reminding him to feed Derek another practice piece. Maloney apologises and quickly pins together a section and passes it to Sean.

'That's right. My students are working towards their Certificate in Applied Fashion Design and Technology,' says Jane.

'What do they do with it? Afterwards I mean.'

'Make a paper aeroplane and fly it out the window,' jokes Mick, earning groans all round.

'Well, some do the course for pleasure, but a few go on to complete the diploma or even get degrees. It depends where their interests lie.'

Brian puts aside his unpicking. 'Thinking about furthering your education, Joey?'

Maloney blushes, shrugs his shoulders. 'Just askin'.'

'I'm not having a go, mate,' says Brian, in that gentle way of his. 'Look at me. When I got here, my head was in a shocking state. It wasn't until I started working in the gardens and doing stitching that I started feeling better about meself. You know the bloke that runs the library, the Doc? It's him that got me thinking about getting the piece of paper to prove I knew a thing or two about growing things in the first place, and here I am today.'

Maloney is not alone in glancing around the sewing room.

Brian smiles. 'Not literally *here*, you silly bugger. I meant I've got me Certificate II in Horticulture and now I'm working on the next one. I'm gunna do the whole diploma so when I get out of here, I can get a real job.'

Jane bestows a smile on Brian. 'It's something to consider, Joey. After all, if you do get parole at the end of the year, a formal qualification will improve your employment prospects immensely. Or maybe you could even apply to join the Connecting Threads Outreach Program. We're always on the lookout for apprentices.'

Maloney goes still, his expression transformed as if a door has opened into a world he has only ever dreamt of. 'Could I do costume design? Is that a course?'

Jane beams at him. 'Yes. There may even be a campus near where you live.'

'Oh,' Maloney breathes. His features twitch with excitement. 'How cool would that be, eh?'

'Super cool,' Jane agrees.

Derek feels a pinch of jealousy. He's never wasted much time thinking about life beyond these four walls. It's too far off and clouded in uncertainty. He watches Brian carefully pull a loose thread from his canvas. Brian's not the smartest tool in the box, not by a long shot, and he's a pretty ordinary sewer, but even he has ambitions despite having more years to serve than Derek. So why doesn't Derek harbour dreams?

'You can do both. Connecting Threads encourages volunteers in the Outreach Program to study as well. You'd be such an asset, being in the unique position to understand both sides of the situation,' Jane says, helping Maloney pin the pieces.

'Imagine what me Aunty would say.'

'What your Aunty's gunna say right now is stop yapping and pass me the next section,' Sean says, snapping his fingers, and bringing them all plummeting back to earth.

Two weeks later, Derek and Sean have finished basting the mock-up. By Derek's reckoning, he's become more proficient with a quick-unpick than the sewing machine. Despite a fair dose of sweat and swearing on Derek's part, as a teacher Sean has been equal parts patient and a perfectionist.

All the Backtackers congregate around the workbench and admire the basted frock.

'Not bad,' declares Mick.

'Aren't you a clever dick, Dezza?' remarks Brian by way of a compliment.

'Thanks to Sean,' defers Derek.

'Wasn't me sitting at the machine, mate,' says Sean, but it's clear to everyone that Sean is pretty proud of his pupil.

'Yes, well, when you've all finished patting each other on the back, how about we see how this baby looks?' Maloney suggests, shivering in the next-to-altogether.

'Joey's right,' Jane says, taking the basted muslin frock off the workbench and spreading it on the floor. Maloney steps into the circle of fabric and she helps him wiggle it up over his hips. Derek can't see much as she fusses with the fit, Maloney with his arms raised in the air turning this way and that.

But eventually she steps away and, Maloney being Maloney, he can't resist the opportunity to parade down an imaginary runway, modelling the wisps of muslin as if he were on the red carpet at the Oscars.

The men study him as he sashays and twirls, laughter put aside for the serious business of assessing their handiwork.

'Jump up so we can get a closer look,' suggests Sean.

Jane moves a chair over to the workbench and lends Maloney a hand stepping up. He shuffles to the centre of the bench and the men close in a circle around him.

'Turn,' instructs Jane and Maloney complies. She measures him from the waist to the end of the fall of fabric at the front, then pins the hem.

Behind, Mick shakes out the excess fabric. 'How long's a train supposed to be?'

'Buggered if I know,' says Derek.

'As long as you like,' comes from above. 'But the last thing you need is the bride going arse over tit, eh.'

Jane, who has had her fingers pressed to her lips throughout this exchange, suddenly says, 'Heels.'

'God, we're not going to have to put up with Maloney in stilettos, are we?' asks Les, who has let curiosity override his misgivings and joined his fellow stitchers.

For an answer, Maloney stands on tiptoes. Jane holds up the fabric, shortening the length. 'Trains can be a nightmare. We either have to make it short enough for her to dance in, or create a bustle to hold the dress up at the back after the ceremony.'

'Or we could attach a wrist strap,' adds Maloney, demonstrating by picking up the hem and revealing hairy brown calves.

Sean takes the fabric from Maloney and rearranges it so it puddles around his feet. 'Tiptoes,' he instructs and, as Maloney complies, Sean grabs a couple of pins and weaves them through the fabric. Satisfied, he says to Jane. 'How high a heel is a bride gunna choose?'

Jane rests her cheek on her hand and thinks for a moment. 'I can't imagine anyone would go for more than a four-inch heel, probably lower. Even when you're used to them, it's tiring to be on your feet all day.'

Derek's gaze drifts to Jane's sensible flat-heeled boots.

'Yeah, you don't want to make that mistake,' says Mick, all serious. 'It had been pissing down the whole week leading up to Samantha's wedding, as well as the day of. It was so bad, we almost decided to wear bloody gumboots, bride and all. Of course, Samantha wanted the photos taken in the gardens, you know, surrounded by the roses and azaleas and shit, despite the fact it was dripping wet. As you can imagine, disaster struck.' Mick shares a knowing look, but the men are clueless.

'I think you'll need to spell it out for them,' Jane says.

Mick grunts, spans his thumb and forefinger as wide as they can go. 'Heels this high, they were. Covered in the same fabric as the dress. And there she was, sunk up to her ankles in mud. There's Kaz, kneeling on my bloody hired dinner jacket, her arse wriggling in the air, trying to undo the straps so Sam can get the damn things off. Meanwhile, Sam's screaming blue bloody murder, her dress hoicked up over her thighs, two of her bridesmaids trying to keep hold of the train with one hand and keep the umbrellas over their heads with the other. The groom and best man were already half cut, so they were next to useless. Bloody debacle.'

'So what did you do?'

'Well, there's only so much crap a man can take. I grabbed her under the armpits and heaved. Out she came like a champagne cork.' He shoves one fat finger in his cheek and makes a popping sound. Laughing, he adds, 'Lucky I'm a big bloke otherwise we both would have ended up flat on our backs. Shoes were buggered, but fortunately Kaz had packed another pair for later, so it wasn't a complete disaster. Hate to think how much the bloody shoes set me back, though,' and he punctuates the story with a shudder.

'Yes, well, so you see my point,' Jane says after they'd all finished commenting. 'What do you want to do, Derek?'

He licks his lips. Christ, who would have thought there'd be so many tiny decisions with such earth-shattering consequences. Making the dress was complicated enough, but now they'd wasted the entire afternoon talking about how long the darn thing should be.

Sean nudges him with his shoulder. 'Puddle it, mate.'

'Or we can make a wrist strap,' Maloney throws in.

'It'll be less fabric if you do it my way,' Sean says, glaring at the brown-skinned boy. Maloney squares his shoulders and gives as good as he gets.

Derek sinks in the middle. Sean's right. And less fabric means less expense – even thinking about money winches him tighter. But he can see Debbie waltzing across the dance floor with her dress attached to her wrist by a pretty strap.

'I think the wrist strap is the way to go. It'll show off the dress nicely.'

Maloney smiles. Sean scowls.

Ah well, it's a done deal now. 'And let's hope she doesn't wear stupid heels,' he adds to soften the blow. Sean's the last person he wants offside. Not only because of the sewing machine but, to tell the truth, the sheer size of the guy terrifies him. He'd hate to be in that kid's bad books.

Chapter 20

There is never any announcement, no forewarning. The guards simply turn up and tell whoever's turn it is that they are conducting a cell search. So when Derek sees Young Carl and Cheryl Blackburn standing in his doorway, he knows what's about to happen. But the timing feels a little suspicious. He's not due for a turnover for at least a fortnight.

Blackburn orders him outside, so Derek lays down the commemorative cushion he's working on and stands in the corridor. A quick recce tells him it is only him and Maloney that have been singled out for special attention on this level. He peeks downstairs and sees Les and Brian are also on the list. The connection is obvious, except not one of them is a troublemaker.

It's the same routine every time. Derek watches as Blackburn empties the contents of his locker onto the bed, followed by his wet pack. There isn't much. Neat piles of clothes, deodorant, single-blade disposable razor, soap, shampoo, a toothbrush, toothpaste and a ChapStick. All prison issue.

'You can keep your toiletries, Brown,' says Blackburn, with a grin.

She's one of the few people who call him by his surname. He knows darn well she only does it to piss him off.

Blackburn picks up the nail clippers lying next to his stitching, then picks up the tapestry kit. The nail clippers are legit – he uses them to cut the threads since scissors are banned outside of Backtackers. Derek holds his breath, waiting for her to tip the contents of the kit all over the floor. He hasn't unbundled most of the threads yet, but still.

Blackburn replaces the kit and lifts up the mattress. She retrieves the bundle of letters, held together with a rubber band. 'How's your daughter's wedding dress coming along, Brown?' she asks, as if continuing the thread of a conversation neither of them have started.

Derek glances at the letters from his dad. It's against the rules to read personal correspondence unless there's a good reason and Derek doesn't plan on giving her one. 'We cut out the proper dress last meeting. I'll make a start on the stitching next week.'

Blackburn drops the mattress back down on the bunk, messing up Derek's hospital corners. 'Looking forward to seeing how you go with that,' she says with a curt nod in Carl's direction.

Derek smiles, keen to get rid of her. It's only after she disappears into Maloney's cell that he wonders at her sudden interest in his wedding dress.

Derek has a moan about it over lunch. 'I hate cell searches,' he says, pulling apart his soggy ham and salad roll. As usual, the tomato has ruined the bread and the lettuce is as limp as a dishrag. And he hates raw onion, it stays on your breath for hours. 'It's like when you're pulled over by the cops. Even though you weren't speeding and you haven't touched a drop of alcohol in days, you immediately start to sweat.'

Parker bites into his roll, either oblivious to the sorry excuse for a sandwich or used to such desecrations in the name of food. 'Stop complaining. You know it's not personal.'

Derek casts aside his sandwich and reaches for the muffin. 'Yeah, but I'm not due, so why are they picking on me?'

Parker heaves himself to his feet and picks up his tray. 'Keep your nose clean, that's my advice. Wanna 'nother coffee?'

Derek declines and watches Parker tack a path through the crims, one unsteady step at a time, that takes him the long way around but avoids the troublemakers.

The Doc slides into Parker's seat, Maloney hot on his heels. The kid puts down his tray then pulls out the thickest book Derek's ever seen him read. It's *Harry Potter and the Philosopher's Stone*.

'Where'd you get that from?' he asks.

'What? Oh. Carruthers lent it to me.'

'He doesn't strike me as a Harry Potter fan,' observes Derek.

'He's been reading it with his son. Gives them something to talk about on their weekly calls, eh.'

Quite a few of the crims do it. They read the same book as their loved ones so they have something in common to chat about on their calls.

'He's moved onto book two, and he thought I might like the first one.'

'And do you?'

'It's all right. Hogwarts doesn't sound that much different from here, except they can do spells.'

'In which case, why don't they simply wave their magic wand and escape?'

Maloney frowns, measures the thick heft of the book. 'Dunno. Haven't got to that bit yet.'

'I have an announcement,' the Doc interrupts, producing a letter from the waistband of his trackpants. He checks he has their full attention before declaring, 'Susannah Cockburn has asked me to become Yarrandarrah's FOYL representative.'

Derek looks to Maloney. The kid shrugs. 'All right then, I'll bite. What's foil?'

The Doc adjusts his glasses. 'The solution to our problems.'

Derek has quite a few problems on his plate. Chief among them being the wedding dress. No one ever told him what a slippery sucker duchess satin could be. But he doubts very much the Doc gives a rat's arse about that.

'FOYL, gentlemen, is the acronym for the Friends of Yarrandarrah Library. This wonderful group of people are working towards stopping the closure of the town library and, in turn, restoring services to the prison.'

'What do they need you for then?' asks Derek.

'I've been sharing some salient details to help the cause.'

'Such as?'

The Doc unfolds the letter and produces a newspaper clipping. 'This is about the last council meeting. Susannah talks about the pensioners and the kids and then she says, "The weekly delivery of books to Yarrandarrah gaol is a lifeline to the men incarcerated within its four walls. The knock-on effect of Mayor Fischer's decision to close the library means that prisoners who have hobbies will no longer be able to receive their monthly gardening, woodwork or stamp-collecting magazines. For those whose eyesight is failing, there will be no more large-print books. And for those where English is a second language, they now have limited resources to improve their linguistic skills."

'I gave her that,' the Doc smiles conspiratorially. 'That's my job. To be her man on the ground.'

Derek has to admit, he's impressed.

'Now for the best bit. "As we are all aware, there is no bookshop in town. For those of us able to afford it, it is a simple matter to make a trip to Corondale or jump online and buy whatever we want. But for the pensioners, the children? Where does this leave them? The Friends of Yarrandarrah Library will not allow this important local resource to be consigned to the pages of history.'"

'She's right, you know,' Parker says, carrying a fresh coffee and a packet of shortbreads. They remain silent while he battles with the wrapper, his hands quivering. Derek's about to help him when the packet bursts open, depositing a biscuit straight into Parker's coffee. 'Buggerations,' he mutters, fishing out the sodden shortbread and laying it on a paper napkin where it collapses altogether.

'You were saying,' prompts the Doc, the corner of his mouth twitching with mirth.

Parker coughs and peers at the Doc through his watery eyes. 'Your girlfriend's right. But rather than give vent to a whole lot of hot air, you lot need to do something practical.'

Derek smothers a chuckle. Parker's braver than he is.

'What do you mean?' The Doc's words are even, but his gaze has narrowed.

'It's all well and good getting the guys to donate books to the library and sending your girlfriend info on the sly, but if you want to save your library, you're gunna need to think bigger.'

The last vestiges of the Doc's good humour vaporises in an instant. 'Like what?'

'Like start a petition.'

Derek leaps into the fray. 'That's not a bad idea, Doc. That way you can prove to Mayor Fischer that the blokes in here value the library service. You can't argue with the numbers.'

'Collecting a few signatures isn't going to save the library,' he grumbles.

Parker gestures to the Doc's newspaper clipping. 'But then you'd have something important to write about. Instead of complaining, it shows you're not going to take this lying down. And you'll have the mayor by the short and curlies.'

The Doc hoots with laughter and leans forward, a wicked gleam in his eyes. 'Now wouldn't that be a sight to behold.'

Maloney puts down his book. 'C'mon, Dezza, time to get going. We've gotta dress to make.'

Derek checks the clock, stands and stretches. 'I'll meet you at the duty desk.' Before he goes, he turns and says one last thing to the Doc. 'I'm not much of a reader, but I'd sign a petition, just on principle.'

The Doc grins. For once, they are co-conspirators and, to Derek's surprise, it feels pretty good.

He goes via his cell and collects his tapestry. On his way to the duty desk, one of the officers hands him a message. 'Bloody hell,' Derek says once he's read it.

'What's up?' asks Maloney, appearing at his side.

'It's my sister-in-law, Sharon. She's coming to visit next Saturday. What on earth can she want?'

Chapter 21

Sharon collapses in her chair, slick with sweat like she's just crossed the finish line in the Turnley Vale Fun Run. 'It's a bloody nightmare out there,' she says, fanning herself.

Derek waits for more information.

'The bus couldn't get through. Some protesters were blocking the main drag.'

Derek looks at her blankly. He has no idea what she's talking about.

Sharon tsks. 'There were people everywhere holding banners and signs. Something about "save our library" and "reading sets you free".'

Ah, now it makes sense. Although, Derek's surprised the Doc hasn't mentioned it, given he has a radio and surely would be the first inmate to know.

'The lady I was sitting next to said it was to do with the mayor.' Sharon scans the visitors' room, as if searching for the woman in question. 'So what's FOYL then?' she asks, returning her attention to Derek.

He gives her the twenty-second pitch because he is less interested in the library agitators than the reason for Sharon's visit.

Sharon harrumphs. 'Good luck with that. Nothing stands between a pollie and a pot of money.' She settles back in her chair. 'We've got more important things to discuss. I'm here about the wedding.'

Derek nods and waits silently. He wants to give Sharon plenty of airspace to give him a bit more intel about Debbie's reaction than Jane had cared to share.

'We went to the florist last week. Obviously, Debbie needs a bouquet for herself and some smaller ones for the bridesmaids and flower girls. Oh, and the buttonholes for the groom and groomsmen.' Sharon counts them up on her fingers. 'Being a bloke you probably don't understand any of this, but you put the word "wedding" in front of anything and the price triples. Flowers, cake, the dress.'

'Ah well, the dress is the least of her worries now, isn't it?' Derek replies with a conspiratorial wink.

Sharon rolls her eyes. 'Yes and no. Lorraine and Debbie are at each other's throats over this blasted dress.' She shifts in her chair. 'Well, not the dress exactly. Debbie's figure.'

Derek sits back in surprise.

'The way Lorraine is carrying on, you'd swear it was *her* wedding. I mean, she's already had two of her own, surely she can keep her trap shut and let Debbie do what she likes.' Sharon shakes her head. 'But no, that would be hoping for too much, wouldn't it?'

Derek wants to ask Sharon what on earth she's talking about, but she's building up a head of steam and clearly won't take any interruptions from him.

'I mean, if Debbie is happy with her weight, then I say good luck to her. There's no point Lorraine sticking her bib in and telling her to lose a few kilos. That's the pot calling the kettle black.'

Debbie balloons before Derek's very eyes. He thinks of the mock-up they made. 'Are you trying to tell me she's got fat?'

Sharon snorts. 'No, of course not. She's buxom, that's all.'

Buxom. That's a loaded word. He'd once described Lorraine as buxom and she almost bit his head off. He'd meant it as a compliment and hadn't expected it to backfire. He's a bit more careful what he says these days.

Sharon plays with her earlobe as she gathers her thoughts. 'To be fair, it's not all Lolly's fault. Apparently, "shedding for the wedding" is a thing.'

Derek opens his mouth to speak, but Sharon holds up a finger to indicate she's not finished yet. 'I'm not arguing the toss either way. The point is, Lorraine's decided Debbie should buy a dress one size too small so she has something to aim for.'

'That sounds like a bit of a gamble,' he manages, although his thoughts are less polite than that.

'You're telling me. Anyway, Debbie's put her foot down. She says Ian likes her the way she is and she wants to buy a dress that flatters the figure she already has. And who can blame her?' Sharon adds, shifting on her own significant haunches.

Derek's thoughts, meanwhile, are caught up on the fact that the Backtackers are making Debbie's dress on the assumption she remains her current size. He's no expert, but if Lorraine convinces her to shed a few kilos, it might cause all sorts of headaches. Then something Sharon said catches up with him. 'What do you mean, "buy a dress"?'

Sharon looks at Derek as if he's a bit simple. 'I said, why can't Lorraine let Debbie choose the dress she wants and be done with it? It's not like *she's* paying for it.'

Derek is struck dumb. Jane said Debbie was over the moon about him making her dress. Naturally, he assumed she'd tell her mother.

'The poor girl has enough on her plate without going on a diet as well. I'm that close,' Sharon holds her thumb and forefinger a centimetre apart, 'to telling my sister to pull her bloody head in.' She sits back and pulls her school secretary look, as if Derek's some wayward pupil sent to see the principal.

'About the dress, Shaz,' he tries again.

'I warn you, don't start me. Ever since Debbie announced her engagement, both of them are on the phone to me all bloody day. How either of them gets any work done is beyond me.' She lowers her voice to a whisper, as if confiding a momentous truth. 'I don't know if the internet is such a good thing, you know. Too much information, too much choice! They're driving me nuts.'

'But I can help,' Derek practically shouts.

Sharon folds her arms across her ample chest, eyes him with suspicion, but remains blissfully silent.

Derek ignores the alarm bells ringing in his head and ploughs on. 'Didn't Debbie tell you? Me and the stitchers are making the wedding dress.' There, it's out now.

Sharon frowns, as if she hasn't heard right. '*Making* the dress?'

'Yes!' He beams at her, his heart fluttering like a little caged bird desperate to be set free.

Sharon drops her chin to her chest. 'A homemade dress.'

It's not a question, so Derek is unsure how to respond. 'What's the difference?'

'You haven't set eyes on her in five years.'

'No, but Jane – the volunteer who runs the sewing group – she went and saw Deb. Measured her up. It's as good as gold, Shazza. You said I needed to show Debbie how much I love her and here we are. Deal's done.'

Sharon looks at him with deep concern. 'Where did this harebrained scheme come from, Derek? You can't seriously think Lorraine, or Debs for that matter, will be impressed by a homemade dress. Not after what you've done,' she adds, with a meaningful look.

'No, no, no, Sharon. You've got the wrong end of the stick. I promise you, it is going to be a beautiful dress. Some of the fellas are seriously good stitchers. You're off the hook. No more emails, no more phone calls.' He chuckles in an attempt to lighten the mood.

But Sharon isn't laughing. She stares at her hands for a long time, adjusting her wedding ring so the stone faces right way up. When she looks back at him, her expression seems sad. 'I'm sure it is a beautiful dress, Derek, but at the risk of sounding rude, if what you say is true, I can't understand why Debbie hasn't mentioned this to me. Or Lorraine.'

She's got him there. Derek doesn't have an answer to that. 'Maybe Debs wanted to surprise Lorraine?'

Sharon rolls her eyes. 'That's one way of putting it. Lolly will be apoplectic if she finds out you're in any way involved in this wedding.'

That hurts, but Derek doesn't dignify it with an answer. It wouldn't matter what he did, Lorraine would always find fault with it.

Sharon stares at the laminate tabletop, chewing her bottom lip. Derek studies the angry pink of her scalp beneath the blonde hair. At last, she lifts her head and speaks. 'It's not often I'm speechless, Derek, but congratulations, you've managed it.'

Derek can't quite meet her eye. She's sapping his confidence, like Lorraine used to do. On one hand, he can understand why Debbie would avoid telling her mother it was him making the dress, given their history. But she should have said something if there were issues. How was he to know the dress was a secret?

Derek shakes off his doubts and draws himself up. 'I can't help you there, Sharon. She's your sister, you figure it out.

And I can guarantee that Debs will have her own reasons for keeping it quiet. But the Backtackers and me are making this wedding dress and that's the beginning and end of it.'

Sharon nods. They sit in silence. It is a bulky kind of silence, filled with uncomfortable lumps. This isn't the conversation Derek imagined he'd have today. And Sharon seems to have aged ten years since she arrived. He feels a bit bad for giving her a nasty shock, but how was he to know she didn't know?

Sharon sighs and gathers herself before she speaks. 'I came to see if you'd had any further thoughts about a wedding gift. But a dress? You're a constant source of surprises, Derek Brown.' And with that, she stands and walks out, her heels clacking across the linoleum floor.

Chapter 22

Jane slips on her best dress, a floral-patterned silk that ends mid-calf with a cowl neck scooped low over her décolletage. It is a little light for the time of year, so she grabs her pashmina and throws it around her shoulders. With a glance in the mirror, she decamps to the kitchen.

'Well, don't you look lovely,' Susannah says, searching through the mountain of paperwork surrounding her laptop. She pulls out a pale green envelope. 'Happy Birthday!' she says, folding Jane in a hug. 'It's a pamper special at the beauty salon in Corondale.'

Releasing her, Susannah fetches a bottle of Champagne from the fridge and pours them both a glass. 'One for the road.' They clink glasses. 'So where's Carl taking you?' Susannah asks between sips.

'Somewhere "special",' she says, using air quotes. 'I've absolutely no idea where, but given how early he's picking me up, it's not somewhere local. And wherever it is, we're staying overnight.'

Susannah raises her eyebrows. 'Flash. He must *really* like you.'

Blushing, Jane changes the topic. 'What about you? What are you up to tonight?'

Susannah gestures to the pile of papers. 'FOYL. Patrick's written me another letter. He says he's started a petition among the inmates that he plans to take to the prison's governor.'

Jane reflects on this week's Backtackers meeting, but can't recall anything of interest outside Derek wrangling the duchess satin for the dress. 'Why's he doing that?'

Susannah sips her Champagne as she rereads the letter. 'You know, advocating for prisoners' rights. We're getting plenty of local media coverage about the closure of the library, but it adds a whole new dimension if we can show it's affecting the inmates' morale. The civil libertarians will be up in arms.'

'But it's only a petition, right?'

Susannah smiles. 'And your point is?'

The doorbell chimes, announcing Carl's arrival. Jane gives her flatmate a long hard look. 'Exactly how far are you prepared to go to provoke Nicholas Fischer?'

Susannah tosses back the last of her Champagne and laughs. 'No comment.'

'Did I tell you how beautiful you look tonight?' Carl asks once the waiter has discreetly served the wine and departed.

'Yes,' Jane says with a smile. 'Twice. You don't look half bad yourself.' Which is true. Dressed in a suit with a gingham shirt and tie in the same shade of purple, he looks good enough to eat.

Carl picks up his knife and fork and carves off a slice of steak. 'So, where were we?'

'The Charity Ball. Giving the keynote address is a real honour, but writing a fifteen-minute speech is much harder than I realised. It's a long way from saying a few words at student graduations in front of a handful of parents, some of whom I went to school with. There'll be hundreds of people at the ball – important people. Every time I sit down to write it, I freeze.'

'I thought you said you were doing a presentation?'

Jane places a morsel of rainbow trout on her fork and tops it with flaked almonds. She pops it in her mouth and savours the buttery deliciousness of the fish. The food is divine. Everything has been divine. 'This place is amazing.'

Carl swirls his wine around the glass and inhales the aroma before taking a sip. 'So it should be. It has three hats.'

And a price tag to match, no doubt. She returns to the matter at hand. 'Anyway, yes, I was hoping to do a slideshow of the dressmaking process, but I haven't heard back from the governor yet about bringing a camera in to take photos, and we're now quite far advanced in the process. If he doesn't hurry up, the idea will be ruined.'

'Don't hold your breath. He's got a million things on his plate. No offence, but I don't think Backtackers is high on his priority list. Let alone wedding dresses.'

'But he's wrong!' Jane clasps her hands together, her meal temporarily forgotten as passion takes hold. 'The dress illustrates how, despite their terrible backgrounds and all the horribleness in their lives, these men are capable of producing things of great beauty.'

'You should write that down.'

Jane picks up her knife and fork, then puts them back down. 'Anyway, I've had a brainwave.'

'Look out.'

'Ha. Ha.' Jane leans forward, making sure Carl is looking at her and not his steak. 'Instead of a slideshow presentation, imagine if I put the actual dress on stage? Then they will see how stunning it is in real life. It will have much more impact than photos.'

In her final flourish, Jane knocks over her wine and a red stain spreads over the linen tablecloth. 'Oh shivers,' she exclaims, scrambling out of her chair to save her silk dress.

A waiter dashes over and begins clearing the mess while another moves Jane and Carl to a different table. He brings over their meals and tops up their wine.

'Sorry,' she says to the waiter once he's done.

Carl grins, amused by her clumsiness. 'That all sounds great in theory, except for one major problem. The wedding is in October. Derek, not knowing that you've lied about taking Debbie's measurements, will have already sent her the dress, so it won't be available for you to borrow in November. Unless, of course, you plan to confess to Derek and he's prepared to forgive you and give you the dress instead, in which case, problem solved.'

Carl's tone declares he knows darn well she has no such plan. Jane studies her hands in her lap, where she placed them to avoid further embarrassment. She can't quite meet Carl's eye as she says, 'I've been thinking about that.'

'I'm all ears.'

'See, I'm assuming Debbie has bought a dress by now and the one we're making will be surplus to requirements.'

'Then why on earth are you making it?'

'You know why. For the men. For Derek …' Jane trails off, skewers peas with her fork to stave off Carl's criticism, because even she thinks she sounds crazy.

But Carl's not done with her yet. 'Barring a major catastrophe, Debbie is not going to be wearing that dress on her wedding day. But if you don't tell Derek the truth, and soon, he will send it to her. He's expecting her to fall over herself in gratitude. And when they both find out you've lied, which they will, what in God's name is going to convince them to lend it to you?'

'I could appeal to their good natures?' Jane suggests with a weak smile.

Carl frowns in disbelief. 'Okay, for the sake of the argument, who's going to model it? You?'

Jane bursts out laughing. 'Me? It would never fit.' She thinks of Joey in that ridiculous hand-me-down bra of June Makefield's – her own modest cleavage certainly doesn't come close. 'I was planning to ask Debbie. I know it will take some convincing, but I think if I could just talk to her without her mother around, I could easily persuade her. Plus, it would be such a great opportunity to show how proud she is of her dad.'

Carl shakes his head. 'What am I going to do with you? Forget about Debbie modelling the dress for you. It's never going to happen.'

'She might feel differently after the wedding.'

'You're overthinking this. If *you* model it, you could wear a cloak over the dress, then fling it off at the end for a big reveal. That would be dramatic. And you'd be standing there looking so beautiful, they wouldn't be able to take their eyes off you.'

Jane's head spins, imagining the picture Carl has painted. He has a point; it would be much simpler than having to persuade Debbie to do it. Then she stops. Carl has been imagining *her* in the dress. The *wedding* dress! She presses her fingertips to her lips to hide her surprise. And, even stranger, the thought doesn't horrify her. She smiles at the gentle man sitting across from her. A man happy to drive more than two hours to celebrate her birthday in this fantastic restaurant. A man thoughtful enough to book the little cottage next door so they can stay the weekend and avoid the long drive home after dinner. Has she died and gone to heaven?

'This is the best birthday I've ever had.' And in that moment she knows that if he asks her, her answer will be yes.

Chapter 23

Derek scans the rec room and spies the Doc at a far table. He makes his way over, and sees the Scrabble board set up, awaiting his arrival. Derek girds his loins and begins to play, opening with VOW. The Doc lays down AZURINE, turning VOW into AVOW and earning a bonus fifty points in the process. Derek sighs. No matter the distractions with FOYL and the library, it hasn't affected the Doc's word power. Maloney joins them, but sits off to one side. He is still reading *Harry Potter*. Not surprising really, as it's a lot thicker than any of his earlier efforts.

Derek manages FEZ off the Doc's Z. He's quite pleased with that. Any way to block the Doc taking advantage of the Z.

'I had a good chat with the gov today,' the Doc says, after playing MYTHS off AZURINE for a triple-word score. He pauses to tote up his points and write them down. 'I presented him with the petition.'

Derek shuffles his tiles, struggling to find a good spot for his Y. 'What did he say?'

'We had a long discussion about the meaning of rehabilitation.'

Derek raises his eyebrows. He's never had that kind of talk with the governor. At last year's annual review, the gov asked him to reconsider his position on seeing the psychologist to help him work through his issues. But Derek doesn't have 'issues'. The last thing he needs is some quack meddling around in his brain, discovering his past life as an Egyptian Pharaoh or, God forbid, discussing the ins and outs of a miserable childhood. For heaven's sake, everyone is unhappy about some aspect of their childhood. If that were the impetus for committing a crime, the whole population would be locked up.

The Doc taps the board. 'Are you going to make your move? I'd like to finish this game tonight.'

Giving up, Derek plays JAM. Not much else to do with a J, a V two Is and an E.

The Doc continues. 'I told him that without access to books, life in here can wear a man down. Better to keep the inmates occupied rather than stewing in their own juices.'

'To which he replied?'

'That there are plenty of other ways for a man to rehabilitate himself.'

Parker joins them and sits there, staring into space. This strikes Derek as odd until he realises what's wrong – no newspaper.

'I reminded him that the queue for any program is a mile long. Look at your sewing circle, Dezza, prime example.'

'You're right there,' Derek answers. 'I was chatting with one of the new blokes, Riley, only this week. He'd been a Backtacker before being transferred here, but it still took him almost ten months to get into our group.' Then he glances at Maloney. It didn't take *him* that long. Why was that?

The Doc studies his rack, either unimpressed with Derek's contribution to the conversation or absorbed in his word craft. 'The gov thinks I'm labouring under the misapprehension that the public care about us having access to books.'

'And you said?'

'I told him he was wrong. I reminded him that learning to read and write allows a man to expand his horizons, develop a trade or gain a qualification. It's money well spent. As opposed to releasing us back into the community the same way we came in, so we'll reoffend and end up back in here.'

'I bet the gov was thrilled to be on the receiving end of a lecture,' says Parker. He doesn't add 'from you of all people' – he's not that stupid.

The Doc chuckles, lays down SHOWERY, and totals his points. 'Anyway, I said that if he wasn't prepared to champion our rights, then I would have to take matters into my own hands.'

'You did not.' As fiery as the Doc's temper can be, even Derek can't believe he'd be brazen enough to question the governor's authority. It's not like *he* closed the town library. Then again, the Doc's parole date is set so far into the future, there's every chance he'll die in here unless by divine intervention. He has nothing to lose.

'So, I told the gov that the guys were getting edgy,' the Doc says, shaking the bag and pulling out a fresh batch of tiles. 'That they're peed off about their rights being violated. I said, "You might be prepared to ignore this petition, but you do so at your own peril."'

Parker's permanent wheeze breaks into a hacking cough. Derek is speechless. Maloney, on the other hand, looks at his book, then across the room at Carruthers.

The Doc follows Maloney's line of sight. 'He's always in the bloody library,' mutters the Doc.

'Even though he buys books himself,' adds Maloney.

'And he's failed the literacy program five times in a row, which is an amazing effort for someone who can read,' Derek says, pointing at the copy of *Harry Potter*.

The Doc scoffs. 'Read? The man's a mining engineer. Of course he can bloody read. I thought he kept failing so he could keep the extra half-day library access.'

Jacko and Ando walk across their field of vision and plonk themselves across from Carruthers. All three men turn and stare at them. Derek drops his eyes to his coffee cup. Maloney lifts the book and shows it to Carruthers, who gives him a thumbs-up. Parker pretends to itch his calf so it's not obvious he's turning his back on them. Only the Doc holds Jacko's eye.

Under his breath, he says, 'The gov said, "I don't care how many signatures you collect, it won't bring back the library books."'

'Yeah, so?' replies Derek.

'And I said, "Next you'll be banning books altogether."' The Doc breaks eye contact and beckons them closer. 'Then the gov got this funny look on his face. He said, "Well, wouldn't that solve a few headaches."'

'Jesus.'

'I reckon there's something fishy going on in the library, and Carruthers is in on it. I think the gov's planning a sting to root it out and, in the process, he's going to cut off everyone's access to the library.'

'He can't ban books. He'll cause a riot,' says Parker.

'He can do what he likes. At least temporarily. All he has to tell upstairs is that it's because he's uncovered a drug ring or whatever.'

'You'll be out of a job, eh,' says Maloney.

Now Derek understands the Doc's strange mood. The poor bloke's been labouring under the misapprehension that the governor supports the library, that he shares the Doc's outrage, when it turns out he doesn't give a stuff. 'What are you going to do?'

The Doc shares a sly grin. 'I will do what I do best.' At Derek's quizzical expression, he adds, 'I am going to stir the pot.'

He turns over the Scrabble score sheet and scribbles down some words. When he's done, he flips the pad around to show them. 'The moment you say books are banned, everybody will listen, inside and out.'

'But they're not,' points out Parker.

'Yet,' snaps the Doc. 'We just agreed it's what the gov wants.'

Derek ignores the list. 'You might get a letter printed in the local paper, but that's about the sum of it.' He expects a dose of the Doc's vitriol in response.

Instead, the Doc simply says, 'Precisely, but you forget we have an ace up our sleeve.'

Derek frowns.

'I intend to pass this intelligence on to Susannah Cockburn. I'm sure FOYL will be thrilled to hear the gov's plans. It wouldn't surprise me in the slightest if the gov was in cahoots with Nicholas Fischer and those two bastards planned the whole thing.'

Derek cannot believe his ears. 'You know that's not true.'

The Doc shakes a finger in Derek's face. 'If you think I am going to take this lying down, you are sadly mistaken. Susannah can handle Fischer and public opinion.' He taps his chest. 'I will deal with the gov.'

And with that, the Doc strides across the rec room, making a beeline for his cell and his stash of stationery, leaving Derek, Maloney and Parker all thinking the same thing: the shit's about to hit the proverbial fan.

Chapter 24

By Thursday, Derek is desperate to get to Backtackers to escape the darkening mood on C Wing. The Doc's been playing Chinese whispers all week, lighting a match with his well-placed words, knowing the rumours will spread like grassfires. Anytime Derek's tried to say a word to the contrary, it only seems to add fuel to the fire. So he's avoided the rec room as much as humanly possible and stuck to sewing and writing letters in his cell. He can't wait for a bit of banter and a few laughs as an escape from the escalating tensions, not to mention his own company.

'It's a violation of our rights,' is the first thing Derek hears as he enters the sewing room. His heart sinks.

'If a bloke uses his own hard-earnt dosh to buy a book, then the gov has no right to refuse him his package,' Mick says, wetting his thumb and threading his needle.

'Too right. I don't know what I'd do if my wife stopped sending me the basics,' Brian says over at the workbench, where he's waiting for the iron to heat up. 'I couldn't stand it if I had to wear prison-issue undies. The thought of all those bums before mine is disgusting. A man has some pride.'

Derek slips into the room and stands beside Sean at the sewing machine.

'Not all packages, you idiot,' Mick replies. 'Just books. Mind you, the way things are going, who knows what bright idea the governor might come up with next? Maybe the buy-up is gunna start stocking Y fronts in every colour of the rainbow. We'll be like fucking Target.'

A chuckle ripples around the room.

'The thing I don't get,' says Sean as he spins thread onto the bobbin in preparation for the day's sewing, 'is that everything we buy from outside has to come from approved retailers anyway, so what's the point?'

'Has anyone heard whether we're still allowed to read to our kids?' Brian goes on. 'Jase and I are right in the middle of the *Ranger's Apprentice* series. He's a teenager for chrissake, if we don't have a book to talk about, all I'll get out of him is the odd grunt.'

'Gentlemen,' Jane interrupts, 'I really want Debbie's dress finished today so we can start on the embroidery and embellishments. I know books are important, but so is our sewing. You're wasting valuable time.'

Astonished, the Backtackers fall silent. But she's not finished with them yet. 'I'm sorry, but it's true. This is neither the time nor the place for such a discussion. You know the rules.'

With that, Jane lays a protective cloth over the workbench, and Derek takes the dress out of its black plastic bag and lays it on top. The Backtackers congregate around it, as silent as worshippers gathered at a shrine.

They've worked like demons these past weeks. Poor Maloney stuck standing on the workbench as Jane moulded him into Debbie's shape. Then it was pin and baste, pin and baste all over again. Sean and Derek feeding the slippery duchess satin through the machine. Brian in charge of the ironing. Mick a much-needed spare pair of hands. But it was worth it.

'It's perfect,' breathes Brian.

'Better yet, we have two months to spare,' Mick adds.

'All that's left to do is sew the hems, then we can tackle the finishing work,' Jane says, straightening the seams. She smiles at the men. What a joy it is to see them so proud, and rightly so. 'Any ideas?' she prods.

'I like Joey's idea of embroidering the skirt,' says Sean, harking back to that long-ago debate about wedding dresses.

Maloney tosses the sandy-haired crim an electric grin.

'Yeah, with the roses,' adds Brian.

Mick sucks on his bottom lip, tilting his head this way and that as he thinks. 'I still reckon we're gunna need some detail on the bodice. It's a bit plain.'

This is met with grunts and head-waggles as the stitchers study the dress.

'Bugle beads might be nice,' suggests Maloney.

'Nah, too gaudy,' dismisses Brian. 'She's a bride, not a drag queen.'

Maloney's smile dims.

Derek feels for him. Without Maloney, this wedding dress caper would have been dead in the water long before they'd even started. 'Well, I think Joey's on the right track,' he says to give the kid a boost.

'It's traditional to include something old and something new,' Jane suggests.

'Yeah,' says Mick, rubbing his knuckles along his jaw. 'Something old, something new, something borrowed, something blue. I remember that.'

'A sixpence in your shoe,' adds Maloney.

'I've never heard of a sixpence in your shoe. What's that for then?' asks Mick.

Maloney rubs his thumb and fingers together and Mick breathes out an ah of understanding.

'It doesn't have to be on the dress itself, but it's worth considering.' Jane's imagination is firing. 'I mean, the bride might borrow her mother's sapphire earrings for instance and that ticks off something borrowed and blue in one fell swoop. But like Joey said months ago, it would be nice to incorporate some meaning into the dress. Like a sort of message, just for Debbie.'

'Blue was my mother's favourite colour,' Derek says, colouring a little at what feels like such a personal admission. The little voice hiding in the recesses of his mind clamours a warning: he's moving into dangerous territory.

Derek keeps his focus on the dress, feeling every pair of eyes glued to the back of his head. Ignoring the little voice, he forges on. 'We'd go on day trips to the country so she could scour those old wares shops for willow-patterned plates and that blue striped stuff. What's it called? Cornishware, that's it.' Then he shuts up because everyone's staring at him, listening to every word. He's said more than he meant to.

Sensing his discomfort, Jane draws the men's attention. 'Well, instead of roses, why don't we embroider some blue flowers on the dress? There are plenty to choose from.'

Brian's face brightens. 'Yeah. You've got cornflowers, delphiniums, periwinkles, irises of course …'

'Forget-me-nots were her favourites,' Derek says to the dress. His head is fuzzy and he can hear his heart pulsing in his ears. The little voice is ringing those alarm bells like a soul possessed. *Not now*, he thinks, wishing he could be alone in his cell, not here talking about his mother surrounded by these men. A memory of the garden as it once was flashes in front of him. His mother on her knees, weeding or planting, humming to herself. Always happiest when she had soil under her nails.

Forget-me-nots were your grandmother's favourite flower, Jane imagines saying to Debbie. *They symbolise everlasting love*, she'll add, to persuade her that *this* dress is the one she should wear on her wedding day. Derek may have just handed her the perfect solution.

Feeling a tantalising surge of possibility, she says to the men, 'Traditionally, people gave bouquets of forget-me-nots or used them to decorate gifts in the hope the recipient would never forget the giver. That's perfect for us, as they are not only blue, but they hark back to something old too.'

Maloney asks Jane for her notebook and pencil. He draws with confident strokes, shading and smudging the pencil on the page with his finger. When he is satisfied, he presents his drawing to the Backtackers.

'We don't want to make the dress look messy with too much fiddly stuff,' he says. 'I reckon we trail the flowers from the point of the train, then up in a panel along the side seam.'

Jane catches on immediately. 'Then it will draw the eye up to Debbie's face.'

'Yeah, exactly. Then if we trail them diagonally from the waist to the shoulder, it will break the line across the bust and make her seem taller and slimmer.'

'Joey, you're an inspiration,' Jane says and she means it. Imagine Debbie in this dress. The blue will match her eyes and the trail of tiny flowers will provide enough visual interest without distracting from the bride herself. 'You really are very good at this, aren't you?'

Maloney shrugs and fiddles with the pencil. Brian and Mick nod. Sean beams at Maloney. Then Jane realises that Derek hasn't said a word. He seems to be miles away. 'Derek? What do you think of Joey's idea?'

On her hands and knees in the vegetable patch, Derek's mother is busy planting seedlings. She turns and smiles at him, one hand shading her eyes against the sun. She waves then returns to her gardening but he can't leave. He loves watching her, the graceful way she moves, her economic gestures. One look from her always floods him with warmth.

'Derek?' Jane tries again.

He turns from the past and tries to swallow the lump in his throat. 'They were my mother's favourite flower, but I don't know what Debbie thinks of them. Maybe we should ask her opinion before we get ahead of ourselves.'

Jane starts. This is not what she wants. Her current plan is for them to finish the dress, then present it to Debbie as a fait accompli. She's confident that when Debbie sees the worth of it with her own eyes, she will recognise the true depths of her father's feelings.

'That's never going to work, is it?' replies Maloney, meeting Derek's eye with a look of complete innocence. 'It's enough your daughter knows we're making her dress. But telling her we're putting flowers on it isn't gunna make sense until she sees it, eh.'

A rush of gratitude surges over Jane. 'Exactly. I think it's nice to have an element of mystery.' She picks up Maloney's sketch. 'To the untrained eye, it can be next to impossible to interpret how a sketch like this transforms into a fully realised design.'

Mick makes himself an unwitting accomplice when he adds, 'Yeah, well, I'm with you on that. The girl's said yes, we don't want to jump the gun here, Dezza. In my experience, women like surprises.'

'Not all of them,' says Les from his corner.

Derek's unconvinced. In his experience, women – well, Lorraine – liked to know exactly what was going on at all times. He'd had no privacy, not even in his own head. She was always asking him what he was thinking, how he felt, and was never satisfied with a 'Fine, thanks,' or a 'Good'.

'Could you at least send Debbie a picture of Joey's sketch, see what she thinks of the idea?' he asks Jane. 'I mean, it's a lot of work to unpick if she turns around and says she hates it.'

Jane's stomach ties itself up in knots. She glances at Maloney, who shrugs and frowns. She lied to protect Derek's feelings, to inspire hope that he could redeem himself in his daughter's eyes. But now his misplaced faith is driving them on a collision course with the truth. And it's all her fault.

'Except, we lose a week while Jane sends the photo, then another week waiting for a reply from Debbie – that's two weeks – and then if she says no, we're back to square one.' Sean looks at them each in turn, checking they are following his logic.

'And we've only got two months to finish the dress. That would leave us five or six weeks at best,' concludes Brian. 'That'll never work.'

'We're cutting it fine as it is,' Maloney chips in for good measure.

Derek looks at the circle of earnest faces, discussing this wedding dress as if lives depended on it. He has the sneaking suspicion he's being railroaded. Part of him wants to insist that Jane asks Debbie's opinion. Part of him wants to follow the path of least resistance and cave in to the Backtackers. He picks up Maloney's sketch. Imagine sewing a secret message onto the dress. Forget-me-nots symbolise faithful love and memories, that's what his mother always told him. On one level, through his sewing, he'd be showing Debbie his faithful love, and reminding her of the shared memories of a happy childhood. And on another level, he'd be wishing her well on a new journey as a married woman, hoping she'll be creating a lifetime of happy memories and enjoying faithful love of her own. It feels right.

He turns to Jane and Maloney. 'Shall we take a look at some colours then?'

Chapter 25

Jane leaves Yarrandarrah feeling rather despondent, her glum mood matched by low cloud and a misty sprinkling of rain, barely enough to dampen the dust. Despite some clever manoeuvring by Maloney, ably aided and abetted by the unwitting Backtackers, she can't escape the feeling that the hole she's been digging for herself has grown another foot deeper. Carl's right. She simply has to find a way to head off disaster. The question is, how?

To distract herself on the long flat road home, she switches on the radio and is surprised to hear a familiar name.

'... and who better to understand the impact of the closure of Yarrandarrah Library than this year's Miles Franklin winner, Charlotte O'Shea. The author of *Pruning the Ghost Trees* today spoke to the ABC about the increasing tensions brewing in her home town.'

Jane recognises the newsreader's voice too. It isn't the local reporter. This is the lady who hosts *Country Hour* on Radio National. She turns up the volume to better hear what Charlotte has to say.

'As a child, Yarrandarrah Library was my refuge. A place to escape from the bullies and the boredom. A place to travel far away from a small life in an even smaller country town. To immerse myself in other worlds. To exercise a right that belongs to us all. This decision to close the library and its outreach services is dirty politics, a human cruelty, and a desperate act.'

Gosh, Charlotte sounds very posh these days. A long way from the shy girl hiding behind her fringe who never said much and never very loudly. Jane turns up the volume again.

'Denying the supply of books to the gaol is nothing short of outrageous. It says we consider prisoners' welfare unimportant. That they are not worthy of such basic entitlements, like the ability to entertain, distract or educate themselves. That what many of us consider a pleasure, to read, is a privilege beyond their due.'

Jane pulls into the driveway behind Susannah's sedan and dashes inside. 'You'll never guess who's on the radio,' she calls out as she races down the hall. But Susannah puts a finger to her lips, urging her to be silent. Together they listen to Charlotte's closing words. 'Libraries are not meant to be profitable in any economic sense. They exist to enrich the human experience. Shame on Mayor Fischer and shame on Yarrandarrah Correctional Centre.'

Susannah leans back in her chair, a satisfied smile on her lips. 'Wow, that was good.'

Jane watches as her friend turns off the recording app on her phone. 'You knew about it,' she says, collapsing into the chair opposite.

Susannah has the grace to look a little sheepish. 'I contacted Lottie via her Facebook page. As soon as I made her aware of what's been going on, she offered to help.'

Jane has a cold feeling in her heart. Susannah has always been competitive, driven to come first whether it was in schoolwork, sport or debating. But she can't fight the feeling that Susannah has lost perspective. This whole election business has hurt her so much, she is blind to the potential damage she is causing. Using the threatened library closure to get back at Nick Fischer is one thing, but dragging the men and women of Yarrandarrah prison into her scheme might cause all sorts of unforeseen problems. 'What do you hope to gain from this?'

Susannah frowns, her gaze narrows. 'There's something going on here. More than closing the library or banning books. From what Patrick's told me, it sounds like the governor has also got a bee in his bonnet about the prison library. I haven't figured out the connection yet but there must be one, mustn't there? Two men, two libraries. I don't know what they're up to, but I intend to force their hand.'

Jane bites her lip to stop the frustration spilling over. She breathes, then says, 'You have to stop adding fuel to the fire, Suze. You have no idea where this could lead.' But even as she says the words, she realises they apply equally well to her own meddling.

Susannah's phone begins pinging notifications in rapid succession. She scrolls through the messages, a smile on her lips. 'Don't worry, Jane, I've got this.' She flashes the screen at Jane long enough for her to see the number of people wanting to talk to FOYL, to Susannah.

'If I'm getting this many calls from the media, imagine how many *he's* receiving,' she says with barely contained glee. 'I'm going to flush out Nick Fischer. Show everyone the real man behind the suit. He's going to regret ever announcing the closure of the library.'

Miserable, Jane makes a cup of tea and takes it to her bedroom. Nick Fischer won't be the only one with regrets. All Jane wants is for Derek and his daughter to reconcile and for Debbie to wear the blasted dress on her wedding day. Is that too much to ask?

Her thoughts drift back to her birthday weekend away with Carl. He never did propose. She'd read too much into what he'd said about her wearing the dress. He really did only mean that she should model it at the ball.

That's another problem that remains unsolved. It's a big enough issue getting the dress to Debbie before the wedding, let alone convincing her to wear it. How is she supposed to persuade Debbie to come and model it for the Charity Ball as well? Forget-me-nots or not?

Jane finishes her tea in one gulp and puts the cup on her bedside table. She turns and stares at her reflection in the mirror as she thinks. Joey's design for the embroidery work is superb. How is it possible that someone so immensely talented could end up in prison?

That's what Connecting Threads is all about. Giving men a second chance. Allowing them to put aside their troubled pasts and find a way to shine. Connecting Threads will be over the moon to have a stitcher of such obvious talents join their Outreach Program. He could even teach some of the volunteers a thing or two.

She smooths down her skirt, imagining the wedding dress complete with the trail of forget-me-nots. That's the most important thing here. To finish Debbie's dress – for Derek's happiness, for Joey's future, for the sake of all the Backtackers who have believed in this project. To show the world this dress that symbolises everything Connecting Threads stands for.

As she stares at her reflection, the image shifts from her in the wedding dress to Debbie. The blue in the flowers picked up by the blue in her eyes. The trail of flowers cutting the line across her bust, reducing it to more modest dimensions. The thought hits her like a thunderclap.

'Of course,' Jane exclaims, clapping her hands and raising them to her lips. Why didn't she think of it before? The answer has been in front of her the whole time. Like all perfect solutions, it is elegant in its simplicity. Jane swirls her skirt around her then descends into a curtsey and smiles at her reflection. 'Truly, I am a genius.'

Chapter 26

At least every three days, Derek gives the top-and-tail a miss in favour of a shower. The infrequency of his showers is not because of his questionable personal hygiene; rather, a visit to the shower block requires a certain level of fortitude.

When he gets there, he nods good morning to the officer patrolling the corridor. Inside, he's surprised to find the block empty given the early hour, and his heart lifts. He puts his towel and wet pack on the bench, removes the soap and shampoo, and turns on the tap. No time to wait for it to warm up – he jumps straight into the frigid water. Five minutes later, he's towelling off when he gets the prickling sensation he's not alone.

He concentrates on drying between his toes, senses on high alert, heart skipping in his chest. Out of the corner of his eye, he sees two blokes, one big, one little, hovering in the doorway. Jacko and Ando.

Derek straightens and knots the towel around his waist. His balls shrivel in their sack and it takes every skerrick of courage to turn and face them. 'All right,' he says, acknowledging their presence with a curt nod.

'All right,' growls Jacko.

Ando looks up at the big bloke, gets the okay, and steps forward. 'You're one of them sewing guys, aren't you?'

Derek switches his gaze from one to the other. He reaches for his deodorant, rolls it on, feigning nonchalance. 'Yeah, what of it?'

A crim enters the bathroom, assesses the situation, and seems to decide he doesn't feel like a shower after all.

Jacko waits until he's disappeared before saying, 'Need a bit of help.'

Derek swallows. Jesus, how the hell did they decide he was up for some dirty work? There must be a queue of blokes a mile long keen to curry favour with Jacko, but Derek Clive Brown is not one of them. 'What do you want?'

Jacko sniffs and hawks out a gob of phlegm onto the bathroom floor. 'I've got a special project in mind.'

Ando grins, dancing on the balls of his feet like some demented puppet. 'Yeah.'

It won't be anything legit, but Derek decides it might be wise to take them at face value. 'Backtackers meets in the education block on Thursday afternoons ...' he begins.

'I know that, dickhead,' snaps the big fella.

Derek shivers, but whether from cold or fear, he's not sure. Standing naked in the shower block with an angry crim is the stuff of nightmares.

Jacko steps forward and jabs Derek in the chest. Derek stumbles and feels the hard edge of the bench jam into the back of his knees. Bending over, the crim picks up Derek's toothbrush where it has fallen to the floor and holds it out to him. Surprised, Derek takes the brush and clutches it, wondering if he can use it as a weapon if things turn nasty.

'See, it's my twenty-fifth wedding anniversary in a coupla months,' says Jacko. 'I thought I'd make me wife something nice, you know, 'cause it's a special occasion.'

Seeing Derek's confusion, he adds, 'Like a cushion with flowers.' He leans in close, hitting Derek with a wave of halitosis that smells like a visit to the tip on a hot summer's day. 'She likes crap like that.'

'Where the hell did that idea come from?' Derek blurts out before his brain has a chance to regulate his mouth.

The big lug looks hurt, then defensive. 'I've seen you and the little poof sewing your fuckin' cushions.'

Ando sniggers, adds a 'Yeah' for good measure.

'It can't be that hard, can it?' Jacko says with all the confidence of a man who thinks the ability to sew on a button is the required skill set for embroidery.

Despite the dire circumstances in which he finds himself, Derek laughs. The idea of Jacko sewing anything is ridiculous. Even ignoring the fact he's missing a few fingers.

'What's so bloody funny?' asks Jacko.

'Nothing. Nothing. But you've got the wrong end of the stick,' Derek says, his voice cracked with relief. 'We don't have a say in what we sew. See, Connecting Threads send us ready-made kits and everyone starts out on simple stuff, like lavender bags. Cushions are a long way down the track.'

He reaches for his t-shirt, but the big man catches his arm. Any attempt at congeniality evaporates. 'Listen here, fuckwit,' he snarls, stabbing one of his few remaining fingers in Derek's face. 'I tried joining your little sewing circle, but it seems I've gotta wait months and I don't have that kind of time to waste. Then I thought, maybe I don't need to join you nannas. Maybe, if I ask Dezza nicely, he'll get me a cushion to sew.'

Derek bites his tongue. He can't afford to laugh in Jacko's face twice. As ridiculous as the thug's request is, Derek's mind skitters to how he can possibly appease him and avoid a thrashing. Maybe he could ask Jane for something simple, like a bookmark.

He can always unpick it and sew it properly later. 'Well, I could try,' he stutters. 'You'll need your own nail clippers …'

'What the fuck for?' snaps Jacko, casting a glance at Ando who shrugs and glares at Derek with his shiny wet eyes.

Derek clenches and unclenches his fist, which has gone kind of numb under Jacko's vice-like grip. 'We're only allowed to use scissors when we're in the sewing room. The rest of the time we use nail clippers to cut the threads. But the thread in the kits is pre-cut so you might get away with leaving the ends dangling and we can tidy them up later.'

Jacko releases his grip and Derek rubs his arm.

'What? The scissors are left in the sewing room?' Jacko asks.

Why the hell would Jacko care about the bloody scissors? Then the realisation dawns on Derek. Jacko's not looking for sewing kits; it's the scissors he wants. Weapons. How's he going to talk his way out of this one?

'Yes. Locked in the scissors box. Only Jane has a key. And the officers. Not me.' *Shut up! Shut up! Shut up!* the little voice screams in his head. It's bad enough he's in trouble; he can't drag everyone else into it.

Jacko paces to the end of the shower block and back, Ando and Derek watching him. Then Jacko repeats the process. Derek risks a glance at Ando, but the little weasel looks as confused as Derek feels.

The thug stands toe to toe with Derek. He's a good head taller than Derek, tall enough that Derek can see the thick hairs sprouting from each nostril and a patch of bristles under the chin that Jacko missed during his morning shave. 'Bring me back a kit about yay big,' Jacko says, indicating the size with his hands, which Derek interprets as roughly that of a small shoebox. 'And I'll give it back to you when I'm finished with it.'

'I can't make any promises …'

Jacko shoves Derek and he falls onto the slatted timber bench. The big man rests one foot on the bench, blocking any chance of a quick exit, and jabs Derek in the chest in time with his words. 'A little birdie told me your daughter's getting married in a coupla months, Dezza. I hear you and that bunch of nancys are working on a wedding dress.' He leans in closer, hitting Derek with another wave of eau de rubbish dump. 'Wouldn't it be a crying shame if something terrible happened to the dress?'

Jacko steps away and stretches out his arms, as if about to envelop Derek in a giant embrace. 'And here's me in the perfect position to help you out. All I'm asking is for you to slip me a couple of tapestries. Ando and me a bit bored now there's no books coming in. Sewing will fill a bit of time. You'll help me out, won't you, Dezza? That's what mates do. They look out for each other.'

'Yeah.'

Derek feels sick. The band around his chest is so tight he can barely breathe. Five years he's spent keeping his nose clean, making himself the smallest possible target. He's a maths teacher, not a fighter. His dad never taught him to be handy with his fists. Said fighting was a last resort, a sign of weakness. But Clive never did time. He's never had to handle himself around men like Jacko.

'I'd hate to think of all that hard work going down the drain.' Jacko shakes his head in mock sorrow, the threat glinting hard in his eyes.

'I don't think Dezza gives a stuff what you think, Jacko.'

Jacko spins around. Derek cannot believe his eyes. Sean fills the doorway, his weight balanced lightly on the balls of his feet. His muscle shirt is dark with sweat. There's a towel slung over one bulging shoulder and his wet pack dangles from a strap wrapped around his fist.

Sean smiles at Derek. 'Better get dressed before you freeze to death, mate.' He saunters over and stands behind Jacko, just out of arm's reach. Not that he need worry. He's got a few inches on the older bloke, and carrying a good fifteen kilos more in bulk.

Jacko must be confident in his ability to go head to head with Sean, though, because he turns around and gives the young crim a look that says, 'You wanna take me on?'

Sean smirks. 'We all know what this is really about, Jacko.'

This stops Jacko in his tracks. 'What d'ya mean?'

'Must be hard, not being able to get your hands on a decent read now the town library's closed. You're gunna have to put that massive brain of yours to work thinking of a better way to sling your gear.'

'Shut ya mouth,' says Jacko.

'Yeah,' says Ando.

Sean polishes his knuckles along his jaw. 'I don't think Backtackers is the opportunity you're looking for, Jacko.' He ambles over to Derek and places an arm over his shoulder. Derek tries not to flinch under the weight. 'Because I'll tell you this for free. We're a team, us Backtackers. If anything happens to Dezza here, me and my mates Mick and Brian will be a bit pissed off.'

Jacko's eyes dart between Sean and Derek. Ando's sneer falters on his lips.

Sean releases Derek and rolls his shoulders. 'So how about you and your little sidekick here go and find something useful to do with your time instead of bothering me mate.'

Jacko's eyes do laps as he assesses the situation before his expression settles into a sneer. 'You know what you can do, O'Brien? I'll give you a hint – it involves sex and travel.'

Sean looks amused, but Derek can see a muscle twitch high in his jaw below the ear.

Jacko risks edging closer. 'Which reminds me, I've been meaning to ask. Does your little boyfriend Maloney know you're only gay for the stay?'

'Yeah,' sniggers Ando.

Sean stares at him for a long minute. With a start, Derek realises he's not surprised to hear that Sean and Maloney are an item.

'I'd be careful where you're heading with that, Jacko,' Sean replies evenly.

'Are you threatening me?' Jacko's confidence is bouncing back. He's circling around Sean, blocking the exit. 'Truth a bit close to the bone?'

Ando sniggers again and moves behind Jacko. Derek notices him slip a shiv out of his sleeve. His guts turn to water.

But Sean stays stock still, his posture relaxed. 'Sounds like you might be the one feeling a bit threatened, Jacko. Worried I might turn up unexpected and request a favour?' He smirks. 'I would, of course, except there's one small problem.'

Sean makes a show of sizing Jacko up, eyes lingering longer than polite on the man's crotch before scanning up to his face. 'You're not my type. I like a bloke who's got something going on between his ears other than filth.'

Jacko's jaw works. Derek can see the panic in his eyes from here. Gay for the stay or otherwise, from what he's seen at Backtackers, Maloney and Sean are willing participants. The last thing any man in Yarrandarrah wants is to be confronted by a crim who's prepared to force the issue. After all, violence comes in many colours, but Sean doesn't strike Derek as that kind of guy. Whereas Jacko's brand of violence only comes in one variety: black and blue.

Eventually, Jacko licks his lips and nods at Sean. 'I'll see you later then.'

Derek watches Jacko and Ando leave. He doesn't realise he's been holding his breath until they disappear from sight and it whooshes out of him in a rush. Dressing quickly, he picks up his damp towel and his wet pack, and faces Sean.

'Thank you,' he says, meeting the young crim's eye.

'Think nothing of it. I'm sure you'd do the same for me,' Sean says with a shrug.

Derek nods, but he knows it's a lie. He's not man enough to stand up to the Seans or Jackos in this joint. He's a lamer, a soft cock, a pathetic loser.

He hurries away before the young crim sees the shameful truth in his eyes.

Chapter 27

'Marriage is the union between two people who vow to love and care for each other for *life*,' the celebrant says, emphasising 'life' as if it were a gaol sentence. Debbie's thoughts flit to her father.

The celebrant offers Debbie a congenial smile, marred by a smudge of lipstick on her prominent front teeth. 'The vows usually say something along the lines of, "it is not to be entered into *lightly*".' Twisting in her plumply upholstered chair, her gaze glides to Ian then returns to rest on Debbie. 'Often couples like to promise they will walk by each other's sides *forever*.'

A glance at Ian proves he hasn't registered the celebrant's point. Instead, when he senses Debbie staring at him, he gives her hand a small squeeze of solidarity.

'And the vows usually include a reference to *fidelity*.'

When neither Debbie nor Ian respond, the celebrant presses her palm to her breast and spells it out for them. 'To be a *faithful* husband and wife *until the end of time*.'

Debbie glances at the page of words containing the vows she and Ian had written together. Words like 'happiness', 'hope' and 'laughter'. She crushes it in her fist.

'Who does that woman think she is?' Debbie explodes, as soon as they are safely inside Ian's car. 'I think we should find someone else.'

Ian puts the key in the ignition and turns over the engine. Warm air begins filling the plush interior. 'Two months out is a bit late to be changing horses, Debs.'

She bows her head and picks at some fluff on her jacket. 'You don't get it. She thinks I'm too young to be getting married. That I'm too stupid to understand this is a commitment for life.'

Ian leans over the console and lifts her chin so their eyes are level. 'If this is your way of saying you want a longer engagement, then say it, Debs.'

Debbie swats his hand away. 'No! No way!' She presses her fingers to her lips and sorts through the mess in her head until she finds the right words. 'I know there's an eleven-year age gap between us, but I think that's a good thing.' She's about to add that she's had heaps of experience with men, but catches herself in time. Last time she accidentally mentioned Ian was not the first, he got a bit antsy. 'You know what you want in life, where you're going. We agreed it's best if we have a couple of kids while we're young and that's easier if we're married, isn't it?'

Ian smiles. 'Three's a better number, that way if there's a falling out two of them will still be talking to each other.'

Ian has two brothers himself, but there's no way she's having three kids. One of each and then she's done. But Debbie's not going down that path again. Instead she says, 'My point is, I think the celebrant has it in for me. Can't we choose someone else?'

Someone who doesn't remind her of her mother. Someone who talks about marriage like it's a joyful prospect.

Ian checks for oncoming traffic in the rear-view mirror, flicks on the indicator, and eases the car out of its parking space. Once on the road, he turns on the radio and hums along to the easy-listening tune.

Debbie takes the hint and stares at her broken reflection in the window, trying to ignore Ian humming in her ear like a midnight mozzie.

They travel the rest of the way in silence until Ian pulls into the staff car park outside Potter & Co. Real Estate Agents. He halts behind her hatchback and lowers the radio volume. 'It's just nerves, Debs. I promise everything will work out fine.'

Debbie gives him a grim smile and pecks his cheek. 'See you tomorrow.'

When Debbie pulls into their driveway, she has to park behind Auntie Sharon's car. She'd forgotten her aunt was coming over tonight to discuss the seating arrangements. That's all she needs – listening to her mother and Auntie Sharon bickering over who should sit where.

She sneaks through the laundry and upstairs to her bedroom, drops her bags and slumps on the bed. In the mirrored sliding door of the built-in wardrobe, her face is blotchy and red. And taped to the glass is a picture of her in the wedding dress.

Debbie takes it down. She's spent hours and hours studying it, trying to reconcile herself to such a dress. It's still a struggle. Too much fabric, too fussy, and now it's too late. Instead of the slimming and elegant dress Debbie had imagined, her mother got her own way. She didn't mind this dress when they bought it, but she's grown to hate it. Every time she pays off another monthly instalment, she wants to kill her mother for forcing the issue.

She thumbs it back onto the mirror and slips off her heels. Unbidden, today's meeting with the celebrant replays like a bad dream. Debbie sighs. She's tired, she's hungry, and she missed Zumba to meet that woman. She hangs up her work clothes and pulls on some leggings and a loose sweater. She pads down the hall towards the kitchen, hoping her mother's left dinner in the oven. She's about to pass the lounge room, when she hears Auntie Sharon say, 'I simply decided it was better not to mention I'd visited him, Lol.'

Debbie steps back into the shadows.

'You went behind my back,' Debbie hears her mother respond. 'Who gave you the right to see my husband without telling me first?'

'*Ex*-husband.'

There is a rattle of ice in a glass. 'And what, pray tell, did you and my *ex*-husband have to talk about?'

Auntie Sharon clears her throat; Debbie cranes forward. 'As it happens, we discussed Debbie's wedding.'

'What?!'

Debbie blinks in surprise.

'Unlike you, Lolly, I think Derek deserves to know his one and only daughter is getting married.'

This is met with silence, but Debbie can imagine the look on her mother's face. It has this way of collapsing in on itself when she is angry or disappointed. Like a blow-up mattress with all the air sucked out of it. The one thing everyone in this family can count on is that Lorraine hates not being the first to know.

Inevitably, her curiosity gets the better of her. 'And what did he have to say for himself, after all these years?'

Debbie edges closer. She can see their reflections in the hallway mirror, but the sisters are too engrossed in their heated exchange to notice her.

'You wouldn't need to ask if you'd ever bothered writing to him, would you?' comes the tart reply.

'Derek and I have nothing to say to each other.'

Sharon sits back in her chair and smiles at her sister. 'Still, it's nice he writes to Debbie so regularly.'

Debbie frowns, mouthing 'What?' and watches her mother to see how she responds.

Lorraine drains the rest of her glass and grips it tight in her fist. 'Derek stopped writing years ago.'

'That's not what he says.'

'And you believe his word over mine, do you? Nice. You've got the loyalty of a snail, Sharon.'

In the mirror, Debbie can see Lorraine going to the cocktail cabinet and pouring herself another vodka. She doesn't offer her sister one, just plonks back down in the armchair, glass in hand. 'So put me out of my misery. Did he have anything useful to say, or were you two just reminiscing over old times?'

Her question lingers while Auntie Sharon squashes a slice of camembert between two wafer-thin crackers and stuffs it in her mouth. When she's done, she says, 'That's right, Lol. If Derek and I hadn't worked together at the high school, you two would never have met.'

'More's the pity.'

Debbie flinches at her mother's dark tone. Doesn't she realise what she's saying? If Mum and Dad hadn't been married, she wouldn't exist.

Sharon flicks a crumb from her lip with her pinky. 'Derek and I discussed his desire to contribute to the wedding. Not financially, of course,' she rushes out to prevent the predictable response.

'I'm all ears. What did he suggest? A set of steak knives?'

'Pull your claws in, Lolly.'

Debbie watches her aunt weigh up whether to share what she knows. Sharon reaches into her enormous handbag and fetches a delicate lace handkerchief. She dabs it at her lips, tucks it in her sleeve, folds her hands in her lap, then drops her bomb. 'Actually, Derek's making Debbie a … wedding dress.'

Debbie gasps and covers her mouth.

'What?!' her mother shrieks.

Auntie Sharon tilts her chin. A smile of satisfaction spreads across her face. 'You heard me.'

Lorraine snatches up her handbag and ferrets around until she finds her silver cigarette case. She trembles as she lights up a fag and inhales the soothing nicotine. 'That stupid, stupid man. Yet another ridiculous scheme of his, thinking he can weasel his way back into our affections. I hope you told him it's too little, too late,' Lorraine snarls, specks of saliva glistening on her lip.

Debbie's heart hammers at a million miles an hour. She rests her head against the wall. Who gave Auntie Sharon the right to interfere? This is none of her father's business. Dinner forgotten, she bounds up the stairs to her bedroom and slams the door. Too bad if her mother and aunt know she's already home. Serves them right. Debbie picks up her phone and pulls up Ian's number. But seeing him smiling goofily back at her from her phone's home screen, she throws it down and storms out of the house.

In the lounge room, Sharon turns to her sister. 'Do you think she heard us?'

Lorraine stubs out her cigarette. Anger gives way to triumph as she registers the concern on Sharon's face. 'You've always been a meddling bitch. But you didn't think this one through, did you?'

Chapter 28

Officer Blackburn meets Jane at reception. They go through the familiar procedure: ID, personal duress alarm, body scan, corridor. Not a word spoken beyond the odd instruction. The woman is all business, but Jane has this creepy feeling. It's not Blackburn, though. There is something going on.

The officers checking the bank of security screens barely acknowledge their presence as the women pass through the airlock. One monitor shows squaddies with dogs, patrolling the security fences, which is highly unusual. Other monitors show Riot Squad teams, dressed in that distinctive gear that make them look like black *Star Wars* stormtroopers, swarming down pathways connecting the various pods of the gaol. Shocked, Jane looks away and focuses on the long white floor of the corridor until they reach the sewing room.

Blackburn unlocks the door and switches on the fluorescent lights. They blink and stutter to life. For some reason, Jane expected the room to look different, but it doesn't. There are the tables pushed together as a workbench. The black plastic bag containing the wedding dress lies on top. The sewing machine sits sheathed in its cover. Next to it is the padlocked box of scissors. Chairs line the wall.

'They'll be here in a minute,' Blackburn announces, unlocking the sewing machine and the scissors box.

Jane nods and places the kits and her sewing tote on a table. She ignores the officer as she starts setting up the room for the day, but she can feel Blackburn's eyes boring into her spine. She's one of those people who thinks wearing a uniform gives her more authority than she really has. But the stout woman annoys rather than intimidates her. 'I could do with a hand,' Jane says tetchily.

Blackburn shoots her a filthy look, but swaggers over to the workbench where the wedding dress lays. Her hands rest on her belt as Jane undoes the knot at one end and carefully peels back the plastic. 'Give the bag a tug and it should slide off,' she instructs. Blackburn does and the dress tumbles with a swish onto the table. Jane catches it before it slides to the floor. 'That was lucky,' she says, determined to control her irritation.

Blackburn scowls. 'Wouldn't matter. You can always dry-clean it.' She picks up the hem and runs her finger over the stitching. 'Pretty, isn't it?' she exclaims, surprising Jane with her approval.

'Yes, yes it is.'

'I'd like a dress like this for my wedding.'

Jane bites her lip to prevent a smile. All she knows about Cheryl Blackburn is that Carl can't stand her. Still, a wedding dress is as good an icebreaker as anything, so she says, 'You should have seen the one I wore at my wedding. Dreadful thing with corsets and layers and layers of underskirts.'

'You married then?' The question is underscored with belligerence, as if Jane's marriage were a crime.

'Was. A long time ago,' Jane hastens to correct.

Blackburn's shoulders lower an inch. 'What happened? Did he dump you?'

Amused, Jane raises an eyebrow. 'No, nothing like that.' Truth is, her marriage was a disaster, but she's not about to share that with Blackburn. Cheryl Blackburn strikes her as a person who'd use whatever ammunition you handed her against you. Jane's probably already said too much.

Jane fetches a paper bag from her sewing tote and puts it on the table, followed by the box of threads from the shelves. The pins aren't in the usual spot. She searches the shelves, keeping one eye on Blackburn, who seems transfixed by the dress. She finds them next to the sewing machine.

The sound of voices in the corridor snaps Blackburn out of her reverie. 'You've done a good job on that dress,' she says to Jane. As she steps towards the open doorway, she turns and adds, 'I might ask you to make mine.'

The container slips from Jane's hand and crashes to the floor, scattering pins everywhere. She kneels among them and starts sweeping them into a pile, grateful for a way to hide her astonishment. Blackburn bustles over to help, but, in her haste, accidentally knocks the bag of tapestries to the floor. 'Whoops-a-daisy,' she says, picking up the bag and putting it back on the table before helping Jane collect the remaining pins.

When they are done, Jane stands and says, 'Congratulations.' She tries to sound as if she means it, but, in truth, she can't imagine this little bulldog in anything as elegant as Debbie's dress. 'When's the big day?'

Blackburn tilts her chin, as if defending herself against Jane's thoughts. 'Yeah, thanks. Soon I reckon. We're waiting for the right time. Y'know how it is.'

Jane doesn't, but the arrival of Mick and Brian saves her from saying so. Behind them stands Carl. She sees the disturbed look on his face and her smile fades.

Returning the pins to the box, she busies herself with sorting through the tapestry kits. The men grab chairs and settle into their favourite spots. Maloney arrives and fetches one of the boxes of tapestry threads. He places it next to the dress and looks around. 'Where's Dezza then?'

Mick looks around and shrugs.

'Sorry, sorry,' comes from the doorway. Derek's cheeks are flushed from exertion. 'Bit busy at the hospital,' he says, joining Maloney.

Mick narrows his eyes. 'What kind of busy?'

Derek glances around and mouths, 'Jugging.'

That sends Mick's eyebrows shooting up into his hairline. Brian looks equally unimpressed. As well they should. Mixing sugar with boiling water makes the liquid stickier and all the more effective at leaving a nasty burn.

'This bloody book-banning's put everyone in a foul temper,' he mumbles under his breath, so Jane won't overhear and tell them off for jail talk.

'Okay, Dezza. Let's look at the colours one last time and make sure you're still happy with what you chose,' Maloney suggests, opening the box of threads and retrieving the bundle stored in one of the compartments. He lays them across the dress.

Derek clears his throat and tries to concentrate. 'I still think we should use a combination of threads. The darker thread will make the flowers stand out when the skirt catches the light. Perhaps French knots in the centre in a golden yellow.'

Maloney picks a range of darker blues and a thread that is not quite gold but has a gleam to it. As he lays them over the fabric, Mick and Brian and some of the other stitchers gather around. From the palest of pastels to almost violet, back and forth they go, switching colours until they agree on the threads to make the flowers.

Maloney bundles them up, glances at Jane, and hands them to Derek. 'Do you want some help with the design, Dezza?'

Derek takes the threads and holds Maloney's eye. 'That'd be good, if you've got the time.'

Maloney smiles. 'Yeah well, I've got a bit on my plate,' he says, indicating the commemorative cushion lying on his chair, 'but I can get you started, eh.'

As Jane unfolds a sheet of tracing paper and spreads it across another table, the cons return to their own stitching and leave Derek and Maloney to it. Maloney grabs two chairs and a soft pencil. Derek sits beside him and watches Maloney sketch a trail of forget-me-nots over the paper.

It suddenly dawns on Derek that Sean is missing and Sean never misses a Thursday. His thoughts return to the shower block. It was a risky strategy, standing up to Jacko. And Sean humiliated the thug by casting aspersions on his prowess in the man department. Or, at least, that's how it looked to Derek. It would have been much better all round if Sean hadn't stood up for Derek. He's not worth the trouble and Jacko's never going to let it go.

For some reason, Jane's thoughts return to the images she saw from the airlock: the fierce dogs, the squaddies. She looks at each of her Backtackers, heads bowed over their sewing, as innocent as lambs. Except what if they're not? How would she know? Maybe there's a reason the men seem so tense. If the Riot Squad are active, trouble must be brewing.

Sean chooses that moment to walk in. Les scuttles behind in his shadow. The young crim reads the room and mouths at Mick, 'What's going on?'

Mick goes to answer, but Jane pulls a chair alongside him and unwittingly splits the pair. She empties the contents of the paper bag on the table. 'So, self-covered buttons, there's a bit of a trick to them,' she begins, trying to whip up some enthusiasm for the subject.

Mick looks at the spill of brightly coloured fabrics and mismatched buttons. 'How's that going to work then? The dress is going to look pretty bloody stupid with buttons of all shapes and sizes.'

Jane curbs the urge to snap at him. It's hardly Mick's fault she's out of sorts. *Breathe*, she reminds herself, then says, 'These are for practice. Given our budget constraints, it's cheaper to buy a packet of plastic buttons and cover them ourselves, and you did say you were keen to learn how.' Jane searches through the sewing machine drawer for a reel of beige cotton.

'Those self-covered button kits are a bit of a rip-off, eh,' says Maloney from his corner of the workbench.

Jane centres a button on a floral scrap and draws a circle around it with tailor's chalk. 'You might surprise yourself, Mick. There's lots you can make out of old buttons.'

'My nanna had a great big jar of them,' says Brian, beaming with fondness at the memory. 'She never threw anything out, that woman. When I was a little tacker, I'd play with them for hours and hours. Matching up the colours and the shapes or making trails all over the carpet. I used to love the gold ones with the crowns on them.' His smile collapses into a frown. 'God knows what happened to them after she died. Mum probably threw them out.'

'Oh, what a waste.' Jane thinks of the drawers and drawers of buttons at the shop. Her grandmother hoarded buttons too, for which Jane is forever grateful.

Brian studies his needlework for a while. When he looks up, there's a tear in his eye. 'I reckon I wouldn't be in here if she'd lived a bit longer. My nan never took crap from no one. It'd be a quick backhander if you ever stepped out of line,' he says, the words wistful with nostalgia.

They all pause to consider this, each reflecting upon their own might-have-beens.

Maloney takes the sheet of tracing paper over to the dress and checks to make sure Derek is paying attention. 'What we do is frame the design and then use running stitch to trace it onto the dress.'

With confident hands, Maloney sets up the fabric, paper and hoop, then picks a sharp needle and grey thread. He anchors the paper to the fabric with backstitch before working running stitch along the line of the design, tracing his pattern. 'I'll get you started on this section and I'll design the next bit while you're sewing. That way we'll be able to see how the design's working as we go, eh.'

Derek pulls his chair over to the workbench and settles into sewing the first flowers onto the train of the wedding dress. He's misjudged Maloney. Thought he was flamboyant, liked being the centre of attention, but he is more than that. More than just a great stitcher.

Soon they are all immersed in their work. The only voices are Mick's and Jane's as she teaches him how to make a small weave around the circle and cinch in the fabric. Eventually, he gets the hang of it and the number of expletives decreases.

They stitch in silence and, before Derek knows it, Blackburn calls time. The men pack up their kits and Jane comes over to help put the dress away while Maloney stores their threads and pattern for the flowers on a shelf above the sewing machine.

Jane farewells the men and watches them head back to their wing, escorted by Blackburn. As she tidies up and locks the sewing machine and box of scissors, her thoughts return to Blackburn's revelations, intrigued by the idea of the woman's impending marriage.

Carl comes in and double-checks she's secured the sewing machine and the box of scissors.

'Does it make me a mean person to wonder who on earth would find Cheryl Blackburn attractive?' Realising that mean is exactly how she sounds, Jane rushes on. 'It's not how she looks; it's her attitude. She's got a real chip on her shoulder. Aggressive one minute, defensive the next, and she never has a pleasant word to say about anyone. Who would want to marry such a person?'

'You never know, she might be completely different away from work,' comes Carl's mild reply.

'You're right, I'm being a cow. Everyone deserves to be loved.'

She waits outside while Carl switches off the lights and locks the door. They walk the long white corridor in silence, Jane castigating herself for her lack of generosity towards Cheryl Blackburn. She can't account for her sudden mean streak.

Carl stops dead in his tracks. 'What the ...?'

Jane looks up.

Carl's face is so pale, she can see each and every freckle scattering his cheeks. She looks around. They are at the airlock. Usually, the officers sit with their eyes glued to the screens. Yet here they are, all standing, hands resting on their belts. Waiting. Behind them stand four members of the Riot Squad.

'What's going on?' she asks, her voice trembling. 'Carl?'

He shakes his head and presses the security code to access the airlock. Once inside, as the door hisses shut, he says, 'I'm sorry, Jane, I don't know.'

The door in front of them slides open and an officer steps forward and propels Jane to the centre of the room. He isn't rough, but the mere fact he is touching her feels like an assault.

'Bags on the table,' he says, indicating her tapestry kits and sewing tote.

Jane does as she is told. Her hand brushes her personal duress alarm. For the first time ever, she wishes she could press the button and call for help.

'This is a routine search of all personnel leaving the premises. Can I ask you, madam, if you have anything you would like to declare at this point?'

Jane manages a small no. She shoots a worried glance at Carl, but he refuses to meet her gaze. He's transfixed by the top of his boots.

'What's this?' asks a guard, holding up one of the tapestry kits.

Confused, Jane looks to Carl, but Carl's no longer there. He's being escorted through a door marked 'Staff only'.

'One of yours?' the officer persists.

Jane nods.

'Why is it taped shut?'

She looks at the plastic ziplock bag. Every Connecting Threads kit comes in these bags because they are easy to open, allowing them to be inspected without damaging the package. But someone has run clear tape along the aperture, sealing it. 'I don't know.'

He runs a finger down a list attached to a clipboard. 'It's not on the list of items you brought in with you today.'

Without thinking, she says, 'But that's ridiculous. I checked it myself.'

The officer slips the kit into a plastic evidence bag and hands it to a fellow guard. 'I'm sorry, madam; you'll have to come with me.'

And with that, he takes Jane to a small white room. It has no windows, nothing at all inside it but a table and three metal chairs screwed into the concrete floor.

Chapter 29

Derek's barely returned to his cell when he hears shouts coming from the direction of the rec room, followed by a loud bang. Someone runs past his cell, then a hand catches on the door jamb and the Doc sticks his head in.

'What are you doing here? Aren't you supposed to be at Backtackers?'

Derek tosses his tapestry on the bed. 'We finished half an hour ago. What's up?'

'The squaddies are all over the joint. It's game on, Dezza.'

Alarmed, Derek joins the Doc in the doorway and scans the corridor.

The Doc wipes sweat from his brow. 'We need to protect our own. Maloney can look after himself. Where's Parker?'

'I dunno. Is he in the rec room?'

'C'mon.' The Doc takes off, assuming Derek will follow. Frankly, Derek would rather stay where he is, but Parker is his best friend and riots are no place for frail old men. Against his better judgement, he hurries after the Doc.

Officers are running the length of the corridor, but they ignore Derek and the Doc as they slip through the gaps. Whatever their business, it isn't with them.

'Double-check the rec room,' the Doc orders.

Derek forces his way through the crims crowding the deck. Everyone wants to see what's going on or spot an opportunity to create havoc. As he passes a cell, Derek sees a bloke heaping toilet paper in the middle of the floor. Another is pulling posters from the wall, shredding them, and adding them to the pile. 'Jesus,' he mutters under his breath.

It's no better two cells down. A crim tears pages from a magazine, adding them to a little bonfire of his own. Derek's seen it before. Setting fires all over the joint triggers the alarm system and distracts the officers from the real game.

From up here, he can see clusters of men around the rec room, but there's no sign of Parker. He clatters down the metal staircase and continues the search, when he receives a tap on the arm. Derek spins around.

'Maloney! Christ! I thought I was about to get domed.'

'Nah mate, not this time. What's the crack?'

'This place is going off. Crims are setting fires upstairs. We need to find Parker and get back to our cells asap.'

'Don't stress, Dezza. Parker knows the score. He's not stupid enough to hang around where there's trouble. He'll be in his cell for sure.'

Derek hears someone shouting his name. He looks up and spots the Doc leaning over the railing, gesturing wildly.

'C'mon,' Maloney shouts and takes off. Derek follows. He knows he's going to pay for all this running later. Maybe he should take a leaf out of Sean's book and use the treadmill once in a while.

Upstairs, they make their way along the corridor towards the last cell. Despite the urgency of their mission, the Doc can't help himself, he stops and yells through a doorway, 'What the hell do you think you're doing?'

Two crims hunch over a small fire. The one shredding pages from a book barely bothers to look up. 'What does it look like, dickhead,' says the other.

The Doc lunges, but Maloney is faster. He grabs the Doc and pulls him back into the corridor. 'Now's not the time, eh.'

The Doc heaves with fury, but gives a curt nod and they proceed. When they reach Parker's cell, the first thing Derek notices is that the door is pulled shut.

'Not good,' mutters the Doc.

'Too right,' Derek adds. The only time their cell doors are ever shut is during lockdown. For the remaining hours of the day, they are wide open. It's the rules.

Maloney scans the corridor. 'No one's looking suss.'

Fear of what they might find on the other side glues Derek to the spot, but Maloney doesn't hesitate. He pulls on the door and it swings open, revealing darkness.

'Maybe the globe's blown,' Derek suggests, more out of hope than anything else.

'Don't be so bloody stupid. LEDs don't blow,' the Doc says, opening the door wider to expand the sliver of light from the corridor.

'Shit,' Maloney exclaims and steps backwards, treading on Derek's foot.

'What is it? What's wrong?' Derek peers over the kid's shoulder and sees Parker slumped on the floor.

The Doc rushes forward and kneels beside the bunk. Derek moves around Maloney towards Parker. Even in this dim light, he doesn't need a medical qualification to see why Parker is so still and silent.

There is blood everywhere.

'He's been stabbed,' says the Doc, pressing two fingers on Parker's neck. 'There's still a faint pulse.' He wipes the blood from his fingers onto his pants, then presses the emergency button above the bed.

'Who would do this?' Derek asks, as the reality of what has happened starts to sink in.

'Look.' Maloney points to the opposite wall where someone has scrawled in large capitals, PAEDO.

A thick pall of black smoke billows down the hall. Derek coughs and moves further into the room.

'Someone's burning more than paper,' the Doc says, ripping open Parker's singlet, exposing a dark mass in his side. 'Grab me a t-shirt,' he orders.

Derek finds one in the locker and tosses it to him. The Doc bundles the shirt against Parker's belly to staunch the flow and Derek glimpses what he must have been like in his professional days: focused, calm, intent on preserving a life.

Beneath the desk, Derek sees Parker's glasses. He bends to retrieve them. The tape has broken and one of the arms is sticking out at an awkward angle. By some miracle, the lenses are intact, but when he tries to re-stick the tape, the glasses fall apart in his hands. He pockets them, his hands trembling almost as bad as Parker's would.

Meanwhile, Maloney searches the cell for a clue as to who did this. He lies on his belly and wriggles under the bunk until all Derek can see is the worn tread on the soles of his sneakers. Maloney swears and, soon after, he slides backwards and clambers to his feet. Held in the hem of his t-shirt is the bloody weapon. Dim as the light is, it's plain to see it's not a shiv, the usual tool for the job. It's a pair of shears, exactly like the ones they used to cut out the wedding dress.

'Well, that certainly narrows down who the likely perpetrator is,' the Doc says drily. He checks his watch and leans on the emergency button. 'C'mon, where are those bastards?'

Derek feels sick. Why would any of the stitchers be stupid enough to single themselves out like this? And snap! His thoughts return to the incident in the shower block. 'It's not a Backtacker. Someone's busted into the education block.'

Maloney's mouth drops open. He tosses the shears on the bunk and bolts out of the cell and down the smoky corridor. Before Derek has a chance to wonder what Maloney is up to, he hears the sound of several pairs of running feet coming from the opposite direction. He gestures to the Doc that they should follow Maloney, but the Doc shakes his head. 'You go. I'll catch you up.'

'You can't stay here by yourself,' Derek protests, scanning the corridor to see if its guards or crims descending upon them, but he can't see anyone yet. 'They'll try and pin it on you.'

The Doc laughs. 'What difference will that make? Let them give me another life sentence. I'm not leaving Parker. No man deserves to die alone.'

Derek starts. He looks at the two men. One dying, the other knowing that, when his turn comes, he will be somewhere within these four walls.

'Prison isn't designed for the ill or the old,' the Doc says softly. 'Men like Parker need carers, not guards. They should have built a nursing home instead of C Wing.'

Derek glimpses the fear in his eyes. That one day his mind or body will fail him, or he will find himself alone and vulnerable. And then it will be the Doc who is lying on the floor next to his bunk, covered in blood.

'Stay safe,' Derek says, then slips into the corridor and takes off after Maloney. As he runs, he sifts through the fragments of information. Whoever tried to kill Parker has to live on C Wing. But why bother breaking into the sewing room and stealing the shears when a shiv would do the job? Surely a Backtacker wouldn't betray one of his own? Nup. His gut tells him that somehow Jacko's involved. And he knows why Maloney took off. He has to catch him. The stupid little bugger's heading straight into trouble.

Derek pulls his shirt over his nose so he can breathe through the smoke. He can barely see his hand in front of him, so he doesn't see the man until he's almost upon him. The man's lounging against the wall, observing the surrounding chaos, coiled tight. Recognition hits Derek in the guts. Their eyes meet and the crim's gaze slides right off him. Because he knows – they both know – Derek hasn't got the balls to challenge anyone, let alone a thug like Jacko.

He runs on, past the unmanned duty desk. Derek shoulders his way through a tide of crims running in the opposite direction. Past cell fires and looters, the wing echoing with the whoops and hollers of mayhem. The security doors separating C Wing from the education block are unmanned and open. Derek pauses to catch his breath and hears the clanging of metal on metal. He looks towards the prison library. Four crims are ramming the door with a metal garbage bin. They stop and glare at him. Derek turns and runs towards the sewing room.

It's quieter down this end, eerily quiet. The damaged fluorescent lights blink and strobe worse than a disco. Derek swears he hears whining, like a kicked dog. He feels his way along the wall until he reaches the door to the sewing room. The noise is clearer now, partly because the door is off its hinges.

'Who's there?' comes out of the darkness.

Bravery has never been Derek's strong suit. He has no inclination to enter a pitch-black room with a whimpering man and God knows who else, hiding in the corners, waiting for his next victim.

'Joey?' comes the voice, high-pitched with hope. 'Did you find someone?'

Whatever his personal feelings, there is an injured man in here. His thoughts return to the Doc, calm in the eye of the storm. Against his better judgement, he enters the room.

He can't see a thing. He can hear the injured man dragging himself along the floor towards him, grunting with the effort. Petrified, Derek pins himself flat against the wall and squeezes his eyes shut.

A hand brushes Derek's ankle. He screams blue murder.

'For fuck's sake, Dezza, you scared the shit out of me,' shouts the guy at his feet. 'Will you shut up? It's me, you dickhead.'

Derek opens his eyes and looks down. A faint halo of hair catches the light. 'Sean? What are you doing here?'

'What do you think I'm doing here?' the sandy-haired crim says, propping himself upright against the wall. 'Turns out our mutual friend found another way into Backtackers.'

Derek squats beside him. 'Yeah, I know.'

Sean rolls his head along the wall to look up at him. 'How?'

'They got Parker with the shears.'

Sean bangs his head gently against the wall. 'I wish Joey would hurry the fuck up.'

'Where's he gone?'

'To find me a fuckin' guard or a nurse. I can't walk.'

Derek notices Sean is clutching his right knee. 'They nobbled you?'

Sean barks with laughter. 'If only. Look further down.'

When Derek does, he wants to throw up. Someone, presumably Maloney, has made a tourniquet out of a remnant of linen from the scrap basket. Below Sean's calf is a bloody mess. 'What … what happened?'

'Fuckin' Jacko cut my Achilles tendon. Let me tell you this for free, it hurts like fuckin' hell.' The breath shudders out of Sean and he clenches his teeth as he struggles to find a more comfortable position. Derek takes off his jumper and balls it up under Sean's knee.

'Thanks, mate,' Sean says, sucking air in through his teeth.

'Why would Jacko do this?'

'The simple answer? He hates poofters.'

Derek's guts roil. 'There's got to be a better reason than that.'

Sean's laugh turns into a groan as pain shoots through him. 'Well, that, and the fact I defended you in the shower block.'

Derek's fear liquifies into anger. 'Then he should have come after me.'

Sean pats his knee. 'That's not how it works and you know it. Anyway, it wasn't about you. Jacko knew I knew.'

'Knew what?'

Sean sighs. 'Jacko was using the delivery of library books to sling his gear. He had Carruthers on the inside and he'd turned a guard to make sure stuff got through security.'

Derek's thoughts immediately turn to Carl. He always thought he was too soft for this job. What if he'd read him wrong?

'When the books stopped coming, he had to find another route. Someone must have told him about Backtackers ...'

'And me being the genius that I am, I told him about the tapestry kits.' Derek sinks in the middle. 'And the box of scissors.'

'You weren't to know.'

Footsteps pound towards them. Out of the semi-darkness comes Maloney, sprinting ahead of a nurse weighed down by a medical kit. He drops beside Sean. 'Sorry it took me so long. It's chaos out there.'

'No worries, mate. You're here now.' Sean manages a small smile.

'Yeah. I'm not going anywhere, eh.' And Maloney rests his hand on the big con's thigh.

Chapter 30

Once the squaddies have got the joint under control, C Wing goes into twenty-four/seven lockdown. Even those in hospital or solitary, Jacko included. While the powers-that-be sort through the mess and deal with the perpetrators, there's nothing for anyone to do but lie on his bunk and contemplate his navel.

Derek puts down his tapestry kit. He's trying to make it last because God knows when they'll return to Backtackers, if ever. He swings his legs over the edge of the bunk and shrugs the kinks out of his shoulders, still a bit sore and sorry after all his exertions. Ordinarily, he loves being alone in his cell, but that's when he had a say in the matter. Now he sees no one and knows nothing. Did Parker survive? What happened to the Doc? Is Sean okay? There'll be merry hell when the Doc finds out about those blokes breaking into the library.

There's no sign of Carl either. A new bloke's handing him his meal trays through the poke hole each day. Percy – his last name, not his first. The crims call him Pecker, which is lame, but kind of inevitable.

By Monday, full lockdown is eased to partial. When Percy opens his cell door, Derek feels like one of those cows you see in videos who've been let out into a grassy spring meadow after being stuck in the barn all winter. He'd click his heels in the air, if he could. But he makes do with a stroll down to the rec room, giving way as some young blokes race past.

Partial means the officers only let out a dozen men at a time. Derek collects his tray and takes great pleasure in taking his pick about where he'll sit. Listening to the level of chatter, it seems everyone's pretty excited to see a fellow human being after three days of their own company.

A tray slides across the table. 'Morning, Dezza. Never thought I'd say this, but aren't you a sight for sore eyes.'

'Doc,' he replies with a small smile. 'What's the news on Parker?'

The Doc butters his toast, spreads it with marmalade, takes a bite, chews and swallows. 'Sorry, Dezza. The stupid bastards hit an artery. Parker had no hope.'

Derek pauses, expecting to feel shocked, sad, something. But there's nothing. Deep down, he must have already known.

'Morning,' mumbles Maloney, slumping into the chair next to the Doc. He picks up a sachet of margarine and flips it between his fingers, reminding Derek of the first time they met.

Derek notes the paleness of his skin and the bruised half-moons beneath his eyes. 'How's Sean?' he asks.

'Sean?' interrupts the Doc.

Derek explains the incident in the sewing room. 'I thought you'd already know. You usually have your finger on the pulse.'

The Doc shakes his head. 'Number one, they've changed the guards' rosters. There's not a familiar face among them and no one's inclined to answer questions. Number two, my usual communication network has been severely curtailed since the gentlemen either side of me are either in hospital or solitary. I might be good at gathering information, but I'm not that good.'

'Fair point.' Derek returns to Maloney. 'So how is Sean?'

Maloney stops flipping the margarine. 'So-so. He'll be on crutches until the tendon heals but, like he says, at least it wasn't his hands, eh.'

'True.' Derek thinks back to that brief glimpse of the intimacy between the pair. He's glad Maloney didn't become the darling of one of the rougher thugs in here.

'I do have some good news to impart,' the Doc throws in, drawing their attention back to him. 'We're all in the clear. Turns out Officer Blackburn has been – how shall I put it – indulging Jacko's intimate desires.'

'You've got to be kidding.' Maloney shudders with revulsion. 'She's got a head on her like a bush turkey.'

'Be that as it may, Jacko had a scratch that needed itching and Blackburn was obliging. Very obliging,' the Doc adds with a smirk.

Derek could do without the image of Cheryl Blackburn and Jacko going at it floating around his head. He distracts himself with a slurp of coffee.

'It gets better.' The Doc's smirk spreads into a grin. 'Apparently, Jacko convinced her they were going to get married.'

'Stop it!' exclaims Derek.

'But she'd lose her job, eh?' adds Maloney.

The Doc laughs. 'I don't think she'd miss working as a prison guard.'

Derek reflects on his chat with Sean. 'Let me get this straight. Jacko's dalliance with Blackburn was so he could get drugs in?'

The Doc leans back and folds his hands behind his head. 'Close but no cigar. When Blackburn was supposed to be checking the books coming in from Yarrandarrah Library for contraband, she was assisting our dear friend Carruthers slipping SIM cards in and out of the books, depending on the direction.'

'SIM cards? What for?' asks Derek.

'Phone numbers,' says Maloney.

'I'm still not with you.'

'Jesus, Dezza, someone who's been banged up as long as you have should know what phone numbers mean. Contacts, all sorts of contacts. Jacko was still running his drug empire on the outside, which means he needed to stay in touch with his subbies. Remind them who was kingpin. That's why the four went over. They were running an important errand for Jacko.'

'And you can't use the wing phones for that,' Maloney adds.

'Not with the kind of sensitive information Jacko had stored on that particular SIM card. Mind you, if Fitzy hadn't been stupid enough to post pictures of himself on social media, he might even have got away with it. But he's never been the sharpest tool in the box.'

Derek's also filling in the blanks. 'Then deliveries from the town library stopped.'

'And they had to find another avenue. Which explains why the gov said banning books would solve a whole lot of problems. He knew about the SIM card racket.'

Derek recalls the incident in the shower. An awful thought sends bile rising in his throat. 'Sean said someone – must've been Blackburn – told Jacko about Backtackers. What if Jane is in on it?'

Maloney frowns at him. 'Nah, you're overthinking it. But whoever was in on this shabby deal, there'll be no more Backtackers until it's sorted.' He absently rearranges the items on his tray.

'Are you going to eat that toast?' asks the Doc.

Maloney shakes his head and the Doc takes his plate.

Chapter 31

Derek's almost back at his cell when the duty officer calls him over and hands him two letters. He waits until he's in his cell where he can read them in private to take a proper look. He recognises his father's trembling script. The other teases him with its unfamiliar cursive.

He puts the stranger's letter on his desk and quickly scans Clive's news. What he reads makes him want to weep with frustration. Usually, his father's frail hand chronicles the minutiae of a shrunken life. But today there is more. He's had a fall. Not a bad one, he says, but he's been laid up this week. He slipped in a puddle of water and went A over T in the loos at the bowlo. He tells Derek not to worry; it's only a swollen ankle. As big as a bowling ball, granted, but he's got the new Candice Fox and Tiddles from next door to keep him company.

The Doc had said the old don't belong in prison where there's no one to care for them. But Clive has ended up with the same fate. Steve won't lift a finger to help him out. If it were up to him, and if they could afford it, Clive would be in a nursing home, out of sight, out of mind. And there's no dutiful daughter to rely upon. Lorraine couldn't stand him, because he was poor and a pensioner and lived in a two-bedroom fibro shack in a street filled with two-bedroom fibro shacks.

Worse, she never wanted Derek to have anything to do with him either. She'd sulk whenever Derek brought Clive over for Sunday lunch, barely hiding her disgust beneath a thin veneer of civility. Her actions rather than her words saying, 'I'm better than you.' It's no surprise she wanted nothing more to do with Clive when Derek went away.

He hopes the neighbours are doing what they can. He'll tell Clive to make sure he rings the doctor so he can access home nursing or meals on wheels or whatever he needs.

Derek picks up the other envelope and sticks his thumb under the gummed flap. Inside are two sheets of paper that look like they've been torn out of one of those spiral-bound notebooks. He flattens the pages on his thigh. 'Jesus,' he mutters, closing his eyes.

He has religiously written a letter home to Debbie every week of the five years he's been locked up. Careful upbeat accounts, absent of any details that might shine a light on his fear and loneliness. No mention of how hard it is to live alongside men who care little for others' welfare or, worse, actively go out of their way to cause harm. Jacko looms large in his mind.

Lorraine only replied the once. Said Debbie was finding it hard enough adjusting to their new lives without his letters reminding her of their reduced circumstances. She told him not to bother Debbie anymore.

Her words had been a knife in the heart. Derek frowns. Had he cried? Well, even if he hadn't shed actual tears, he'd shed them inside.

Lorraine had no right to tell him what to do. It wasn't her cut off from the people she loved. So he'd kept on writing to Debbie, hoping Lorraine would pass the letters on regardless of her bitter words. After all, Debbie's always been their glue and time's supposed to heal all wounds. One day, he'll be out of here and on that day, he will face Debbie with a clear conscience because his letters prove he still cared. This matters more to him than the fact Debbie never writes back. He understands why. Lorraine, that's the why.

Derek studies the handwriting. Though he can still tell it's Debbie's, he can see how it's changed over the years. Debbie's old handwriting had fat letters and little circles dotting her i's and j's. Her words jammed together like biscuits in a tin. Now it's a strong cursive with rounded letters, and y's with loopy tails that hook into the line below. He fingers the paper and wonders what this change says about Debbie's transition to adulthood.

There used to be a set of *World Book* encyclopaedias on the shelf in the lounge room – another of Lorraine's whims. He'd forked out good money for a source of knowledge, which was then largely ignored. Occasionally, he'd pull one out to check a fact or help Debbie with a school project. He'd sit on Debs' bed and read to her about industrialisation or the solar system, while Debbie doodled on her thigh in biro. She hated homework. School was her social network, not a place of learning. She was far more interested in her appearance, the latest trend or whatever being cool dictated at the time. And Lorraine never seemed to worry, saying, 'They pick up more than you realise, Derek.' But he was never convinced. There were plenty of Debbies in his classes – probably more than most, being maths. 'You have to apply yourself if you want to learn,' he'd told her. But the expensive encyclopaedias gathered dust on the shelf.

One thing he does remember, though, is how the *World Book Dictionary*, split into two thick hardback editions, had a row of letters in different styles, one of them cursive, scrolling across the top of the page where the new section began. Seeing Debbie's elegant handwriting, maybe she did eventually get those dictionaries off the shelf. Laboured over her writing, copying the cursive until she had reinvented her handwriting and, in a way, herself.

Clearing his throat, Derek begins reading the words written in Debbie's strong flowing hand. He only manages two sentences before he has to stop. He puts aside the letter and stands at the washbasin, runs the cold tap, and cups his hand beneath it, slurping the water as it escapes through his fingers. Derek scrubs his face and drags a hand across the nape of his neck. Then he picks up his towel and scours his face, avoiding his reflection in the dull metal square that serves as a mirror above the basin.

He returns to his bed and picks up the letter. Derek reads it aloud, hoping to dissipate the power of her words, sharp and to the point.

Dear Dad,

I bet you're surprised to get a letter from me after all these years. Don't worry, I haven't become sentimental. Far from it. I already know you know I'm getting married in October (BTW, thanks for the engagement card!), but I've just found out you're making me a wedding dress!!!! Auntie Sharon told me. I'm still in shock. What are you thinking??? Oh that's right, you're not!!!

You haven't even seen me since I was sixteen years old. You have no idea what my life's been like. I had to change schools; we had to sell the house. All because of you and your stupid addiction.

You used to go on and on about the way Mum spent money, but at least she didn't throw it away. It wasn't your friends talking about you behind your back, saying, 'How dumb is Debbie Brown's dad?'

And what, because I'm getting married, you suddenly think you can make it up to me? How can you be so

stupid? I'm glad you won't be at my wedding. I don't
want you to have anything to do with it.

I hate you for what you did to us. I will <u>never</u> forgive
you. The only wedding present I want is for you to stay
out of my life!!

Underneath she had written *Love Debbie*, but then scratched
out the word 'Love'.

Derek resists the urge to screw up the letter and throw it
against the wall.

Debbie never came to the trial because Lorraine insisted she'd
miss too much school. That was a first. Though he was grateful
Debbie had not witnessed his humiliation. But she came to the
sentencing hearing. Dressed in her pleated skirt, neat blouse,
blazer, and straw boater with a ribbon round the rim. Her
private-school uniform soon replaced by the cheap synthetic
one of Turnley Vale High, a school devoid of Olympic-size
swimming pools, rolling lawns, and computer labs fitted with
the latest technology. Once upon a time, Lorraine had declared
Turnley Vale High unfit for Debbie, attended as it was by the
riff-raff, the newly immigrated, and the lefties who believed in
free education. People like Derek.

Hands shaking, he skims over the words, catching on the
phrase 'stupid addiction'. How can she call him an addict?
Because he liked to go to the club for a quiet beer after work?
It was his way of unwinding, of dulling the noise of a day spent
teaching reluctant children trigonometry and calculus. That's
all it was. A couple of quiet beers and a chat with whichever
member of the committee was loitering about.

So what if a quiet beer included a flutter on the pokies?
There was never anyone at home at that hour anyway. Lorraine
would be ferrying Debbie around to one of her after-school

activities or they'd be at the mall buying another useless piece of tat.

He could easily have gone home via the drive-through bottle shop for a couple of longnecks instead, like Dad used to. Maybe he would have, if it weren't for the memories of Clive slouched over a beer at the kitchen table. A sad old man drinking on his own because one day his wife ran away, never to be seen or heard from again. No thank you. Derek preferred the camaraderie of the club – not that there was much chit-chat among those feeding coins into the machines. He'd sit on a beer for hours, unwilling to leave his lucky machine for a piss or a refill. Mesmerised by the rhythm of pressing buttons and watching the spades and hearts and diamonds spin.

Derek stands at his window and stares out at the patch of quadrangle, willing his pounding heart to still. He can see the junkies, glued in the corners like dust bunnies. Their eyes are hollow, their cheeks sunken. They're twitchy, stinging for their next fix. How dare Debbie call him an addict? He's nothing like them.

He spins around and stares into the dull sheen of the metal mirror. His eyes are clear, his cheeks ruddy but full. He holds out his arm and studies his steady hand. He has a job at the hospital. He has his stitching.

'I'm not a loser,' he shouts at his reflection. 'I'm not my father,' bursts forth and he crumples on his bed, holding the sobs in his chest.

She hates him. She'll never forgive him.

A burning rash of anger engulfs him and sweat pours from his body. Lorraine with her airs and graces and petty snobbery, as if wearing fancy labels makes you a better person. Jesus, she's wasted a pretty penny ensuring she wore all the top brands, from her shoes to her undies to her carefully made-up face.

Her lips twisting with distaste any time he walked in carrying a shopping bag from Lowes or Target. He used to open the credit card statements with trembling hands. Gasp at the tumbling list of shops and dollars.

And Debbie wants to call *him* an addict. Isn't spending your weekends traipsing around the mall spending money on stuff you don't need an addiction? What about lining up at the crack of dawn to get in early on the Boxing Day sales? Buying the latest mobile phone, television, coffee machine. How did they expect him to pay for it all?

Derek didn't have to do the books; there were accountants aplenty among the membership. Too many accountants, doctors and lawyers, like any golf club. But Garry Johns was a penny-pinching bastard who'd preferred to let Derek ingratiate his way into the inner sanctum rather than having to play politics choosing which accounting firm would get the work. Using Derek meant no one was offside.

It took years before anyone noticed Derek's pilfering. A little here, a little there. As the credit card numbers soared, Derek had to grow bolder, but he was never greedy. Maybe not all of the takings from the pro shop made it to the bank. Or the Mother's Day raffle didn't earn quite as much as they'd hoped. Easy to manipulate the gaming machine revenue. False invoices for the caterers. Adjustments to the bar's receipts. The odd losing streak on the pokies never helped, but, the way he figured it, the club got some of its money back that way. He only ever took what he needed. Who would have thought it would add up to almost three-quarters of a mil? The judge threw the book at him. Derek had to be punished for outsmarting the auditors for so long.

Derek flings himself on the bed, burying his head in the pillow to absorb his cries. A sharp corner digs into his cheek.

Sewing for Beginners. He sits up. Studies the old-fashioned black sewing machine on the cover with the name of the machine painted in gold lettering. He thumbs through the pages, releasing chits of paper that drift to the floor. Picking one up, he reads the note he wrote to himself. *Must backstitch first*. His smile is sour. About his feet drift scores of other little notes. Reminders of how desperate he was to do a good job, to impress his fellow stitchers, Jane and Debbie. Derek hurls the book across his cell. It hits the wall and plops into the toilet.

'Shit, shit, shit,' he cries and clambers off his bunk.

Fortunately, the book is too big for the bowl. It is wedged sideways and only one corner is in the water. Derek grabs his towel and dabs at the wet pages. The words 'Violet Dempsey' have bled into a watercolour of faded blue. 'Bloody hell,' Derek mutters. 'She'll never believe it was an accident.'

He fans the pages of the book open on his desk so they'll dry. He'll have to apologise to Jane for the damage, but that's all he'll be apologising for.

Chapter 32

Jane burrows under the doona. It's not the chill of the crisp winter morning that keeps her in bed. She's cocooning, she knows it, but she has every right to wallow in self-pity. In the kitchen, the toaster pops and the kettle rumbles as it comes to the boil. Her phone chirrups announcing an incoming call from Carl. She ignores it. Jane doesn't want to talk to anyone, especially him. She closes her eyes and lets her mind drift.

A gust of cool air slaps her legs. Susannah stands at the end of her bed, the doona in hand. 'Get up. I've made breakfast.'

'Go away, I'm not well.' Jane makes a grab for the doona, but, with a flick of the wrist, Susannah flings it to the floor.

'It's your favourite. Raisin toast with cinnamon sugar. Get up before it's cold.'

Jane pulls the pillow over her head. 'Bring it to me in bed.'

'No way, Jose. You've spent two weeks feeling sorry for yourself. The pity party is officially over.' Susannah fetches Jane's dressing gown from the hook behind the door and dangles it in front of her. 'Now, get up.'

With a sigh, Jane lurches upright. She catches a glimpse of herself in the mirror. Her hair is a medusa mess of greasy curls. Susannah helps her into her dressing gown and slippers. 'That's better. Now, one foot in front of the other. Follow me.'

The plate of hot buttered toast undoes Jane's resolve. She

demolishes it in the time it takes Susannah to pop more raisin bread in the toaster and top up their mugs of tea.

Susannah butters the fresh batch and dumps the plate of toast in front of her. 'We need to talk.'

Jane concentrates on adding honey to her tea.

'I know those accusations were hurtful, but you were cleared of any involvement.'

'That doesn't—' Jane begins to protest.

Susannah holds up a finger. 'Uh-uh. Let me finish. This Cheryl Blackburn woman has lost her job over it, not you.'

'I can't go back, Suze. I feel ...' Jane searches for the right word '... sullied by the whole experience. How can I look the Backtackers in the eye ever again? They'll think I'm a criminal.'

Susannah frowns. 'Did you just hear yourself?'

Jane turns an interesting shade of pink. 'I mean it. I've been lying to the men for months in order to get the dress made. Then I'm caught red-handed for something I didn't even do. It made me realise, you know, that even a white lie can have unintended consequences.'

Susannah shrugs and steals a triangle of toast. 'Everything has consequences.'

'Yes, but what if those consequences get out of control? I deliberately lied to men who trust me. As soon as I tell them the truth about the dress, they are going to hate me. I will never be able to return to Backtackers. My career at Connecting Threads will be over. I'll forget about the Charity Ball. I'll be running a haberdashery shop in some out-of-the-way country town and teaching at TAFE one night a week until I am old and shrivelled and nobody loves me.'

'I'll always love you, idiot. Even though you did steal my Cabbage Patch doll in first class.'

'I gave it back.'

'No, you threw it over the back fence. That's not the same thing.'

'I was ashamed.'

'And listen to you now. Beating yourself up because you're feeling guilty.' Susannah goes to steal another corner of toast, but decides to put more bread in the toaster instead. She turns and leans against the kitchen bench as it cooks. 'Anyway, the riot had nothing to do with you. It was the result of the escalation in tensions over the banning of books.'

Jane shoots her a scathing look.

'Save your filthy looks, it won't change the truth. If Nick Fischer hadn't closed the library and stopped deliveries to the prison, the smuggling ring may very well have continued along its merry way, and you would never have got tangled up in that mess.'

'That's a pretty long bow to draw, Suze.'

Susannah arches an eyebrow. 'I beg to differ. You're not the only one facing consequences for their actions. I admit, Fischer could never have envisaged the chain reaction he set off. The riot has made front-page news across the country. Rumour has it those four going over the wall is linked as well. The Twittersphere is in meltdown.'

The word to describe the look on Susannah's face is glee. The polar opposite of how Jane feels about her meddling. She wishes she could get back under the doona and stay there until after Debbie's wedding, after the Charity Ball, until things calm down. Not Suze, though.

The toast pops and Susannah flicks it onto the bread board. 'I intend to insist upon an extraordinary council meeting to reverse this library closure and restore order once and for all.'

Turning, Susannah sees Jane's miserable expression and softens. She sits back down and places a hand over Jane's.

'Look. No matter how you feel personally, you can't let the men down. They look forward to Thursdays, and so do you. You've made all these promises ...'

'Empty promises.'

Susannah shakes her head. 'You're wrong. You've promised these men you will make this dress. Tell them you plan to make it the centrepiece of your keynote address at the Charity Ball. I bet you they will be over the moon and won't give a toss whether Debbie wears it or not.' She pins Jane's gaze with her own. 'You cannot desert them now.'

Jane slumps in her chair. Susannah's words have found their mark. Connecting Threads has already emailed her to advise they are cooperating with the gaol's internal investigations and to assure her that no charges are being laid against her. However – and this was the thing – they admonished her for not exercising due care and caution in her dealings with the men. Jane isn't stupid. She can read between the lines. They meant she has become too familiar. She needs to put her relationship with the Backtackers back on a professional footing.

The doorbell chimes and Susannah checks her watch before calling out, 'Coming,' and disappearing down the hall. It's a bit early in the day for visitors. Jane hears the murmur of voices and, before she can escape, there stands Carl.

Susannah leaves him hovering in the doorway while she fills the kettle and puts it back on to boil. Then she disappears into the bathroom and shuts the door. The shower is turned on, as is the radio, and Susannah sings along.

'She has no shame,' Jane offers to Carl, as Susannah misses the first of many notes.

Carl smiles and gestures to the vacated chair. 'May I?'

'Of course.' Jane refills the teapot so she doesn't have to look at Carl's sad face. She finds a packet of shortbread creams in the pantry and spills four onto a plate, then puts the biscuits and a cup of tea on the kitchen table.

Carl splashes milk into his mug and wraps his hands around it. 'How are you?'

Jane shrugs and sips her tea.

'I've been temporarily shifted to the women's pre-release unit,' he continues. 'We're having a great old time sharing a thousand ways to use mince. I'm building their repertoire so their kids don't have to put up with burgers or bolognaise every night when Mum gets out.' Carl smiles, but it struggles to reach his eyes.

Jane's not interested in small talk. She's been avoiding Carl for a reason. And now he's sitting in front of her, she won't let him leave until she has the answer to her question. 'On the day of the riot, Cheryl Blackburn told me she was getting married soon.'

Carl gives her a strange look, goes to speak, then decides on a shortbread cream instead. He swallows and washes it down with some tea. 'She was in a relationship with one of the prisoners, Mark Jackson. She was ...' He pauses, considers his words then opts for, 'useful to him. He'd do or say anything to keep her on side, but the brutal truth is Cheryl's not the type to be flicking them off with a stick. It probably didn't take much.'

Despite herself, Jane feels a surge of pity for the woman. To take love at any price, for any value, rather than to be alone. Cheryl Blackburn isn't an island when it comes to selling herself short. What was it her mother said when she found out Jane was seeing Carl? Don't fish off the company wharf. Jane's current circumstances aren't much better. 'Did you know what was going on?'

Carl winces, but remains calm. 'Yes. It was an undercover operation, so we were under strict orders to keep it under wraps. But given what happened, I wish I had warned you to be careful.'

Jane leaps to her feet and retreats to the far corner of the kitchen, as far from Carl as she can possibly get without leaving the room. 'You could have told me to double-check my belongings at the end of the meeting.'

Carl bows his head, presses his thumbs into his eyes. With a huge sigh, he looks up at her pleadingly. 'I was between a rock and a hard place. I'm sorry.'

Jane bites her lip. She will not cry. She will *not* cry.

'I wish we could go back to the night of your birthday and pick up the threads from there,' he says softly. 'I wish none of this had happened, especially when it did, because you and I were getting someplace, weren't we?'

Jane bats away his words. She doesn't want to believe him and, even if she did, it's not possible to reverse time and fix every wrong. Otherwise, they'd all be doing it. 'I think we should call it a day.'

'Please don't do this, Jane. I love you.'

Jane deflects Carl by seeking the view from the kitchen window. Frustration quickly turns to anger. She turns on him. 'What's the point of telling me this now? Didn't the riot make it obvious that we can't be together and work together? It's too …' She tries to find the right word in the jumble of her brain, but all she can come up with is, 'messy.'

'Life's messy. That's the nature of the beast.'

'Not like this it's not.'

'Jane, please look at me.'

Jane glances his way, a small concession. Enough to see that Carl is distraught. Enough to hurt.

'One of the reasons I came here was to tell you that I've decided to resign. I don't think I'm cut out for prison work.'

Curiosity gets the better of her. 'What will you do instead?'

'Go back to my training. Maybe open a little café. Full breakfasts, light lunches type of thing. I always liked cooking, but not the hierarchy of the kitchen, which is kind of ironic given I ended up being a prison officer.'

'Whereabouts?'

'There's plenty of empty shops on the main drag. People must be bored with take-away from the milk bar.'

Despite herself, Jane's first reaction is relief that Carl is not planning to leave Yarrandarrah. She's trying to break up with him, not ride him out of town. 'I'll be telling everyone to eat there. You're an excellent cook.'

'Thanks,' Carl says. He sighs and studies his palms as if reading the lifelines and divining his future. To his hands he says, 'I also thought it might make it easier for you to return to Backtackers, without me hanging around like a bad smell.'

Jane's heart sinks. Even when she tries to do the right thing, it flies back in her face. Carl's words make her feel like a real heel. Now she feels sorry for him. That's not the way it was supposed to work.

Carl stands and jangles his keys in his pocket. 'The Charity Ball's in November. The Backtackers will need to put their skates on to finish the dress in time.'

'It's not that simple.'

'Isn't it?'

Chapter 33

Derek lies on his bunk and waits for a new day to dawn. It's Thursday again. Three weeks since the whole riot fiasco. Two and a half weeks since Debbie's letter. The sky fades to grey, then cracks open, and a faultline of light washes the sky pink. He relieves his bladder, checks the time, and waits for the sun to spill over the horizon.

He eats breakfast alone. No Parker to chat about the weather and read out titbits from the newspaper. Apparently, no family has claimed his body, leaving Parker like lost luggage at a railway station.

The Doc's off gathering forces to defeat Nicholas Fischer in the upcoming council meeting about the fate of the library. Maloney will be eating breakfast with Sean in his cell. Good. Plenty of time to cogitate in peace about this afternoon's Backtackers.

Derek arrives at the duty desk at twelve-thirty on the dot. This will be the first time he's been anywhere near the admin block since he found Sean in the sewing room. An unsettling feeling overtakes Derek as he walks, escorted by Officer Percy. Where they normally turn right, they chuck a left. There are new tubes in the overhead lights, and the walls have been patched but remain unpainted. They stop at the literacy room.

The officer runs a scanner over Derek's tapestry kit, then grunts at him to raise his arms. He gives him a once-over, then indicates Derek is free to go inside.

Derek looks around. Jane has done her best to convert the space into a sewing room. In the centre of the room, two tables have been jammed together to form a workbench. Mick and the others have rearranged the chairs to suit themselves, but there's no sewing machine and there's no Sean.

'Good afternoon, Derek,' Jane says, rising from her chair.

Derek blinks. Jane wears a high-necked blouse with sleeves that cover her wrists. Her hair strains to escape a tight bun and a long skirt ruffles the tops of her boots. The only familiar thing about her is the little pendant watch dangling around her neck and the furrows of concern marking her brow.

He manages a croaky hello.

Jane's fingers drum a nervous rhythm on her chest. She glances at the guards lingering in the doorway and clears her throat. 'How is that commemorative cushion coming along? Almost finished?'

Derek holds out his kit. 'Done.'

'You'll be needing another one then.' Jane takes it and hastens over to a table in the corner. She shoves the kit in the bag without even a glance at the completed piece. No words of praise, no quiet smile. Derek grimaces.

A noise in the doorway snags his attention. Percy is putting Maloney through the same rigmarole.

Forgetting all about Derek, Jane hurries over to Maloney, and whispers, 'How are you?'

The boy shrugs and the furrows in Jane's brow deepen. 'And Sean?' she presses.

'He reckons he'll be back in a week or two, once he can put a bit more weight on his leg.' Maloney scans the temporary sewing room. 'Nothing for him to do here anyway, eh?' is all he says about the missing sewing machine.

He nods hello to Derek, goes over to the workbench, and stares at the black plastic bag.

'Do you need a hand?' Mick asks, laying aside his work and lumbering over. Without waiting for an answer, he unties the knot and the dress slips out. 'She's looking good, mate.'

Maloney thanks him, then asks Jane where the thread box is.

'You gunna stand there all day?' Brian growls at Derek's side.

Startled, Derek switches his gaze between the wedding dress and the spare chair next to Brian and chooses the chair. He stares at the dress with its growing trail of flowers shimmering against the fabric. It truly is quite beautiful. Who would have thought the Backtackers had it in them? Then a voice breathes in his ear: *I hate you, I hate you, I hate you.*

Jane joins Maloney at the workbench and passes him the box of threads. She catches Derek's eye and he looks to the floor. He feels sick. He's been pouring his heart and soul into making a dress for a girl who will never forgive him. *I hate you, I hate you, I hate you.*

'Shake a leg, mate, you haven't got all day.' Mick's sneakers are millimetres from the tips of Derek's own. But he can't move. The poison of Debbie's words trickles through him. He's nauseous with her hate, his own hate, for the man he became. The man he is.

'I can't,' is all he manages as the band constricts around his chest.

'What do you mean, you dumb bastard?' mutters Mick from above.

'Is everything okay?' slides in Brian.

Derek stands up, forcing Mick to step back. He looks around at their depleted numbers. Frank and Vince have been busted back to basic for lighting fires in the riot. The new kid, Jarrod, is as jumpy as a cat in a sack, Mick won't get a decent stitch out of him today. Les is huddled in his corner. The others are bent over their stitching, but they'll be straining to catch every word. His gaze flits from Jane to Maloney and back again. Emotions tumble inside him like clothes in a dryer. Anger, humiliation, betrayal. Derek's had days to prepare for this moment. Calling Jane out in front of the Backtackers makes him sick to the stomach, but he has to put an end to this nonsense. She's left him no choice.

Derek looks Jane straight in the eye, and forces out the words. 'Debbie wrote me a letter.' He pauses to let his words sink in. 'I was a bit surprised to hear that she knew nothing about the dress.'

'What are you talkin' about, mate?' comes from Riley.

'Are you sure? Jane went and visited her in person.' Suresh glances from Derek to Jane.

For her part, Jane goes completely still. It takes every ounce of willpower to hold Derek's gaze, to accept his accusation. The hurt on his face breaks her heart. But she deserves this and won't look away.

Derek shifts from one foot to the other, the faint squeak of his rubber soles on the lino audible in the silence. 'She told me she won't have a bar of it.'

'It's a bit late to be pulling the pin now, isn't it?' says Pete.

'Does this mean the wedding's off?' asks Ahmed.

Derek eyeballs Jane, mustering every skerrick of dignity he has left. 'She made her feelings crystal clear.' *I hate you, I hate you, I hate you* rings in his ears.

Jane has to clench her fists to stop herself burying her head in her hands. The hate in Derek's eyes shrivels up her insides. Finally she glances away, to break the unbearable contact, and sees the dress. The beautiful, beautiful dress. Jane catches Maloney's eye. The poor boy looks done in. Diminished without his veneer of sass and attitude. Younger.

'I'm sorry,' is all she can manage. 'I've been trying to find a way to tell you ...' She trails off. She's been full of promises these last few months, but all Jane's actually done is avoid the truth until it became impossible to ignore.

Derek doesn't bother answering Jane. *I'm sorry.* Is that the best she can do? If she thinks taking advantage of him then tossing him an apology will make him feel better, she is sadly mistaken.

Jane wishes the floor would open up and swallow her whole. Who did she think she was, coming here with her do-gooder intentions, riding roughshod over these men's feelings? Connecting Threads accused her of having been over-familiar with the Backtackers. And they were right. How much does she really know about any of them? She has shown no respect for their lives or their pasts. Who cares if her heart was in the right place? She has single-handedly ruined everything.

Maloney moves from behind the workbench and stands beside Jane. 'It's not all her fault. I knew from the start.'

His words are a sucker punch to Derek's guts. Maloney's one of them. The anger Derek can't direct at Jane, he hurls at Maloney. 'You lied to me? What the hell for? If it wasn't for me, you wouldn't even be in Backtackers. Where's your bloody loyalty?'

'What are you on about?' Mick asks, cutting between the two men.

Derek tries not to laugh. He's never hit anyone in his life and he's not about to start. Not with Percy watching him like a hawk from the doorway. This lot aren't worth being busted back to basic for. 'Are you in on the joke too?'

Mick shrugs. 'I'd love to help you, Dezza, but I've got no fucking idea what you're talking about.' He turns to Jane and Maloney. 'Anyone care to share the big secret? No? What about you, Brian?'

'I'm as much in the dark as you, Mick,' says Brian. He glances at the other men and gets blank stares from everyone.

Mick crosses his arms over his chest and glares at Derek. 'Looks like we're back to you, mate. Care to share what the fuck is going on?'

Derek looks around the sewing room. The one place in his sorry existence that felt safe. Where the camaraderie made him feel a little like a normal person. Where he could be distracted from the fear, boredom and loneliness that percolate through his days. His gaze returns to Jane. She looks distraught and part of Derek longs to put a calming hand on her shoulder. But he can't forgive her. Because Debbie hates him. Jane's meddling has made him a fool in the eyes of the one person in this world who matters to him. Worse, Jane's made Derek look like he was trying to weasel his way back into Debbie's affections, when all he was trying to say was 'I love you'. Jane can't expect him to forgive her for that. He simply can't.

Maloney's fiddling with the box of threads, not looking at anyone. Derek wills the kid to look up, to meet his eye and defend the indefensible. All this nonsense about how the dress symbolises love and hope and new beginnings. It's been nothing but a tissue of lies and deceit. What a stupid idiot he's been paying an ounce of attention to a single word that has come out of their mouths. He feels used and the feeling makes him sick to the core. 'I'm done. This charade is over.'

With that he walks over to Percy and tells the officer he's not feeling well. Percy's not fooled, but he can smell a scene coming and he can do without the paperwork. 'Best come with me then.'

Derek doesn't look back, although the effort nearly kills him. He feels like he's leaving part of himself behind. The good part. The part that made living in this shithole bearable.

Chapter 34

Derek arrived at today's meeting determined to confront Jane and left realising he had just said his goodbyes to Backtackers. She and Maloney had given him no choice. Mick and Brian said they knew nothing about it. The question is, can Derek believe them? Whichever way he cuts it, the trust and friendship that was the backbone of the stitchers has been destroyed. He should feel angry. Instead, he feels cast adrift, like a spaceman untethered from his rocket ship.

Derek looks around the neat confines of his cell. This is it. No sewing to fill the hours. No friendly banter now Parker's dead. He lies on his bunk and wraps himself in his blanket. Safe within its folds, he silently fumes about all the wrongs inflicted upon him and licks his wounds.

He'd stay there forever, except he has to eat and do his shifts at the hospital. These are the only two things that get him out of bed each day. Well, that and the call of nature.

It's on a day when he's working his shift at the hospital that Officer Percy appears out of the blue and says, 'There you are, Brown.'

Derek spins around and knocks his elbow on a shelf, right on the funny bone.

'Did I startle you?' the guard asks, a glint in his eye.

Refusing to let him win the round, Derek shrugs and swallows the salty taste of pain.

'I have some bad news,' Percy goes on, although, to Derek's ears, he sounds particularly cheerful about it.

Percy's a big bloke; his shoulders almost touch the doorframe. Stuck in the small supplies room, his arms wrapped around a bale of toilet paper, Derek has nowhere to go. He braces himself, waiting for the blow.

'Your father's died. Thought you might like to know.' With that, Percy raps his knuckles on the door jamb and spins on his heels.

The words hammer a rhythm in Derek's head. He clutches the toilet rolls to his chest and bursts out of the airless cupboard into the artificial brightness of the corridor. It's empty. Officer Percy has left in a hurry.

He dumps the toilet rolls on the bench outside the cubicles and stares into the polished steel mirror, sees Clive looking back. His father is dead. How? The man had a sprained ankle. What went wrong? Not a word from Steve, no details at all. Only the bald facts: your father's dead.

Derek forgets to load the loo rolls, hose out the urinals or check the soap dispensers in his rush to sign off. When the duty officer questions him, he barks, 'My father's died,' and the officer shuts his mouth. It takes all Derek's willpower to walk, not run, back to the sanctuary of his cell.

How he longs to close the door and secure his privacy. Instead, he lies on the bed, turns to the wall, and closes his eyes. He waits for tears that refuse to come. The single overriding thought is that he is now an orphan. All alone in the world. It frightens him.

His father might have been pretty useless, but he'd had a good heart. And to be fair, his father's failings were no worse than most men of his generation. There was no need to cook, clean, iron a shirt or fold a sobbing child in his arms. That was women's work. And then Maureen ran away, bleaching all the colour from their lives, and leaving Clive to figure out how to raise two boys, one angry, one sad, both lost.

Derek gets a prickling sensation on the back of his neck and shivers. Has he been asleep? Maybe. He rolls over and sits up, the world around him swaying like he's on a ship at sea. There in the doorway is Young Carl. 'What are you doing here?' Derek asks.

Carl chuckles. 'Nice to see you too.'

Derek swings his legs over the side of the bunk, waits for the world to stop swimming. 'Yeah, sorry. I meant, I thought you were working the women's wing.'

'I've taught them everything I know: meatloaf, Swedish meatballs, chilli con carne, chow mein and tandoori chicken burgers. So I'm back here to make sure you lot are behaving yourselves.'

Derek's head remains foggy. He shuffles over to his hand basin, splashes his face and towels off. 'Well, you haven't missed much.' The silence that follows this declaration tells Derek that Carl knows that's a load of BS. 'My dad died,' he amends.

'Yeah, so I heard. I'm sorry to hear that. It must have come as a terrible shock.'

Derek squeezes his eyes tight against a sudden memory of standing at the front gate on his eleventh birthday. He'd checked the letterbox twice for a card. Nothing but the electricity bill and a letter from the motor registry. Him watching the postie tootle down to the next house, tears streaming down his cheeks.

Derek clears his throat. 'Do you know what happened?'

'Heart attack. According to your brother, a mate from bowls found him in his favourite chair.'

Derek can see his father in that chair, the cushions moulded around the bulk of him. The TV remote weighing down the paper, folded at the crossword, on the wobbly side table. 'At least it was quick.'

'There is that I suppose.'

Derek's fingers tingle. He needs his sewing. Something to do with his hands, something to soothe his soul. At a loss as to what to do, he rubs the back of his neck. 'Did Steve tell you when the funeral is?'

'That I don't know. I can check if you like.' Carl runs his thumbs around the waist of his trousers. 'Are you going to ask permission to attend?'

The thought hadn't even occurred to Derek.

'There's no harm asking,' Carl prods.

'I don't like my chances,' Derek says, eyes on the floor. 'It's a seven-hour round trip. They'd have to put me on the milk run.'

What sort of funeral would a man like Clive have? There'd be no one there except him, Steve, maybe a couple of mates from bowls. If they'd read the obituary column in the local rag, someone from the factory might turn up. Not enough people for a wake. Hardly worth the bother of a funeral, with so few to remember him. And Steve would whinge at the expense as a way of reminding Derek that the money was coming out of his pocket.

'At least you could put your hand on your heart and know you tried. Nothing to regret later,' urges the ever-optimistic Carl.

Regrets. Now that's a long list. But Young Carl's standing there, brimming with kindness, and Derek doesn't have the heart to hurt his feelings. 'Okay. I'll ask.'

Carl keeps hanging in the doorway. Derek longs to ask, 'Haven't you got somewhere else to be?', but Carl clearly doesn't since he's dithering about. He pops his head out the cell door, looks left, looks right, then steps back inside. Derek's immediate thoughts are that Carl's about to defend Jane's actions. After all, those two are an item. He's bound to take her side. Except Carl says, 'Look, if you want, I can put in a recommendation for you to see a counsellor.'

'Jesus Christ. As if I'm going to let some nutjob tinker around inside my head doing who knows what damage.' He's done his compulsory counselling. Sitting in that sterile classroom with the chairs arranged in a virtuous circle surrounded by drug addicts. Every single one of them making up excuses for why they ended up liars and cheats and murderers.

'Talking about the past doesn't change anything. Trust me.' Derek hesitates. Clive used to say the same thing. He remembers how his father's lips would zip tight at the mere mention of his mother's name. Not Dad, not Steve, no one wanted to remember Maureen. Except Derek.

Carl looks less than convinced. 'Right. Well good luck with the gov. I'll see you at muster.'

Chapter 35

Derek has no intention of asking the governor for favours. But the conversation with Carl has put him at odds with himself and suddenly his cell feels two sizes too small. He sniffs his armpits and pulls away. Jesus, he stinks. He rolls on some deodorant and changes his t-shirt. Now he's ready to brave the rec room.

When he gets there, nothing has changed. Before him is a sea of men in green, eating, arguing, communing. He spies the Doc, crackling with energy. It's as close to a friendly face as Derek is going to get. He makes his way over.

'Look at this!' the Doc says by way of greeting, shaking a letter in Derek's face. '*The Guardian* wants to interview me. Or in Susannah's exact words, "*The Guardian* are keen to meet the man at the centre of the FOYL campaign." She's written to the gov asking for permission.'

Derek takes the letter and reads the fulsome praise. 'Do you like your chances?'

The Doc laughs. 'Why wouldn't he? It's a good-news story and it might diffuse some of the heat from the riot, not to mention the four going over the wall.' He takes back the letter, folds it along the creases, and pockets it. 'Susannah is a wonderful champion, but imagine if I have my say? I'll be able to tell the world how restricting access to books is dangerous and inhumane.'

The Doc may want to paint himself in a benevolent light, but Derek's not so sure. To his eye, the Doc's motivation seems less about access to books and more about him preening under all this attention. He better be careful. When this FOYL campaign is done and dusted, the Doc might find himself right back in the same place he started.

'Yeah, well, no one likes a tall poppy,' says Derek. 'Opinion could go either way.'

The Doc harrumphs and returns to reading his mail. Derek goes to fetch a coffee and when he returns, Maloney has joined them.

'Guess what?' he begins, staring up at Derek with those big brown eyes, the very picture of innocence.

'Your Aunty's out of hospital?'

Maloney frowns. 'Nah, she got out weeks ago.'

The Doc shuffles his paperwork into a pile to clear some space. 'Is it the TAFE course? You got in?'

'Yep,' says Maloney and palms him the letter. The Doc presses his glasses to his nose and reads.

Derek remembers that Backtackers meeting. How Jane had been all over Maloney like a rash, singing his praises, telling him how a piece of paper would change his life. And bloody Brian egging them on. Obviously, the Doc's thrown his weight behind the scheme too.

'Congratulations, Joey. Well deserved,' the Doc says, folding the letter and returning it.

Seeing them grinning like a pair of fools sours Derek further. All this joy and none of it his.

Maloney taps out a rhythm on the tabletop. He's so wired, he can barely keep his bum on his seat. 'It gets better. The gov's sent my case for review.'

'You're on a roll,' says the Doc.

'If I get early release, I could be out by Christmas! Thanks to you Doc. If you hadn't taught me to read, none of this would have happened, eh.'

The Doc beams at Maloney like he's a prized pupil. Derek remembers the feeling well. 'Hmm, I'm not sure I can take all the credit. You can lead a horse to water et cetera. You're a quick study, Joey. He shows up us old blokes, doesn't he, Dezza?'

Derek drains the dregs of his coffee and crushes the paper cup. 'I'm not sure I'm following your logic here.'

'I mean that your girlfriend Jane obviously thinks Joey has talent, given she supported his application. Then there's all that help he's given you with the dress.' The Doc grins at Derek. 'It's been quite the godsend, that little frock, hasn't it?'

Derek looks from the Doc to Maloney. The kid's head is bowed, his attention focused on running his fingernail along the creases of his letter. Why does he get the sense that the old bastard is having a joke at his expense? 'Don't know what you're talking about. The dress is as dead as a dodo.'

The Doc feigns surprise. 'No! You can't leave the dress unfinished. What a waste.'

Derek is sick to death of the Doc's manipulative behaviour. He's had to put up with it ever since they moved to C Wing, and he's bloody over it. 'Don't you dare lecture me. Debbie doesn't want the dress and what the hell am I supposed to do with a wedding dress? It's not like I can wear the blasted thing.'

The Doc's back at him in a flash. 'For starters, you could raffle it. Maybe sell tickets to the posh lot at that Charity Ball Joey was telling me about. You could use the funds to buy books for the library. I'll even arrange to put a faceplate in them that says, "Donated by Yarrandarrah Backtackers". Wouldn't that be a great legacy?'

'Stuff that for a game of soldiers. You reckon you're so well informed? Did Maloney bother telling you about his little scam?' Maloney's head drops further. He's ashamed of himself, and so he should be. Derek sneers at the soft curls of his head. 'No, of course he didn't. Doesn't want anyone knowing how he was using you, me and Jane. Means to an end, that's all we were.'

The Doc's smirk disappears. 'This is between you and me, Dezza. Leave Joey out of it.'

'I've gotta go anyway,' Maloney replies, scrambling to his feet. 'I promised I'd look in on Sean.'

The Doc waits until he's gone, then leans in close. 'The thing I've always liked about you, Dezza, is that you're a well-balanced bloke. You've got a chip on each shoulder.'

Anger flares in Derek's belly. He's had a gutful of this smart alec.

'Don't give me the evil eye, Dezza,' the Doc admonishes, his smile widening. 'Anyone who cares to pay attention knows you look down your nose at the "real" criminals. "All I did was rob a golf club,"' he says, mimicking Derek's voice. 'Not very original, I admit. Although probably safer than holding up a 7-Eleven, granted. But what you conveniently choose to ignore is that here you are, rubbing shoulders with us junkies and murderers because you too were caught.'

Tension snakes through Derek's body and his hands curl into fists. 'Who the hell are you to cast judgement? At least I'm not serving life for murdering innocent old ladies!'

Spittle lands on the Doc's cheek. He laughs as he flicks it away. 'Touché, Dezza. Touché. But, you see, there's a difference between you and me. I've sat in court, watched those sons and daughters boo-hooing about their poor old mums. The same old duck they never bothered to visit, or visited just often enough to make sure she didn't cut them out of her will.

Because even though they didn't give a stuff about her, the last thing they wanted was for the RSPCA to get the lot. No, they were quite happy paying someone else to wipe her bum and spoon-feed her slop not fit for a pig. Not one of them showed an ounce of gratitude when I put the sad old love out of her misery instead of letting her linger on and on and on, waiting for death to claim her. It wasn't them that had to look into their mother's sad watery eyes every single day and hear her whisper, "I wish I would die."'

Derek burns to smack that insolent smile from the Doc's jaw. The gall of the man to make it sound like he'd done everyone a favour. But the Doc's only paused to draw breath.

'See, I'm not in denial. I can look you in the eye and say, "I'm not sorry for what I did." If I'd euthanised my pet dog, I wouldn't be here. That's the hypocrisy of the situation. But I know who I am. Whereas you think shaking hands with the one-armed bandit sets you apart from the smackies who would kill – ha, who am I kidding, *did* kill – for the sake of a hit. Well, pull the other one, mate. You're an addict just like them. Somewhere in that shrivelled soul of yours is a sad little boy whose mummy didn't love him enough.'

Electrified, Derek springs to his feet. 'Who are you to judge? You're a bloody psycho.' He's sixteen again, finally big enough to get his brother back for a lifetime of taunts and threats and nastiness. 'Gambling's nothing like taking drugs. It doesn't hurt anyone.' But as soon as the words leave his mouth, Debbie screams at him *I hate you, I hate you, I hate you*. And he's there, snot pouring out of his nose, his brother, Steve, holding him at arm's length, while Derek writhes and cries, 'I hate you, I hate you, I hate you.'

The Doc sits there, arms crossed. 'Do it. You know you want to.'

Derek looks around him. They've drawn a crowd. Crims are begging them to start something, blood lust shining in their eyes. The sight scares the anger right out of him and Derek deflates. The Doc can say what he likes, Derek's not one of them. He's never been that kind of man and he never will be.

Exhausted, he pushes his way through the crowd and heads for the stairs. He's desperate to curl up on his bunk and wipe the entire episode from his memory.

'You did the right thing,' Carl says as Derek enters his cell. 'Whatever the Doc said, it wasn't worth it.'

Derek shrugs him off. He's thirsty. He gulps water from the tap, then splashes his face. Derek stares at the man in the mirror, water streaming down his cheeks. He opens his mouth and whispers, 'I hate you, I hate you, I hate you.'

Chapter 36

Derek refuses to leave the sanctuary of his cell. Through the long lonely hours of his self-imposed exile, he relives and reshapes his confrontation with the Doc. All the things he could have said, should have said. How dare that man compare his crimes to Derek's? They are nothing alike. Yet the truth of the matter rises up out of the dark muck of his memories and forces Derek to bear witness.

There he is, pulling into the car park at the golf club, next to the spot reserved for the Club President, often empty on an early weekday afternoon. He makes a point of not hurrying into the club, stopping by the pro shop to study the upcoming games on the board: four ball Ambrose, stableford, mixed rounds. Derek liked to keep his weekends fully booked. Out of the house by seven for a seven-thirty tee-off. He dutifully writes Lorraine's name next to his for a mixed round, wishing it were otherwise. Then he strolls up to the club house, past the putting green, pausing for a quick chat. The bar holds a few old codgers, retired men with no reason to hurry home, worse for wear after an afternoon spent at the nineteenth hole. Derek orders two schooners of ale for himself, then heads to the alley of poker machines tucked discreetly away from the floor of the club.

Two beers and a quiet corner. His ritual. A way to avoid going home to Lorraine's incessant demands and the dreaded letterbox. The relief when it is empty, the clenching when it isn't. The rising panic when he opens those windowed envelopes and unfolds the pages within. The belt winching tight around his chest as he scrolls the extent of Lorraine's excesses, the ever-spiralling decrease in his bank balance, and the criminal interest rates banks charge for the pleasure of keeping him in debt. He's had to start drawing down on the mortgage, forging Lorraine's signature on the documents, because those rates are less extortionate than those charged on credit cards. Robbing Peter to pay Paul. As he transfers another three, four, five thousand dollars into the bank's coffers, the waste makes him physically sick. Each night, he stays at the club longer and longer.

The odd windfall keeps the devil at bay. Elated by the feeling of having a few extra hundred in his pockets, he'd splurge on a bottle of Champers for Lolly on his way home. Then he'd go to the letterbox, open another bill, see the dizzying numbers, and hide the Champagne in the filing cabinet.

'You've got to stop, Lorraine,' he pleads, cutting up her bloody credit cards for the umpteenth time. 'You'll have to increase your hours at work if you want to keep spending like a drunken sailor.'

But new cards appear like magic puddings. It's as if the banks and the department stores have nothing better to do than to give money away. His golf game falls apart, blowing out from single figures to twenty-four. Twenty-four, for heaven's sake. The only sanity in his day is the two quiet beers in front of the machines. Borrowing from the club is the only way to keep the wheels on the show. It's easy enough to do when you're the bookkeeper.

'How could you do this to me?' he pleads with Lorraine.

Derek throws back his head, gasping for air. His chest feels like it's going to explode. Sweat pours off him as if he has run a marathon. He picks up the tail of his t-shirt and presses it to his face. Presses harder to stop his hands shaking. He leans on the desk, sees his stack of stationery, the unfinished letter to Clive.

The words echo in his head. He's heard them before. When Mum left. He's hiding in his bedroom in his striped flannelette pyjamas, the ones with the trains on them. He's desperate for a wee, but he's stuck in the shadows, terrified by his mother's incandescent anger, the bleakness of his father's face. 'How could you do this to me?' his dad asks her.

God help him, Derek loved that woman. How he begged her to take him with her. But she refused.

Derek slumps on the chair at his desk, picks up the stationery and fans the pages. He finds his pen under the unfinished letter. Derek straightens the stack of paper so the edges line up, flattens the pages and begins to write. He writes until the pen runs dry. He finds another and writes on, broken memories cramming every page. He writes of his mother as he prefers to remember her, wearing the long white fur with the blue oriental silk lining that she inherited from her grandmother. Of her gold bedspread with the peacock throw cushions. Of her elegance and beauty, even when she was wearing the cheap synthetic uniform of the local supermarket chain. Of how she'd take his hand in hers and dance across the shag pile, crooning the song in his ear, him drunk on her floral perfume, heady in the warmth of her embrace. Then the back door would whine and Dad's boots would scrape on the wire mat and the magic would disappear in a puff.

She loved him best, she always said. How could she leave him to the torments of Steve and the blank wall of his father?

He writes until his fingers cramp and his stomach clenches in hunger. Somewhere in the middle of a night, the paper runs out, and, as the moon keeps watch, he begins writing on the wall. In the corner where no one will see, along the bottom where the skirting board should be, next to his locker, under the desk, and on the back of the door.

He writes on though his pen has run dry, until it is all said. Then he curls on his bed, exhausted by the act of confession, and sleeps a dreamless sleep.

When he wakes, he stumbles to his feet and looks out the window to see a dawn. The clouds are backlit in pink. They look like a school of jellyfish drifting through the shallows. Derek turns and traces the tentacles of scrawl trailing around the room and feels buoyed by his words. He crawls back into his bunk and sleeps again, his mind wandering free.

Chapter 37

Derek floats up from the sea of memories. He looks at his watch, but the battery's dead. He swings his legs over the side of the bed. When he stands, his pants slip down his hips. He runs his tongue over his teeth. Disgusting. Energised, he strips to the waist and washes his hair, gives all the bits that count a thorough reminder of soap, and brushes his teeth. A lick of deodorant and a fresh change of clothes and Derek Clive Brown is ready to rejoin the world.

The cell door swings open and the officer on duty gives him a quick up-and-down. 'Feeling better, mate?'

Derek smiles at the officer. 'Much better.'

He steps through his day, a lightness in his tread matching the lightness in his heart. That's all he needed: a good night's sleep. Several of them. By the time dinner comes around, he is starving. Derek grabs a tray and finds a quiet spot at the back of the rec room. He's sitting there, eating his meal, minding his own business, when a tray bangs down opposite. Derek's head shoots up and his eyes meet those of Sean.

The crim says nothing. He removes the plate of corned beef, mash, and carrot and pea medley drowning in parsley sauce from his tray. He shakes out the paper napkin and lays it across his lap. Opens the sachets of salt and pepper and sprinkles the contents over his meal. He carefully spears a bit of everything onto his fork and loads it into his mouth. When he finishes chewing, he finally speaks.

'You've been missed at Backtackers.'

Derek plays with his food. The corned beef is overcooked to billy-o and the parsley sauce has congealed into a leathery layer over the meat. The bright spot in the meal is the jelly and custard. But hunger always wins, so he carves off another slice of beef and chews.

Sean breaks his bread roll into pieces and swipes some sauce off the rim of his plate, waiting for his reply.

Derek knows that whatever he says, his words will be reported to the Backtackers, to Jane, so he makes his message clear. 'If you've come to talk about the dress, forget it. There's no point and we've lost too much time between the riot and everything else anyway.'

Sean chews on his bread, washes it down with a slurp of water. 'You know something I don't?'

'I doubt it.'

Sean laughs, loud enough to draw attention from some of the neighbours and a nasty look from the guy on his left. He takes a final swipe at his plate, leaving it cleaner than a dog would. 'What are your plans for the dress then?' Sean presses, swapping his plate for the jelly and custard. 'The blokes reckon we'll need to get a wriggle on if we're going to get it finished in time.'

This stops Derek in his tracks. He'd been working on the assumption that he wouldn't be returning to Backtackers. For starters, it'd be awkward and he's probably not welcome anymore. He's been thinking he might try his hand at woodwork. Cubby houses can't be that hard to make. 'What?'

'It's four weeks to the wedding, Dezza.'

Derek's last mouthful sticks in his throat, glued there by the mash. He washes it down with coffee. 'I'm well aware of that, thanks.'

Sean eyeballs Derek. Derek holds his gaze, though it's killing him.

'Making the dress was never about your daughter,' Sean says.

Derek is slow to hide his surprise.

Sean smiles at this. 'No one ever thought she'd wear the bloody thing. You can't honestly think we're that stupid.'

'Then why?' is all Derek can manage.

Sean discards his spoon and swipes his finger around the inside of the container to make sure he has captured every last skerrick of dessert. He licks jelly and custard from his finger and says, 'We're not animals in a zoo; we've got a choice how we spend our time.'

Derek shifts in his seat. He suspects he's about to be on the receiving end of a lecture and he's not much in the mood for being preached at.

'None of us expected to find salvation sewing cushions and quilts, but let me tell you something.' Sean stabs the air with that same moist digit. 'Before I went, I used to think Backtackers were a bunch of nancy boys, but I was prepared to try anything rather than spend another minute in me own company. Couldn't believe how the stitching ate away at the loneliness rather than let the loneliness eat me. It's a precious gift, Dezza. Not one to give up lightly.'

'Lovely sentiments, Sean, but I'm done with stitching. I've got my job, I'll be fine.'

'Cleaning toilets? The only thing a man can reflect on with his head inside a toilet bowl is how disgusting some people's personal habits are. What are you saying? Aren't we good enough for you?'

'It's got nothing to do with Backtackers. I'm simply being realistic.'

Sean tucks his hands under his armpits and glares at Derek. 'Bulldust. You've cracked the shits because Jane told you a porky and Maloney backed her up. And somehow you think that gives you the right to punish the rest of us.'

The words find their mark, but he'll be damned if he gives Sean the pleasure of showing it.

'I've got something to show you,' Sean says, reaching into his pocket and withdrawing a folded page with a ragged edge where it was clearly ripped from a magazine. He smooths out the creases. On the page is a quilt – a very old quilt, judging from the photo. He spins the page around so Derek can read the caption: 'The Rajah Quilt'.

'You know what this is?' Sean doesn't wait for a reply. 'It's a friendship quilt. Two hundred convicts made this. Crims, just like you and me. It's a beauty, isn't it?' He pauses to admire the photo. 'I borrowed it from the library,' he says without a trace of irony.

Sean searches the lines of text until he finds the spot he wants. 'Listen to this: they only bring it out of storage every few years because it's too fragile to be on permanent display. Imagine that. Anyway, these women were on one of the first convict ships to come out here. Not the First Fleeters, but a later group of ships. And do you know why they called it the Rajah Quilt?'

'Because that's the name of the ship they were on?' guesses Derek, glad to contribute, but wary about Sean's direction.

'Yeah. These women were stuck on the *Rajah* for months on end. Locked in the bowels of the boat in the cold and damp. Only allowed out a few hours a day and mostly then for work. You following my drift here, Dezza?'

'Yes, Sean. I'm following.' A little too well, he suspects.

The big crim grins. 'Good. So some, what d'ya call them, benefactors, yeah, some Good Samaritans, back in England, decide that in order to pass the days, what these women needed was something to stop them going stir crazy.' He leans closer, lowers his voice. 'You gotta remember, most of them were being sent to the arse-end of the world for crimes they didn't commit or for stealing handkerchiefs from rich pricks. I bet they were bloody grateful to have something to keep their hands busy. I reckon even those who didn't want to sew, or didn't know how, realised that the point wasn't to make a quilt. It was about sticking at something in the face of adversity. All them ladies stitching, hour by hour, added up to tell their story. It just goes to prove that beautiful things can come from dark, lonely places, doesn't it?'

Sean pushes the slip of paper across the table and Derek studies it. The central panel has birds swooping around a loose wreath of flowers. There is an exquisite central border of patchworked diamonds and yet more flowers. He can see the women gathered around their growing quilt, stitching and chattering, their heads filled with hopes and dreams. Wondering if this distant island might offer more than fear and deprivation; praying that instead they might find a place to flourish.

Sean retrieves the page, folds it back along its creases and slides it into his pocket. Standing, he finds his crutch and tucks it under his armpit. Before he goes, he offers some parting words. 'That dress is our friendship quilt, Dezza. It's time you made your presence felt at Backtackers.'

Chapter 38

Derek thinks about those poor women as he mops the floor of the treatment rooms in the hospital. Stuck in the hull of a squalid, rat-infested ship for months on end. How did they manage to keep the quilt clean as they worked on it? He moves backwards down the corridor until he reaches the toilets. Someone's in the middle cubicle. Out of habit, Derek makes sure he doesn't look, as the half-door is as close to privacy as a man gets. He sings out hello so the fella knows he's there and keeps mopping. As his mop gets close to the cubicle, he can't help but glance under the door and spots a pair of very familiar sneakers.

'Maloney, is that you?'

When there's no answer, Derek decides to risk a peek over the top. Maloney's fully dressed, sitting on the metal rim, head buried in his hands.

'Jesus Christ, are you all right?'

Maloney shakes his head and sends Derek straight into panic mode. 'What's happened? You look like death warmed up.' He swings open the door and grabs the kid under the armpits. He tries to haul him to his feet, but Maloney refuses to budge. 'Jesus, mate, you've gotta help me here.' Derek squats before him. 'Are you hurt?'

'I'm okay,' the kid mumbles.

Derek's not so sure. For once in his life, he's desperate for someone to enter the toilet block, but the officers stay in the corridors as much as possible and these loos are only for the in-patients, not the general population. He scans the room, searching for an explanation as to why Maloney's sitting there like a broken puppet, but there's nothing.

At a loss, Derek stands – his knees can't take squatting for any length of time. He hovers in the doorway. He'll keep the kid company and talk to him until he feels like sharing his troubles. It's as good a plan as any.

'I'm sorry I haven't seen you for a while, I've been a bit preoccupied.' Derek taps his pocket and takes out the shortbreads he was saving for later. He opens the packet, and snaps a biscuit in two, then realises where he is and slips them back into his pocket. 'I've been reflecting on my problems. You know, what got me in here in the first place, that sort of thing.'

Maloney glances at him. Derek reckons the kid looks pretty pale. 'Do you want me to scrounge up a sandwich and a cuppa? You look a bit peaky.'

'I'm all right.'

Derek nods, but he can't agree. Maloney's hands lay palms up on his thighs, revealing the pads of his fingers pockmarked with tiny pinpricks. 'You're keeping up your sewing then?'

'Yeah. Passes the time.'

'Sure does. Working on anything in particular?' Derek's mind turns to the Charity Ball project. They must have finished the cushions by now.

Maloney tries to ease himself upright, but collapses halfway through the effort.

'Here, let me give you a hand.' Derek grasps Maloney's arms and feels the tug of the dead weight until Maloney gets his feet under him. They end in an awkward embrace. Maloney staggers and Derek tightens his grip. There is so little of him, it feels like he's holding a child.

'Steady there. You've been sitting down too long.' The warmth of Maloney's body is a balm. A sense of peace descends on him.

'Did I tell you I got a letter from my brother, Steve?' Maloney still feels a bit wobbly, so Derek shuffles backwards then eases the kid down on the bench opposite the basins and sits beside him. 'Turns out Dad was sitting on a goldmine. It's unbelievable what people will pay for a quarter-acre block half a mile from the beach. Even one with a fibro shack on it.'

Maloney rests his head against the wall and closes his eyes.

'Steve and his wife are planning a trip to Europe. Vickie's never been overseas, so she's pretty excited.' Derek rubs his thighs as the cold seeps up from the icy floor through his sneakers. 'Means I'll be able to buy Debs a decent wedding present too. I might go to the library, get some ideas.'

Maloney opens his eyes. 'The dress.'

Confused, Derek stares at the kid. 'Oh well, the dress, yes, well, no point thinking about it. I'm sorry I wasted your time.'

Maloney shakes his head. 'Finish what you start. That's what the Doc said.'

'Mmm, I'm not sure that applies in this case.'

Maloney lurches upright, weaves a drunken line to the washbasins. He scoops water into his mouth and pours a handful over his head. He rubs it through his hair, shakes himself like a dog and returns to the bench.

'You haven't told me why you're in here,' says Derek. 'You're not sick, are you?'

'I wanted to be alone.'

Derek looks around the sterile toilet block. 'But you can do that in your cell.'

Maloney yawns and rubs his face. 'I heard back from the gov.'

'Yeah?' Derek brightens for a moment before realising that good news is shared, not secreted away in a quiet corner.

'I got parole. I'll be out in October.'

Derek doesn't know what to say. Early parole is the holy grail, but Maloney's not looking like a ray of sunshine. 'That's great,' he offers.

'I guess. But Sean's still got four years to go.'

The penny drops. Derek searches for words of comfort, but, finding none that fits the circumstances, he keeps his trap shut.

'What if we're not strong enough to last that long apart?'

Derek remembers Jacko accusing Sean of being 'gay for the stay'. He tries to find a diplomatic way into the question, but decides on the direct route. 'Do you love him?'

Maloney looks up at the ceiling, tears leaking from the corners of his eyes. Derek takes that as a yes.

'Well, that's a start.' As unfamiliar as this territory is, Derek tries to put himself in the kid's shoes. It's not that different from him and Debbie. Love is love, in all its shapes and sizes. 'Your Aunty needs you too.'

'Maybe.'

'What do you mean "maybe"? It's all you've talked about for months.' Trouble is, it's a lousy set of cards. Maloney's had his heart set on early release, but he hadn't counted on what that would cost him. Derek tries to bolster the boy. 'The world's your oyster. By the time Sean's out, you'll have finished your TAFE course and you'll have your piece of paper. The pair of you will be facing a bright future.'

'Yep,' Maloney says, the tears flowing now, his shoulders shaking, his hands clenched in his lap.

Derek feels himself well up. He flails about, trying to find something else to say to make things better. 'I don't understand, Joey. You should be happy.'

Maloney shakes his head. 'You know nothing about me. You see the little guy who's a real good stitcher. "Isn't Joey clever how he can read now and how he's got into his course?" But I don't deserve it, eh.'

'Don't say that.'

Maloney picks at the broken skin on his fingertips. Derek wants to tell him to stop, that he'll make them bleed, and he can't afford to get blood on his sewing.

'It's like I've been rewarded for being in prison.'

Derek's antenna goes up. 'I'm not really following you,' he says carefully.

'I got those eight years for a reason. Now look at me. Walking out of here with a lot more going for me than when I came in. All because of other people. The Doc taught me to read. Thanks to Jane, I found out about me course. And if it wasn't for you, I'd never have met Sean. But none of it changes who I am on the inside.'

'I doubt that very much. Leaving here a better man than when you entered is something to be proud of.'

Maloney hunches in on himself, like an echidna curling into a ball. 'Mum and her boyfriend were having a blue. Inside their caravan, screaming at each other. I took a can of petrol from the shed and splashed it everywhere. Lit a match. I just wanted to smoke 'em out.'

Derek holds his breath. He longs to console Maloney, make excuses for him, but the boy's revelations shock him into silence. He thought the kid was in for nicking cars, not murder.

'I was sixteen. Old enough to know what I was doing. But the judge took into account that Mum's boyfriend had beaten the living snot out of me because I refused to sell his drugs to me school mates. Plenty of people knew he called me a useless little shit.'

Derek winces. How many times has he met kids just like Maloney? Violence, drugs, alcohol, poverty. It's a wicked brew that few escape.

He looks at the boy beside him, tears flowing down Maloney's neck, darkening the front of his t-shirt. Derek can guess what happened next.

'Turns out he'd smashed her unconscious. She couldn't get out. I couldn't save her.'

'Did you try to?'

Maloney pulls down the waistband of his pants. Beneath his Y fronts snakes puckered skin. 'The door was locked from the inside. I smashed the rear window, tried to get in that way, but the metal was burning hot, eh.'

Derek digests this. There are so many excuses he could offer right now. You were a young man fuelled on testosterone. You were hurt. Angry. Your mum was in trouble. But Maloney's bound to have heard them all a million times or more. And he knows, from experience, it does bugger all to make you feel better.

Maloney dries his face on the hem of his t-shirt and turns to Derek. 'Making that dress is the one thing I really wanted to do.'

'Why?'

'Wedding dresses are symbols, eh. Love, hope, that kind of shit. My Aunty could sew anything, but the poor woman ended up with four boys – no one to make pretty dresses for.' Maloney chuckles at this, the memories warm in his eyes. 'So she treated every girl who came to her like her daughter. Every detail of every wedding dress was filled with love.'

'She sounds like a beautiful woman, your Aunty.'

'Yeah, she is. See, you all thought the reason I wanted to make the wedding dress was so I could earn brownie points towards getting early parole.'

'Wasn't it?'

'Nah. Okay, maybe kind of. But the main reason was to say sorry to me Aunty. To make a dress so beautiful, she might be a bit proud of me despite what I done.' Maloney sinks in on himself again. 'I thought if I did that, maybe she'd let me live with her when I got out. I've got nowhere else to go, eh.'

Derek wonders how this dress has taken on a life of its own. Everyone's invested in it and each for their own reasons. Sean banging on about friendship. A 'sorry' dress for Maloney. What did Derek want out of it? To also apologise? Or to beg Debbie's forgiveness, show her how much he loves her? Can a dress be all those things and more?

Maloney stands, tucks his hands into his armpits and steps across the small space between the hand basins and the toilet wall.

'Once Aunty made a wedding dress for a young girl from up the coast. A lovely soft grey silk it was. But the girl got hit by a drunk driver in town and died before the big day. Everyone told Aunty not to bother finishing it, said the dress was bad luck. Even I said, "No point now, Aunty." And she said, "There's every point in the world."'

'Yeah, well, I gotta say, I'm with you on this one.'

Maloney waggles his finger. 'Nah, I was wrong. We finished the dress and Aunty put a bag over it and hung it in the wardrobe. Then a few months later, this other girl comes into the shop. Came from a screwed-up family, but a nice girl, eh. She shows Aunty a hundred dollars. I'll never forget her counting it out, one grubby note after another. See, she'd been hiding it from her dad. He used to nick it so he could go down the pub and be the big man and shout all his mates a drink.'

Derek cringes. That sounds like him. He's been blaming Lorraine for all the stuff she kept buying while he was busy chucking it down the pokies. Always the first to shout a round of drinks after golf, never knowing if the credit card would be declined or accepted. They were both as bad as each other.

'Aunty made a fuss of her, took the cash, and told her to come back in a month. Said she'd make her the nicest dress money could buy. The girl was so excited. But you know how much wedding dresses cost, Dezza. A hundred bucks don't go far.'

'So your Aunty gave her the dead girl's dress.'

'Hang on, it's my story, let me tell it my way. A month later, she comes back, eyes like saucers she's so excited. She stands in front of the full-length mirror as Aunty nips and tucks. The whole time, this girl is staring at her reflection, like she can't believe her eyes, eh. Aunty sweeps up her hair and pins it. I dig out a pair of old heels we keep to check the hem length. The girl twirls in front of the mirror, rubbing the fabric between her fingers, saying, "I look like a princess" over and over again. Sent her away to get married in the dead girl's dress, her thinking it cost a hundred bucks. Aunty could have sold it for heaps more. But she said to me, "That's why you finish what you start, because you never know what good it can do."'

'Did the girl ever find out the truth?'

'Nah, that would've spoilt it for her, eh.'

Derek goes to say more, but Maloney cuts across him. 'I know what you're gunna say, but you're wrong. You only started this dress because you thought your daughter wanted it. And when she cracked it, you gave up in a huff. Left me and all the other stitchers hanging. Well, too bad, so sad. Just because she hurt your feelings didn't give you the right to hurt ours. And what's the use of a half-finished dress? Your daughter may not wear it, but someone will. Some girl who's saved every penny so she can wear a nice dress on her wedding day. And who knows, maybe there's still a small chance your daughter will wear it on hers – but there won't be any chance at all if you don't finish it.'

Derek's cheeks burn. 'It's too late. The wedding's just weeks away. We'd never get it done in time.'

Maloney's familiar smile spreads across his face. 'Says you sounding so sure.'

'What d'you mean?'

Maloney jerks his thumb at the door. 'C'mon.'

Derek can't believe his eyes when he steps inside Maloney's cell. Beautiful waifs modelling haute couture cover the walls. He studies them more closely and realises Maloney has drawn on the pictures. Arrows point to waistlines and there are scrawled comments about fabrics and cuts. Beside them are sketches showing variations of the same dresses, but with different necklines and trims.

'I never knew you could draw,' says Derek.

Maloney crouches down and drags a black plastic bag from beneath his bunk. He lays it on the bed, unties the knot and slides it off, smoothing the creases of the dress. Debbie's dress. Except it's not. Or at least, not the dress Derek remembers. An exquisite pattern of forget-me-nots trails along the hem and up the side panel of the skirt. Soft blues and touches of navy and gold are wreathed together until they gather in a bouquet at the hip.

'I haven't finished yet,' Maloney says.

Derek stares at the dress. 'When did you do this?'

Maloney shrugs. 'At night. Nothing better to do. Like I said, I like to finish a job.'

'But I told you not to bother.'

'Yeah, well, I figured that since none of the Backtackers had ever made a dress, we may as well keep going. So they could see the end result. This dress has a bit of all of us in it.' Maloney turns over the dress and points at a row of self-covered buttons. 'Mick did these.' A trail of tiny forget-me-nots stitched in the same white as the dress curl around the buttons. 'And Sean's been working on the veil. It's one of those ones that hangs all the way to the floor. He's been putting a spray of flowers on it. Lucky he's patient. It's pretty fiddly work.'

Maloney's generosity, and that of all of the Backtackers, humbles Derek. He's embarrassed by his petulance. 'I don't know what to say.'

'I reckon you should ask Jane to take a photo and send it to your daughter. She might change her mind.'

Derek smiles at Maloney's eternal optimism. 'Debbie's pretty stubborn. I don't think even a dress this beautiful will change her mind about wearing it.'

'I meant change her mind about *you*.'

Derek blinks. For a moment, he dares to imagine Debbie's face if she did lay eyes on this dress. Sean's words come back to him. How things of beauty can come from dark, lonely places.

'It doesn't matter that you didn't make it by yourself, Dezza. If it weren't for you, this dress wouldn't even exist. You let us help you and look what we can do.'

Derek shakes his head, surprised at the sudden lump in his throat. 'It isn't right. I don't care what your Aunty says. That girl who bought the dead girl's dress was desperate. Debbie ...' He hesitates. Maybe Maloney is right when he says the dress is a 'sorry' dress. But you can't say sorry to someone and expect them to accept it. They've got to be able to tell that you really mean it. 'Debbie hates me. Nothing I can do will ever change her mind about that.'

Maloney snaps the plastic bag over the dress, reties the knot, and slides the bag beneath his bed. When he turns around, hurt is written all over his face.

'Don't look at me like that,' says Derek. 'I can't give her the dress, Joey. It's not right. It's me who's sorry. Debbie will never appreciate all the love poured into it.'

'So it's better to leave it in a plastic bag to grow mouldy?'

'I don't know how many different ways I can say the same thing. It doesn't matter that it's the most beautiful dress in the world, she will never wear it.'

Maloney sinks onto the bed. 'I think you're making a big mistake.'

'That's why we're here, mate. To pay for our mistakes.'

Maloney shoots him a scathing look. 'What about Jane? Don't you think you owe it to her?'

'Jane? The woman lied to me.'

Maloney jumps to his feet and faces Derek. 'Who are you to judge?! Jane was just trying to help. You can't hold that against her.'

Derek's thoughts turn again to the Rajah Quilt, and those poor women who lived in much worse conditions than he endures. Their futures uncertain, their families torn apart by their desperate actions. Their dreams were invested in every stitch of that quilt. Every bird and flower, a symbol of hope. Maybe, in a roundabout way, that's what forgiveness means: never giving up hope that things will be better.

He looks at the boy before him. A complicated boy with a heart as big as an ocean. Derek will never be able to repay Maloney for what he's done. Worse, he's going to miss the cheeky bugger when he's gone.

'I think you've underestimated your Aunty,' says Derek. 'You don't need to prove anything to her. From everything you've told me about her, she cares a lot about you.'

'I killed her sister.'

Derek contemplates this. It's one thing to strive to make a better man of yourself; it's another thing to expect to be forgiven for past crimes because of it. 'You need to show her who you've become. That's the best way to say sorry.'

'That's why I have to finish the dress. To prove there's still some good in me.'

'Blind Freddie can see the good in you, Joey. She doesn't need a dress for that.'

Maloney crosses his arms and arches an eyebrow. 'I could say the same about you.'

Chapter 39

The FOYL campaign is victorious. Derek leans against his cell door and watches the Doc parade along the deck like a conquering hero, complete with a mob of sycophants trumpeting his success. He's not close enough to hear what they're saying, but he is curious enough to follow the crowd down to the rec room.

Derek finds a spare spot up against the wall. He can barely see the telly over all the heads and it takes the familiar theme tune of the ABC News for the chatter to subside. Anchorwoman Jocasta Delaney begins.

'Tonight, a community celebrates as Yarrandarrah Council votes down the closure of the local library and the sale of the site to developers. Councillor Susannah Cockburn, had this to say:

"Mayor Fischer attempted to ban books in this town and punish those people to whom the local library means everything. Those unable to make the two-hour round trip to Corondale to borrow a book. Our preschoolers who look forward to their weekly story time. The local prisoners who rely on the library for entertainment and education. Nicholas Fischer chose to ignore the simple fact that libraries are about more than mere books. They are a place of respite, a place to improve our minds or heal our souls. On behalf of the Friends of Yarrandarrah Library, I'd like to thank the council for giving our community back its library."'

A roar of approval rings out around the room. The Doc, who's sitting near the front, receives backslaps and high-fives from the men surrounding him.

The footage switches to Nicholas Fischer standing outside council chambers facing down the media. The crims hurl boos and catcalls at the TV.

'Let me say this—' he begins.

'Will you be handing in your resignation?' interrupts a journalist.

'No, I will not. I have set a clear agenda for economic reform in Yarrandarrah and I intend to deliver on that promise.'

'But clearly the overwhelming majority vote against you makes your position untenable?' asks a polished brunette, thrusting her microphone at the mayor.

The wind picks up his forelock and blows it about his face, momentarily making him seem wild and deranged. Derek chuckles at the unintended comedy. Surely the man knows that the only honourable thing to do is fall on his sword.

Back in the newsroom, the camera zooms in on Jocasta Delaney. 'With me is the person who spearheaded the campaign, Councillor Susannah Cockburn. Thank you for joining us, Susannah. How does it feel to sit here tonight having succeeded in saving Yarrandarrah Library?'

It's funny matching up the petite blonde with a gash of red lipstick on camera with the picture Derek had in his head. Susannah's not at all how he imagined.

'Libraries should never be measured by profit and loss,' says Susannah. 'Their value goes beyond the balance sheet. And in the end, banning books is a false economy. The council's job is to service the community, not deprive it of its lifeline to the world. Today's decision is the triumph of common sense over commercial interests.'

Jocasta glances at her notes and back to camera. 'Now I understand that an active member of the FOYL campaign was an inmate himself, Patrick Lyall, is that correct?'

'Yes. Pat is an excellent example of how, with the right programs and encouragement, lives can be turned around.'

'In what way? My understanding is that he's serving a life sentence for murder.'

'That's true. However, here is a man who has accepted his due punishment and, rather than giving into bitterness and recriminations, decided to pursue a path of reform. Patrick gained first an honours degree, then a PhD in English literature. He currently works as the prisoner librarian at Yarrandarrah gaol. That passion, that dedication, and the knowledge he has acquired, has made Pat a valuable contributor to the FOYL campaign and its ultimate success.'

The interview moves on to delve further into the machinations behind the vote, but Derek's no longer listening. He's in shock. He knew the Doc was an arrogant prick, but this really takes the cake. He ducks and weaves through the throng, desperate to confront that lying hound.

'You've got a bloody hide.'

The Doc turns, a smug smile twitching at his lips, as he basks in his moment of glory.

'You're not a real doctor.'

The Doc crosses his arms, affecting a relaxed pose, but his eyes are wary. 'I am indeed. I have the piece of paper to prove it.'

'You're not a *medical* doctor,' Derek splutters. 'When you killed all those women, what were you? An orderly? A cleaner?'

The Doc's good mood evaporates. 'I am a doctor of letters.'

Derek throws his hands in the air. 'How bloody appropriate. A doctor of letters.' His defiant tone echoes the Doc's. 'But you've been quite happy for everybody to believe you're a trained medical practitioner.'

A few of the crims stare at the pair in confusion.

'I never actually said that. It was assumed.' He stands now, towering above Derek, but Derek refuses to be intimidated.

'You earnt the men's respect because they thought you were smarter than them. You convinced everybody that you'd put those old women out of their misery.'

'And they'd be right.'

Derek grinds his fist into his palm, fighting the urge to clock the smug bastard, but he refuses to give him that satisfaction. 'There's a world of difference between a doctor making that decision and a cleaner. Between being a man of compassion and a ... a ... a psycho.'

The Doc darts a nervous glance at the remaining men. The looks being returned are curious, suspicious, for Derek has hit the nail on the head. In here, murder is not judged by the death itself, but whether the victim got what they deserved.

'I was not a cleaner,' the Doc says quietly.

'Well, what were you then?'

The men wait silently for an answer.

The Doc nervously clears his throat. 'When I was transferred here, I couldn't believe my luck. I knew no one. How often does that happen? You're always running into blokes from other prisons.'

Derek wonders where he's going with this. No one cares where the Doc was before Yarrandarrah.

'When I got my first degree, the blokes started calling me "Doc" as a joke. When I moved here, the nickname stuck.

People assumed I was a medical doctor; I just never bothered to correct them.'

Derek snorts. 'But you sure made it work for you.'

The Doc acknowledges this with a shrug. 'As if I'm going to jeopardise my chance to be treated with a bit of respect. No longer spending my days worrying if I'm going to be necked, knifed or harassed. To live my life without fear.'

Derek can't argue with that. There's no doubt C Wing is a reward for good behaviour. A place to serve your time working in the garden or building stuff in the workshops, maybe even day release if you're lucky. The Doc's not alone when it comes to wishing for a meaningful existence.

'So who are you really?' Derek presses.

The Doc goes to resume his seat but thinks better of it. He gives Derek a knowing smile. 'Now there's a question, isn't it?'

'This isn't about me,' Derek snaps.

'I'm just someone looking for a peaceful life. Not unlike yourself, Dezza.'

'We're nothing alike. I could never hurt another human being.'

The Doc doesn't even flinch. 'You know, the funny thing is, when I was first sent down, I had zero interest in rehabilitating myself. But one of the rare benefits of these fine institutions is that a man has time to think, which is lucky, because it took me a long time to appreciate that I was in here for a very good reason. That whether I saw it as a punishment or an opportunity was entirely up to me.'

The Doc smiles at Derek and sits back down. He taps the arm of his reading glasses against his bottom lip. 'I will die in this place. But at least I'll be remembered for a good deed or two. What will be your legacy, Dezza?'

Most of the men have lost interest by now and wandered off to share the gossip, leaving Derek and the Doc, face to face. The Doc's question lingers between them like a bad smell. Derek has nothing to say. He can't think of a single thing he's done to be remembered for. Inside and out, he's been a nobody. Someone who fades into the background, letting others be the life and soul of the party, lead the charge or take the initiative. That's always been his core strategy. So why does it suddenly make him feel like he's wearing a pair of slacks that's two sizes too small?

The Doc gathers his glasses and book. He moves around Derek, then says as he passes, 'I suggest you take a long hard look at yourself before pointing the finger at others, Dezza.' As he crosses the rec room, the Doc stops to accept a handshake, a backslap, and a word from Young Carl before he climbs the stairs.

Derek decides he may as well head back to his cell too. He nods at Young Carl and, as he passes, the officer says, 'He was a nurse.'

Derek stops in his tracks. 'You knew?'

Carl shrugs. 'Of course I knew. He's on my watch.'

'But why didn't you say he was lying?'

Carl gets that dumb look he often gets when he's thinking. 'He wasn't, though, was he? He *is* a doctor, of sorts.'

Derek shakes his head. The Doc sure knows how to make everyone dance to his tune. He grabs the handrail to haul himself up the stairs when the man himself appears at the top.

'Joey!' he shouts.

Confused, Derek looks around at Carl, then back again.

'Hurry!' The Doc waves him up before racing back along the deck towards Maloney's cell.

Words scream in Derek's head; *no, no, no, no, no.* He scrambles after the Doc, terrified one of Jacko's poofter-bashing cronies has dealt out his punishment, or Maloney's fear of leaving has pushed him into doing something stupid. He arrives at Maloney's cell and sees the Doc standing in the middle of the room, his face rigid with shock.

Derek scans the room. The beautiful waifs in their haute couture have vanished. So have the sketches. He takes in the empty locker. The cleared desk. The naked mattress and pancake pillow. A blanket folded at the foot. 'What have they done with him?'

The Doc removes his glasses and presses his thumb and forefinger into the corners of his eyes. 'Nothing.'

'We should check the hospital. He wasn't well the other day. What if he needs our help?'

Derek is halfway out the door, when the Doc yells, 'Stop!'

He turns. Waits.

'Look next to the door, Dezza.'

He searches the bare surfaces on the outside of the cell until his eyes alight on the blank slot on the wall. It takes his brain a few moments to catch up with what he sees but when it does, it hits him hard. 'He's been ghosted.'

The Doc traces a finger over the vanity basin and sniffs it. 'The joint's already been cleaned. He must have gone on the milk run.'

Derek recalls the day in the hospital toilets. 'He got the news.'

'Meaning?'

'Maloney got parole. He told me he's out in October.'

'Jesus. Why didn't he tell me?'

'You were too busy saving the world.'

Derek thinks of the last time he was standing in this cell. He knows it's probably pointless, but he has to see for himself. He gets down on his hands and knees and peers under the bunk.

'What are you looking for?' asks the Doc.

'The wedding dress.'

'Why would it be under the bed?'

Derek shuffles backwards and uses the edge of the bunk to get to his feet. 'It's not. Christ knows where it is.'

'It'll turn up.'

Derek doubts that very much. It's probably sitting in lost property waiting for his release. Either that or Maloney has taken it with him. Strangely enough, the idea has appeal. Maybe it'll be another dress for Maloney's Aunty and some girl with big dreams and a small budget.

The Doc sighs and takes a final look around. 'I wonder where they took him.'

'Someone must know.'

'They'll never tell us. You know the rules.'

The Doc meets him at the door. They stand there, the emptiness pressing at their backs.

Clearing his throat, the Doc says, 'We never even got to say goodbye.'

Derek swipes his sleeve across his eyes. 'Or thank you.'

Chapter 40

Speculation about Joey's ghosting lasts only as long as it takes for the powers-that-be to ship someone new into his cell. There are plenty of other distractions in the weeks that follow, not least being the return of newspapers and the regular delivery of books to the prison library. The Doc's relishing the restoration of order to his fiefdom and, in many ways, the whole of C Wing.

Derek has enough on his plate without worrying about what everyone else is up to. The Doc hit a nerve when he questioned what Derek's legacy will be. On the upside, he has about a year and a half left to ponder an answer to that. The more immediate issue lies on his desk in front of him. A letter a week adds up to a fair old stack of mail when you look at it. But Debbie's one letter to him has got him thinking that maybe he overestimated Lorraine. Here was he thinking she'd do the right thing where Debbie was concerned. But it sounds like Debbie has no idea he's been writing to her. No wonder she is furious with him.

He turns to the blank pages in front of him. This will be his last letter to Debbie. He won't rest easy until he tells her he is sorry. Whether she gets the letter is another question altogether but he will feel better for writing it.

Except apologising isn't as easy as it sounds. Does he come straight out with it? Or is it better to couch it in terms that shows he understands her feelings? He's weighing up the options when there's a knock on his door. It's Young Carl.

'Morning, Dezza. Another gorgeous day in paradise. You wouldn't be dead for quids, hey.'

Derek puts down his pen and sniffs. 'I'll take your word for it. So, put me out of my misery. What's on today's menu then?'

Carl doesn't miss a beat. 'I've heard it might be yum cha.'

Derek thinks of steaming baskets of dumplings, crunchy piles of salt and pepper squid, and, his personal favourite, plates of Chinese broccoli glistening with oyster sauce. 'That's a bit fancy, isn't it?'

Carl grins, running his thumbs inside his waistband. 'Well, we've plenty to celebrate with Mayor Fischer resigning. Now that Susannah Cockburn's taken on the job in caretaker mode, things are looking up.'

'She'll be a breath of fresh air, that's for sure.'

Despite his defiance, Nicholas Fischer failed to weather the political storm. Turned out the rumours he was receiving kickbacks from his developer mates were true. Someone caught him on camera receiving a brown paper bag full of cash.

'The jokers reckon he'll soon be joining you lot in here.'

'That tour you took him on might prove to be quite instructional then.'

They both chuckle. Derek waits for Carl to move on, but the young bloke keeps hovering in his cell like he's got something on his mind. Derek's tempted to ask him what, but he figures the officer will tell him sooner or later.

Carl fidgets a bit more. Scratches behind his ear, shifts his weight from one foot to the other. 'I've got a bit of news of my own,' he says finally.

Derek's thoughts immediately fly to Carl's relationship with Jane. Is Carl about to announce their engagement? He girds his loins, not sure he's too thrilled to be the recipient of that kind of news.

Carl straightens as if he's delivering the news to the governor, not an old fart like Derek. 'I'll be finishing up at the end of the month.'

'Well, that *is* a surprise,' Derek says, and he means it too. 'You got a better offer?'

Carl smiles and shakes his head. 'Nah, nothing like that. I've decided to go back to my first love. I'm going to open up a café in town.'

'Good for you.'

'Thanks, Dezza. Truth is, I don't think I'm cut out for this job.'

'Nah, you're wrong there.' Derek stands up and goes over to Carl. 'You're a good bloke, Officer Petty. It's been a pleasure to be under your care.'

Carl turns a bright shade of pink and the poor guy doesn't know where to look. Then Derek does something he'd never have dreamt of a few months ago. He puts out his hand and says, 'Congratulations.'

Young Carl looks at Derek's proffered hand, then takes it.

'It's been years since I've shook another bloke's hand,' Derek says, flexing his hand, surprised at how strange it is to feel another person's skin on his.

'Yeah, well, don't go making a habit of it,' Carl jokes.

'No worries about that.'

Carl turns to leave. 'You'll be all right without me. You've got Backtackers to keep you on the straight and narrow.' He hesitates in the doorway. 'I take it you'll be going back. Dress or no dress, you're a stitcher. The place isn't the same without you.'

Derek thinks of Maloney. Backtackers won't be the same without him either. He hopes that famous Aunty folded the boy in her arms and held him there for a good long minute. He thinks of Sean and the Rajah Quilt, and says, 'You betcha.'

Derek arrives and hovers in the doorway of the sewing room for a moment. He takes stock of the familiar sight of men bent over their stitching and a small flower of joy blooms in his chest.

'Hello, stranger,' Jane says, looking up from her work, a tentative smile on her face.

Derek glows. He's missed her so much these past few weeks. From her warmth to her perennial optimism, Jane is a good soul. She made a silly mistake. Haven't they all been guilty of that at least once in their lives?

'Well, ain't you a sight for sore eyes,' says Brian, tossing his tapestry on a chair and giving Derek a nod of welcome.

'Gee willikers, who's the new bloke?' Mick adds with a wink. 'Standards must be slipping.'

'Yeah, they let all sorts in these days,' says Les, scurrying past them to his corner.

'Ha, ha, bloody ha,' Derek says, trying not to look too pleased at the warm reception.

Jane looks at him expectantly. 'I guess you'll need something to work on.'

Derek deflates. As illogical as it is, a small part of him had hoped he would come to Backtackers and there would be the black plastic bag laid out on the workbench, the same as every other week. It's a crying shame that dress has disappeared.

'Afternoon, everyone,' comes from the doorway. There stands Sean, and Derek can't help but think of Maloney's misery about leaving his love behind. Sean looks tired. Right there and then, Derek vows to keep an eye on the fella, for Maloney's sake, and Sean's.

'Is that what I think it is?' asks Mick, lumbering over to the doorway.

Derek's gaze drops. Draped over Sean's arm is the black plastic bag.

Jane's hands fly to her mouth. 'Oh my goodness.'

'Can you give us a hand, mate?' Sean asks Mick. 'I'm still a bit unsteady on my pegs.'

'Of course,' Mick replies, galvanised into action. Derek clears the table and, as Mick lays down the bag, the rest of the Backtackers congregate around the workbench.

Derek unties the bag. In his haste, the dress slithers out, but he catches it before it hits the floor. Straightening, he drapes it over his arms and holds it up to catch the light.

'Oh my.' Jane presses her hands to her lips as if in prayer and pride wells inside Derek. If only Maloney could see the look on her face.

She gathers the skirt and runs it through her fingers. 'Your needlework is exquisite.'

'What?' replies Derek.

Jane beams at him. 'This project has certainly fine-tuned your skills, Derek. It's faultless. You should be really proud of yourself.'

Derek gets a prickling sensation rising up the back of his neck. Like he's been busted doing something wrong.

'Lucky we've still got three weeks up our sleeve,' Mick says, turning the dress over. 'Look at this!' He elbows Brian and points at the tiny flowers entwined around the self-covered buttons.

'Very impressive, mate,' says Brian.

'I reckon that's your best needlework ever,' Derek adds, glad the focus has turned elsewhere.

Mick's eyebrows disappear into his hairline. 'Me? With these hands?' He raises them to illustrate his point. There's no denying they're not a delicate pair.

'And Joey said you did the hand-stitching on the handkerchief sleeves,' Derek throws at Brian. He's got a sneaking suspicion he knows where this conversation is going.

'You've gotta be kidding,' says Brian.

Derek turns to Sean for final confirmation. 'And apparently you're working on the veil.'

Everyone bursts out laughing.

'That little—' Mick begins, but Jane interrupts.

'Yes, well. It seems it's Joey who's had the last laugh.' She turns to Derek. 'Joey was nervous about the dress being left in the sewing room after the riot, so he said he'd return it to you.' She gathers it in her arms and holds it against her body. 'I never guessed this was what he was really up to.'

Jane swishes the dress in front of her, then takes a few tentative dance steps in the limited space of the room. Her face shines against the soft shimmer of the fabric. There's no doubt about it, it's a dress fit for a princess. 'Such perfect work,' she says. 'What a shame it will never be worn.'

'I've thought about that,' says Derek, pleased to have a solution to this particular problem. 'Apparently, Joey's Aunty is always on the lookout for spare dresses.'

'That's very noble of you,' Jane replies, although she sounds less than thrilled by the idea.

'Does Dezza know about the Charity Ball?' tosses in Mick.

Jane stops, the dress limp in her arms.

Derek looks at Mick questioningly, but he doesn't elaborate. Brian is suddenly crackling with energy. He takes the dress from Jane and lays it on the workbench. 'I seem to recall Joey planned a seeded bodice with a double row around the neckline.'

'A crumb catcher,' corrects Sean.

But Derek refuses to be distracted. 'What about the Charity Ball?'

Jane fiddles with her pendant, eyes downcast.

'Well?' he prompts, glancing around, but even Carl's studying his clipboard as if learning the contents by rote. 'For goodness' sake, fellas, what the hell's going on?'

Mick clears his throat and looks to Jane, who gives him the nod. 'Jane's doing a little more than delivering our cushions for the ball this year.'

This is hardly earth-shattering news. Derek waits for more information. Jane picks up the story. Tells him about her invitation to be the guest speaker at the Charity Ball. How, ages ago, she'd had this idea to use the wedding dress as the centrepiece of her speech. 'Members of Connecting Threads from all over the country will be there. I thought it would be the perfect opportunity to showcase your wonderful work.'

'See? We have to finish the dress now, Dezza. For Jane,' Brian says, grinning his broken smile.

'Not just for Jane,' mutters Sean.

'Imagine Jane up on stage, wearing our dress to the ball, telling everyone all about us,' says Mick, puffed up with pride.

That's all very well, but Derek's heart was set on his original idea. He'd planned to ask Jane to get him a nice big box filled with tissue paper and a long satin ribbon to tie the whole lot up in a bow. He'd even gone so far as to imagine the look on Joey's Aunty's face when she unwrapped the box and saw the dress.

'You don't have to, Derek,' Jane says, failing to hide her disappointment at his reaction.

'Course he does,' grumbles Mick.

'Especially after all the work we've put into it,' Sean slips in.

'Now, gentlemen, that's not entirely fair. We made the dress for Debbie,' Jane chides, the little frown furrowing her brow, 'not for the Charity Ball.'

'Yeah, but now we know she's not gunna wear it, don't we?' Brian replies, blundering over the sensitivities in his size-ten boots. 'We may as well get some benefit out of it.' He grins at Jane. 'You'll be like Cinderella.'

Jane turns a deep shade of crimson, and Derek notices Carl swallow a smile. Maybe she's the real reason Carl's decided on a career change. His gaze shifts to Mick, who winks at him, then lands on Sean. His words echo in Derek's head: *That dress is our friendship quilt.*

He returns to Jane. Imagine her parading about in the wedding dress in front of all those posh buggers in their penguin suits. Wouldn't that be something? The idea tickles his fancy. It would be a wonderful way to show her that he forgives her for lying to him, without having to embarrass her by putting her on the spot. And really, the more he thinks about it, what better way to repay Jane for her thousand small kindnesses?

Jane clears her throat. 'I didn't mean that I'd actually wear the dress, Derek. It's not actually my size. And if you think there's any chance Debbie might still want the dress, I can always just take some photos or ...'

But Derek's made up his mind. 'I've spent far too long deluding myself about my relationship with my daughter. And I'll be damned if I see months of hard work amount to nothing.'

Derek looks at his fellow Backtackers. Even the ones not involved in making the dress have been barracking from the sidelines. It's been a team effort. Taking the dress to the ball feels like the right way to honour Maloney's hard work and to thank the Backtackers. He turns to the men and says the simplest of words: 'I think it's a bloody brilliant idea.'

Chapter 41

When Derek gets the message that Lorraine's coming to visit, he reckons it can't be good news. She's had five and a half years to avail herself of the pleasure – why now? As he waits in the visitors' room, he keeps flexing his hands, feeling the tension fire through his muscles. He really doesn't want to see his ex-wife. Not for the obvious reasons. Truth be told, he's glad she divorced him. They should have put their marriage out of its misery many moons before. No, the thing is, though he might have changed for the better on the inside, the outside is a different kettle of fish. Lorraine won't see the good in him.

Although the minute he sees Lorraine bustling into the room, his own insecurities go flying out the door. She looks terrible. No, frazzled, that's the word he wants. She plonks herself down in the chair opposite, mopping her face with a tissue.

'What's the matter, Lol?' he asks. No point beating around the bush.

'It's a disaster,' she declares and bursts into tears.

This gives Derek pause. 'More information?'

She fans her face with her hands as if this will be sufficient to dry the tears flooding down her cheeks. 'Debbie's hysterical. I've completely ruined the wedding.'

By Derek's calculations, the wedding is supposed to be ten days away. 'Have they called it off?' he asks, trying not to sound too chuffed at the idea. Marriage is not for the faint-hearted. Debs would be far better off backpacking through Europe. Getting a bit of life experience under her belt. Like he should've done.

'I wish,' Lorraine says, and immediately looks guilty. She blows her nose hard, drawing the attention of the other visitors.

'I'm not a mind reader, woman.'

Lorraine heaves a deep sigh. 'I didn't mean to. I was distracted.' Seeing Derek's mounting frustration, she hurries on. 'It was full of creases from being in the bag so long. I thought I'd give it a press and hang it up so there'd be one less job to worry about.'

Ah, she's talking about Debbie's wedding dress.

'I was right in the middle of ironing it when Auntie Bev called, and you know how she loves a chat.'

Derek nods. Auntie Bev is a champion talker. She makes Lorraine look like a rank amateur.

'She was carrying on about somebody in the retirement village who'd borrowed her good teapot and hadn't returned it. When she asked them about it, they denied all knowledge. Half the people in that village are losing their marbles, I can't understand why she goes around lending her stuff to such people.'

Lorraine draws breath. Derek knows better than to interrupt his ex in full flight, so he waits for the rest of the story.

'Anyway, I'm busy trying to sort this all out and I've completely forgotten about the dress, haven't I? I'm out on the patio blathering on about teapots when I notice this awful smell. I turn around' – she looks at Derek, eyes like saucers – 'I turn around and the bloody ironing board's on fire.'

'Jesus Christ, Lol! What did you do?'

'Well, obviously, I hung up on Bev and called the fire brigade.' Lorraine frowns. 'I think someone else must have already rung them, because they were there in a flash.' Her face collapses again. 'The smoke was so thick, I couldn't get into the laundry to grab a towel and wet it. Then this fireman's pounding on the front door, so I dash out to the patio and call out to them, telling them to come through the back. The whole brigade rushes up my side passage and, before I know it, I'm being manhandled out into the garden.'

He can see it now: the dress in flames, bits of ash floating around the house. Typical bloody Lorraine. Then it occurs to him. 'Where was Debbie?'

Lorraine hiccups. 'She'd spent the night at Ian's. She wasn't even there to help.' More tears flow and Derek waits for her sobs to subside. 'Eventually, they let me back in. The police had to be called and everything. The fuss, I can't tell you. I still can't get the stench out of the house.'

'But how did the fire do so much damage?' Derek ventures. He's never seen Lorraine's new house, but it's hard to imagine how ironing a dress created such destruction.

Lorraine blows her nose and pulls herself together. 'I'd set the ironing board up in the kitchen. I had the skirt – oh you can imagine it. Well, actually, you probably can't. She'd gone for the full catastrophe with a long train, so it would puddle behind her as she walked down the aisle. Terrible thing to iron. No matter how I arranged the dress over the board, I couldn't stop it touching the floor. And then' – Lorraine's shoulders shudder and heave as she struggles to muster her self-control – 'the iron must have tipped over. All that organza. Whoosh! Up in flames.'

Derek cannot believe his ears. It takes every effort not to laugh out loud, but he can't quite manage to suppress a smirk.

'The skirt melted into the ironing board. I'll have to get a new one.'

'Can't you just replace the skirt?' Derek asks.

'You don't understand. The firemen used this special yellow foam. The dress was white.' Fresh tears course down her cheeks. Having run out of tissues, she resorts to using her sleeve to soak them up. 'A three-thousand-dollar wedding dress. Ruined,' she wails.

That wipes the smile off Derek's face. 'Three thousand dollars!'

She shoots him a killer look. 'Ian helped pay for it.'

Typical Lorraine. Incapable of denying Debbie anything, especially when she wasn't spending her own money. But that's no longer his problem. 'What now?' he asks in the most reasonable tone he can manage.

'That's why I'm here, Derek,' Lorraine huffs as if it should be obvious. 'Since the house is unlivable, we're stuck at Ian's mother's. Debbie's not speaking to me and Ian's mother, well, she's a piece of work, that one.' Lorraine sniffs. 'Full of airs and graces, as if living at Pelican Shores makes her someone special.'

Derek tries to put himself in Lorraine's shoes. 'It's fair enough Debbie's upset about the dress, but there's no point flogging you after the damage is done.'

'Thank you, Derek.' Lorraine dabs her eyes with her sodden collection of tissues. 'She hasn't been very reasonable lately. Wedding nerves.' Lorraine hesitates, fiddles with her wrist where her watch should be, then says, 'Debbie told me about the letter she wrote you.'

Derek sits back. *I hate you, I hate you, I hate you.* Ah well, she has a point.

'I told her what's done is done. It's time to leave the past in the past.'

Derek smiles. He can see right through her. There is no way on earth Lorraine would ever say anything like that.

'I told her there was no need to be nasty. That you couldn't help yourself at the time.'

She leans forward. Despite the rules about covering up, he can see the blunt line of her cleavage. He's certain she's batting her eyelashes at him. Unfortunately, since her eyes are red-rimmed and the mascara has settled in the creases, it fails to have the desired effect. Derek stays mum, curious to see where Lorraine's heading.

'I saw Steve the other day. He told me your news.' Lorraine tries a consoling look but she's a terrible actress.

The penny drops. Of course that's why she's here. But he's not giving Lorraine an inch. Not after all the water under their particular bridge. 'What news would that be, Lol?'

'You've had a bit of a windfall, what with Clive ...' She pauses, no doubt in an attempt to seem delicate. '... passing over to the other side.'

He has to suck on his cheek to stop himself grinning from ear to ear. Lorraine isn't here to mend bridges. She's heard he's cashed up and she can't wait to get her hands on it. And he can't resist having a bit of fun at her expense. 'It's a shame Debbie made it crystal clear she wants nothing to do with me.'

Truth is, it would be easy to slip Lorraine a couple of grand. He could even give her their wedding dress, if not for the fact Debbie wouldn't wear it in a million years. All the Backtackers' hard work stashed in the attic and forgotten.

Lorraine settles back in her chair. 'She acted in anger. We're all guilty of that at some stage in our lives, aren't we?'

Christ, straight out of the daytime soaps. Lorraine's got a hide lecturing him about guilt, but she has a point. Part of him wants to punish Lorraine, to withhold the money out of spite. But there's another part of him – the good in him – that thinks it's perhaps time he forgave her. Especially if it means helping Debbie. 'How much do you need?'

Lorraine's face floods with relief. 'Oh Derek, I can't thank you enough.'

She names a figure that, six months ago, Derek would have declared obscene. Now he's a bit more au fait with weddings, the amount doesn't surprise him at all. Even so, he knows his ex-wife far too well. This particular leopard will never change her spots. And for once in his life, Derek's not going to let her get away with it. Forgiveness is all well and good, but it doesn't mean a man has to be stupid about it.

'It's ten days till the wedding. By the time I stuff around trying to get you the money, you won't have time to buy a dress. So how's this for an idea: I'll send you a dress. That way we cut out the middle man.'

Lorraine's jaw drops. She dabs at her eyes like a frantic bird. With a shudder, she replies, 'Can't you just give me the cash?'

Oh, what a familiar tune that sings in Derek's ear. He smiles. 'Not this time, Lol.'

Her mouth opens and closes, but, for once, no words come out. Then her face hardens and she looks like her old self. 'It's not *your* dress, is it?'

Naturally, his first reaction is to defend himself, but what would that achieve? The only way he'll get Debbie into his wedding dress is to lie. Does that make him a bad person? Jane with her soft brown eyes and generous smile looms before him. 'Here's the deal. I'll arrange for a stunning wedding dress to be delivered to your door. But on one condition.' He sits back. Lorraine's lower lip quivers. 'Under no circumstances is Debbie to know I had anything to do with it. I don't care what story you dream up about where the dress came from, just don't mention my name. Understood?'

Because at the end of the day, Debbie doesn't need to know the truth. If she loves the dress, if it makes her happy on her wedding day, what more could a man ask for?

Lorraine blinks. Her brain's whirring so fast, he can almost smell the smoke. Then she breaks into a smile and Derek knows why. She just realised he's gifted her a way to redeem herself in Debbie's eyes. 'I won't breathe a word.'

'Do me one more favour.'

Lorraine looks wary.

'Send me a photo of Debbie in the dress. You know, so I have a keepsake.'

Lorraine crosses her heart like a child. 'I will, Derek, I promise.'

He hopes that, for once in her life, Lorraine's word is her bond.

As he watches her prepare to leave, he feels a bit sorry for her. This wedding business must be emotionally draining, let alone travelling seven hours to beg Derek to save her arse. Poor Lorraine's not used to such pressure.

When she reaches the doorway, Lorraine turns and mouths the words, 'Thank you.'

Derek gives her a thumbs-up before heading back to C Wing. He might have solved Lorraine's problems, but he now has a major headache of his own. How the hell is he going to get the dress back off Debbie in time for Jane to show it at the Charity Ball?

Chapter 42

Debbie rolls over in the cramped single bed that used to be Ian's, flicks open the Venetian blinds and peeks outside. It's a perfect spring day. Not a cloud in the sky. She swings her legs onto the floor, wriggles her pink toes and admires the glow of her golden calves. She's never had a spray tan before, probably never will again, but she has to admit, it was worth it.

Downstairs, Ian's mum, Nicola, or Nikki as she prefers to be called, pops the cork on a bottle of bubbles. In the middle of the island bench is a tray of ham-and-cheese croissants from the local French patisserie and a carton of freshly squeezed orange juice. Alcohol-soakers – something to line the tummy and soothe the nerves. Ian's staying at his best man Gavin's place, so it's women and children only. Auntie Sharon will be here soon, along with Ian's tribe of nieces and nephews signed up to be flower girls, pageboys and ring bearers.

Nikki passes Debbie a glass of mimosa, a cream satin slip peeking through her kimono. Combined with the gelatinous pink face mask and the halo of hair rollers, she has the startled look of a Japanese cartoon character. She catches Debbie staring and winks, saying, 'Got to look my best for the big day.'

Not knowing how to respond, Debbie sips her cocktail.

'Give me one of those, would you?' Her mother totters through the doorway, her hair squished flat from where she's slept on it. She has yet to slap on the thick layer of anti-aging cream filled with secret ingredients that will transform her complexion with its expensive youthful dew, and looks every day of her forty-plus years. Lorraine plonks herself down on one of the bar stools at the island bench and her dressing gown gapes open, revealing lingerie in an eye-watering shade of pink that Lorraine would call 'watermelon' but is probably 'bubble-gum'.

Nikki hands her a glass, which she drains in one gulp. 'I love a Buck's Fizz.'

'Mimosa,' Nikki mutters under her breath, as she wipes the drips off the marble benchtop.

Lorraine rolls her eyes. 'Same thing.'

Nikki fetches an elaborate pair of tongs from the cutlery drawer, places a croissant on a gold-rimmed plate, and passes it to Lorraine. 'Actually, no. A Buck's Fizz is two parts Champagne to one part orange juice, whereas a mimosa contains Champagne and orange juice in equal measure. Makes it less alcoholic.'

She turns to fill the coffee machine with water, so doesn't see Lorraine's livid expression.

Debbie knocks back the rest of her glass and takes her phone off the charger. She sees a half-hearted text message from Garry, wishing her luck. He's in Queensland on a fishing trip he swears he'd planned long before they announced their engagement. The thrill of not having to deal with her stepfather today far outweighs the insult of him failing to turn up. With any luck, a marlin will eat him.

She checks the time. 'You'd better chuck on some clothes, Mum. I promised Maddie we'd be at the salon by ten.' Her bridesmaid, Maddie, and her colleagues at Shear Beauty are doing hair and makeup as Debbie's wedding present. Then it's back here to get dressed and off to the reception centre. Debbie eyes the bottle of Champagne. She'd love another but they can't *all* be tipsy on her wedding day. She shoots a glance at her mother. Heaven help her if she ruins anything else.

'Stop touching your hair, Debs,' Maddie demands when they pull into the driveway three hours later. 'You'll wreck it.'

Debbie regrets saying the girls at Shear Beauty could do what they liked. Every time she blinks, eyelashes the size of butterfly wings crash into her cheeks. She's wearing more shades of eyeshadow than she has in her entire makeup bag and she probably should have said no to plumper lips. She has to keep touching herself to make sure the real Debbie is still in there.

She opens the front door and almost collides with a half-dressed little girl squealing as she runs down the hall being chased by a herd of little boys in suits. Auntie Sharon follows hot on their heels.

She grabs the balustrade and pulls up short. 'Hello, love. Don't you look nice?'

Debbie glances at her trackpants and rumpled t-shirt. 'Thanks, Auntie Shaz.'

Lorraine harrumphs and pushes past them, making a beeline for the kitchen. Sharon purses her lips and moves aside, pulling a hoity-toity expression in her sister's wake.

Debbie swallows a smile. 'Mum insisted on it,' she says, in reference to her mother's hair. 'She thinks she's channelling Jackie Onassis.'

'More like she's walked straight off the set of *Dynasty*,' snorts Auntie Sharon.

'Quick! Let's escape while we have the chance,' Maddie whispers, tugging Debbie up the stairs. Debbie giggles and mouths an apology to her aunt. As she closes the bedroom door behind them, Maddie says. 'No offence, Debs, but three hours of your mum is about my limit.'

'You should try living with her,' Debbie says, checking her phone for messages.

Maddie slips off her work shoes and dumps her bag on the floor. 'What do you keep looking at your phone for? He's not going to pull out, Debs. Ian really loves you.'

'I'm checking the weather forecast,' Debbie lies. What if the venue's been flooded or Ian's been struck down with some deadly virus? But her phone remains blank and silent.

'I'm dying to see your new wedding dress,' Maddie says, sliding open the wardrobe door and pulling out the hanger. She holds the dress against her body and checks her reflection in the mirror. 'Oh. My. God. This is *divine*. Where did your mum find it?'

'No idea. She wouldn't tell me. She just says I should be grateful she solved the problem.'

Maddie lays the dress on the bed. She lifts the skirt and checks the seams. With a tsk, she opens up the bodice and runs her hand along the lining. 'There's no label.'

'So?'

Maddie crosses her arms and tilts her head. 'Like no manufacturer's label? No cleaning instructions? Wherever your mum got this dress, it wasn't from a shop.'

'But it must be.' Truth be told, Debbie hasn't given much thought to how her mother managed to find the perfect dress on such short notice. 'Mum's stashed the box at home somewhere. The receipt's probably still in it.'

'Well, anyway, it's heaps nicer than your first one,' Maddie says, fetching her bridesmaid's dress from the wardrobe. They chose emerald green silk to match her eyes. She lays it alongside the wedding dress and examines the effect. 'It looks nice with the blue flowers, doesn't it?' Maddie whips out her phone and uploads a picture of the dresses, hashtagging it #matchmadeinheaven and adding a few love heart emojis for good measure.

'Forget-me-nots,' says Auntie Sharon, entering the room. 'They were your nanna's favourite.' At Debbie's astonished look, she adds, 'Maureen, her name was. She was long gone before your time, darling. I have a box of your dad's stuff somewhere, filled with Maureen's things. Her favourite colour was blue and forget-me-nots were her favourite flower. How clever of your mother to remember.'

'What do you mean?'

Auntie Sharon studies the dress. 'Amazing,' she says. She looks like she wants to say more, but she gives herself a little shake and smiles at Debbie. 'Something old, something new, something borrowed, something blue. The dress is new and the flowers are blue.' Auntie Sharon passes Debbie a small wrapped gift. 'This is something old.'

Debbie carefully unsticks the tape. Inside the paper is a white handkerchief with lace scalloped edges and the initials AR embroidered in one corner.

'That was your other grandmother's. My mum, Ada. And I thought you might need a hankie today. So now you have something old.'

'Now all she needs is something borrowed.' Maddie looks around the room, as if the answer is lurking somewhere there.

'What about this?' comes from the doorway. Nikki joins them. She holds out her hand and nestled in her palm is a beautiful diamond and sapphire bracelet. 'Ian's father gave this to me on our tenth wedding anniversary. I'd like you to have it as my wedding gift to you.'

'But it's supposed to be something *borrowed*,' butts in Maddie.

Nikki laughs. 'All right, I'm *lending* it to you for the day. But be careful not to lose it so I can give it to you later.'

Debbie feels her chest tighten. It takes all her effort not to burst into tears. Wedding nerves, her mother keeps telling her, but Debbie's not sure that is exactly it. She clutches the hankie tight in her fist. She'll be walking down the aisle as her mum has before her, and as Auntie Sharon and Nikki and Ada and Maureen have. Generations of women, each wearing the most beautiful dress they've ever worn, looking into a bright future with the man they love. All of a sudden, she misses her dad.

The doorbell rings, galvanising the women into action. 'That will be the photographer. Shall I send her up?' asks Nikki, dashing the tip of one finger under each eye and heading out the door.

'Give us a couple of minutes, will ya? We're not decent,' says Maddie.

'Tell me something I don't know,' Auntie Sharon throws over her shoulder, following in Nikki's wake.

Debbie has to dress in stages. The photographer takes shots of Maddie doing up the fiddly self-covered buttons and pretending to fix Debbie's hair. When she is finally dressed, they have to wrangle the flower girls, pageboys and ring bearers for group shots on the stairs. Then they head to the garden, where Nikki lays down an old bedspread for Debbie to stand on so the train doesn't get dirty. 'We can't ruin those beautiful flowers,' she says.

Lorraine, stiff in her silk shantung day suit, manages to slurp Champagne and roll her eyes at the same time. Everyone ignores her.

The fleet of wedding cars arrives at the reception centre at precisely ten to two, but Lorraine taps the driver on the shoulder and tells him to go around the block. As they sail past the garden, Debbie glimpses white Balinese flags bearing the words 'Together Forever' fluttering in the breeze. The guests are already seated, the smart ones wearing large hats, the less so fanning themselves with the program. She spots Uncle Steve in his dark suit and reflector sunglasses, sitting on the steps of the rotunda, looking like a gangster.

The next time around, they arrive a fashionable few minutes late. The photographer waits, ready to capture Debbie as she disembarks. The crowd turns to watch the fuss of all three women extricating themselves from the car while juggling the wedding train, high-heels, bouquets and veils. Maddie straightens Debbie's skirt, hands over the wedding bouquet, and adjusts the folds of the long veil that almost touches the ground. The music starts and Debbie glides into position. She tries her best to look demure, locking her jaw so she doesn't grin like a madwoman. When Uncle Steve extends his crooked arm to her, for a flash, Debbie wishes he was her dad. She squashes the thought and takes her uncle's arm. He winces under her vice-like grip, but keeps the beat as he measures their walk down the aisle. Whispers follow them. 'Doesn't she look beautiful?' 'What a stunning dress!' And Debbie basks in their admiration, turning pink with pleasure at the look on Ian's face when he lays eyes upon her.

The ceremony goes without a hitch until the exchange of rings, when Debbie's hands tremble so much, she almost drops the ring when she tries to slide the thick band over Ian's knuckle. Then he lifts the veil and kisses her and the guests burst into applause. The celebrant whisks them over to a table, where they sign the register. With the formalities completed, the celebrant signals to the guests and announces, 'Ladies and gentlemen, may I present Mrs Deborah and Mr Ian Smith.'

Debbie cracks a huge smile – bugger her makeup. Now she's married, her real life can begin. She's so excited she could cry. Mum already is; Debbie can see her dabbing at her eyes with the corner of a tissue.

'Free at last,' she thinks, as Ian slides his arm through hers. She rests her hand on his, admiring the flash of her ring against her dress. It is gorgeous. Everything is gorgeous.

At Ian's signal, they walk back down the aisle, laughing under a shower of confetti. The photographer leads them to a secluded part of the garden and positions them beneath an archway covered in flowers, while the caterer sends waiters through the crowd bearing trays of Champagne and canapés.

'Stunning dress, Lolly,' Sharon says, passing her sister a glass of bubbles.

'Isn't it?' Lorraine sniffs. For the life of her, she can't stop crying. It must be the emotional exhaustion. Or maybe it's the relief of knowing that in a few hours' time, this will all be over and she can take off these damn heels and her bra. She fortifies herself with a gulp of Champagne. 'Although this wedding's a bit over the top. Ian's obviously got more money than sense.'

'Pull your claws in, Lolly,' Sharon snaps, before acknowledging the photographer who is waving them over for the family photos.

That Nikki is already standing there, clutch purse tucked under one arm, draped in a simple dress that shows off how skinny she is. Lorraine swipes another glass of Champers from a passing tray and waddles over to join the wedding party.

'Did you take a nice photo of the dress?' she checks. Derek will kill her if she forgets. As if she hasn't got enough on her plate already.

'For God's sake, Mum,' Debbie cuts across before the photographer can answer. 'She's got heaps of photos. Stop worrying.' She waggles her empty glass at Ian and her dutiful new husband goes in search of Champagne.

Lorraine bites her tongue. After all, it's not *her* big day. She's only the mother of the bride, forced to wear the same day suit she got married in since Garry had put his foot down when she mentioned she'd like a new dress. He says she spends like a drunken sailor. Imagine if he was here today. He'd have a heart attack at the amount Ian's thrown about.

The photographer scrolls through the shots and Lorraine peers at the screen. 'Have you got a close-up of the flowers on the dress? I can't really see them.'

The photographer assures her she has.

'Well, take a couple more, just in case. I need to be able to see the detail.'

Debbie tries not to fidget as she is forced to stand still for yet another five minutes while Ian sips her Champagne.

Lorraine taps the screen with a violent purple nail. 'That's the one I'll send.'

'Send to who?' Debbie asks, trying to tiptoe to prevent her stilettos sinking in the grass.

Lorraine waves the question aside. 'The bridal boutique wants a photo of you in the dress.'

'I don't know why they'd care.'

Debbie chases after Ian and her Champagne. Lorraine watches her go. It really has been a terribly long day.

'Almost got caught out, Lol,' Sharon says, popping a smoked salmon blini in her mouth.

Lorraine pulls herself up to her full height, all the better to look down her nose at her sister. 'I have no idea what you mean.'

Sharon chuckles as she watches her unsuspecting niece trot after her new husband. 'I'm not as stupid as you think, Lol. I know exactly where you got that dress.'

*

Deflated, Lorraine heads into the reception. Her feet are killing her. She needs to sit down. Most of the guests are way ahead of her. Nothing like a free feed to get people queuing out the door. More Champagne floats about the room on large trays. She finds her spot at the main table. As the mother of the bride, her seat is between her ex-brother-in-law, Steve, and Debs' friend Maddie. The good news is that skinny Nikki is on the other side of the table, next to her son, far enough away that Lorraine won't have to speak to her. Lorraine sits down and eases off her heels under the table.

The degustation menu starts with oysters in three different dressings. There is a retro prawn cocktail with a lime aioli to follow. And so it goes. By the time the waiter announces the wagyu beef braciole, Lorraine's having trouble breathing. Damn these support undergarments Debbie insisted she wear. They've sucked everything in all right, but now the food's got nowhere to go. She eyes the menu in front of her, half hidden by the four different types of wine glasses. They are yet to serve the kingfish ceviche. She has no idea what that is, but she hates fish. Dessert better be good.

Lorraine's eye alights on Debbie. She's buzzing around the room, lapping up compliments, thoroughly at home at the centre of the universe. Women keep picking up the skirt of the dress, clearly raving about it. Thank God Derek can't hear them. He probably thinks throwing a few grand at a wedding dress makes him the big hero. At least it's not that homemade jobbie he tried to fob off on her. Mind you, he'd probably give his eye teeth to be here today, enjoying this all-expenses-paid extravaganza, all gooey-eyed at the sight of Debbie. She can almost feel the warmth of his hand on her thigh. Startled, she realises there *is* a warm hand on her thigh. Lorraine turns and registers that Steve is speaking to her.

'Sorry, I missed that. What did you say?' she asks.

Already half sloshed, he jabs at her plate. 'Are you going to finish that? I'm bloody starving. There's not much food, is there?'

Lorraine pushes over her plate of beef rolls and watches him demolish them in two bites. He'd choke if he knew that was thirty bucks' worth of steak. Always been a tight wad, that Steve, not like his brother.

He belches and wipes his face with his napkin. 'Right, time for a quick piss, then I'm up,' he says, nodding towards the microphone stand.

Steve's speech has the merit of being short, because, the truth is, he knows bugger all about Debbie. Next up is Ian. He struggles out of his chair, like a map that's been folded the wrong way. He pulls a set of palm cards from the inside pocket of his jacket and clears his throat.

'Debbie is the light of my life,' he begins and Lorraine inwardly groans.

He rabbits on about Debbie's beauty and how she brings sunshine into every day. Clearly, he doesn't live with her. Yet.

'Looking at her today, I'm sure you can all see why I had to marry her. I could not let her get away. To my wife, Deborah.' He raises his glass and a murmur rolls around the room, her name a quiet prayer for good luck.

Of course, no one mentions the mother of the bride, without whom none of them would be there. Lorraine sniffs and pours herself another glass of wine from the nearest bottle, mingling red with white. Who cares? It all goes down the same way.

Debbie, who had actually managed to sit down for the speeches, now rises to her feet and joins her husband at the microphone. 'I know it's not traditional for the bride to speak. But there are a few people missing today that I'd like to acknowledge.' She gestures to Ian for a glass of water, but doesn't complain when he passes her more Champers.

Debbie takes a sip and collects herself. Lorraine hopes it's emotion and not the grog that's got the better of her.

'My granddad died a couple of months ago. He was eighty-seven; thirteen short of his hundred. The cricket fans in the room will know what I mean. All Pop wanted was to make eighty-eight. He would have been really annoyed.'

There are a few 'To Clive's, the clink of glasses, and applause from Steve.

'I also want to thank Uncle Steve for stepping in today, since Dad couldn't be here. I know he didn't deserve to be, but it still feels pretty strange not having your dad at your wedding and I just wanted to share that.' Debbie's hand flutters in front of her face as she gulps back tears.

Lorraine can't believe it. All she's heard for the past five years is how much Debbie hates her father. Now it's *Boo-hoo, I miss my dad.* The girl has definitely drunk too much.

Debbie draws a deep breath. 'But I want to end on a happy note. Where are you, Mum?'

'Right here.' Lorraine waves and smiles through gritted teeth. Right here on the same table where she's been totally ignored for the entire dinner.

Debbie smiles and nods through gathering tears. 'Mum's been a rock since Dad went away. Especially this year. There's a lot more to organising a wedding than I'd realised before I said yes to my darling husband. I've got to thank my mum for all her help.'

There is a general chuckle acknowledging the truth of her words, a few raised glasses in Lorraine's direction. She preens and nods to show her appreciation.

'And I can't forget Ian's mum, Nikki. She's been terrific. I'm very lucky to have her as my mother-in-law.'

Nikki laughs and presses her hands to her heart, mouthing, 'Love you.'

Lorraine's smile freezes on her face.

'I don't know if any of you know the story, but this wedding was almost a disaster. Mum burnt my wedding dress!'

There are gasps and oohs. Lorraine has the sudden urge to slither under the table. She's going to kill Debbie. That child has no tact.

'But Mum's never been afraid of a challenge. Here I am, carrying on like a complete idiot, and Mum's saying, "I'll fix it. I'll fix it." Well, of course I didn't believe her, did I? But Mum, I want to say, I was wrong.'

'Can we get that in writing?' some wag yells and the room swells with laughter.

Debbie shakes a finger at the smart alec. 'I'm not joking. You should have seen me. The wedding is, like, days away. There's no money left for a second dress. But Mum walks in carrying this massive box and inside is this.'

Debbie makes her way to the centre of the dance floor. She still has the microphone in her hand and she's so close to the speakers that when she twirls under the lights, they squeal in protest.

'Sorry about that,' she says, moving into the full beam of the spotlight. The skirt billows, revealing the wreath of trailing flowers. The beading twinkles in the light. 'Mum won't tell me where she got it or how she could afford it, but thank you, Mum, for saving the day and finding me the most beautiful wedding dress I have ever seen.'

There is a loud rain of applause and the thunder of feet stamping the floor. Debbie totters over to where Lorraine sits, and stretches out her arms for an embrace. Lorraine rises, her neck aflame with embarrassment. They share an awkward hug. Debbie kisses her cheek, then turns and smiles to the audience, saying, 'My mum's the best.'

Sharon smiles too, thoroughly enjoying the sight of her sister turning the same colour as her day suit. After all these years, Derek Brown has finally managed to pull a swifty on Lorraine. The crafty bugger. What a shame she can't stand up and announce it to the room. Wouldn't that make this a day to remember?

Ian gathers Debbie in his arms. The spotlight plays on the happy couple as they stumble their way through the bridal waltz. Her cheeks are high with colour, her eyes alight with love, as the man of her dreams sweeps her across the parquetry. Debbie's dress shimmers under the lights.

Halfway through, Steve walks over and taps Ian on the shoulder, asking for permission to cut in. Ian and Debbie exchange an awkward glance before Ian hands his wife to her uncle. Sharon watches them, wishing it was Derek taking Debbie in his arms, twirling her around the floor, mumbling 'one, two, three; one, two, three' to keep count. That child has no clue how much her father loves her. How it kills him that he lost her. That no matter how old she grows, she will be her father's little girl until the day he dies.

Sharon brushes a tear from her cheek. She hates to say it, even if only to herself, but sometimes there is no justice in the world.

Chapter 43

On her lunchbreak, Debbie pops into the post office and sends the first batch of thank-you cards. Then she ducks into the drycleaners to pick up the wedding dress. She lays it on the back seat of her hatchback and makes sure the car's locked before detouring via the Japanese place and grabbing a teriyaki chicken salad bowl.

She spots Maddie across the plaza, sitting on one of the benches under the liquidambar tree, and joins her. They chat amicably about their day so far.

'So what are you going to do with your dress?' Maddie asks, taking a sip of her green smoothie as she watches Debbie devour her salad.

'You sure you don't want some?' Debbie asks, offering her the bowl.

Maddie waves her away. 'Nah, it's my fast day. I'm eating with my eyes.'

Debbie snorts and shoves a forkful under her friend's nose. She waits until Maddie accepts a sliver of julienned carrot and sucks it down. 'What are you supposed to do with pre-loved wedding dresses, anyway?'

'Sell them on eBay and use the money to pay off your credit card.'

Debbie winces. Ian doesn't know that her old credit card, the one in her maiden name, is maxed out. Maybe Maddie's right. Selling the dress is no different from returning unwanted wedding gifts. After all, it's not her fault some people didn't use the gift registry, and who needs two coffee machines? The extra five hundred came in handy. And the dress would be worth heaps more than that.

'Yeah, I don't know. Do people even wear second-hand wedding dresses?' She opens another tiny fish of soy sauce and throws it over the salad. She's no fan of vegetables, but Ian's gone back to being a health nut since they returned from their honeymoon and she feels obliged to show support now that they're married.

Maddie steals a slice of teriyaki chicken. 'Did you ever find out where it came from?'

Debbie stops chewing as she considers the question.

'I still think it's suss that it had no labels,' continues Maddie. 'What was in the box?'

'I forgot all about that. It must still be in the wardrobe at Mum's. I was planning to pop in and see her on the way home. I can check then.' She wasn't planning anything of the sort but, now she thinks about it, she may as well store the dress there. No point cluttering up her new wardrobe.

Debbie's pleased to see the driveway's empty when she pulls up, but, to be sure, she sings out hello when she enters the house. Silence. Perfect. She carries the dress upstairs, but when she opens her old bedroom door, she receives a nasty surprise.

'Well, that didn't take long,' she mutters, taking stock of the room. The least offensive item is a set of golf clubs leaning against the wall in one corner. But it gets worse from there. A treadmill overlooks the fifth fairway, and facing the mirrored sliding door of the wardrobe is a gym station. On the bed appears to be a damp pair of black spandex exercise shorts in XXL.

Debbie picks them up between her finger and thumb and flings them onto the seat of the gym station. She lays the plastic bag on the bed and opens the wardrobe. Hmm, that's strange. There's no sign of the box. It must be in Mum's room.

Her mother's bedroom is a shambles: clothes piled on chairs, abandoned coffee cups and a bed that looks like they left in a hurry. The mess makes Debbie feel like she's intruding. She'll grab the box, take it back to her room, and pack the dress in there.

She searches the walk-in wardrobe, but she can't see it and she's not tall enough to see what's on the top shelf. Debbie runs down to the laundry and fetches the stepladder. With the added height, she spots the box right at the back of the shelf. If she stands on her tiptoes, she can just hook it with one finger, but it's wedged in somehow. Debbie searches the room for something she can use to add a bit more height. Then she hits on a genius idea. In the lounge room, she grabs the A–K and the L–Z editions of the *World Book Dictionary* and stacks them on the top step of the ladder. The extra few inches are just enough to help her wriggle the box closer. Once she can properly reach it, she pulls it to the edge of the shelf and, in the process, knocks another box to the floor.

'Damn,' Debbie curses, as a bunch of old letters and cards scatter over the floor. She climbs down and puts the dress box on the bed, then kneels on the floor to scoop up the letters. Garry wouldn't be too thrilled knowing Mum had held on to her old love letters. No wonder she hid them.

Curious, Debbie flips over a letter and freezes. The envelope isn't addressed to Mum; it's addressed to her. She examines the other side. The return address is Yarrandarrah Correctional

Centre. She thumbs her way through the stash of envelopes. Every single one has her name on it. Out of habit, she pulls her phone from her pocket and presses Ian's number, but as she listens to it ring, she ends the call. It's probably best to find out what's inside the envelopes first.

She picks one up and inserts her finger under the flap. The glue is so old, it's barely stuck down. Inside is a birthday card with a glittery number sixteen on the cover. Debbie reads the message, then opens the next one and the next. She lays them out in ascending order; a card for each birthday. Then she sorts the letters, using the postmark to place them in chronological order. There are years' worth. Why has she never seen them?

Debbie rests on her haunches and studies the top shelf where the box had been stashed. Where nobody would find it. By someone who knew that Garry, despite all his fancy gym equipment, was too fat and too lazy to bother climbing a stepladder to have a good poke around.

By someone who let Debbie think her father didn't care enough about her to bother writing a single letter. Not even for her birthday.

Debbie scrambles to her feet. She's breathing hard, caught between tears and fury. She shoves the letters and cards in the box and takes it out to the landing. She returns the stepladder to the laundry, the dictionaries to the bookshelf, then carries the dress box to her old bedroom and removes the lid.

Maddie's right. Why is there no label on the wedding dress? Debbie tears out the layers of tissue paper and shakes them. Nothing. Where's the receipt? She tips the box upside down, expecting to see the name of the shop printed on the bottom. Still nothing. Debbie growls in frustration. What has her interfering mother been up to? She'll go through every last one of Garry's credit card statements if she has to.

Then she spots it. Wedged in the seam of the box is a card. Debbie pulls it out and studies the image on the front. The logo says 'Connecting Threads', in a font designed to look like it's been sewn by a needle and thread. Debbie frowns and turns it over. Sees the name 'Jane Watts', a mobile phone number, and a handwritten message: 'Please call me.'

Debbie closes her eyes and dredges up a memory of a woman in a floral sundress with dark curly hair. She said she ran the sewing group at the prison. She'd said something else too. What was it? 'Your father is a very fine stitcher.'

Debbie stares at the wedding dress laying on the bed and sinks to her knees. He'd written her letters, lots of letters, and she'd only ever written him one. *I hate you, I hate you, I hate you* rings in her head. Her hands fly to her mouth. Oh no. What has she done?

Chapter 44

It's chaos backstage at the ballroom. Jane has obviously watched far too many Hollywood movies, as the so-called dressing room is less grease paint and glamour and more a mess of pins and hair brushes. Not to mention the stench of stale sweat. There are stressed-out people running everywhere. Yet, it's still exciting and nerve-wracking and somehow wonderful.

'How are you feeling?' Carl appears at her side bearing a mug of tea he has scrounged from the grubby kitchenette.

Jane wraps her hands around its comforting warmth. 'Terrified.'

Carl moves to embrace her, but stops and smiles instead. 'You'll be fine. You look gorgeous.'

'And so does the dress,' Susannah adds, sipping on Champagne.

Jane gives them a watery smile. 'I don't think I can stand in front of a thousand-odd people and speak.'

'Don't be ridiculous,' says Susannah. 'We've practised it a million times, and you have your notes if you get stage fright.'

Jane's hands fly up in horror. She goes to pat her pockets, but of course this dress doesn't have pockets.

Susannah withdraws a sheaf of paper from her handbag. 'Looking for these?'

Jane almost melts with relief.

'Maybe it's you who needs this glass of bubbles,' Susannah says, trying not to laugh. 'What d'you reckon, Carl?'

Carl just stands there in his evening suit, with matching cummerbund and bow tie, grinning like a fool.

'And look at you all spruced up,' she continues. 'Anyone would think it was your wedding day.'

Carl winks at Susannah. 'Not yet.'

And Jane smiles for real this time. Not yet, but soon.

A young couple enters the dressing room. Carl moves out of their way so they have access to the bank of mirrors with its ring of bright globes.

'Thank you so much for coming tonight,' Jane says to the pair.

'I wouldn't have missed it for the world,' Debbie replies, leaning into the mirror as she reapplies her lipstick.

'What's that expression they say in the theatre for good luck?' Carl sucks on his bottom lip, trying to recall. 'You know, it means the opposite of how it sounds?'

'Break a leg,' says the young man to his reflection.

Carl beams at him. 'That's it.' He turns back to Jane. 'Break a leg. And remember, we're sitting at the third table on your left, so if you feel like you're losing your nerve, look at me and I will send you good vibes.'

Despite herself, Jane laughs. 'Good vibes? How will I know?'

'Because he'll look like this,' Susannah says, contorting her face into a stupid expression.

'You know I won't be able to see you in the dark?'

'Yes, but you'll know I'm there.'

'Five minutes please,' whispers a short woman wearing enormous headphones. She splays her fingers to reinforce the message, then scurries away to her next task.

Carl blows Jane a kiss and puts out his arm for Susannah. 'Mayor Cockburn?'

Once they leave, Jane peeks through the curtain. The Governor-General, relaxed and confident in her effortless suit, delivers her speech as if she and the audience are scrunched up on the couch having a cosy chat. And here's Jane, a sewing teacher from the middle of whoop-whoop, about to share the same stage. Imagine that.

Jane feels the sudden urge to pee.

'It's only nerves,' says Debbie, who has finished checking her appearance and now stands quietly in the wings.

'Do you think?'

'Remember to breathe,' adds her companion.

When the MC announces her name, Jane walks on stage, shakes the Governor-General's hand, and places her speech on the lectern. She grips its wooden edges and, remembering the young man's words, takes a calming breath.

'Good evening, Your Excellency Lady Bolton, members of the board, ladies and gentlemen. My name is Jane Watts and I am the sewing teacher at Yarrandarrah Correctional Centre.'

She leans away from the microphone and clears her throat. To her left, a few faces peer up at her out of a sea of darkness. He's in there somewhere; she can actually feel the good vibes.

'I want to tell you a story. It's not the kind of story you're used to hearing at the Connecting Threads Charity Ball, but it is a story that demonstrates the power this organisation has to transform lives.'

Jane rests her hands on her notes. Susannah's right. She doesn't really need them. This has been her journey too, and she knows every word by heart. Jane tells the audience about her Backtackers, describing Mick and Brian, Sean and Maloney, and, of course, Derek. Little details to show what kind of men they are. She paints a picture of lives far removed from the extravagance of a two-hundred-dollar-a-head dinner in a five-star hotel ballroom on a warm night in late spring. The few faces she can see are with her, their desserts untouched.

'Ultimately, making this wedding dress has been a labour of love, in every sense of the word. Almost to a man, not one started out knowing how to make a wedding dress. No one was sure the dress would even be completed, let alone be worn.' If only the audience knew how the library closure had almost derailed the whole project. That she had almost lost her job. But tonight is not that night.

'There is much more to a wedding dress than making a fine gown that flatters the figure and comes up well in photos.' She smooths down the skirt of her dress and the audience chuckles.

'These days, we can get caught up in the details and lose sight of the fact that, at its heart, a wedding is about the love shared between two people. A love so great that they want to pledge, in front of their family and friends, their eternal desire to be as one.'

Jane searches the crowd for Carl, sure he will shine out of the darkness, lit by the love in her words.

'This dress contains a small part of Connecting Threads and a larger part of every single man who helped make it. My Backtackers might wear prison greens, but every time they pick up a needle and thread, they create things of beauty. They have poured so much of their love into this dress and sent it out into the world filled with their hopes. My words cannot do them justice, so I think it's best that, rather than me talking, I let the men's needlework speak for itself. Your Excellency, ladies and gentlemen, it gives me great pleasure to present our wedding dress.'

Jane steps away from the lectern and moves to the side of the stage. The spotlight follows her, then the room is plunged into darkness. In a heartbeat, the lights come back up, but they're not focused on Jane. The spotlight shines on a bride hidden beneath her veil, holding a tumbling bouquet. Mendelssohn's 'Wedding March' swells around the ballroom, and the bride walks demurely, as if in a chapel, lingering in the audience's admiration. When she reaches Jane, she sinks into a deep curtsy and Jane curtsies in return. They join hands and Jane holds hers high. The bride turns a slow pirouette, the skirt flaring and sparkling under the bright lights. Behind them, a screen springs to life, projecting an image of the dress a thousand times bigger. Applause erupts at a table to their left and spreads across the room. Someone stands up. Then another. People pop up all over the ballroom. Jane's cheeks hurt from smiling so much. The bride squeezes her hand and Jane fights back tears. She can't see the bride's eyes beneath the veil, but she hears her whisper, 'It's time.'

Jane returns to the lectern. She swallows against the lump in her throat. 'Ladies and gentlemen, thank you so much ...' She trails off, waiting for the applause to die down.

'As many of you already know, this year Connecting Threads instigated its Outreach Program. It is modelled on a similar post-prison program run by Fine Cell Work in the United Kingdom called "Open the Gate". The purpose of both programs is to provide a path to formal qualifications in machine and hand-stitching skills. But more importantly, it provides released prisoners with purpose and structure to help them rebuild their lives on the outside. Our aim is that, eventually, some of these former prisoners will return to the Backtacker network through volunteering.'

There are murmurs of approval. Jane holds back until there is silence.

'It makes me immensely proud to announce that one of Yarrandarrah's Backtackers will join the next intake commencing in January. Ladies and gentlemen, will you please join me in congratulating Joey Maloney.'

There is a smattering of applause as people look to the wings to see this new recruit. There is confusion as the bride lifts the veil, carefully unpins it, and passes it to Jane. Maybe it's the combination of alcohol and surprise, but it takes a while for the realisation to dawn that she is a he. After all, it's not every day you see a man in a wedding dress.

Of course, Joey being Joey, he's loving every minute of it. It's been ages since he's had centre stage and he has no intention of squandering his moment.

While Jane explains the finer details of the dress's construction, he sashays up and down the front of the stage like it's a catwalk, proudly showing off the dress that changed his life. He even blows a kiss to the Governor-General, who throws her head back and laughs, much to the relief of the head of Connecting Threads.

Jane winds up her speech, then walks to centre stage and meets Joey. They join hands to take their final bow. This time, the applause is deafening.

Chapter 45

The Doc sticks his head in the doorway. 'You up for a game?'

Derek stops writing and rests the pen on the page. The letter-writing habit has proven hard to shake, so he's decided to channel his energies into keeping a journal instead. It's like talking to himself and, like sewing, it allows him to sort through his thoughts and feelings. 'Would it make any difference if I said no?'

He and the Doc haven't spoken much since Maloney disappeared. That kid was their glue, and, after their stoush, they kind of came unstuck. Or so Derek thought.

'C'mon, live dangerously,' says the Doc. 'I've run out of things to do now I've saved the library. Although I see you've started a new project.' He nods at Derek's bed, where pieces of fabric are mapped out in a grid-like pattern.

'Sean's got it into his head that now I can use a machine, it's time I learnt some "real" sewing.' He doesn't mention his resolution to look out for Sean for Maloney's sake, or the fact that Sean's not the only one who's lonely since Maloney left. 'But I don't know if I'm cut out for quilting. All that fiddle-faddling about. Give me a tapestry any day of the week.'

In his usual fashion, the Doc sets up the Scrabble board on the desk, forcing Derek to move his stationery onto his bunk.

They each pick a tile and Derek has first go. He racks up seven tiles and chuckles.

'You know something? I reckon I'm in with a chance this game.'

The Doc snorts. 'Dream on.'

They play the first few moves in silence, both concentrating on besting the other. But as they settle into the game, Derek strikes up a conversation.

'So what's next on the agenda, Doc?' he asks, shuffling his tiles. He's hoping to capitalise on the triple-word square with his X.

The Doc lays down QUIZ and totes up his points. 'I've decided to go back to uni.'

This stops Derek in his tracks. 'What? Three degrees aren't enough for you?'

'The FOYL campaign taught me a lot. Susannah Cockburn thinks I'd make a terrific advocate for prison reform. I'm going to study psychology.'

Derek can't believe he's hearing this. 'Mate, even if you're God's gift to advocacy, the only place you'll be championing prisoners' rights is on this side of the razor wire.'

The Doc grins. 'Yeah, but imagine the havoc I'd create with a psych degree and the knowledge of a crim.'

The perfect place to use his X leaps out at Derek and he lays down EXPERTLY, using an L already on the board.

'Nice one, Dezza,' the Doc says, jotting down the score. 'That puts you twenty in front.'

'Told you I was in with a chance.'

'Knock, knock.' Young Carl stands in the doorway, looking mighty pleased with himself. He's been that way ever since he and Jane announced there'd soon be more wedding bells in the air. Mick joked that the Backtackers might have to dust off their dressmaking skills for another run, but Derek's not sure he's got the ticker for it. One dress is enough for this old man. Still, never say never.

'Christ, are you still here? I thought you'd resigned,' the Doc says, feigning disgust.

'The gov asked me to stay on until they'd recruited my replacement. You're stuck with me for one more week then I'm out of here,' says Carl. 'Free as a bird.'

'Yeah, don't rub it in.'

Carl taps his watch and points at Derek. 'Don't forget, you've got a visitor straight after lunch.'

The Doc raises his eyebrows. 'You better be careful, Dezza. You've had more visitors in the past twelve months than I've had in twelve years. I might start to think you're becoming popular and decide you need to be taken down a peg or two.'

Derek draws the J and the K and lays them on his rack alongside an O and an E. 'Always the joker, aren't you, Doc? Watch me wipe that smug smile off your face.'

Derek lays down his tiles, the K earning triple points. The Doc writes down the score and hoots with laughter. 'Well, things are looking up, Dezza. I believe you've just won your first round of Scrabble.'

'Miracles will never cease,' Derek says with a straight face, but he's laughing on the inside.

Chapter 46

Derek sits in the visitors' room, his leg jiggling like a spider in a rainstorm. How many years has it been? She's a married woman now. He has the photo to prove it. But seeing his daughter in the flesh? His leg jiggles that little bit harder.

Then, all of a sudden, she appears on the other side of the room, searching for him. Her hair's tied up in a ponytail and her face is free of makeup. She looks sixteen again. Except she isn't.

She walks across the room with the loose-limbed ease of youth. Derek grips the table to stop himself flinging his arms around her. 'Hello, Debs,' he croaks.

'Hey, Dad.' Debbie shifts from one foot to the other. This place is weird. All the men dressed in the same drab shade of green. All of them grey and wrinkled, even the ones who aren't that old. Like her father.

Realising she's out of her depth, Derek indicates for her to sit. He can't take his eyes off her.

This is the closest they've been in nearly six years. She's grown taller, lost the puppy fat, and her hair colour seems lighter. Derek realises she's staring at him too, so decides he'd better say something.

'Congratulations.'

'Thanks.'

'You enjoying married life?'

'S'all right,' she says, raising one perfect eyebrow.

What a stupid question. It's only been two months, of course they're still having fun. Derek blushes and looks away. He doesn't need thoughts like that floating around inside his head, especially ones involving his baby girl. He decides to skip over the whole 'how was your honeymoon' question, but he doesn't have another one in the rack.

Debbie searches her father's face for a trace of the man she remembers. He's put on weight and his hair has thinned at the temples. She watches him rubbing one thumb over the other. He's more nervous than her. 'Dad,' she begins, but stops. She rehearsed the words all the way here, but she'd imagined saying them to the father she remembered, not the damaged man in front of her.

Derek can see she's in trouble, so he throws her a lifeline. 'How's your mother then?'

Debbie blinks. Her mother? God, imagine if Mum knew she was here – she'd have a fit. 'Fine, I think. I haven't had the chance to see much of her since the wedding.' Or more specifically since the screaming match about the hidden box of letters.

Derek can tell she's being a bit coy with the truth, but it's not his place to pry so he lets it go through to the keeper. 'And what about Auntie Sharon, she well?'

Debbie seems more comfortable with this question. 'Yeah, she's good. She sends her love.'

Derek smiles.

'She said to tell you she'll come to visit in the new year.'

'It'll be nice to see her again.'

Debbie shifts in her chair, settling in now she's on firmer ground. 'I've also been promoted at work. I'm a senior property manager now. The boss says I've got potential.'

She beams at her father, clearly seeking his approval.

'That's wonderful, Debs. I'm pleased for you.' And he is too.

Enough stalling. She needs to just spit it out. She squares her shoulders. 'I came to thank you for the wedding dress.'

Surprise sends Derek's gaze straight to the laminate tabletop. 'You don't need to thank me, love,' he murmurs. Christ, Lorraine must have told her, after he specifically asked her not to.

Debbie snatches his hand and forces him to meet her eye. 'Yeah, I do. I wrote you a really nasty letter and said some things I now feel really bad about.' She sucks in her breath, then makes herself go on. 'I spoke to Jane.'

Her father looks confused. Debbie realises he has no idea what she's talking about. She explains how she found Jane's card in the dress box. 'So I rang her, you know, demanding an explanation about where the dress came from, and she told me everything.'

Derek hopes not. Jane of all people would keep Backtackers' business to herself.

'Then after I'd got over the shock, she said she had a favour to ask.'

'What kind of favour?'

'Jane asked me to lend her the dress for the Charity Ball. At first, I was like, "no way", but then she explained how much it would mean to you and the other blokes who helped sew it and I thought, "That's the best way I can say thank you." So I said yes.'

Derek doesn't know what to think. Here he was feeling bad for letting Jane down, and she's gone straight to the source and got the dress herself. He's kind of relieved. 'Jane never mentioned any of this,' is all he can think to say.

Debbie grins. 'It's not Jane's fault. I said I'd lend her the dress on one condition. That I got to tell you face to face.'

Derek looks around to where Young Carl is standing guard, eyes dead straight ahead, pretending he's not listening to every word. 'You knew,' Derek says to him.

Carl gives the slightest of shrugs.

Derek will have to wait until he's back on the wing to get the full story. He's not letting Young Carl off the hook for this one. Then an idea pops into his head. 'Did you wear it then?' He can see Jane standing in front of all those big wigs with Debbie parading about in their wedding dress. 'You two good-lookers must have gone down a treat.'

Debbie shakes her head. 'Not me, Dad, I was in the audience.'

'What? Who modelled the dress then?'

'You're not going to believe it when I tell you.' Debbie grins, crossing her legs. She knows she should build up this moment, create a sense of tension, but she can't contain herself. 'Joey Maloney said to say hello.' And Debbie thoroughly enjoys seeing her father's face go from shock to joy. 'He did a much better job modelling than I ever would have.'

A million thoughts and questions shoot through Derek's head. How did Jane find Maloney? This must mean he's out on parole. Was his Aunty thrilled to see him? Has he started his course at TAFE? 'I wish you'd taken a photo. I'd loved to have seen that with my own eyes.'

'Jane said they're doing a whole spread on the Charity Ball in the next Connecting Threads newsletter. She's ordered a copy for each of you.' Debbie's smile disappears. She crosses her arms on the laminate tabletop. 'Joey said it was all thanks to you. That you convinced the Backtackers to work on the dress and made sure everyone stayed motivated until it was finished.'

Derek squirms in his chair. 'I don't know about that, love.'

Debbie raises one eyebrow. 'Jane said the same thing.'

How is he supposed to respond to that without calling Maloney and Jane out-and-out liars? He can't understand why they're giving him all the credit instead of telling Debbie that it was *them* who rescued *him*.

'I wish you'd been there, Dad.' She paints him a picture in words. She tells him how the audience reacted when they saw his beautiful dress. Her chest had ached, she was so proud of him. 'Afterwards, they showed photos of me and Ian from the wedding, and Jane motioned for me to join them on stage and the audience applauded even harder.

'Then the head of Connecting Threads came up to thank us and ask if they could borrow the dress for an exhibition they're holding at the Museum of Modern Art next year. It's called "A Stitch in Time" and it's going to show all sorts of sewing made by prisoners to commemorate the twenty-fifth anniversary of Connecting Threads. How cool is that?'

Derek's head whirls. Their dress has assumed a life of its own, twirling from one event to another. 'All I ever wanted was for you to wear it, Debs. Now it's been showcased at the Charity Ball and being put in an exhibition. Imagine that!'

Debbie smiles at him, a dimple forming in her cheek. 'You've got to admit, Dad, it's heaps better than being left hanging in a wardrobe.'

Who would have thought that making a dress could bring so much joy?

'Time, Dezza,' Young Carl says over his shoulder.

Debbie checks the clock on the wall. 'Already? But I only just got here!'

Although that's not quite true. She's been here well over an hour. The time has flown. Derek's joy evaporates. Almost six years since he's seen his little girl. Who knows how long it will be until he sees her again?

'You have to go, miss,' Carl says gently.

Debbie nods, but still doesn't move. The dimple has disappeared. 'I'll come and see you again, Dad. Soon.' She ducks her head and blinks away tears.

'That'd be really nice, love. Thank you.' How he longs to take her in his arms and breathe her in. Bottle up her scent, so he can hold her close whenever he feels like it. But there'll be none of that. 'Give my love to your mum and Auntie Sharon.'

'I will.'

And he says the words he's written a thousand times, wondering if he would ever be able to say them to her face again. 'I love you, Debs.' He gulps. There's a lump in his throat that's hard to get past. 'To the power of infinity.'

Debbie sobs, tears cascading down her cheeks.

Derek has to steel himself so he doesn't end up blubbering too. 'I'd like to write to you, if that's okay?'

Neither of them mentions the missing letters. Derek realises it's enough he wrote them; it doesn't matter if Debbie hasn't read them. And Debbie, having read every word twice over, has enough threads from the past five and a half years to be able to weave them into her own story.

'I'd love that. How about I write to you first so you have my new address?'

Derek smiles. 'Sounds like a plan.'

And with that she stands and walks towards the door.

Carl hustles him along but, before he leaves the visitors' room, Derek can't resist one last look at the girl – the young woman – who is the light of his life. The only good thing to come from his marriage, but what a jewel she is.

He watches as Debbie stops, her shoulders quivering. She presses her sleeve to her face, then dashes a finger beneath each eye. He doesn't want her to cry. He wants her to be happy forever. What father doesn't want that?

She turns around and he does something he hasn't done since she was knee-high. He presses his fingers to his lips and blows her an enormous kiss. It floats across the visitors' room, above the heads of the grim men in green and their families. When it reaches Debbie, she snatches it from the air, smacks it to her lips, then mouths the words, 'To Finny and back.'

Author's Note

Back in 2014, I worked as Books Editor for the online women's magazine, *The Hoopla*. Apart from producing a weekly literary column covering reviews and news, I also did one-off interviews with authors. On this occasion, the author in question was Esther Freud and her forthcoming book, *Mr Mac and Me*.

In preparation, I read some articles Esther had written for *The Guardian*. One in particular, sent my imagination into overdrive. Freud wrote about the charity Fine Cell Work, which operates in prisons throughout the British Isles teaching inmates needlework and quilting. Much of this work is at an impeccable standard. Pieces can be found hanging in the Victoria and Albert Museum, Buckingham Palace and Elton John's home. Places like Colefax and Fowler sell their cushions, which end up scattered over beds and lounges in private homes and National Trust sites.

Strangely, my immediate response was: imagine if I was a bloke in prison who wanted to make a wedding dress for my daughter. Strange, because while the prisoners make quilts and cushions, altar runners, and even embroidered penguins for the Antarctica gift shop, they definitely do not make dresses. Strange too as, at that time, I knew no one who had ever been incarcerated and the only gaols I'd set foot in were those historic ones where the sandstone is crumbling back to dust.

Not long after, I happened to see Johann Hari's TED Talk, 'Everything You Think You Know About Addiction is Wrong', which led me to read his book *Chasing the Scream*. Addiction is a fascinating subject but often only thought about in its guise as a drug-related issue. However, as a Sociology major, the addictions I find fascinating are the socially acceptable ones: technology, shopping, food, alcohol. I love the idea Hari posits that the opposite of addiction is not sobriety but connection.

Now I had a character who wanted to make a wedding dress, who was in gaol as a direct result of his addiction. An addiction fuelled by the lack of connectedness within his immediate family who were also addicts of their own making as many are in this disconnected century.

Research often leads a writer down many rabbit holes. It can be tricky to know which ones are time wasters and which will turn out to be pure gold. For starters, I read several memoirs about life behind bars. Erwin James' memoir, *Redeemable*, talks about how gaols fail when they are about punishment rather than helping people break the cycle that leads them into the prison system. James served many years for murder and began writing for *The Guardian* while still incarcerated. His articles are fascinating, especially (to me) the ones about the incredible saga that engulfed the Tory government in 2014 when they made legislative changes to the Incentives and Earned Privileges Scheme and, inadvertently, banned books. A public outcry ensued with many famous authors adding their voice to the general outrage. I just had to turn it into a subplot.

All stories require an element of world-building and must include those authentic details of everyday life that underpin the events that unfold. To that end, I have read numerous PhDs, newspaper articles, department of justice handbooks for inmates and visitors, posts on prison chat room forums and pretty much anything and everything I could lay my hands on. As corrective service departments are run by state governments in Australia and are not uniform in their approach, I have taken the liberty of cherry-picking the procedures and protocols that have best served the story. Therefore, Yarrandarrah Correctional Centre is a completely fictional hotchpotch of various systems.

Inside knowledge came via various retired correctional officers and other people who worked in prisons who were kind enough to answer questions small and large on life inside. It was terrific to have affirmation that my gaol, my inmates, and the lives of the cast of *The Dressmakers of Yarrandarrah Prison* might be fictional but the story is entirely plausible. It's not the version we know from perennial favourites such as *Prisoner*, *Wentworth* or *Orange is the New Black*, but as one of my experts so wisely said, 'You can't view gaol through a single prism.'

In order to try and get the details right, below are some of the written sources I found invaluable. As always, all the mistakes are mine, as are any liberties I may have taken in the pursuit of story.

If you would like to know more about Fine Cell Work, make yourself a cuppa and pop onto their website at www.finecellwork. co.uk. I promise you a fascinating and inspiring read.

List of primary sources

'Experiencing the use of Australian prison libraries: a
    phenomenological study', PhD thesis, by Jane McDonald
    Garner BBus (InfoLibMgt) RMIT (July 2017)
Policy Directive 3 Hierarchy of Prisoner Management
    Regimes by Government of Western Australia Department
    of Corrective Services (31 March 2009)

Policy Directive 19 Prisoner Hygiene – Personal, Clothing
and Bedding and Policy Directive 57 Induction Program
for Persons Working in Prison by Government of Western
Australia Department of Corrective Services (no date
provided)

Section 4: Inmates Earning, Expenditure and Buy-Up and
Section 9: Inmate Private Property, Corrective Services
NSW Operations Procedures Manual (October 2016, v 2.1)

Daily Operations and Activities, Inmate Mail Operations
Procedures Manual by Corrective Services NSW (3
September 2014)

Prisoner Handbook: Your Rights, Obligations and the Law by
Legal Aid Western Australia (Last modified: May 2016 [v 3])

Profile of Violent Behaviour by Inmates in NSW Correctional
Centres by Jennifer Galouzis, Research Officer, NSW
Department of Corrective Services (Corporate Research,
Evaluation and Statistics Research Bulletin No. 25, March
2008)

'A day in the life of an Australian Residential Inmate', Prison
Talk Online Community (prisontalk.com) (March 2004)

Problem Gambling and the Criminal Justice System by the
Victorian Responsible Gambling Foundation (January
2013)

Gambling Motivated Fraud in Australia 2011–2016 by Warfield
& Associates (August 2016)

'Prisons taking role of care homes and hospices as older
population soars' by Amelia Hill, *The Guardian* (20 June
2017)

'Prison food service in Australia – systems, menus and inmate
attitudes' by P. Williams, University of Wollongong, Karen
L. Walton, University of Wollongong, M. Hannan-Jones,
Queensland University of Technology (2009)

Reading Group Questions

*Isn't spending your weekends traipsing around the mall spending
money on stuff you don't need an addiction? What about lining up at
the crack of dawn to get in early on the Boxing Day sales? Buying the
latest mobile phone, television, coffee machine. How did they expect
him to pay for it all?*

Question 1: One of the themes the novel explores is
addiction. The main character, Derek, is in gaol for embezzling
funds from the golf club to fund his gambling addiction. He
looks down his nose at the drug addicts he is in gaol with, and
he holds his ex-wife, Lorraine, partially responsible for landing
him in gaol because of her blatant consumerism. How has the
novel changed or reinforced your views on addiction? Is Derek
right when he says spending money on stuff you don't need is
a form of addiction?

*'Guest lists and seating arrangements are easy.
How you look is the only thing that matters.'*

Question 2: The upcoming marriage of Derek's daughter,
Debbie, is central to the narrative. In Chapter 8, where the
reader first meets Debbie, she is trying on wedding dresses.
How does the author use comedy in scenes such as this to
challenge social norms (such as how a bride 'should' look on
her wedding day) and explore social issues?

Jacko risks edging closer. 'Which reminds me, I've been meaning to ask. Does your little boyfriend Maloney know you're only gay for the stay?'

Question 3: The central conceit of *The Dressmakers of Yarrandarrah Prison* is that the dressmakers are all men. Most of the action in the novel happens within C Wing of the prison, and most of the characters are male. In what way do these things allow the author to explore ideas about masculinity?

'It was about sticking at something in the face of adversity. All them ladies stitching, hour by hour, added up to tell their story. It just goes to prove that beautiful things can come from dark, lonely places, doesn't it?'

Question 4: In Chapter 37, Sean shows Derek a picture of the Rajah Quilt as a means of convincing Derek to return to Backtackers. How true is Sean's assertion that 'things of beauty can come from dark lonely places'?

Question 5: The dressmakers all belong to a sewing group called the Backtackers, which is run by a fictional charity called Connecting Threads. How does this sewing group exemplify the author's premise that people can transcend their backgrounds and circumstances to become their better selves? And is this premise right?

'Couldn't believe how the stitching ate away at the loneliness rather than let the loneliness eat me. It's a precious gift, Dezza. Not one to give up lightly.'

Question 6: One of the core issues in the novel is the mental health of the men incarcerated in Yarrandarrah Correctional Centre. How does the novel articulate the value of groups like the Backtackers in helping inmates deal with their mental health issues?

'As a child, Yarrandarrah Library was my refuge. A place to escape from the bullies and the boredom. A place to travel far away from a small life in an even smaller country town. To immerse myself in other worlds. To exercise a right that belongs to us all.'

Question 7: The novel explores the role of libraries in a community as well as the right of every individual to have access to reading materials. Why are libraries important to the story?

'I got those eight years for a reason. Now look at me. Walking out of here with a lot more going for me than when I came in. All because of other people. The Doc taught me to read. Thanks to Jane, I found out about me course. And if it wasn't for you, I'd never have met Sean. But none of it changes who I am on the inside.'

Question 8: The Doc, the prisoner librarian, is serving a life sentence for murder. Maloney is in for manslaughter. What do these two characters say about the idea of rehabilitation? Is it possible for anyone to be rehabilitated, and are prison sentences an effective means of rehabilitating criminals?

Of course, no one mentions the mother of the bride, without whom none of them would be there.

Question 9: The character of Lorraine verges on caricature. Apart from providing comic relief, what purpose does she serve in the novel?

Question 10: The story is mainly told from three character's points of view: Derek's, Debbie's and Jane's. How does this structure affect the reader's ability to empathise with each character? Is using multiple points of view an effective storytelling technique? We also see snippets of thoughts from the other Backtackers throughout – what do these insights add to the novel?

Question 11: The sewing teacher, Jane, is desperate for the men in Backtackers to have a group project they can work on, which is why she seizes on the idea of making the wedding dress. Apart from facilitating the making of the wedding dress, what function does she play in the story?

Acknowledgments

The more stories I write, the more I realise that every story has its own journey. I wrote the first draft of this novel in August 2017. Needless to say, it was a very different beast then than the polished version I present to you today.

Thanks to the kind and guiding hands of Kathy Hassett and Anna Valdinger from HarperCollins Publishers, who both made the novel structurally stronger and challenged me to dig ever deeper. Some days I honestly didn't think I had it in me. Thanks too for the wonderful editorial support of Rachel Dennis, the meticulous proofreading of Pamela Dunne and the insightful sensitivity reading from Melanie Saward. It is a joy to be working on the marketing and publicity campaign with Jordan Weaver-Keeney.

The people who worked on the cover design deserve a special mention. It's not every day that someone hand-stitches your book cover. So thank you to designer Emily O'Neill and her super-talented stitching mum, Sandra O'Neill. The cover is exquisite and I am humbled by this generous act.

And lastly, always there, quietly working her literary agent magic is Tara Wynne from Curtis Brown Australia. We have been on quite a journey together and I couldn't ask for a better person to have my back.

There have also been writing and reading buddies who have generously read earlier versions of this story. I have to thank Michelle Barraclough and Joycelyn Bowles for their feedback right back at the beginning. And a big thank you to Catherine Szentkuti for stepping up to the plate a bit later on to read yet another of my novels in its semi-formed state. Thanks to Pamela Cook, author, podcaster, writing teacher and champion of Australian writing, for her insights as well. And thanks to my friend, the talented artist and teacher, Sue Paull, who, right near the end, generously shared so many insights about life inside. The story is stronger because of you.

Thanks too to Craig Cooper, founder of Cooper Street Clothing, for a lovely lunch and lessons in how to make a dress. For inspiration, I must also thank the Chatters from the Chat 10 Looks 3 Facebook group who generously shared their wedding stories in the full knowledge that fragments may end up inside these pages. Some did. If it were not for these women, Lorraine would not have been quite so awful. Thank you one and all.

I live and write on unceded Murramarang Yuin country and wish to specifically express my respect and gratitude to the Murramarang people and pay respect to their Elders, past, present, and future.

Since moving here, I have been so fortunate to meet some wonderful people and forge great new friendships. Chief among them included our local bookseller and publisher, Garry Evans. Sadly, Garry passed away in early 2019 and didn't get to see this book finished. I miss his sly sense of humour and his bolstering pep talks when writing felt like a slog. We are all grateful for his legacy and that his family, particularly his wife, Michelle, keeps this community in books and provides a hub where we can hang out.

And speaking of wonderful booksellers, I'd like to sign off by thanking each and every reader, the booksellers who gently guided them towards this novel, the librarians who made sure there is a copy on their shelves, and everyone who tells their friends and families that they must read this book. Your support warms my heart.

Last, but by no means least, thank you to my family – Paul, Imogen, Matilda and Beau – for hearing my ideas, bringing me cups of tea, and allowing me the space to create stories.

meredithjaffé
Newsletter

If you would like to know more about what I am up to, what I am reading, listening to, and working on, or even what my bookish friends are up to, then my newsletter is the perfect place to read all the goss. It will hit your inbox every couple of months and will be about a one-cup-of-tea read. Plus, I'll sneak in a few giveaways along the way, because who doesn't love a freebie? Sign up at meredithjaffe.com

After 30 years of marriage, can there be any secrets left? The charming new novel from the author of *The Dressmakers of Yarrandarrah Prison*.

Diana Forsyth is in the midst of planning the Big Party, a combined celebration of her husband Will's 60th and their 30th wedding anniversary. The whole family is flying in and, unbeknownst to Will, Diana is planning a Big Surprise.

But then she finds a torn scrap of paper hidden inside the folds of one of his cashmere sweaters, with the words, *I forgive you*. And all of a sudden, Diana realises she's not the only one keeping Big Secrets.

As empty nesters who have just downsized from the family home, she and Will are supposed to be embracing a new promise of glorious freedom – not revisiting a past that Diana has worked *very* hard to leave behind.

A witty, poignant and insightful exploration of marriage: the choices we make – or don't make – the resentments we hold, the lies we tell and what forgiveness really means.